PRAISE FOR *THE*

"A great romp of a read."

—Cokie Roberts, ABC News correspondent

"O'Brien manages to be both topical and engrossing."

—*Kirkus Reviews*

"A terrific novel. I have attended a number of ladies' lunches in my time, but none as exciting or revealing as this!"

—Nina Totenberg,
U.S. Supreme Court Correspondent,
NPR

"A riveting capital and Capitol crime story."

—*United Methodist Reporter*

AND FOR *THE CANDIDATE'S WIFE*

"A savvy, compassionate look at how a presidential campaign is put together—and how easily one can fall apart."

—*Chicago Tribune*

"An authentic and compelling political story. The author clearly knows her territory."

—*New York Times*

"Fast-paced, highly readable . . . It's an absorbing story with dead-on observations."

—*Philadelphia Inquirer*

"A provocative and timely book—in fact . . . a little ahead of its time."

—AP Special Features

St. Martin's Paperbacks titles
by Patricia O'Brien

THE CANDIDATE'S WIFE
THE LADIES' LUNCH

The Ladies' Lunch

Patricia O'Brien

St. Martin's Paperbacks

This book is a work of fiction. Names, characters, places and incidents are either products of the author's imagination or are used fictitiously. Any resemblance to actual events or locales or persons, living or dead, is entirely coincidental.

Published by arrangement with Simon & Schuster

THE LADIES' LUNCH

Cover photograph by Herman Estévez.

Library of Congress Catalog Card Number: 94-16075

ISBN: 0-312-95789-0

Printed in the United States of America

Simon & Schuster hardcover edition published in 1994
St. Martin's Paperbacks edition/February 1996

St. Martin's Paperbacks are published by St. Martin's Press, 175 Fifth Avenue, New York, NY 10010.

10 9 8 7 6 5 4 3 2 1

For Martin S. Thaler

1932–1992

Reader and Friend

CHAPTER 1

"Time's up, counsel." Judge Sara Marino's biting command stopped cold the meandering plea of the attorney standing before her in U.S. District Court.

"But—" he started to protest.

"Sit down, counsel. You've been over that ground."

The entire courtroom fell silent as Judge Marino leaned forward and pointed with a long, slender finger toward the milk-faced, slightly balding man in an expensive suit seated at the defense table. "Stand, please," she said.

The lawyer hurried quickly back to the table where his client—a man more used to hospital operating rooms than courtrooms—was rising on obviously wobbly legs. "Just our luck to get Marino," the lawyer mumbled under his breath.

"Doctor, you obviously think you're entitled to make yourself a rich man practicing medicine, which is fine, but not the way you and your colleagues went about it," Judge Marino began in the low, even voice some lawyers had come to dread. "You have violated the anti-trust laws. By secretly banding together to set your fees, you forced patients to pay much more than was fair or just. I remind you, a medical license is not a license to steal. I've seen no evidence presented that convinces me you did other than deliberately betray your profession and your patients. Accordingly, I feel I have no other choice but to impose the maximum sentence under the law. I sentence you to two years in the federal penitentiary, without eligibility for parole.''

The defendant paled as a collective gasp swept the courtroom. ''Plus a fine of two hundred thousand dollars.'' Judge Marino paused as a slightly plump, middle-aged woman in the front row began to cry loudly. For just an instant, their eyes met, and then Judge Marino banged her gavel down. ''Court dismissed.''

''Jesus,'' breathed the man with the milk-colored skin.

''We'll appeal, don't worry,'' whispered the lawyer.

His client all but hissed his shocked and wounded response. ''That bitch is going on the *Supreme Court?*''

''Keep it down,'' Coleman snapped, glancing in Sara's direction. But Sara Marino had already stood, strode through a partially open curtain behind the bench, and disappeared. Safely out of sight, she paused and breathed deeply. Much as she liked to keep her hand in at the District Court level trying anti-trust cases, the moment of sentencing still took a lot out of her. The bastard was guilty, all right, but there was no pleasure in sending a man to jail. That woman must have been his wife. She suddenly longed to get back to the less emotional Court of Appeals—for a few weeks, anyway.

Sara Marino hurried from the courtroom to her chambers, high heels clicking sharply against the gray marble hallway floors, glancing at her watch as she shrugged off her heavy black robe. She'd be late for lunch if she didn't get out of here fast.

''Got the documents?'' she asked, thrusting out her hand toward a young law clerk with thinning hair who had been waiting for her patiently.

''Yes, Judge, right here.''

Sara scanned quickly, anxious to be out of the stuffy confines of the courthouse, still sobered by the course of the case just concluded. Greed was the same, no matter who initiated it, but she hated seeing a doctor turn corrupt.

"Guess you're glad that one's over," the clerk said shyly, breaking into her thoughts.

"Not for outside these walls, Aaron, but I can't stand characters who think nothing's at stake except money. What else is up?"

"*People* magazine wants shots of you in your robe."

Sara shrugged. "Sure, here in chambers?"

"In your *bathrobe*. At home, I guess." Aaron was trying to hide a smile. "For the personal touch, they said."

"In my bathrobe?" Sara arched an eyebrow. "That's ridiculous, I'm surprised they don't want me in the bathtub, too."

"Well . . ." he started, reddening.

Sara looked startled for an instant, then broke into a laugh. "Why, Aaron," she said. "You're making a joke—just when I'm leaving the court, you're loosening up!"

"I guess." He was reddening more, but actually looking pleased with himself as Sara returned to the job of signing the documents with her large, loopy scrawl. It probably shows a bigger ego than I should have, she thought. But her meticulous eye scanned each paper, missing no detail, before she handed them back to Aaron and sent him on his way.

The minute the door closed behind him, she moved into the private washroom off her chambers and turned on the faucet, splashing cold water across her face. She stared critically into the mirror. Dark brown hair shot with gray, swept back and cut crisply short, exposing high, strong cheekbones. She smoothed a touch of powder over a nose still sunburned from a bike ride last weekend. The eyes were serious, the brow high, the chin firm, even stubborn; a good, Italian chin. Not bad for forty-seven, she thought, crumpling a paper towel and tossing it into a wastebasket.

Slowly, she walked out of the washroom while pondering the fate of the man whose decision to nominate her for the Supreme Court had changed her life. President Goodspeed was really gone: working on a speech in the Oval Office one minute and slumped over his desk the next, dead of a heart attack. Unbelievable. And there was no use pretending her nomination was the top priority of the man who had taken his place. The very thought of Dick Sayles deepened the lines in her brow. That wavy hair, the little-boy smile. . . . Would Faith be at the Ladies' Lunch? Surely she'd break away from the White House, at least for half an hour. Faith would tell her if anything was going wrong with the nomination—if she wasn't too steeped in her own troubles.

Sara pulled on a yellow blazer and hurried down the corridor. She touched the phone slips wadded in her pocket and suddenly remembered she hadn't returned Faith's calls. She quickened her step through the corridor to Constitution Avenue, feeling a familiar guilt even as she nodded pleasantly to an elevator operator who responded by beckoning her closer.

"Judge," the woman whispered conspiratorially. "Your slip is showing."

Exasperated, Sara glanced down. "Again?" She hurried outside, stepped up to the curb, and thrust her arm in the air, trying to see if there was a passenger in the back seat of the cab pulling up for her. Good, it was empty and the windows were closed—it was air-conditioned. She heard the shouting just as she opened the door, and glanced quickly to her right. There she saw a small, angry group of mostly elderly people with hand-lettered signs. "Stop the murders!" one man yelled, spotting her on the curb. "Stop the murders! Stop the murders!" the others instantly chanted. With a sigh, Sara jumped in the cab, slammed the door, and let it speed away.

* * *

The House bell began to ring. Three rings; a quorum call. Carol Lundeen's administrative assistant wheeled away from the televised House proceedings he had been watching in his cramped corner of the congresswoman's office and barked:

"Carol! Your amendment is up! Right now!"

"Whoops, I've gotta get to the floor right now, sorry," Carol Lundeen breathed, jumping up with quick apologies to the reporter on the other end of the phone and to the two slightly stunned lobbyists sitting in her office. She ran out the door of her room in the Cannon Office Building, a blur of energy capped with brilliant red hair. Her wiry, athletic body headed for the Capitol at a quick trot. Within minutes, she was on the House floor arguing in a strong, rolling voice for a mandatory life sentence for repeat child abusers. In the heated debate that followed, her eyes kept straying to the clock above the chamber. Get to the vote, damn it, she thought. I'll be late for lunch. An hour later, the maternal and child health bill passed—minus her amendment.

"Why'd you bail out?" she whispered angrily to a colleague from New Jersey.

"We'd have risked the whole bill," he whispered back. "I owe you, okay?"

"You bet you do."

"Congresswoman," said a reporter outside the chamber. "You worked hard for that, how do you feel?"

Carol shrugged, a little weary. "Like I just pulled my head out of a Cuisinart, how do you think I feel?" she said to the reporters clustered around with their notebooks and busy pens. "We'll get it next time, okay? Sorry, guys, I've got to run." She ducked through the Speaker's lobby and out of the Capitol, stopping to shake hands with a few eager constituents from her Maryland district. Damn, this job got frustrating at times. At least she had no trouble getting a cab.

* * *

"Maggie, push the 'send' button. I need your desk."

"In a minute." Maggie Stedman frowned, trying not to hunch her tall frame too close to her computer screen—bad for the eyes or something. But her column wasn't wrapping up right. Her nose went close to the screen, and her fingers stayed tense over the keyboard. The tiny pie-shaped cubbyhole at *Washingtonian* magazine was stifling. Ah, she had it. She typed fast.

"I can't wait all day . . ." The assistant editor had an irritatingly thin voice.

She hit the "send" button and groped with her foot for the shoes she had kicked off under the desk, before swinging around in her chair to face him. There were freckles sprinkled like pepper over her pale skin and her gray-purple eyes were determinedly friendly. "Any changes, call me at lunch. I'm at Galileo's, in the wine room."

"Oh yeah, the monthly Ladies' Lunch, right?" She could tell he was irritated that the column had gone off her screen before he could get a good look. "You run with a fast crowd, Maggie."

"We've known each other a long time."

"So what do you talk about—besides the state of the nation?"

"Look, I know you're itching to get at the column; it's on your computer, Danny."

"Give them all my regards. You *should* be the most knowledgeable reporter in town."

The dig found its mark, and Maggie shut off her computer slightly more forcefully than necessary. She still was only a free-lancer writing without a contract; very dicey. She pushed that worry from her mind for the moment and thought about her friends: Carol would probably have a good Hill story. Leona was probably making elaborate plans for some kind of party to celebrate Sara's swearing in. And Sara—was there a date yet for her confirmation hearing? This was the first chance they'd all had to get together since Goodspeed's death; would it change anything? Maggie smiled, anticipating one of Faith's rapid-fire monologues—she could be very funny about maneuverings at the White House. On the other hand, Faith hadn't been joking much lately, and that was the truth of it.

Galileo's was buzzing with the usual lunch crowd as Maggie walked in the door and headed straight through the narrow, elongated room with its graceful cream stucco arches toward the enclosed wine room at the rear. This was a favorite room, a room made cozy by floor-to-ceiling racks of wine on every wall. But the best part, the part the members of the Ladies' Lunch liked the most, was the privacy. She spied Sara just ahead, noting the slight pauses in the conversations of the other diners as she passed; the nudges of recognition. God, it must be exciting, she thought. Sara's been appointed to the Court and she's my friend. Maybe it isn't going to her head, but it's going to *mine*. She felt a sudden twinge of alarm as she hurried forward, wondering if Sara would be different now, less breezy, less open. . . .

Suddenly Leona Maccoby's cheerful, delicately boned figure popped in sight around the corner of the wine room. Maggie sighed. How Leona managed to stay thin while constantly testing recipes for her catering business was a secret her friends had given up trying to discover.

"Sara! Maggie!" Leona greeted them happily, oblivious to the heads turning at the sound of her voice. "I'm so glad you both could make it, that's a feat these days, isn't it? There's so much happening!" Her voice lowered. "Poor Goodspeed . . . Sara, you've got to tell us what comes next."

"What comes next is, I need a safety pin." Sara looked down at the barely visible edge of lace beneath her skirt, then glanced questioningly toward Carol, who was swinging the strap of her bulging purse over the back of a chair.

"Really, Sara, you've got to go shopping and get new stuff," Leona protested.

"I will, I will."

"Don't worry, Leona, we'll have her decent in a second; I've got a pin somewhere," Carol said. She shoved her hand inside the bag and emerged with a huge safety pin, which she handed to Sara as the friends gathered around the white-clothed, rectangular table.

"Unbelievable, isn't it, Goodspeed dead?"

"It's a killer job."

"Worse and worse."

"He was a pretty good president, all in all."

"What will Sayles be like, do you think?"

"Who knows? At least he's young and healthy."

"I wonder if he'll shift people at State?" Leona worried. "I've got such *good* catering deals with them now."

"Faith will know."

"You think so? Good," Leona nodded, looking relieved.

"Nice dress," Maggie said to Carol, although in truth she thought Carol looked a little bit like a schoolgirl in a wispy, long number with a string tie in the back.

"Too young for me, huh?"

"No," Maggie said quickly.

"Maggie, you're such a diplomat. Faith will tell me the truth." Carol's springy crop of curly red hair bounced as she sat down very matter-of-factly. "Honestly, sewing is all that keeps me from going nuts at home."

Sara, her slip fastened, exchanged glances with Maggie and Leona. Then she pulled out the chair next to Carol and reached for a bottle of mineral water as she sat down. "Are you and Bart going to Jack Valenti's screening tonight?" she asked, pouring a glass for Carol. "I hear Al Pacino's going to be there."

"Questionable," Carol said, her voice slightly strained. "I have a choice—go by myself, or stay home and play housewife. So what do you think?"

They glanced at each other again. Things seemed to be getting worse for Carol and her husband lately. "Maybe you two ought to think about seeing somebody," Sara suggested.

Leona said, as casually as she could, "A friend of mine has a terrific therapist . . ."

"Not when I've got my friends to whine to," Carol protested quickly. "Anyhow, he'll be happier now that he's got the commission for the Sheridan house in East Hampton. Sara, you did it right, not getting married."

It was one of those curves Carol had a way of throwing, and Sara poured the fizzing water into her glass more slowly than necessary. But then she shrugged inwardly as she had many times before. Carol was Carol.

"Where's Faith?" Carol said, taking in the table. "Skipping lunch, do you think? On another diet, or something?"

"She *says* she's sworn off hot fudge sundaes," Leona said, pursing her lips slightly. "With Faith, you never know."

"Wish she'd hurry. I've gotta get out of here for a two o'clock press conference on microwave radiation; think I'll have any luck getting reporters to pay attention when I tell them their microwaves are frying their kids' insides?" Carol said.

Maggie pushed at her wilting hair. "You will if they're under thirty-five."

"Too bad Joe Beecham isn't under thirty-five," Carol said. "He's the one who needs convincing."

"You support his Centurion submarines if he votes for your health bill?" Maggie felt suddenly mischievous.

"Why don't you give up writing and run for Congress? You've got the instinct," Carol parried. "By the way, did you hear another poor guy got yanked off a ventilator and died?"

"I saw the AARP demonstrating," Sara said.

"They've got old people on every street corner today," Maggie offered.

"The crazies are popping up, too," said Leona. "I heard they assaulted some doctor in Idaho for refusing a heart transplant." She twisted in her chair, peering around the corner of the room. "Where *is* Faith?" she asked impatiently. The group wasn't complete yet, and Leona loved to have everybody there. "Late as usual; guess what?" She nodded at Maggie with a bright smile. "*Vanity Fair* okayed Maggie's idea for a piece on Sara, isn't that fun? Aren't we happy for Maggie?"

Maggie winced. Leona's exuberance did underscore the fact that she hadn't had many good assignments lately. Leona caught the wince and hastily turned to Carol. "We all know Maggie's the best feature writer in town," she said firmly.

"Of course she is," Carol said, turning to Maggie. "Now all you have to do is get her cautious judgeship to talk."

Sara laughed and threw her hands in the air. "I'll talk; for Maggie, I'll talk," she said, and Maggie felt better.

That dealt with, Leona switched topics. "I thought the Style item on me was a pain; where'd they get off hinting I had a face-lift?" she said.

"Maybe a tape recorder at this lunch?" teased Carol.

Leona waved airily. "Sandi Snow's awful since she got that gossip column, it's gone to her head . . ."

"Maggie, your hair looks great," said Sara.

"Velcro rollers," Maggie said promptly.

"Really? They work?"

. . . Now they were relaxing. It always took a few minutes, but they were settling in comfortably with each other in the ritualized fashion they had established over time. Soon they were exchanging scraps of information about the upheaval at the White House and Sara began sharing her nervousness about the new president. "I don't have any reason, I suppose," she said.

"You're worried?" Carol frowned.

"Not exactly worried . . ."

"Faith will give you a read on what's going on."

"I'm hoping," Sara said, after a pause.

"We can find out things," Leona said briskly. "We're good at that."

"You're one of the best judges in the country," Maggie reminded. "Sayles would be a fool not to stick with you. People would be *furious.*"

Sara glanced around the table fondly at her friends. We're pretty good at this, she thought; we've been building our own private network for fifteen years. "Do you know how long we've been coming to these monthly lunches?" she asked suddenly.

They paused, each doing mental computations.

"Just after my miscarriage," Carol volunteered. It had been an abortion, actually, but no one contradicted her. Carol had a way of rewriting personal history, and they were all resigned to that.

"I'd just leased my first catering truck," murmured Leona.

"Since way before Jim died," Maggie said. She felt a little self-conscious bringing up her long-dead husband, but his death had marked a passage. She wondered sometimes if the others understood.

"Leona's the one who kept us together," Carol said, restlessly flipping her napkin into her lap. "I never would have worked as hard at it, to tell the truth. I wish the waiter would bring those menus, I'm going to have to get out of here."

"Oh, I was just the one who kept the fax numbers up to date, that's all," Leona said lightly, which was true as far as it went.

Sara picked at a slice of flaky Italian bread, looking at her friends in turn, a little surprised herself at how long it had been. "Funny, isn't it—how fast the time went?" That sounded a touch wistful, so she quickly went on. "Leona, when you wanted to buy that catering company? I crossed my fingers for you when I did the paperwork, I thought you were *nuts.*"

Leona laughed. "What about when you prosecuted that ball player who raped the girl in the limo? I thought you were *tough.*"

Carol wasn't slipping quite as easily into the reminiscent mood. She looked at her watch and glanced toward the door, a slight frown on her face. "Where do you think Faith is?" she interrupted. "Wouldn't she have called if she wasn't coming?"

They all fell silent and Sara suddenly felt the phone messages in the pocket of her blazer weigh heavier on her conscience.

"Something funny is going on," Carol said bluntly. "I saw her the other night at a reception. Maybe I'm sticking my neck out . . ."

Now it was Leona fiddling, this time with an untouched glass of iced tea in which the ice was rapidly melting. "She hasn't been the same lately," she ventured. "Goodspeed's death must have hit hard."

Maggie noted Sara's expression changing. She wondered: were they going to talk honestly? By their own unspoken code, they never gossiped at lunch about each other. Could they keep pretending? As she considered what to say next, Carol's beeper went off.

"I told them not to call me unless there was a vote," Carol muttered, looking slightly embarrassed. This was not a group where a beeper made a person look important. She rose and moved toward the telephone, vanishing around the corner that led to the ladies' room.

"I've had this feeling," Leona was delicately tentative. "Faith's been depressed, don't you think?"

Maggie and Sara exchanged quick, reluctant glances,

checking the other's reaction. Neither spoke. Flushing, Leona moved to safer ground.

"Well, let me tell you what Donnie Graham said to me at this party last night, you won't believe it . . ."

Before she could continue, Carol appeared in the doorway, her face ashen.

"What's wrong?" As if by signal, the three seated women rose in some kind of stumbling accord. Maggie moved toward Carol the fastest, gritting her teeth as she hit her knee against a chair.

"What's the matter, why are you so pale?"

"The President's been shot! That's it, isn't it?"

Carol shook her head. And then they heard: Faith Paige, press secretary to the President of the United States and a member in good standing of the Ladies' Lunch, had died an hour ago—suffering a violent death in the rapids of the Potomac River, just below the tumbling waters of Great Falls.

They all began talking at once, babbling over each other's voice with the agitation of people who don't know what to say. "What are you telling us?" Maggie blurted. "How did it happen? Why was she there?"

"The Associated Press says it could be suicide," Carol said in a shaky voice. "No witnesses—but she drove there alone."

The faces of the women turned white as they shrank back from the news. "My God," Sara whispered in horror, "Are you saying she drowned herself?"

"They don't know . . ."

"I don't believe this!" With a high-pitched wail, Leona swept her hand out and knocked over a water glass.

Maggie shivered at the sound, turning around. Only then did she focus by chance on Sara. Her friend's face was totally without color, but there was something else: for whatever reason, Sara didn't look at all surprised.

CHAPTER 2

Sara paced back and forth like an animal caught in a cage. Across from her, watching, Maggie sat slumped into one of the oversized sofas in Leona's living room.

They had fled together to Leona's house in Kalorama, the closest refuge, a leafy, affluent enclave of embassies and the kind of stately homes that had always struck Sara as lonely and empty. One didn't say that to Leona, of course—but this afternoon the house felt lonelier and emptier than ever. The rumble of thunder from outside was all that filled the void left as they kept asking each other the same unanswerable questions.

"Could it have been an accident?" Maggie's words hung awkwardly in this vast room suited more for cocktail parties than the language of grieving, like notes of a song sung flat. She curled tight into the scratchy brocade of Leona's sofa, shivering, wishing there was a blanket handy to pull up to her chin. She looked hopefully to her friends, waiting for one of them to agree.

"It could have been," said Sara, still pacing. "She loved walking on the towpath."

"It was morning, maybe she just went up there and tried to sit on a rock and slipped," chimed in Leona.

Sara couldn't keep it up. "Not all the way to Great Falls, not with the hours she kept at the White House. Anyhow, she was a strong swimmer. Excuse me." She reached for a Kleenex from a box Leona had placed on the coffee table and blew her nose.

The steamy weather outside broke, suddenly and spectacularly. Lightning crackled across the sky, and they fell silent. Only Carol was missing. Walking out of Galileo's, Carol had announced she was going directly to the morgue. Her eyes had been almost wild. "I want to see for myself," she told them.

Maggie felt hot tears sliding down her cheeks. She couldn't take her eyes off Sara's grim, pale face. Was she hiding something? Leona didn't seem to notice anything strange—she just kept rushing back and forth from kitchen to living room with wine and stupid trays of crackers and cheese that nobody wanted. Now she was mopping up drops of spilled wine with one of the pristine white linen napkins the cook had stacked on the tray. What was the matter with her?

Leona glanced up and saw Maggie watching her. "I'm not losing it," she said quickly. "I'm just so stupefied, I can't . . ." But her mouth was quivering. "Has anyone notified her mother, do we know? Her other friends—"

"The White House will," Maggie said, hoping she was right. "They'll handle everything, telling the President, all those things." She felt suddenly nervous, wondering why she wasn't thinking like the reporter she was trained to be.

"The police are probably already interviewing Mrs. Paige," Sara broke in authoritatively, almost in her normal voice. "Maybe even the FBI, depending on who asserts jurisdiction. The investigation will move fast, Maggie. Everybody in town knows by now." She seemed strengthened by her own words.

The others turned to her questioningly.

"What about us? Will they interview us?" Leona asked.

"Of course," Sara said. "They'll show up any time."

"What do we tell them?" Leona's voice was tense.

"Whatever you think is relevant," Sara said, gently. She hesitated. "You're not required to reveal anything, you know. Not without a court order."

It was an odd thing to say. They sat quietly for a second or two, not quite making eye contact with each other.

"But—shouldn't we still call her mother? Tell her how sorry we are?" Leona asked uncertainly. "She can be volatile and odd, I know, but Faith was her only child . . ."

"You're absolutely right, this wipes out her family," Sara said quickly, feeling chagrined. Leona's instincts were operating better than her own.

"Somebody's got to plan a funeral. It should be here, with the President attending, not off in that place in Virginia where she's from that nobody's heard of; maybe Mrs. Paige will let me plan it." Leona squared her shoulders. "I'm good at that," she said. "I know how to put a party together, so I should be able to do a funeral—God, I sound ridiculous!" She slammed down the tray in her hands, cracking it so hard against the glass coffee table, a goblet of wine tipped perilously toward the edge.

Sara reached forward and grabbed the goblet just in time. "Look, we're all confused right now," she said, again gently. "We'll work out the details. The hard thing is absorbing the news. It's so horrible."

"You've always known her best, haven't you?" Leona said almost pleadingly. "Am I right? Sara, do you think she killed herself? If she did, *why*, for God's sake?"

"I didn't know her as well as you think," Sara said. "I only wish—" But then her voice failed her and she couldn't finish.

Okay, I'll say it, Maggie thought.

"Maybe she was murdered." Maggie's words felt like a verbal shiver. Was it her imagination, or had Sara turned a shade paler?

"Remember that woman who was murdered on the towpath, oh, I don't know, fifteen years ago?" Leona ventured.

Sara let herself fall heavily into the sofa. "Anything's possible," she said. "Sure, Faith could have been assaulted and thrown into the river."

"But by whom? Why?" Maggie was challenging herself now; it was too awful. But if Faith committed suicide, why weren't there any signs? Suicide meant total despair. If that's what happened, then clearly *she* hadn't known Faith well at all, or she would have detected something. Had she missed key signs? If so, why? How? What were they? She looked at Sara, wanting to probe—but uncertain, she paused.

The three women fell silent again; no one quite knew what to say next. They were smart, savvy women who recommended each other for jobs and for the top Sunday talk shows, shared copies of the latest *Official Airline Guide*, chatted at parties and had lunch together once a month. Now their certitude was gone; it all seemed misplaced, buried like stray coins under a sofa cushion. Here they were, by virtue of being Faith's friends, charged with trying to hold the slippery fact of her death steady in order to study it, so they could make some sense of it, understand it, maybe come to some conclusion. But where to start?

"What could have gone *wrong?*" Maggie burst out finally.

"I was just thinking," Leona ventured slowly. "Every time I call, I get her answering machine. And she doesn't—didn't—call back. Maybe she was pulling away. People do that, you know, when they're thinking about killing themselves."

"But Faith wasn't depressed," Maggie objected, wondering now, as she said the words, if they were entirely true. "She loved her job, she had lots of friends, everybody liked her."

"Who knows?" whispered Sara.

"Maybe she was having financial problems," Leona said with some hesitation.

"With all the money in her family?" Maggie shook her head, unconvinced. "That's hard to believe." She thought about what little she knew of Faith's mother—the imperious Ruth, widow of a Secretary of State and granddaughter of a senator; the proud descendant of a long line of monied Virginians and reportedly not the easiest of mothers to please. Faith liked to joke that her mother had never forgiven her for being born female. Faith could make you laugh with jokes like that, and then later you would find yourself wondering exactly what had been so funny. There was always a bite to her words. . . .

A sudden heavy knock—a flurry of murmurs in the hall—and suddenly Carol stood like some determined gladiator, framed in the doorway to the living room.

"Hi, everybody." Her voice was hollow, filling the room an instant before she did. Carol was not one to waste an entrance.

"Was it awful?" Leona whispered.

Carol started to respond, then stopped. The waistband of her floaty summer dress had gone limp with the heat and she looked more now like an orphan waif than a schoolgirl. Her face was pale. "Can I have a drink?" she said instead. "Scotch, please. Single malt, if you've got it." She settled into a chair as Leona moved swiftly to the mirrored bar tucked behind the bookcase. "It took forever. . . ."

Sara asked the most obvious question first. "Is it Faith?"

Carol hesitated again. She had asked herself the same question when the morgue attendant lifted the sheet. Was it Faith? It was a face—no, something less than a face; something bloated and gray, a child's drawing of a face, all defining planes and curves obliterated.

"Yes, but I could barely recognize her," she said weakly.

Sara bowed her head.

"She was gray. . . ."

Maggie covered her ears with her hands. "Stop."

"Well, you asked," Carol said, slightly stung. "A park warden fished her out of the river, they told me. No gun, no weapon of any kind. Her body was badly battered, but they're talking suicide." The steel in Carol's back seemed to bend a bit as she slumped back into her chair, reaching out for the drink that Leona silently offered. Her hand was trembling as she took it. She was left forever with the awful memory of Faith's body on that slab.

"Did you talk to anybody at the White House?" Maggie asked.

"I tried to get through to Sayles, but he was closeted with Jack Patton," Carol said. "He just inherited the guy and now he's *always* closeted with him." Disdain for the president's tight-lipped chief of staff crept into her voice.

"Have they sealed her office?" Sara asked quietly.

"I don't know, but I hear Patton plans to search her files himself first with the police just standing by. He says he has a right to remove privileged communications."

"No, he doesn't." Sara said sharply, sweeping her hair back from her brow in sudden agitation. "She wasn't the President's attorney."

Carol threw up her hands. "Patton does what he wants to, you know that. He hasn't even put out a statement on her death yet. The reporters in the press room are going nuts and Faith's staff is running in circles." A flicker of pride crossed her face; she was not able to resist a small boast: "My staff got my statement on the wires within an hour. Some team, those guys."

"Honestly, Carol," Sara clearly felt no patience tonight with Carol's instinct for self-promotion.

"Well, I have a job to do," Carol shot back.

"Okay, okay."

But it wasn't okay. A short, uncomfortable silence ensued, and then Carol rallied. "The press will be all over us," she said.

"Why us?" Sara was caught off guard.

Carol shot her a heads-up, reproachful glance. "Faith had an important job and we have important jobs and we're linked and this was a screwy way to die," she said. "Someone with everything in the world going for her doesn't just hurl herself off a rock unless there's a reason, does she?"

"If that's what happened," Leona broke in.

"Whatever, you can bet we're going to be asked a thousand questions about her job, her mental health, her love life—you know reporters." Carol pushed the last word out like a hard and bitter grape.

Maggie clamped her mouth shut fast. Her own days as a reporter at the *Post* were long over, but if she started defending the business, she'd probably end up apologizing for it. "It's partly because of you, Sara," she said. "Your nomination. It makes us part of the story, whether we like it or not."

"Money," Leona said stubbornly. "It was money. She was worried, I could tell. She always *used* to answer my calls."

A sudden sound caused Maggie to glance at the doorway. Justin Maccoby, Leona's husband, was leaning against the door frame. He always looked filled with secrets, she thought. People try to look that way in Washington, but Justin, who hadn't taken many years to amass a fortune from his brokerage firm, had the real credentials. Now he was advising government leaders around the world and arranging the kind of economic development deals that no one completely understood.

"I heard you were all here," he said. "I'm sorry." He leaned forward, flicking on a light, filling the darkening room with a soft, comforting glow. His gray hair was wet from the rain, and it glistened in the light as he rested his hand on his wife's shoulder. Leona's small fingers fluttered upward and danced uncertainly. The words settled over the four women, chilling them anew. Outside, the wind was blowing now around the hollows of the house, producing a high-pitched mournful echo.

"President Sayles said to tell you he's shocked and deeply sad," Justin went on.

Carol's eyes flew open wide. "You saw him? Just now?"

"I was over there on other business," Justin said with a quick, self-deprecating gesture. Even now, in the midst of this turmoil, there was a shimmer, a hint of satisfaction in his words. "Let's catch the top of the news," he said, moving to a television set at the end of the room. He opened the cabinet door and turned on the set, releasing the full-volume voice and image of ABC's Peter Jennings.

". . . The nation's move toward rationing health care unleashed more violence today. Anti-euthanasia groups clashed with police outside the Wisconsin state capitol, charging a national conspiracy against the elderly. . . ."

"Those people are over the top," muttered Carol, half to herself as Justin switched channels.

"The death of White House Press Secretary Faith Paige remains a mystery tonight," intoned Dan Rather on CBS, forcing them all to attention. "U.S. Park Police investigators say that severe lacerations found on Paige's neck could have been caused by sharp rocks in the swift-flowing waters of the Potomac—but authorities have not ruled out the possibility of murder. The White House will not comment yet on the possible cause of death, but whispers abound. Was it suicide? If so, why would a successful woman with no history of depression take her own life? That is one question official Washington is asking today as the nation's capital is plunged"—Rather paused, dark brows furrowing—"once again into painful self-examination. Was it overwork? The cruelties of a town that demands a high price for success? Was it—"

"Turn it off," Sara demanded.

"Why?" protested Carol. "Look, they're interviewing Marge Beckerman. That's a joke, she's been on Prozac for years."

"Turn it *off.*"

Justin glanced at Sara's face and switched off the set. They all turned to her, but the phone rang before anyone could speak. Everyone jumped, except Justin. "This will be the President," he said, reaching for the phone, noting their surprise with clear satisfaction. "He wants to convey his regrets to you all."

There was silence as he spoke. "Hello? Yes, Mr. President." Again, silence. "Yes, she's here." Justin turned to Sara with a contained but triumphal flourish. "He wants to talk to you."

Automatically, Sara reached for the phone. "Hello, Mr. President," she said, in as businesslike a voice as possible.

Again, not a sound in the room. Dick Sayles was the man on the other end of that line. Eight years ago, he was just an average California lawyer who had barely managed to win a Senate seat. Then, two years ago, Luke Goodspeed plucked him from obscurity and made him his running mate for his second term. And now—

"Yes, it's a terrible shock. Yes, we knew her for fifteen years." Sara was holding the receiver tightly and the skin around her softly polished nails was white. "Yes, I know, you did, too." Her eyes suddenly widened and she listened intently for a few moments. "The timing is important," she said carefully. "The police—that's right, Mr. President. Of course." Her eyes flew to Leona with a question. "We don't know yet about the funeral, but there'll be a memorial service here."

Leona was nodding vigorously, her face pinched with strain.

"Yes, we'll see you there. Of course." Again a pause. "We can certainly make an arrangement to do that afterward. Thank you. Yes." Her voice sounded unnatural, even to herself. She hung up the phone and turned to her friends.

"He damn well better come," Carol said.

"Don't be so fierce," Sara said with a small smile. "He will."

"What did he say?"

"They found a bottle of anti-depressant pills prescribed by her family doctor in Virginia in her desk. Along with the names of some psychiatrists."

Justin nodded briskly. "Depression. I'm not surprised," he said. "Faith had her moods, we all know that."

"That doesn't necessarily mean anything," Maggie said, an edge creeping into her voice.

"Don't misunderstand," Justin said with a slightly weary smile. "Surely we can admit in this room that Faith was showing some signs of instability." He paused.

There was no response. Each woman froze as if the music had stopped.

"Remember the party after she got the White House job?" he continued with an added thread of impatience. "Surely you remember how manic she got—and after only a few drinks. That's a fair description, I would say."

"She doesn't drink much usually," Carol said defensively. "I mean—she didn't."

"Think about it," Justin said, warming to his analysis. "A beautiful, single woman with a cold, repressed mother, a failed marriage and no children."

"Faith *liked* being single," Carol snapped, a little more testily than necessary. "She didn't want to be tied down to one man. After that disastrous marriage to the guitar player, she'd had enough."

"I think she was having trouble with money," Leona said. Her voice was agitated. "Justin, you helped her with some of her investing, what do you think? Why doesn't someone listen to me?"

"Because it doesn't make sense," Justin snapped at his

wife with a certain practiced ease. ''She was a rich woman, remember? God, Leona!''

''She had other problems.''

Justin looked at Sara swiftly. ''Like what?''

His interest was too quick, and Sara was irritated with herself. ''Not everything went right in her life,'' she said with a shrug. ''Does it for anyone?''

Justin started to speak but Carol broke in. ''What was Sayles asking us to do?'' she said, turning to Sara.

''He said Faith's mother wants us to go to her house and choose something for her to wear''—Sara swallowed with sudden difficulty—''for the funeral.''

''But, what about the police? Have they searched the place yet?'' Carol asked.

''They're doing it in the morning,'' Sara said. ''I started to tell him we had to wait, but he knew that. Nothing can be taken out of the house that could be possible evidence.''

Justin let out an exasperated snort. ''A dress is evidence? Come on, Sara, don't be so legalistic.''

Sara appraised him coolly, irritated by his condescending tone. ''The law's the law, Justin, and I assume you respect it,'' she said.

''Of course I do, but we have a straight case of suicide here.''

''What makes you so sure?'' Carol demanded.

''There's no sign of foul play, no reason to suspect it, and she was profoundly depressed,'' Justin said. ''What else do you want?''

Sara glanced at the others, and saw her own skepticism mirrored in their faces. ''No one saw her go in the water,'' she pointed out. ''The circumstances were definitely mysterious. The police won't drop it, I guarantee you. We'll all wonder.'' She suddenly wished Justin would leave. They needed to talk more, the four of them. They needed to be alone.

''I'm not satisfied, for one,'' said Carol, suddenly energized. "Nobody's convinced *me* unless we find a suicide note."

"Another reason for checking the house ourselves," Justin said. "Obviously, if there is one, it might clear up loose ends, but we don't want the police pawing through Faith's things—and we certainly don't want reporters turning this tragedy into a circus."

"Sure, Justin," Carol said with a hard glint in her eye. "And if we do go over there and find something, we'll do the right thing and bring it to Patton first. That's what's being said here, isn't it?"

"Not at all."

Once again, a silence fell over them.

"I know who's pulling the strings, and so do you."

"Carol," Leona said, glancing swiftly, placatingly, at Justin. "Patton's no choirboy, but everything isn't a conspiracy, for heaven's sake."

"That's right," Justin said with a small smile. "Will you handle getting the clothes, dear?"

Leona relaxed visibly. "Of course," she said.

"After the police have finished their search," Sara cut in calmly, locking eyes with Justin. He shrugged, and glanced away.

The usurping of Leona's loyalty wasn't much of a surprise, but Carol was stung. "I intend to be there, too," she said, glancing at the others. "Look, Jack Patton is a born snoop. All he cares about is whether she left anything around that might cause him trouble." Her voice grew firmer. "I think Patton figures we'll do his snooping for him because none of us wants Faith's life to become public property. And don't tell me I'm wrong, Justin."

The atmosphere had turned sour. Maggie looked at her friends and felt the responsibility to make sense of it all, but where to begin. . . . Going to Faith's meant walking in on a life barely over. Who would pack up her things? The lovely old antiques and that beautiful Persian rug and those funny little wood carvings from Prague she loved so much—who would wrap it all up and ship it off to, where? To her mother?

"Carol, somebody has to get clothes for Faith," she said. "Why not us?" Instantly, she realized her mistake. Carol wanted an ally, not a debate.

"Sara, you've got the most at stake," Carol said, changing focus as she swiveled in Sara's direction. "I should think you'd be pretty wary of that guy."

"And what makes you think I'm not? Look, I don't like him and he doesn't like me. That's no secret in this room, but we barely know each other."

"He's never wanted you to get the Supreme Court seat," Carol said. "He's been against your nomination from the start, right? He got pissed off over something."

Sara started to reply, but thought better of it. Carol would calm down, she always did. But a weariness was descending, a weariness so overwhelming she felt she could curl up right now on the sofa and sleep.

By now Justin was on a second important phone call—and when he pushed the "hold" button and strode from the room to take it privately elsewhere in the house, the sourness began to dissipate. Odd, Sara thought fleetingly—we can't find whatever is natural for us with him here.

"Remember when Faith fixed you up on a date with that congressman who talked nonstop about himself at dinner, Maggie? And afterward Faith yelled at him for not treating you right?" Leona's voice was tremulous.

Maggie managed a ghost of a grin. "Faith always followed through. Nobody did it better."

"You know, you read the papers and you worry about cancer and estrogen and power lines . . ."

"But not whether a friend might commit suicide."

Sara lifted her head. "Or might be driven to it."

Maggie turned, the question now on her lips—

The doorbell rang.

Leona opened the door to two men, one hunched into a beat-up yellow slicker and one with a tiny, almost dapper mustache. Both wore the kind of professionally blank expressions that belie the nature of the task at hand.

"Leona Maccoby?"

She nodded. Involuntarily, she shivered.

"I'm from the Park Police, ma'am," said the man in the raincoat, "and this"—he nodded at his companion—"is Agent Leo Forman from the FBI. I think you know why we're here. May we come in please and ask you a few questions?"

Leona stepped back slowly and beckoned them in. "You've saved yourself some time," she said, leading them back into the living room, and nodding toward her suddenly wary friends. "You've got the whole Ladies' Lunch at one shot."

"Good," the FBI agent said. "That saves us a lot of time." It seemed to Leona he narrowed his eyes as he surveyed them all, one by one.

An hour later, the four women sat silently, drained. The two investigators had left, finished finally with their persistent, low-key, polite questioning: Did they know any reason why anyone would have wanted to kill Faith? Any reason why she would kill herself? What about problems on the job? Her financial history? "We don't know," Leona said finally, almost despairingly. "Maybe she was depressed, maybe she had financial problems—but we don't know anything else."

Now Sara was pulling herself up from the sofa, looking far smaller than the judge who had only hours ago presided over a courtroom sentencing. Her eyes were haggard. "Look, this has been a terrible day," she said. "Hope nobody minds if I head on home?"

No one objected.

"Let's talk tomorrow," Carol murmured.

"The taxi stand is right down the street," Leona said, rushing for the phone.

"Thanks," Sara said, pulling on her yellow jacket. "The rain's stopped. I'd rather walk. No, don't get up, I'll let myself out."

Hands jammed into her jacket pockets, head bent, she walked from the room. Outside, she trudged toward Connecticut, finally hailing a grimy Yellow Cab and sliding into the back seat with exhausted relief. Her fingers closed tight over several pieces of paper in her pocket, crunching them into little balls. The phone messages. Slowly she pulled them out and smoothed them straight, one by one, on the seat next to her. Pink fragments, already half-torn, each carrying a searing indictment.

"Call Faith," said one.

"Faith. Please call," said another.

"Need to talk." said the third.

That was all. Just three. All from yesterday afternoon; all unanswered because she had been listening to the evidence against a shoddy doctor and dreaming about what she would do the day she was able finally to don the robes of a Justice of the Supreme Court. All unanswered because she was too busy. . . .

Sara stared straight ahead, seeing nothing, allowing herself finally to concentrate fully on what these crumpled slips of paper meant. I let down a friend, she told herself. Totally, irrevocably. Those weren't messages from a woman letting go of life, they were messages reaching out for help. Admit it, she thought, bracing against sudden nausea. Maybe if you had taken two minutes to go through all the phone messages at six o'clock last night instead of looking through them this morning, would Faith be lying dead in the morgue? If you hadn't been impatient the last time, if you hadn't anticipated being sucked into another complicated conversation. . . .

Sara forced herself to take a deep breath, mustering her

counterarguments. No one could see into another person's soul. Survivors always felt guilty, suicide (was it suicide?) was inexplicable. She rolled down the window and watched the heavy, wet trees of Kalorama slip past as the cab traveled in sputtery bursts toward Connecticut Avenue. Then she rested her forehead against the window frame and two stinging tears squeezed out of the corners of her eyes and slipped silently down her cheeks. Others began to follow.

The Oval Office was very quiet now, the drumming rain on the windowpanes the only sound. The man in the tufted leather chair pushed back abruptly from his desk, a signal of dismissal. He took a few steps, walking with a slight limp. He was tall; strong bones and a fine nose, but his hair had an unruly character to it that gave him the casual look of an adolescent boy. His face held the remains of an early summer tan.

The angular, tow-headed assistant White House press secretary stood quickly. "We're all set, sir," he said nervously, clutching a piece of paper. "This'll be in the press room bins in ten minutes."

"Should've been there an hour ago," Dick Sayles replied flatly. The midwestern twang he had worked years to suppress was present in full force.

"Doesn't matter," said a thick, gravelly voice. Its owner leaned against the wall with the ease of a man in comfortable surroundings. Jack Patton had a soft face, dominated by narrow eyes and heavy lids that made him look slightly sleepy or even slightly foolish, an impression no one had twice. His reputation as a political strategist was rightfully legendary. He existed in something of a cold, hard political Hall of Fame, having moved through the back alleys of politics (dispensing enemies with flair) to the governorship of a midwestern state, and then on to the White House. He was loyal, smart, and lethal. "None of those guys missed a deadline, no matter how they scream," he said.

The aide nodded automatic assent and hurried out. It was not for him to contradict the chief of staff; no way. Patton straightened and stretched, all the while watching the jutting, almost delicately carved chin of his commander-in-chief.

"It's tough," he said carefully. "I know you worked with her on the Hill for years, but—"

"Don't say it."

"I have to. It solves a few problems."

Sayles settled back into his chair and began a gentle rocking motion, staring at nothing. "She liked tennis, did you know that?" he said. "She was pretty good—had a great serve, as good as a man's. . . ." He focused on Patton with obvious effort. "I can't believe I'm talking about tennis, for Christ's sake." The rocking continued. "She told me I wasn't missing anything because of this." He gestured toward his leg. "She said that too much sun on the court could fry a person's brain." He chuckled softly. "Not too subtle a message."

Patton took a tiny step sideways, distancing himself from Sayles's reminiscences. "Her behavior deteriorated," he said pointedly.

"She was a good press secretary, the best. You know it."

Patton nodded slowly. "She did a great job fielding the networks on that gay-bashing case in Transportation," he conceded. "No doubt about it."

Sayles waved a hand, brushing the words away as if they were cobwebs. "She's dead," he said, speaking the word as if it came from some alien language. "I still can't believe it."

"It's a blow, but we all have to pull ourselves together and go on."

"Fuck that. We should've seen it coming."

The atmosphere was suddenly more charged, and the two men stared at each other. "I don't agree," Patton said.

"She was right on the edge; no telling what she might have said or done, even something damaging to you. You had to stay out of the line of fire. I'm telling you—I was right." Then, after a slight pause, "You can't agonize, sir. You did your best." He watched and saw to his satisfaction that his deferential "sir" had found a mark.

Sayles straightened in his chair and offered the hint of a smile. Patton had effectively reminded him of his new role, and he took grateful refuge in it. "I tried," he said. "Thanks, Jack."

"Any time, Mr. President." Patton turned to leave. "You could use a few minutes alone, I'll bet."

Sayles reacted as if it were a novel idea. "Yes," he said. "I believe I could."

Patton's fireplug shape vanished through the door and Sayles leaned back once again. For the next ten minutes, he did nothing but stare fixedly at the ceiling.

The house was quiet as Maggie stepped through the doorway and walked on tiptoe through the dark living room toward the light from the master bedroom. The light probably meant that Michael was spending the night. Either that or he was madly faxing copy for tomorrow morning's paper. She stopped and quickly thumbed through the day's mail on the hall table, her heart thumping as she pulled out an envelope from the mortgage company. She was late again, she'd have to call—she glanced quickly at the rest of the mail. No check yet for the *Washingtonian* piece. Why did it always take so damn long to get money out of these magazines? She tiptoed on down the hall; her son, Jeff, would be asleep. She would stop and kiss him, and then try to creep into bed unless Michael was still awake. Part of her hoped he was. She had not left Leona's house until midnight, not left until Leona had gone through three double vodka gimlets, until Carol broke through the day's strange hold and hugged her goodbye, until Justin disappeared, and until she had comforted Leona and consumed an entire bottle of white wine all by herself.

"Maggie," Leona had grabbed for her hand as she left. "Let's you and I go to Faith's house tomorrow morning, early. Justin's right, it's a good idea to get this over with. We don't need to run into the police and, God, the reporters."

Maggie was instantly wary. "What about what Sara said? We can't . . ."

"All we're doing is getting a *dress*, for goodness sake," Leona interrupted. "We're not taking anything the police might want. Maggie, please, come with me."

Maggie hesitated, but she was very tired. "They'll probably be there before us, anyway," she said. Maybe Leona was right. Just get it over with.

Now, as she walked down the darkened hallway, a floorboard creaked under her feet.

"Mom?"

Jeff's voice pierced the silence. "Hi, honey," she whispered, pushing at his bedroom door. "Why are you awake?"

"Don't bullshit me, Mom, I know what's going on."

She walked into the room and saw her son propped up on two of the Mickey Mouse pillows he had clearly outgrown. Buy the kid some new sheets and pillowcases, she told herself, adding it to her mental shopping list. He's almost ten years old.

She sat on the edge of his bed and suddenly felt his thin arms wrap around her.

"Michael said your friend died, he said maybe she killed herself," Jeff whispered, and something in his voice warned her to focus totally.

"We don't know for sure," she whispered back, pulling him close. "She drowned, Jeff. I don't know how it happened."

"Was she mad at somebody?"

"I don't know."

"Maybe she was sick, like Daddy was."

How rarely he spoke of his father any more. It jolted her. "I don't know," she said helplessly.

"Maybe somebody killed her." She could see his face now, white in the darkness, and she felt chilled.

"The police will check that out."

"Did you cry?"

Maggie tried to think back and sort out the last terrible twelve hours. Had she cried? Sara had. Leona had. Carol must have cried in the morgue, why else would she have been so cranky and angry? She couldn't remember; she must have. But had she sorrowed enough, or were her real feelings frozen by shock?

"Yes," she said. She was too tired to sort out her feelings; too tired to deal with the aching confusion that felt lodged deep in her bones.

Jeff stared at her matter-of-factly. "I don't believe you," he said.

She paused. "Why not?"

"You never cry."

"You can cry and still be strong."

"Mom!" He giggled and punched her with a Mickey Mouse pillow. "Give me a break."

If his voice hadn't been quite so shrill she might have been diverted. "Nothing's going to happen to me," she said, lightly punching him back.

"Maybe you'll die, too."

"No, Jeff."

"But—"

"Hey, remember that great base hit of mine last week? I'm more than strong, I'm tough."

"Mom, you got tagged out at *second.*"

"A lousy call."

"Yeah." She saw his grateful face looking at her and yearned to cover it with kisses, but he would think she was treating him like a baby. Instead, she settled for another hug.

"See you in the morning, Mom."

"Sleep tight, son. I love you."

Maggie stood and turned toward the door. Michael Bitterwood was standing there. His glasses were on top of his head, giving him a slightly professorial yet rakish look. He was clutching fax paper in his left hand—just as she had thought, his story for tomorrow's *Post*—studying her with those startingly blue eyes that always seemed to see everything.

"I knew he'd prop himself awake until you came home," he said with a small grin as she stepped back into the hall.

"Thanks for staying tonight, Michael," she said gratefully. "Did he watch the news?"

Michael nodded. "He was watching when I came in the door. You know CBS led with Faith?"

There was no discernible reproach in his voice, but Maggie felt shaken. She nodded. "I should have called him and told him myself. I didn't think."

Michael put his arm around her shoulders and gave her a rough, awkward squeeze. "Got a message for you," he said.

She waited, almost as if for another blow.

"It's from some book agent, a guy who said you'd probably recognize his name."

"What was it?"

"Teleki. Janos Teleki."

"For me?" She was astonished.

"Yeah. Is that somebody good?" He was watching her closely.

"Michael, he's one of the top book agents in the business. Of course I've heard of him. He's got a half dozen clients on the best-seller lists right now."

"Well, he was very excited. Wants to talk to you about doing a book."

"On what?"

Michael shot her a slightly exasperated, slightly wary glance as they walked down the hall and into the bedroom, as if to ask where on earth had she been in the last twelve hours.

"He didn't tell me that," he said. "But I can guess."

Maggie pressed on. "What?" she asked eagerly. "On what?"

"On Faith, on Sara—on your Ladies' Lunch, I guess," he said. "What else?"

CHAPTER 3

"I can't believe this." Leona's voice was indignant as she stepped into the tiny kitchen of Faith's house in Georgetown shortly after sunrise. "They've already been here. The radio's on!"

Maggie felt a hot itch of prickly heat spreading under her armpits. It was another sweltering day and she was sorry she had agreed to come, sorry they had known where Faith kept her spare key. She secretly hoped Leona was right, but her instincts told her otherwise. "More heat," the WTOP announcer barked. "Another—" Maggie flicked out a hand to turn off the radio, wondering too late if she should have done that.

"I think we're the first," she said. "Faith must have left it on. I don't like this. I think the police *should* be here."

"Not if Patton can keep them away."

They glanced at each other uneasily. Together they looked in silence around the tiny kitchen. Then they saw a note in the middle of the table: "Ladies' Lunch, twelve o'clock, don't forget!" They stared at it.

"It's from me," Leona said slowly. "I faxed it to her night before last. She was coming to lunch."

Maggie shivered. The note, the radio on. . . . What happened here yesterday morning? "At least she was thinking about it," she said.

"I think she was coming."

Instead of answering, Maggie pulled open the door of the freezer, took out two ice cubes from a full tray, and held them tight to her forehead. She flicked off the automatic icemaker and stared at the freezer contents. A tub of Safeway's nonfat frozen peach yogurt and a package of very gray beef stew meat was all she saw. She couldn't trust herself to answer Leona. If she did, she would show her fear. Why weren't the police here? How could Patton keep them away?

Suddenly conscious of the dryness of her mouth from last night's wine, she took one of the cubes and began sucking it gratefully. "We don't need to do this, not right now," she said. "Let's lock up and get out of here."

Leona seemed to be losing some of her resolve. "We have to go upstairs first," she said, after hesitating briefly. "I know, you feel like an intruder, and I do, too. But I have this feeling that maybe we'll find something that will give us a reason—" She broke off.

"We're not taking anything except clothes, Leona." But Maggie followed her silently up the stairs and into the small, high-ceilinged bedroom that was Faith's, feeling worse with every step. Everybody had secrets; small ones, big ones. The things you shoved into drawers and cabinets or scrubbed with Comet before company came. And Faith now had lost her right to her secrets. Her clothes lay in a jumble about the room; bras, stockings; a gray silk Armani jacket bunched carelessly in a chair. Books. A box of paperclips on her dresser. A plastic tray filled with lipsticks in gold and silver and ebony cases. A photo album, open on the bed. A pile of letters held together by a rubber band.

The room was terribly hot and Maggie felt sweat trickling from her scalp. She spied an ancient air conditioner resting at a slight angle on the window sill and moved to the window to turn it on. It wasn't working. How had Faith been able to sleep? Surely, living with a broken air conditioner in Washington in summertime meant having a life out of control.

"Maggie, look." Leona was gazing down at the photo album.

Maggie stared at a photo of the five of them sitting in a boat, laughing and sunburned, their arms over each other's shoulders, taken during that weekend they spent together at Key West. Five years ago. You could see the beginnings of a fiery sunburn on Faith's recklessly bare arms in the high noon heat. Maggie felt herself trying to peer deeper, to see more, but all she could see was what she remembered: the lighthearted leader of the group, the one who had planned the trip, made the arrangements—made it come off. Her eye strayed to Sara and paused. Sara's eyes, shaded by a sunhat, were a slash of darkness across the photo. . . .

Leona leaned forward, studying the photo. "No clues here," she said.

Maggie nodded in agreement.

"Faith was kind of edgy then, remember?"

Maggie nodded again. Yes, Faith had turned morose on the trip, but they had all concluded it was because she was worried about getting a job offer from Goodspeed's administration. They were always sympathetic to the dips and surges in each other's careers. Faith had been forgiven.

Leona gazed at the photograph and her tone turned melancholy. "How come we only went away together once?" she said.

"Oh, you know." Maggie stopped. The two of them looked at each other sorrowfully.

"We were always too busy," Leona said quietly.

Maggie reached out and closed the photo album, startling her friend.

"It's okay to remember the good times," Leona said.

"It just makes me wish . . ."

"Well, me, too."

Maggie wasn't sure what to say, so she moved to Faith's dresser and picked up the letters held with the rubber band, flipping them quickly. "Mostly bills," she reported.

"What's under them?"

Maggie glanced down at a sheet of paper torn raggedly from a notebook covered with columns of scrawled figures. Leona moved quickly to her side and picked it up. She studied it briefly, her eyes suddenly lighting up.

"I told you," she said triumphantly. "Faith was having financial problems. God, you can hardly *read* it."

"She had terrible handwriting, remember her rule? Never write anything you can type."

"Look, she's subtracting stuff, coming up with big minuses, see how she keeps scratching things out and refiguring?" Leona held up the paper.

"Maybe she was just adding up her bills."

"I think it's obvious," Leona said, reaching for the pack of mail. "Justin's supposed to know everything; well, maybe he doesn't." She rifled through them quickly. "You're right, they're mostly bills. A letter from her mother." She hesitated, staring at the envelopes, then put the pack down. "No threatening letter. No suicide note."

"So you're satisfied?"

"You mean, am I through poking around?"

Maggie looked taken aback and Leona laughed. "God, Maggie, you're the reporter. I would think you'd want to know more."

"I get tired of picking up rocks and looking under them." Maggie blurted it out, hoping she didn't sound overly dramatic.

"At least you try," Leona said with a slightly different laugh. "I don't pick them up at all." The rays of morning sun streaming through the window touched the corners of her mouth, tracing deepening commas of shadow. "But I want to understand what happened,'' she added.

Maggie smiled wanly. ''So do I.''

Together they looked silently around the hot, stuffy room. Maggie could smell faintly the spicy sweet scent of the special Hungarian soap Faith had ordered last month from a catalogue. Faith loved ordering from catalogues. Clothes, dishes, furniture, anything. She would pore over them, ordering the strangest gadgets she could find—and then be furious when her purchases didn't live up to expectations. She had high standards for everything and everybody. Maybe too high.

''I'm just going to say one thing,'' Leona said.

''What?''

''Faith spent a lot of money. I mean, a *lot.* And you know it.'' Leona said it with the calm certitude of a woman who knew what ''a lot'' was.

Maggie studied the determined line of Leona's chin, wondering—not for the first time—how her friend managed to be both vague and absolutely dead-on at the same time. Silently, she watched Leona walk over to Faith's closet and swing it open. Surprisingly, it was relatively neat.

''What do we need?'' Leona asked uncertainly.

''I suppose we should have talked to the funeral director.''

The two of them stared at Faith's clothes, completely nonplussed. Not shoes, Maggie thought confusedly. They won't show. Certainly not pantyhose. Underwear? Did you dress a corpse in underwear?

''Let's just choose a dress,'' Leona whispered. ''Something pretty and soft that she liked to wear.'' She pulled out an apple green silk tunic. ''This?''

Maggie shook her head. ''It wasn't her best color,'' she said.

''That won't matter,'' Leona said with tears in her eyes.

Maggie hated this job now; she wanted it over with fast.

"There," she said, pointing to a royal blue wool dress with an embroidered collar. "That's the one she wore the night we gave her the big party at your house, remember?"

"God, she was gorgeous," Leona said, removing it carefully from the closet. "Nobody should be that gorgeous." She flushed, catching herself, and looked around. "Some jewelry?"

They stared at each other indecisively. "Maybe Mrs. Paige would want to decide that," Maggie said finally.

"But this dress looks bare without something—"

"Okay," Maggie said, opening Faith's jewel box and pulling out the first pair of earrings she could grab. This whole venture was getting bizarre. "Let's bring these. I don't think they're real gold, so it's probably okay."

Leona's face brightened as she fingered the simple crystal hoops rimmed in gold. "These are the ones she wore the night of the party," she said. "They're beautiful. Good pick, Maggie."

Maggie knew she couldn't bear to stay in this house one more moment. "Let's go," she said.

"Okay," Leona replied. But she didn't move.

For a moment, the two of them stood silently and looked around.

"Are we overlooking something?" Leona asked nervously.

Maggie realized she had the same feeling. "Leona, are we just buying this idea that she committed suicide, or do we really believe it?" she asked suddenly.

"Who would murder her?"

"I don't know."

They stared at each other.

"Look, go on down—I'll be right there. I need to find a bag to put this stuff in."

Maggie turned with relief and started down the stairs. She had done her job as a friend; now she wanted to get as far away from Faith's house and Faith's life and Faith's death as possible.

For a long moment, Leona stared after her. Then, swiftly, she checked the drawers, opening them silently, rifling their contents with care. She had to be careful. It would be so embarrassing if Maggie caught her doing this. She opened a box of cream-colored notepaper, rummaging fast. Then she stopped.

She had found what she was looking for.

Later that morning, Sara found herself sitting on the narrow Federal-style bench outside the Oval Office, resisting the impulse to glance again at her watch. The secretary was watching her casually. When Jack Patton had called and asked if she were free to "drop by in about an hour," she had felt herself go cold inside. You didn't "drop by" on a president, not on any president, even if it was Dick Sayles closeted behind that door with Jack. Something was up. On the other hand, she had questions about Faith and this was as good a time as any to ask them. Carefully.

Sara again caught the secretary watching her and automatically stiffened her spine. It was a reflex that probably came from her father's early training. "Posture, Sara, posture," he used to say in his comfortable, low rumble while he stared at her over those funny-looking half-glasses that made him appear to be everybody's favorite old-fashioned family doctor, when he was much more than that. It was their code word for "toughen up," and she still used it to admonish herself, long past the times when she had most needed the advice: when her mother died, when she first applied to law school, when she faced the truth and realized no man was probably ever going to take care of her, so she'd better learn to take care of herself. Now she was a nominee to the Supreme Court, waiting to see the President of the United States. Not bad, she told herself grimly. But the taste of glory, of having reached the mountaintop, had somehow diminished in the wake of Faith's death. She shifted, irritated. Sayles should hurry up. She was not some supplicant. Idly, she stared down at her shoes. Funny, Faith was always the one telling her the gold buckles and bows had to go. Faith was always . . .

Sara shivered. It would sink in eventually.

The discreet murmur of the secretary's voice on the intercom broke through her reverie. Sara gazed levelly at the woman guarding access to the most powerful officeholder in the world and gave her a small, controlled smile. Just what was this summons about, anyway?

"Judge Marino?"

"Yes."

"The President can see you now. Please go in."

"Judge, how good of you to come," Jack Patton said, rushing forward as she walked through the door. "Please accept our condolences, I'm so sorry. I understand you and Faith have been friends for many years. It was a great loss, for you, for the President"—he nodded in Sayles's direction—"for all of us."

"Yes, it was." She had no wish to endure Patton's lugubrious condolences any longer than necessary, but her words, to her own ear, sounded inappropriately crisp. "Thank you," she added, sensing that no matter what she said, she would irritate Sayles's chief of staff. So what? I don't fit into his sense of the fitness of things, Sara thought, aware that she was masking her face with a smile. So let him think I'm a middle-aged spinster with a tough, corseted mind—he always has, anyway.

"Sara," said Sayles. He was holding out his hand, willing her forward, forcing her to look directly into his eyes. It was the gesture of an old acquaintance. "Faith was my friend, you know that. We went back a lot of years." A small, sad chuckle. "More than I care to remember."

Sara, marveling briefly at how presidential he already sounded, focused on his eyes. He's acting, she thought suddenly. He's following a script on how he should perform and what he should say. There could have been chalk lines on the carpet, the staging was so deliberate.

"Faith certainly considered you her friend," she said. "She was your champion for a long, long time."

"Yes. . . ." His voice was vague, tapering off.

"You wanted to speak to me?" she prodded.

"Oh, just to give my condolences in person."

Sara paused. "That's very kind of you," she said, not quite sure why the script seemed suddenly so lame.

"The least I can do," he said. The charm he was known for, the warm ease, was bottled up, corked, and put away.

"Mr. President," she said quietly, stumbling ever so slightly over his title. "I have to ask you something."

The muscles in Sayles's handsome face tightened and his eyes flew to Patton.

"Go ahead."

"Was anything going wrong for Faith? Here at the White House?"

She saw his eyes widen, and her instinct was to thrust home with more questions. Be careful, she warned herself. You can't grab him by the throat and push him into a corner, not this soon after Faith's death. But if these men knew something. . . . In the ensuing silence, she felt her fingers turn cold. Her eyes darted back and forth between the icy stillness of Sayles's gray face and the glowering intensity of Patton's.

"That's an odd question," Patton interrupted sharply.

Sara released Sayles from her gaze and turned directly to Patton, relishing the challenge within the challenge. "I'm asking you if she was under undue pressure," she said. "Perhaps about her job. We all know she set high standards for herself."

"You're not implying she killed herself because of problems here, are you?"

I'm fishing for something even more important, you bastard, Sara thought. "How do you know for sure it was suicide?" she asked swiftly.

Patton ignored the direct question, reshaping it. "I grant you, Faith was unhappy. Are you surprised? Did she talk about her work here?"

The atmosphere in the room was uncomfortably charged. Sara knew these men could be intimidated, she knew how to make it happen. But she had her nomination to protect. "Rarely," she said. "But, on occasion—yes." She knew better than to balance herself on the razor's edge. Not in front of Patton.

"That's all right, Jack," Sayles murmured.

But Patton appeared not to hear him. "Anything you can tell us?"

"Nothing relevant."

"Try me."

"No, there's nothing." And if that wasn't true, it was none of his business. She had learned what she needed to know—they were indeed in a hurry to close the book on Faith's death. All she could do now was hope she was wrong on why.

"Hell," growled Patton, suddenly amiable. "She had a heavy workload these past few weeks; to tell you the truth, she did seem a bit overwhelmed, but there was nothing disastrous in the air. Right, Mr. President?"

"Right," Sayles said. But this time, Sara noted, the actor missed his cue by a millionth of a second.

"It's like the President told you yesterday, Faith was looking for professional help." Patton cleared his throat. "Emotional problems, I suspect. We had no idea how bad it was, to be honest."

Sara turned her attention back to Sayles, noting how different he looked from the man she remembered from only a few short weeks ago. The affable nature that had made him a favorite of White House reporters had been supplanted by something else, something hard to define.

"We were friends for a long time," she said. "I'd like to find out from you as much as I can." Her tone was reasonable and she sensed both men relaxing. Sayles walked slowly around the desk and sat down in his chair, swiveling, staring out the window, a somber, reflective look on his face. But Patton was giving her his undivided attention.

"Faith was having trouble separating her personal from her professional life," Patton said. He let a short pause fall. "She had something of a volatile personality, Judge. I think you know that."

Again Sara glanced at Sayles, vainly trying to catch his eye. But he was still staring out the window and Sara felt an edge of anger nibbling at her natural caution. "Faith loved her job here," she said, deliberately not raising her voice. That, she had learned on the bench, was the best way to force someone to pay attention. "She was as loyal a member of this administration as they come."

"I know that," said the man in the chair.

"She was a person who would suffer greatly if she felt people she respected didn't deal straight."

She could see Sayles stiffen as he swung to face her, the small cleft in the middle of his chin deepening as he tightened his jaw. Deal with it, she thought almost savagely.

"Well," he said in a calm enough voice, "Faith took things very personally, as you know. But she was a special, charming human being who was well liked around here." He paused and drew a long, audible breath. "I care about the people who work for me; always have," he said. "Just because I'm sitting in this chair in this office doesn't change that."

For just an instant he seemed like the Dick Sayles Faith used to describe.

"I trust this conversation is off the record, Judge," Patton said, forcing his unspoken challenge to the fore. Sara hesitated for half a heartbeat, mostly to make Patton wait.

But there really was no choice.

"Yes," she said. "Of course it is."

"Your confirmation hearings are coming up soon," Patton said, switching topics with practiced ease. "Should go smoothly; you're a top pick, Judge. President Goodspeed did the country a service."

"Thank you," she said, stiffening. There was nothing in his words, but the tone—she would think about that later.

"We'll be back to you for the pre-hearing briefings," he said cordially, moving toward her to signal the end of the meeting. "You'll get grilled real good. Part of the game, of course. But we don't want the opposition tripping you up." He touched her shoulder and squeezed it companionably. "Thanks for coming. We'll talk soon."

Sara moved lithely away from his hand. "I'm sure we'll see a lot of each other," she said coolly. She faced Sayles. "Goodbye, Mr. President."

Sayles too had stood, but he didn't walk toward her. Even here, he hated to be seen limping. He smiled from behind the desk—a gaunt, lifeless smile—and she had this sudden impression of a lonely man trying not to pick a scab. I have company, she thought, for as much comfort as that gives.

They stared at each other. Then she smiled back just as lifelessly and left the room.

The door clicked closed. Patton turned to Dick Sayles and for a long moment, the two men stared at each other.

"She knows," Patton said softly.

The sun was already high when Maggie threw a towel over her shoulders and scanned the straining bodies of her fellow exercisers at the Washington Health Club on Connecticut Avenue. It was eleven o'clock, a reasonably private time before the noon rush. She quickly spotted Carol and worked her way past the machines to the vacant Stairmaster next to her friend.

"Maggie, did you know Leona blindsided us? She went to Faith's house this morning—without telling us?" Carol's voice was impatient and hurt as she pedaled.

"I went with her, actually."

Carol cast Maggie a look of astonishment. "Why? After what Sara said? I thought we were doing this together!"

"Leona wanted to get it over with, and I went along, that's all," Maggie said. She wondered briefly if she should feel quite so defensive, but it was too late to worry about that now. "We got some clothes for Faith to wear, that's all. We were glad to get out of there."

"Well—" A high-pitched, tinny sound cut through the whirr of the machines. Carol made a face. "Just a minute." She reached for a cellular phone balanced precariously on a magazine stand in back of the handlebars. "Tell him I'll be there by noon," she barked to an invisible aide. "Get out those papers on the microwave study—yes, *those* papers! Right—right. Noon, Room 23, tell him. Did we get the *L.A. Times?* Okay."

Maggie didn't feel as patient as she usually did with Carol's frenzied, fractured phone calls. "Carol . . ."

Carol clicked the phone off and slammed it back onto the magazine stand, unapologetic, ignoring the glances of a few other exercisers. "Sorry," she said. "I've rescheduled that press conference, these things are a bitch, you know how it works. So why didn't you call me?"

"I told you, it was impulse," Maggie said, feeling defensive. Why did she let herself slip into this? "It felt weird being there. You're welcome to take my place next time."

"No note? No booze?" demanded Carol in her best give-me-the-facts tone. Maggie envisioned her scrawling questions on a piece of paper before rattling them off and had to remind herself it was Carol who had mustered the guts to go to the morgue yesterday.

"No," she said. "Nothing."

"What was by her bed?"

"A phone number on a piece of paper."

"Whose was it? Are you checking this out?"

"Atchison and Keller."

Carol's response was puzzled silence.

"The air-conditioning people," Maggie said, suddenly impatient. "The air conditioner was broken."

"That doesn't sound like someone planning to commit suicide. Where's the autopsy? That should be followed up. I'm calling the police. Who'd she talk to there? Did she—"

Maggie pushed down hard on the pedals, the sweat breaking out on her forehead, welcoming the sense of pitting herself against the strength of the machine. This was Carol, the bird dog, hammering, hammering.

She glanced quickly at her friend. No, it was more than that. Carol was biting her lip with furious concentration and climbing with excessive fervor. Frantic, almost. . . . She wanted to ask if Carol had seen and wondered about Sara's reaction to the news of Faith's death at the restaurant, but she hesitated, then decided to hold her tongue.

"Look, I've told you all I know," she said. "What do *you* know?"

A short silence, broken only by the labored breathing of both women as they studied each other in the mirrored wall facing them.

"More than I want to," Carol finally said.

"God, Carol, what am I supposed to say to that?"

"Look, Mrs. Paige called this morning and started screaming for a congressional investigation," Carol said, her face redder with each thrust downward. "She says it's my responsibility as a member of Congress to figure out what happened to her daughter."

"Has she talked to the police?"

"She refused. Told them she was too distraught."

"Strange woman."

"You bet."

They shared a short companionable silence, broken by an abrupt confidence from Carol. "Bart and I had another fight. He's always telling me I'm selfish and self-absorbed. How can he say that? Especially right now. God, all I'm thinking about is Faith."

It was the unspoken question in Carol's voice that moved Maggie. "I know—" she began.

"Honestly, I work my ass off, and to hear him say *that*. . . ." Carol was waiting.

"I'm sorry, Carol, it must be tough." She hesitated, feeling a stir of resentment. She had to be careful not to impose her own submerged sadness on Carol. "I suppose if that's what he thinks, it's a reality, at least for him."

"It isn't true!"

"You still need to listen to him." She started to say more, but Carol's mouth was set in a familiar way, and Maggie instead gave vent to her own sense of loss. "I wish I had listened more when I had the chance," she said. Unfair, she knew it was unfair.

"I can't compete, Maggie. I'll grant you, nothing's worse than having your husband die."

"I laid that on you, and I'm sorry."

"It's just too many things at once." Carol wasn't interested in talking about Bart any more. "It scares me, you know, to think of how much of a loner Faith was."

"Me, too."

Carol pushed harder, leg muscles straining. "I've been thinking about it. She didn't let anybody in too close . . . though I can't say I tried all that hard."

"Maybe none of us did."

"She only opened up once with me. Talked about her mother."

"She never got too personal with me, ever." The realization made Maggie sad.

"Sometimes you try to figure people out, and nothing computes. Damn, Bart gets to me."

Maggie glanced at the clock, anxious now to leave, but Carol was on a roll.

"I can't even figure out why I'm on this damn Stairmaster. I just do it because it's the thing to do. How do I figure out what happened to Faith if I can't figure out myself? And look at Leona, putting up with that self-important prick . . ."

"Who gives a lot of money to things we care about."

"Thanks, you said that nicely. Things like my reelection campaign. I know, it makes me a hypocrite, but Leona's completely blind when it comes to Justin."

"Who isn't, when it hits too close to home?"

"There you go, Maggie the philosopher." Carol started to grin, and then the grin faded. "Do you realize—this time yesterday, she was probably still alive?"

The realization, the reminder of finality, swept over them both.

"I miss her. I miss Faith."

Maggie looked at Carol's reflection in the mirror and impulsively reached out to comfort, forgetting where she was. Her foot slipped.

"Watch out!" Carol grabbed for her arm, but she regained her balance, heart thumping.

"Thanks, that was dumb of me."

They smiled at each other in the mirror this time, taking in the gleaming black and chrome mechanically moving landscape behind them.

"We look so busy," Carol said, almost absent-mindedly.

"We're supposed to," Maggie replied.

They pedaled on toward noon in silence, both thinking about that.

Later that afternoon, Maggie sat in her chair at home, carefully stretching leg muscles that ached more than usual after her morning session on the Stairmaster. Sitting in front of the computer screen for a couple of hours straight rarely made her restless, but this afternoon was different. She had found Jeff's empty cereal bowl in the sink when she got back from the health club, left in his mad dash for school—and encrusted as usual with dried Raisin Bran. The old dishwasher never got that stuff off. Would she ever get this kid trained to rinse his dishes? The flash of familiar irritation had still been with her when—was it only an hour ago?—she had reached for the telephone to return the call of Janos Teleki.

Fifteen minutes later, Maggie had hung up the phone, all thoughts of cereal bowls gone from her mind. She wandered around the kitchen, absorbing the offer she had just received. She, Maggie, should write a book. About her friends. What was unbelievable was Teleki's confident voice telling her the market was very, very good, he had already shopped the idea around, and he could probably get her, oh, in the neighborhood of half a million.

You're kidding.

Well, that's optimistic. But it'll be healthy, I promise. Not including paperback rights, of course.

Of course.

The tingle of shock was still moving through her body.

It could be a fabulous book, said the confident voice. A book about women succeeding, about success and tragedy and achievement and loss—listen, it's all there. A human story set in the backbiting world of power in Washington. And who better to do it than Maggie Stedman?

Who indeed?

Put together a quick proposal, ship it to me. Let's get moving. It's contingent, of course, on Sara Marino getting that Supreme Court seat. Then your friends become a hot story.

The money, the money, how could she get him to repeat the sum so she could be sure she heard right?

How much did you say?

Half a million. Hey, it's possible.

Why me?

You're a writer, aren't you? And you happen to be in the right place at the right time—and part of the right story. Need I say more?

What about Faith?

Faith?

Faith Paige.

Well, of course. You have to tell all about her, too. She's the tragic figure. The woman who reached too high, perhaps?

I don't think that's what happened.

Well, whatever. What do you say?

I don't know—I don't think I can do it.

What do you mean?

I can't write about my friends, I'm sorry. You're wasting your time.

Not many people get this kind of offer, you know that, don't you?

I'm sorry—

Look, don't turn this down so fast. You'll regret it.

I told you, it's not possible.

Think about it.

What's to think about? I can't do it.

You may change your mind.

I doubt it.

For half a million?

I have other writing commitments.

None like this.

No, none like this.

If you change your mind, call me. Soon.

I won't, but thank you.

And now she sat staring at her computer screen and the words she had written there, thinking about what half a million dollars meant: independence and a chance to start over. A better school for Jeff. Maybe a move to New York, an apartment, not a huge one. Most important, a chance for security. What was she going to do if her insurance got canceled? She was already two months behind. . . . And where was she going to come up with the twelve hundred for last month's mortgage payment? The life insurance was dwindling so fast, it was scary. Why hadn't Jim bought more? She tried to check tears of self-pity. Give him a break, she told herself, he was young and vigorous and never thought he'd develop cancer and die. She sighed then. Face it, you're on your own. And this was the first and only real pot of money she'd ever been offered.

And still she stared at the screen, thinking about her friends and what it would mean to write about them. Would that make them meal tickets to her security? A profile written with Sara's cooperation for *Vanity Fair* was one thing; a book was another. The high-gloss cast of Sara's nomination seemed enough to carry a magazine story. But Faith's death changed everything.

Wearily, she shook her head. The old questions were all there: What was she afraid of? What did she stand to lose? They were the same questions she had struggled with before, a year ago, shocking everybody by quitting her job at the *Post.* Even now, if she closed her eyes, she could hear the whispers. She could read the glances and hear the subtexts of the words. They believed she left because she was not tough enough for the job any more. Maggie Stedman, not tough enough? Nobody would have dared say that before last year.

The peal of the phone broke her reverie.

"How'd it go?" Michael said.

"Fine," she said automatically. "We got some clothes for her, that's all."

"No evidence of a high-level White House plot to blow up Ankara?" His attempt at humor was a little heavy, but she found herself smiling.

"No evidence of anything," she said. "What do you think? Why is the White House resisting a criminal investigation?"

Michael lowered his voice as he answered, and Maggie—with a slightly wistful pang—imagined the crowd of reporters around him in the *Post* newsroom.

"Patton's still claiming everything points to suicide, but we're calling for one in tomorrow's paper," he said. "Let's see if he keeps stonewalling. When's the funeral?"

"Day after tomorrow."

"Want me to go with you?"

"Thanks, Michael. I'd like that."

"I'll be there."

She hung up and sat quietly, wondering why she had said nothing to Michael about the sudden overwhelming, incredible prospect in her life of making a lot of money. Maybe even half a million dollars. And then she looked once more at the words on the screen: "*The night Faith Paige took over as President Goodspeed's press secretary, we hosted a party. Who are we? Her four friends; her lunch group. It was a great party.*"

She stared at the words she had written, willing them to say more. Her fingers moved slowly to the keys.

"*Maybe that's when it all began.*"

When all *what* began?

Her head was aching. She turned off the computer.

CHAPTER 4

The huge interior of the Washington Cathedral was glowing with light and almost half-full as Sara slipped into a middle pew next to Maggie and Michael.

"Look," she whispered. "It's Kate Goodspeed." And there she was, the beautiful, dark-haired widow of the former president, walking slowly toward her place at the front of the cathedral, her complexion pale, her expression resolute.

"Poor woman, she's had a terrible time," Maggie said in a low voice.

"She's still one of the classiest people in this town," Sara replied.

Suddenly the organ filled the cathedral with stately, sorrowing music. Faith's funeral had begun.

Sara, riveted by the sight of the rose-covered coffin in front of the altar, hardly heard the sermon. Faith was in that thing. . . . Sara's fingers were digging into the wooden railing of the pew when she felt Maggie give her sleeve a tug. "Are you all right?" She nodded, a little too quickly.

Maggie cast her a doubtful look, then settled back and thumbed through her hymnal as the minister finished and the choir began to sing. She blinked to clear her vision, but the page numbers were a blur. No matter, she thought miserably. All any of us can see is that terrible coffin.

Maggie glanced across the aisle at Leona, who sat with Justin, her small features half-swallowed by a hat swathed with black veiling. Catching Maggie's eye, Leona smiled valiantly. She was vaguely aware of Justin checking out the crowd, noting all who had come, and she swallowed a twinge of annoyance. Justin couldn't be expected to deal with a major event in Washington solely on one level, not even Faith's funeral, but couldn't he at least pretend? She too thumbed randomly through her hymnal, thinking obsessively of the anguished scribblings she had found in Faith's room. Faith's death had something to do with money, she was sure of it, even if Justin didn't believe her. But if anybody could figure out what happened, Justin could, she told herself. The thought made her contrite. Why was she criticizing Justin? He was just being himself.

Carol sat behind Leona with Bart Lundeen at her side, a black beret squashing down her coppery hair. She had half-expected her husband to bury himself in his architectural drawings and not come with her this morning, but he'd come through, she would grant him that. Carol stared at the back of Mrs. Paige's tidily coiffed head, wondering what particular hell awaited a mother who lost a child. She shivered, resisting the answers.

Back on the other side of the aisle, Maggie felt a nudge from Michael. "You're being watched," he whispered. She glanced around, catching the eye of a woman with blond hair wound high on her head and the sharp, long neck of a very thin bird. Sandi Snow, the gossip columnist; what was she doing here? Collecting tidbits for her next book? Sandi could parlay nothing into a nasty item and very little more than nothing into a best-selling book. . . . And what about me? Maggie asked herself silently. If I sign that contract, what would I be doing?

The unseen choir launched into the splendid cadences of

"Oh God, Our Help in Ages Past," signaling the end of the funeral. Now the coffin was being borne down the aisle by six pallbearers: the two senators from the state of Virginia, the recently elected governor of the state, Faith's burly, red-faced deputy from the White House, an unknown second cousin from Richmond, and an elderly uncle who didn't look quite up to the job.

Regal and tidy in black bouclé wool and with her chin high, Mrs. Paige rose from her pew and accepted the quickly offered arm of the President of the United States. After her came Laura Sayles, the president's wife. A tall, gaunt woman with half-moons of shadow under her eyes, Mrs. Sayles had an understated strength to her that was already driving some reporters crazy. She didn't quite fit the accepted models painstakingly constructed for the wife of an American president, but then, neither had Kate Goodspeed. Seemingly oblivious to this, Mrs. Sayles firmly took hold of her husband's other arm and the three of them walked slowly down the aisle. When Dick Sayles passed their pew, Maggie could have sworn Sara recoiled, ever so slightly. She glanced at Michael and saw his eyebrow arch. So she wasn't seeing things.

"Maggie, let's get out of here," Sara whispered under the somber music. Her eyes were wet, and the veins in her hands were raised and blue. She looked strangely nervous.

"It's over," Maggie whispered back. "Ten more seconds, and we're out the door."

The crowd was shuffling out, aisle by aisle, and soon, mercifully, it was their turn to leave the cathedral. Sara stood at the door facing Wisconsin Avenue and inhaled deeply, grateful for a slight breeze blowing from the north, watching President Sayles and his wife as they walked slowly toward their waiting limo. They were talking, but she couldn't hear a word.

"I told you, I'm not going to the cemetery," Laura Sayles was saying to her husband in a low voice as they approached the car. She spoke through her teeth, a trick learned long ago when she first found herself surrounded by cameras.

"We have to," Dick Sayles responded.

Laura Sayles looked at her husband with a flash in her eye. "Not me, my dear," she said. "Not me." And with that, she climbed into the gleaming black limo.

Sayles hesitated for a fraction of a second. Then he climbed in after his wife. Almost immediately, the car swung silently away from the curb, did a quick U-turn, and headed with a Secret Service escort back down Wisconsin. The siren began to wail and the mourners in the milling crowd outside the cathedral paused and watched.

"That was a fast exit," said a heavy, drawling voice directly behind Sara's right ear. "Now all he has to do is learn how to be President. Right, Judge?"

Sara turned and smiled. Amos Berman, the senior senator from New Jersey, her chief Hill sponsor for the nomination, was hitching up his trousers with an elaborate gesture and grinning conspiratorially. Good old Amos. He wore a seersucker suit and scuffed shoes. He had a forehead covered with liver spots and a round nose covered with spider veins that turned pink at the tip. He loved playing to the hilt the caricature of the crusty old lawmaker, but he was canny and smart and took no guff from anybody, and he had pushed hard for her nomination. She owed him a lot.

"I'm sorry about Faith," he said quietly before she could answer. "She was a fine woman, a good person; better than those guys deserve." Amos didn't bother hiding his contempt for the new regime at the White House.

"I can't believe she's gone."

"Pretty terrible. They're still calling it suicide—you agree?"

Sara took her time before answering. "I don't think we have enough facts yet," she said.

"Spoken like a judge." He stared up at the intricately

carved gargoyle on the stone facade above them with seemingly fascinated interest. "Talked with Sayles lately?"

"Yes, briefly," she said. "A few days ago."

"What's your feel for the guy?"

Sara drew a deep breath. She should be careful, even with Amos. "He seems self-absorbed, maybe not quite in charge yet."

"Okay, so you're a judge, Sara," he said gently. "To put it another way; when your boss is the President and he drops dead, how do you convince people you're up to wearing the mantle? That's the question. And the answer is—"

He looked at her expectantly, a faint twinkle in his eye.

"You tell me, Amos."

"—The answer is, you cover your ass. That's what Sayles will do. And Jack Patton, as long as it serves his own purposes, will help him do it." He patted her hand and started to move away through the crowd. "Watch yourself, kid," he said with a parting glance. "Remember, successful ass-covering in this town means somebody else's gets kicked."

"Sara!"

It was Leona, beckoning her over to a small circle of mourners surrounding Mrs. Paige. Sara moved forward, noting as she did the tightly pressed lips of the older woman accepting murmured condolences. There was something formidable about her small figure, her careful, cadenced movements. This was not a woman who hugged.

"Mrs. Paige?"

"Yes." Her hand was tiny, the skin glued tight to fragile bone. She held it out, stiffly, to Sara.

"She was a wonderful friend," Sara said simply.

A nod. Then, in a flat voice: "I want to know how my daughter died. It was *not* suicide, I'm convinced it was not."

"Do you know something?" Sara asked as quietly as possible. "Do you have any idea?"

"No!" Mrs. Paige took a small step back. "I simply cannot imagine it happening!"

Sara bit her lip. You would think some of her vaunted judicial discretion might have surfaced, she told herself, but no—she had blundered in and upset this woman. "I'm sorry," she began.

"Don't be sorry." Mrs. Paige interrupted, her eyes abnormally wide. "Just *do* something."

"How could any of us know what was going on in Faith's mind?"

Everyone turned in the direction of Leona's voice, who blanched at the sudden attention but pushed on. "It's just that she must have been under terrible pressure—"

Mrs. Paige was staring.

"She worked hard and there've been all the changes at the White House. . . ."

Leona was foundering, so Sara spoke up. "It's possible she did kill herself, Mrs. Paige," she said reluctantly, not wanting to voice her deeper concerns. "We can't rule that out."

"Well, I can," Mrs. Paige snapped. She pointed directly at Carol with a shaking finger. "You're in Congress," she said. "I want something done and I'm waiting for someone with the courage to do it. You people think this can be swept under the rug, that's what you think. What sort of friends are you?"

Carol flushed. At least a dozen people were listening now. She caught from the corner of her eye a flash of blond hair and realized Sandi Snow had moved in closer to catch every word.

"Congressional investigations don't bring back the dead, Mrs. Paige," Bart Lundeen said suddenly in a flat, matter-of-fact tone. "And Faith's dead."

Ruth Paige drew in a sharp breath and looked at him as if he were a piece of spoiled meat. "Don't lecture me about reality," she said furiously. "Faith was worth ten of you.

She would have gone far, she was brilliant, she was—''

It was several seconds before Sara realized Mrs. Paige was crying. It took a sudden flash of sunlight hitting those hard blue eyes at just the right angle to show the moisture collecting under crepey lower lids that were one wink away from spilling their contents down her carefully powdered face. Meanwhile, the flush on Carol's face was deepening from embarrassment to indignation and the tightening cordon of mourners was edging closer, ever so politely, with no one intending to miss a word—especially Sandi, who had the alert look of a heron about to grab a fish. If this becomes some kind of confrontation, Sara realized with alarm, Faith's funeral will be trivialized.

''You are absolutely right, Mrs. Paige,'' she said, thrusting her arm firmly around the woman's tautly held shoulders. ''You deserve a full explanation for this tragedy and we will do everything in our power to make sure you get it.'' Deliberately, she lowered her voice and spoke slowly. ''But today is the day we mourn.'' She paused. ''The whole city is here, Mrs. Paige. Everyone important. . . .''

Mrs. Paige seemed all suspended energy, like a bolt of lightning quivering in the air, but the sound she emitted was that of a kitten whimpering. Then she nodded silently, and the hard glaze over her eyes began to melt as she turned and walked away. The gathering crowd emitted a collective sigh of relief (or was it disappointment?) and began to drift off. Mrs. Paige was shriveling back into the role of the bereaved mother of a dead daughter, and there was nothing particularly dramatic about that.

Sara, Leona, Maggie, and Carol stood in a ragged semicircle, looking at each other. And as they tried to muster unity, Sandi Snow stepped into the group.

''My goodness,'' she said lightly, in the lilting southern accent she had nourished since her early days in Georgia. ''You four are such *formidable* women.''

''Oh, for heaven's sake,'' Carol began, but Maggie

nudged her into silence. Sandi might be hard to take, but her power was real.

"First, my condolences, really and truly." Sandi managed to look properly doleful as she moved close enough to let her voice drop to an almost conspiratorial whisper. "What do you'all think really happened? Leona, it sounds like you think she committed suicide, but Sara—I mean, Judge Marino—you sound like you're thinking *murder.* Something is going on, isn't it? Isn't this just the most *tragic* development, after Goodspeed's death, do you think there could be a connection? Do you think. . . ?"

Sara knew better than to leap in with any clarifications. But Sandi was pressing closer. "We've got nothing to say," she told her.

Sandi shot Maggie an appraising glance. "Well, you're a reporter, Maggie, you know how it is. I'm just trying to do my job. Are you writing about this?"

It was a chance shot, and Maggie flushed red, unsure how to respond.

"Why, I do believe . . ."

"This really isn't appropriate," Leona said with surprising crispness. "None of us have a word to say about this to you, and you'll just have to understand."

"Ladies." Sandi rolled her eyes and flashed a helpless smile. "I'm being so thoughtless, I'm so sorry, do forgive me, Faith was your friend, so close to you all." And with that, she floated back into the crowd, leaving them all wondering what they had done to themselves—and to Faith.

"Good for you," Carol said.

"I can't stand that woman," Leona moaned.

"Let's not waste time worrying about her," Sara said, as comfortingly as she could, but a pinch of fear had lodged in her heart. Together, they trudged toward the cars waiting to take the funeral cortege to the cemetery. Leona and Carol, with Justin and Bart, climbed into one waiting limo, and Maggie and Sara started toward the one next in line.

Suddenly Sara stopped. "I'm not going to the cemetery, Maggie. I can't."

"Why not?" Maggie asked, astonished.

There was no satisfactory way Sara could answer. The need to console Mrs. Paige had rubbed something raw and she needed time alone. "It's just too much to take," she said.

Maggie glanced over at the cluster of reporters and photographers clustered behind a yellow plastic ribbon stretched taut across the driveway. "Those guys will wonder why," she said uncertainly, nodding in their direction. "I think they expect us all to play this out in the usual way."

"I don't feel like performing," Sara said, "not today." There was something in her voice that gave Maggie the courage to ask the question she needed to ask.

"If I'm over a line, just say so," she began, searching Sara's face. "But you weren't surprised when we learned Faith was dead, were you? Do you know something we don't?" She knew she should leave it at that and wait, but she was nervous and unable to stop from babbling on. "I mean—I felt you weren't surprised at all. It was as if you were expecting—" She couldn't finish.

Sara gave her a small smile. "So it showed?" she said.

"Yes."

"Oh, Maggie." A short pause. "Faith wasn't happy."

They were at the cars; standing close together on the sidewalk. The sound of engines revving up cut through the air, and people were glancing their way.

"Why wasn't she happy?" Maggie said with overwhelming urgency.

"She was scared, I know that much." Sara was choosing her words carefully, too carefully for Maggie. "I didn't know she was desperate. I still can't believe . . ."

"*Why* was she scared? And desperate? What happened?" Maggie sensed her voice getting pushy but it was hard to stop. "Her mood swings weren't so bad. I mean— it's something else, isn't it?"

Sara clenched her fingers around the strap of her purse. "Work," she said vaguely. "A lot of things." She touched Maggie's shoulder. "Look, I've got to get out of here. Please, be a friend and make up some excuse for me."

"We'll see you tonight at Carol's?" Maggie asked, trying to stall.

"Yes, but let's keep it quiet."

"Oh, we will. It's our own private goodbye."

Sara nodded. Then she walked briskly away, leaving Maggie with no choice but either to run after her or to climb into the last empty car waiting to depart.

Frustrated, Maggie ducked her head and entered the car and found herself alone in the back seat. She settled back as the car pulled away from the curb and joined the funeral procession. Then, in a gesture automatic and well learned and almost frighteningly easy to put once again into play, she snapped open her soft, pouchy shoulder bag and rummaged for a notebook and pen. Balancing the notebook on her knee, she scribbled quickly, writing down every word of their short exchange, pushing back guilt as she did it. Writing down a conversation with a friend was a little dicey, but this was okay, it was fair. It was fair because Sara was hiding something. . . .

She stopped, staring down at her notes in horror.

"What am I doing?" she whispered. Quickly she ripped the page out of her notebook, tore it into shreds, and stuffed the pieces into the shallow ashtray on the car door.

"Mom! We're outta peanut butter!"

"Put it on the list!" Maggie shouted as she kicked off her shoes in the crowded foyer, noting for the twentieth time the chips and scratches in the floor molding. The whole house was shabby; it needed a paint job. "And turn down that TV!"

Jeff's aggrieved face popped through the dining-room door. "There's no list on the refrigerator," he said accusingly. "You took it when you went to the store and you forgot peanut butter."

Maggie leaned over and tried to brush his forehead with a kiss before he could dodge. With a small lurch of her heart, she remembered how only last year he would automatically present his face for a kiss at any point in the day. Now, sentiment was reserved for bedtime. "I'm a failure as a mother and you'll never get over it," she said lightly.

Jeff was fast. "That's my line," he said with mock disdain and disappeared back behind the door. "Hey!" he yelled through the closed door. "I just remembered! Call Mr. Habecki!"

Maggie stood still. "Teleki?" she shouted back. "Do you mean Teleki?"

"Habecki, Teleki—something like that."

"Jeff, how many times have I told you to get the name right and write it down?" she yelled. "This is important!"

His face popped through the door once again, his nose wrinkled tight. "Hey, Mom, don't have a cow," he said. "I'm sorry."

Okay, it was an overreaction. "Where's the number?" This time her voice was calm.

"By the phone. Oh, the *Post* called, too. Some woman about health insurance."

Maggie froze. So they weren't going to send any more warning notices; this was it. She would have to start shopping again for a policy, and then hold off payment for a while. What were you supposed to do when you didn't have a full-time job?

She hesitated, staring at the phone. And then she dialed slowly. Teleki had probably changed his mind, anyhow. She couldn't write that book, so why was she calling him back? Maybe he wanted to tell her it wasn't such a good story after all. Washington stories didn't interest people.

Washington stories bored people.

He answered on the first ring. His voice was amused; expansive.

Have you decided?

She breathed deeply. I told you, I can't write that book.

You aren't breaking a law, Maggie.

No, just screwing my friends.

He laughed. Write something down, all right? Give it a chance.

She stared at the phone and said nothing.

I've sounded out the right people, and there is definitely interest and we are definitely in the right ball park financially. Give me five pages, okay? I've seen your interviews; you're good at human interest. You could make your friends famous. That's good, not bad.

Give me a week or two.

Don't sit on it, Maggie. Somebody's going to do it, it might as well be you. Start writing. It's a winner.

The sun had set, leaving a brilliant glow in the sky, when Leona, Maggie, and Sara gathered at Carol's townhouse that night. They parked their cars and walked up the sidewalk, reaching the steps to the house at almost the same time. By unspoken consent, they had shed their funeral clothes in favor of pants, shirts, and sandals, and Leona carried a package of holiday jams she had snatched from the kitchen before leaving the house. They all felt scattered and tired, at a point in an unforgettable day where finishing sentences would be a challenge.

But when they met at the foot of the steps, they seemed to revive. "I couldn't watch the news tonight," Sara said, grabbing a jar of Leona's jam just as it was about to slip out of the bag and onto the sidewalk. "But at least the investigation doesn't seem to be producing any evidence of murder."

"I wish I hadn't," Maggie said. In her arms, cradled

oddly like a wedding bouquet, was a bouquet of tulips. Yellow ones, Faith's favorite. "It's like being robbed of something private. Sounds stupid, I guess."

Sara's eyes lit with instant understanding. "Or watching a public autopsy."

Maggie nodded and started to reply, but Leona interrupted.

"What are you carrying?" she asked, glancing down at Sara's left hand as the three of them ascended the stairs to the opening door.

Sara couldn't resist a pale grin. "Faith's birthday cards."

"Oh, God!" Maggie laughed. "Those great cards she always sent!"

"I've got some from ten years back," said Leona. "They're classics, aren't they? Funny as hell—"

They all felt slightly better as they approached the door where Carol stood, waiting.

"Great flowers, Maggie," Carol said with grace. They walked together into the living room and stopped, looking around. Carol had flickering candles on every surface. The place looked a little like a funeral home and Maggie felt a nervous impulse to make a joke, but she refrained.

"I know, it looks like a funeral home," Carol said, surveying her work critically. "Faith would laugh."

"It looks absolutely appropriate, and she'd be touched." At least half of that was a true statement, Maggie told herself.

They all took seats on Carol's comfortable, sofas and looked at each other.

"Who wants to start?" Carol asked.

"I will," Leona said unexpectedly. She stood and walked over to the fireplace, pulling a single piece of paper from the pocket of her white linen pants. "I wrote something out after the funeral," she explained. "I wanted to write a poem, but I made a botch of it. So I thought about the things we shared and what they told me about her life, not her death." She cleared her throat.

"Faith and I were both crazy about politics," she began. "We met during the New Jersey presidential primary when we were sent out as a team to canvass for votes in Newark." She smiled. "We were two kids just out of college, getting doors slammed in our faces, slogging through the ice and snow together—but Faith made it fun. She set up a game: Would the housewife in the Cape Cod at the end of the block invite us in or throw us out? We'd keep score on who guessed right the most, and that got us through a couple of tough weeks. I thought I'd get *frostbite*, it was so cold."

"Who had the highest score?" Carol asked.

"Faith, of course," Leona said. "Always. She was always there for a friend, too. Last year, at the White House Correspondents' dinner? The zipper on my dress broke. Faith had a pile of safety pins in her handbag and she hauled me into the bathroom and fixed it on the spot." Leona smiled again. "You should have seen her, frowning, talking with all these pins in her mouth—but she was supposed to be up on the dais with the President. Instead, there she was, pinning me together. Now that's a friend." And then she sat down.

Carol took her place, her back determinedly straight. "Faith was one of the smartest friends I've ever had," she began. "She could get a press release out in nothing flat and she knew how to keep Goodspeed from stepping on his own message. I know how hard that is, I've had to avoid doing it enough myself." She looked around at the others, clearing her throat. "I know she hated to get sentimental; I do, too. Once we saw a dog get hit by a car on our way to lunch—Faith sat down in the street with the dog's head in her lap and talked to it until a fire truck came. By the time they got there, the dog was dead. I was furious because they took so long, but Faith just kept talking to the dog."

She paused. "I don't do this sort of thing very well," she said.

"You're doing fine," Sara said.

"There should be music or something," Carol said. She waved her hand to take in the room. "These candles are silly."

"No, they're not," Maggie said.

"Go ahead, Maggie, you do it now. You two were always laughing together."

Maggie stood slowly and looked at the small group of women. They all looked oddly waxen, and if they did, she knew, so did she. "We don't want to forget who she really was," she said. "We don't want to forget because if we do, we lose something of ourselves. We're trying to keep snapshots of her, I guess." She drew a deep breath. "She was someone I could always laugh with. Not just me—people gravitated to her; remember that laugh? So throaty and full—she loved to have a lot of people around her. And nobody could tell you the plot of a movie with more feeling than Faith. Sometimes I couldn't remember whether I had actually seen a particular movie or whether Faith had told me about it. She made the stories vivid."

Maggie looked around at her friends, feeling a weight of sadness and a sense of loss that had eluded her both in the cathedral and at Faith's graveside. "She made *life* vivid, and we benefited. . . . Faith shouldn't be dead, that's what I feel the most." Overwhelmed, she sat down.

Sara stood, sensing something extra was expected from her. "Faith was a hiker, like me," she began. "We never did anything ambitious together because there wasn't enough time—but she joked a lot about going to the Oregon Cascades and hunting down 'Big Foot.' Her plan was, we'd find him, bring him back, be credited with the great anthropological discovery of all time—and never have to work again." She smiled and swallowed hard. "We owe our friends a part of ourselves, but when a friend like

Faith dies, it's too late to give. I was born and raised a Catholic, and I guess that makes me the most religious one here. Right? Buffalo, New York, as Italian as they come." She tried to smile again as the others nodded.

"A part of me still believes in redemption and an existence after death, which isn't very fashionable at the moment. But it comforts me, anyhow. . . . Faith deserved better than she got. She was a joy to be around. And when she needed"—Sara was having a hard time completing the sentence—"when she needed help, she didn't get enough."

"Don't cry," Leona said softly. "It's okay."

Sara took a deep breath, steadying herself. "I think it would be appropriate," she said, "to say a silent prayer."

They bowed their heads, united in a strange and unusual intimacy. Never had they been quite so bound by a shared emotion as they were at this moment.

"Faith, we won't forget you," Leona said finally.

The four women sat quietly, bound and yet separate, each trying to hold on to a sense of the living Faith as long as she could. "Do you hear something?" Leona said suddenly. They all froze, listening. A murmur of voices; flashing lights through the window. . . .

"I don't believe it," Maggie said. "It's a camera crew!"

Leona had moved swiftly to the window, keeping herself hidden behind the curtain. "It's *two* camera crews," she reported. "What is the matter with them? Didn't they get enough at the funeral? Can't they leave us alone?"

Angrily, Carol flicked off the lights, plunging the room into total darkness. They heard a shout from outside and could see clearly now a reporter waving a microphone. "We'll just sit here and wait them out," Carol said as she clenched her fists into tight balls. "There's a time and a place, and this isn't the time and it isn't the place."

So together they huddled closer in the gloom, saying little if anything. Someone rang the bell, loud and long, but no one moved. They sat there for a long time, trapped by their own identities, unwilling to move into the light.

Three days later, Maggie hurried her step through the wide, marble corridors of the Cannon Office Building, reaching Carol's office just as an aide with an armful of papers and a slightly mad glint in her eye came rushing out. The aide paused, eying Maggie suspiciously.

"Can I help you?" she said.

"I'm here to see Congresswoman Lundeen," Maggie said. This was someone new she didn't recognize. "She's expecting me."

Annoyed, the aide freed one hand from her burden and brushed back a long strand of blond hair. "Sorry, I didn't catch your name?"

"I'm Maggie Stedman."

Instantly, the aide's face cleared. "Oh, sure; oh God, I'm sorry, I thought you were just another reporter. Hey, come on, she's been on the phone all morning drumming up sponsors for her nursing home bill, but she's definitely expecting you for lunch. Come on in."

At that moment a second aide brushed past them both and threw open the door to Carol's office, handing Carol a message as Maggie entered the room.

"Hi," Maggie said, assuming it might take a minute or two to get Carol's full attention. But Carol was staring at the piece of paper in her hand.

"Hey, Carol, it's me, Maggie."

"Can you believe it?" Carol interrupted in a befuddled whisper.

"Believe what?"

"There's no money left."

Maggie was momentarily confused. "No money in the budget for your nursing home bill?" she asked stupidly.

"Faith's money," Carol replied. "Look, this story just came over the wire." She rose part way from her chair and leaned against her desk, offering the piece of paper. "What do you think?"

Maggie stared at it. She had the dim impression the two of them were reacting much too slowly to something important, but she couldn't quite wrap her mind around what was happening. "Faith's money?" she echoed.

"Her money is gone—not just hers, her mother's money, the family money."

Maggie held in her mind for just an instant the fleeting memory of the tiny woman in black wool at Faith's funeral two days before. "Good God," she said, her mental image of Ruth Paige's protective wealth crumbling. "How did that happen?"

"I haven't the faintest idea. But I'll tell you who damn well should know and who damn well should care."

"Who?"

Carol's eyes narrowed until they were as tight and focused as those of a fighter entering the ring.

"Justin, that's who."

Maggie took one last gulp of stale coffee from a Styrofoam cup found behind a potted plant in Carol's office; Carol had a crack team for issues but nobody in her office ever seemed interested in replacing coffee cups. Right now, her head was buzzing with too many questions and too much caffeine as she listened to Carol field press calls on the news: Mrs. Paige's lawyers had announced half an hour ago that a substantial fortune—supposedly in a joint trust, with her daughter as custodian—had disappeared. Mrs. Paige still had considerable real estate holdings in Virginia, but the financial clout of the Paige family was definitely diminished. And there was no apparent explanation.

"I wish I could get off this phone long enough to call Justin and make him explain what the hell happened," Carol said, holding her hand over the receiver. "These reporters are talking like Faith gambled it all away. . . ." She searched Maggie's face for a response, her eyes on neutral.

"Impossible," Maggie said. Her voice faltered. She didn't believe Faith had done something awful with her mother's money, and she was sure Carol didn't believe it either. "Call the others."

The phone buzzed again. "Hello?" Carol's face brightened. It was Sara—calm, reliable Sara. "Sara, have you heard? What do you think?" She listened silently, then glanced up at Maggie. "She wants to talk to you," Carol said.

"Maggie." Sara's voice was weary.

"Sara, this is crazy."

"We've known all along something was going on. Maggie, I think we should postpone that *Vanity Fair* piece, I really do."

Maggie's stomach twisted into a sudden knot. "But—why?" she blurted, already knowing the answer to her question.

"I feel we're walking on Jell-O," Sara said, almost pleadingly. She hated pulling the rug out from under Maggie's project, but what was the alternative? "I've got five calls here from Sandi Snow that I have no intention of returning. But this news about Faith's lost money worries me. What comes next?"

"I don't know," Maggie whispered.

"Oh, Maggie, I'm sorry, I know you need the money, but we don't know enough yet about Faith's death. We could find ourselves in a mess if we're not careful."

Maggie couldn't think of anything to say. Her hands began to tremble. Ten thousand dollars down the drain, just like that. She needed to say something, but for just a minute it was the money she was thinking about; the money she had been counting on. In another part of her brain, she understood perfectly. She would have decided the same thing if she were in Sara's shoes. But wasn't there an alternative? Wasn't there a way to—was she saying these things out loud? She was babbling something, but what she was really thinking about now was the growing stack of bills on the hall table at home.

"I understand," she managed, "You're right, Sara, I know that, but—"

"I'll find a way to make it up to you," Sara said. "Right now we need to hold ourselves together and find out what happened to Faith."

She had indeed babbled something; apparently it was coherent. Sara was saying goodbye and telling her once again that she was sorry and she was glad Maggie understood.

Maggie said a quick and unnecessary goodbye to Carol—she had already shifted her attention to a line of constituents waiting in the crowded reception room. Maggie tripped over the polished brown oxfords of a veterinarian from Howard County, smiled a hello at his wife, and made her way out the door, thinking primarily at this point not about Faith or the missing money or Carol's anger or Sara's caution but of just how precariously she had her own financial life patched together.

"Okay, where are we going?"

Michael swung the wheel of his aging Ford to the right and turned onto MacArthur Boulevard. Maggie tipped back the seat and answered him with her eyes closed.

"Where do you think?"

"Lock Seven."

"Naturally," said Jeff from the back seat, sounding bored. "That's where you always want to go."

"I love the canal," Maggie said. "And it's the prettiest part of the towpath."

"It's just trees." Jeff was being pulled from his *Aladdin* video and he didn't like it. "Can I have some gum, Mom?"

Michael flipped a package of gum over the seat without glancing around. "Take the whole pack," he said.

"Jeff, don't put all that gum in your mouth at one time," Maggie ordered.

"Already did," came the muffled reply.

Michael glanced at her with a small warning smile, but she knew better than to take Jeff's bait.

"You might choke to death," she ventured. "It's a horrible way to go."

Suddenly Jeff's arms were up on the seat and she could smell the fresh soapiness of his skin. "If I do," he said solemnly, "I leave all my earthly possessions to you, and it's legal because Michael's my witness."

Maggie reached backward impulsively and yanked a lock of his hair.

"Ouch!" he yelled.

The mood in the car had lightened considerably as they made a U-turn at the bridge and headed back on Canal Road toward Lock Seven. The tires bumped over the gravel of the clearing cut from the roadside for parking. It was early; they were the first to arrive. With Jeff running ahead, they walked past the old caretaker's cabin and crossed the bridge spanning the lock which once lifted barges traveling northward up the canal. The air was still fresh. Maggie swung her arms free, searching the sides of the path for the bright blue patches of fragrant sweet william. If there was any still blooming, she'd put enough flowers together for a bouquet and take them home.

"So, talk," said Michael. His hands were shoved into the back pockets of his jeans and he was exhibiting considerable interest in the heavy foliage hanging over the thin ribbon of water to their right.

"I've lost the *Vanity Fair* assignment," she said. "Sara backed out."

"You need money?"

She smiled. "Got any to give away?"

"Sure." He was serious. "Five hundred dollars, any time you need it. Or more."

Maggie felt a sting of tears. Michael labored under huge child support payments and even offering five hundred dollars was a lot for him.

"Something else's on your mind," he said. "Something more important, if I'm not mistaken."

"What are you, a mind reader? I'm wrestling with a book proposal idea."

"Oh, sure—Teleki's seductive little proposal."

"I haven't told you about it. . . ."

"Maggie." Michael took her hand and moved it up to his forehead. "I'm smart, remember? Enough to have picked that up, anyhow."

"He says he can get me half a million dollars," she whispered.

Michael froze in his tracks. "Wow," he managed to say.

"So I've got to decide whether I can go ahead. Maybe I can write it in a particular way—"

"You've always wanted to write a book."

"Yes." She hesitated. "But about my friends?"

"Well, that's a problem. Have you talked to them about it?" he said.

A short silence. Maggie kicked a pebble out of her way and walked a little faster. Michael's legs were longer than hers and he wasn't slowing his gait.

"No."

"I guess you have to, Maggie."

"I know," she said simply. "But it's the wrong time."

Michael squinted into the sun, watching Jeff run ahead of them up the path. "Look, I understand what's happening," he said. "You're tired of banging out travel pieces and profiles."

"It's true, I'm hustling assignments to do *anything* all the time, and it all feels like lightweight junk," she said with a sigh, pushing back her hair. "Mostly, I'm sick of not knowing where my next dollar is coming from." She kicked at another pebble, wondering if she sounded too whiney.

"You could come back to the *Post.*"

"They wouldn't have me."

Michael waited to answer. "Someday, you've got to let go of what happened."

"Easier said than done." Her heart skipped a beat, but her voice stayed steady.

"Maybe I'm overstepping to push this, but you've got to do it some time."

"I can't talk about it."

"Look. You wrote a story; you did your job. When Senator Fairbanks died, you felt terrible; worse, you felt responsible. But you didn't kill him, Maggie."

"Fairbanks shot himself because my story outed him," Maggie said flatly. "His whole family fell apart. Come on, Michael—that's the truth."

She looked away, and they walked again in silence. This was the first time the subject had been broached in a year, and she was shaking. It was hard enough explaining it to herself, how could she explain it to anyone else?

"What I'm saying is, you don't have to shut yourself out the way you've done," he said doggedly. "I worked with you, I know how good you are. You're fair, you're honest; you were a good reporter. You're a good writer now, but you're stuck on blaming yourself."

Maggie pressed her lips together, wishing she could absorb what Michael was saying without responding too quickly. She reached for his hand and in silence the two of them continued down the path. "Nobody at the paper wants someone back who fell apart the way I did," she said finally.

"If they don't, it's because you've pulled away from them, not the other way around."

"Once they realized how guilty I felt, they got nervous," she insisted. "I violated a—a code."

Michael raised his arms. "Code? What code?" he said. "*The Washington Post* isn't the Catholic Church, Maggie. It's not the U.S. Army and it's not the Mafia, for Christ's sake! You make a mistake . . ."

"No, not just a mistake," she interrupted. "I made a terrible, unforgivable mistake."

He was giving up, passing on the issue. "You make a mistake, you learn, you move on—look, have it your own way."

In a perverse way, she was glad he had brought it up. It had been sitting there between them, a boulder in the road, for a full year. At least now he couldn't think she was avoiding the subject. She had made her point, even though she didn't feel any better. . . . Right now, what she needed was enough money to pay next month's bills. That's what it all came down to, didn't it? Money to pay the bills.

It was late Saturday night. When the phone rang, Sara squinted to read the hazy illuminated numbers of the clock on her nightstand. She blinked. My God, twelve-thirty.

"Did you hear that awful story about Patton?" Without even a hello, Leona was whispering the news in her best dramatic fashion.

"Leona—can it wait for the morning?" Sara said groggily.

"No! No, wait, *listen.*" Leona giggled. "It's too awful, too good really, to wait. He blew up at May Brenden, you know, the *New York Times* reporter? He called her a bitch, right out there in the White House press room. She was demanding to know why the White House hadn't let the police and the FBI search Faith's office by themselves, and he blew up. Said she'd never get another story out of him. God, Sara, how can anybody stand that guy?"

Sara was awake enough now to realize Leona was very drunk. She could almost hear the liquor flowing through her voice. This wasn't like Leona. She liked her wine, it was true, but she was much too savvy to let herself slip this far.

"Hey, don't you think you should go to bed?" she said gently.

"No! Why should I go to bed?" Leona was indignant. "I want to talk about people; did you see Nat Gordon at the funeral? Tawdry little man, everybody fawning over him for seats in his box at the Panther games, he has more power than *anybody.*"

"Leona, I'm dead tired."

"No, listen, I've got more stories about Jack Patton, everybody ought to hear them. Carol was right, he's a terrible man."

Sara heard Leona take time out for a gulp. "You're going to have a colossal hangover," she warned.

"I've earned it," Leona said. "I know what you're thinking. And I know what the others are thinking, too."

Sara didn't want to hear this, she just wanted to burrow deep into her pillow and try to fall into the sleep that had been so elusive these past few weeks.

"Let's talk tomorrow," she suggested.

"What you're thinking," Leona said, forming the syllables with elaborate care, "is that Justin wrecked Faith's finances and lost all her money and her mother's money. I'm right, aren't I?"

"I know nothing of the sort," Sara said. "I've got no right to jump to that kind of conclusion; I'm sure there's an explanation."

"Carol was all over me today. I'm sick of her righteousness, I really am." The words were running together now. "She insulted my husband, claiming he had to know what was going on. Well, he didn't. I don't know what Faith did, but I'm telling you, Justin isn't involved." Leona let out a hoarse sob. "And okay, maybe we shouldn't have gone to Faith's house . . ."

"That was a bad move, Leona. I can't pretend otherwise.'' The truth was, Sara had been appalled when Maggie had shamefacedly admitted to the early morning visit.

''But everything is aboveboard with my husband!''

''I believe you, okay?''

A silence. ''You do?''

Sara paused. Leona had an artless quality that went beyond naivete. Oh, that wasn't fair. There was another word she wanted—but digging it out of her brain at this hour was too much trouble. Right now she wanted more than anything the chance to fall back asleep.

''Yes, I do.''

A long sigh slipped over the wires and Sara could almost visualize Leona drooping like a wilted flower.

''I'm so glad,'' Leona said uncertainly. ''Really, I'm so glad.'' A pause. ''I hope I do, too.''

Another pause.

''I can't believe I said that.'' Her voice was astonished. ''Goodnight, Sara.''

The phone clicked and the line went dead. Sara let her head sink onto the pillow and tried to go back to sleep but it was impossible. She shifted positions; punched her pillow. She had that meeting tomorrow and she had to get some sleep, but all she could think about was Faith. She hadn't responded . . . why hadn't she responded? She lay there, staring at the ceiling, following the shadows as they worked their way like tiny tentacles across the plaster. It seemed like hours, but finally her eyes grew heavy. She slept. Maybe, if she were lucky, she thought before slipping into unconsciousness, it was too late to dream.

CHAPTER 5

"Good morning, Judge."

Sara found herself looking closely at the man standing in the committee-room doorway. He was of medium height, spare and muscular, and dressed in a crisp white shirt and khakis. He had a wide, relaxed smile. This must be Barney Cassidy, she thought with interest. He didn't look like the kind of man who would have spent twenty years shepherding bills through the labyrinth of Congress, but maybe his cheerful ease came from the fact that he had finally broken away from the political grind.

"Hello," she said, extending her hand, liking him immediately. "You're my guide through the Senate for the next couple of weeks?"

"Yes, ma'am." His grin was warm. "I need a break from the boring job of making money—finally."

She laughed.

"Good, I made you laugh." He turned suddenly diffident. "I'm sorry about your friend, Faith Paige. I understand she was special."

Sara kept her smile steady. Ten days now, and each morning she awoke unable to believe the reality of Faith's death. She was walking into this committee room for her first prehearing briefing, going on with her life as if nothing had happened—while Faith lay buried in the ground. It was unfair. Horribly unfair.

All this, somehow, he seemed able to read. "I guess you never quite get over it," he said quietly as he followed her in.

"How's the consulting business?" she asked to make conversation as she sank into a padded swivel chair that wobbled a bit on its base.

"On a scale of one to ten? Oh, about a seven, I guess. Actually, getting pretty lucrative. But I'd much rather be showing you the ropes up here, Judge. *That's* a ten."

He was flirting, ever so slightly, and Sara had to smile. Not many men had the self-confidence to do that around her any more.

She looked around. This meeting was supposed to be a quick run-through of the political necessities of the next couple of weeks, but she felt a lump of fear she had been unable to swallow down since Faith's funeral. Next to her, with a sour look on his face, was Tray Bingham, the graying, shriveled Senate Majority Leader. He cast a grumpy glance at Sara.

" 'Morning, Judge," he said.

She nodded, scanning the rest of the table: from the other end, Amos Berman shot her a grin. Next to him sat Jack Patton, looking busy and restless. His eyes were scrutinizing each person in the room in turn, but he gave her an affable wave of the hand. Three staffers with tight, concentrating faces completed the table.

Bingham cleared his throat, a raspy, unpleasant sound. "Welcome, Judge," he said, small blue eyes staring inquiringly from beneath heavy-beetled brows. "We're here to give you an idea of what to expect in the next few weeks, with help from our White House friend over here. Right, Jack?"

A curt nod from Patton.

"Well, now." Bingham launched into a lecture on the various stroking techniques Sara would need to employ as she made her Senate rounds, taking the opportunity to go into various pet issues of his own. "They're not going to ask you how you'll actually vote on some of the cases, Judge, but they'll be getting a sense of how you *feel.* You understand? For example, I'm concerned about rationing health care for old people, you understand? We've got all these new state laws making it too *easy* to pull the plug on them and I'm—"

"Let's move along, Tray." Patton, slumped deep in his chair, looked bored. "You're on a tangent."

Bingham glared at this affront to his authority. "We're all busy men, Jack," hc said. "You have pressing business back at the White House?"

"Always, Tray. We're used to getting things done." The emphasis on "we" was unmistakable.

"Does that include releasing everything you know about Faith Paige's death?" Bingham shot back. "Seems to me you folks are moving mighty slow on that."

"The police have no complaints."

"How come you kept them out of her office?"

The atmosphere was suddenly charged, and Patton's eyes turned ice-cold. "We've given the police everything they need. She killed herself."

"You're got a friend of hers sitting in this room, Jack," Barney broke in. "Are you absolutely sure?"

"Absolutely."

All eyes moved to Sara, whose own eyes had turned frosty. What arrogance! Patton thought he could make something true simply by saying it. "Nobody's explained the missing money," she said.

"Nothing will surface that changes the obvious facts, I'm sure. You think differently?" Patton asked his question of Sara with almost bland curiosity.

"Maybe I will—when all the facts are in."

No one spoke. Bingham suddenly stood, his wizened face tight as a raisin. "Well, we'll just finish this up right here," he said. "We'll meet tomorrow. Judge Marino, Mr. Cassidy here will brief you on your first Hill meetings and get things moving along. That way our busy White House person can get back on the job." He was plainly furious. But Patton hardly seemed to notice.

As they all pushed back their chairs, Sara saw Amos's puzzled frown. He nodded to her and Barney, and the three of them left the committee room and walked down the hall.

"What do you think?"

"Patton? He makes me long for Marty Apple." Barney looked disgusted.

"Goodspeed's handler? Yeah, a tough old bird, but nothing like this guy," agreed Amos.

"It's more than arrogance," Sara said.

Amos paused. "Yep, it is. Seeing the President's chief of staff keep an eye on his watch when he's supposed to be monitoring the course of a Supreme Court appointment is . . ."

Sara leaned over and took a long drink from the water fountain tucked into the marble walls at the end of the hall. The water felt cool on her lips. Was she going to say it, or was Amos?

"You don't do that," Amos finished. "It's too important."

So it was up to her. "Unless you don't want the nominee."

Amos and Barney glanced at each other uncomfortably. Both were silent.

Now Sara knew that worrying about the lump of fear in her throat was totally rational.

Leona patted a little extra powder on her nose and surveyed the results critically. The tension of the last ten days was telling on her. She was anxious to talk to Justin about Faith, but it was frustratingly hard to get time alone with him lately. Her day today had been exhausting: interviewing three new waiters, trying to perfect a risotto dish that wouldn't go soggy in transit, and buying the produce for tomorrow's State Department reception. Maccoby Caterers was getting too big for the kind of hands-on work she enjoyed most . . . for heaven's sake, these were small worries. She was a very fortunate woman, wasn't she? So why had she hit the liquor cabinet and made that ridiculous call to Sara?

"Leona? Ready yet?"

Quickly she twisted the lid off the aspirin bottle and gulped down two pills without water, a trick that struck Justin as a little too efficient when he caught her doing it.

"Justin, we need to talk," she said, as he stepped through the door to the bedroom. With a sinking heart she saw he was in a tux.

His smile was neutral. "We're due at that buffet for Governor Idelson at Union Station. It's formal, remember? Why don't you wear the Bob Mackie?"

Leona squirmed in her chair. She had no interest in going out tonight. "Needs alterations," she said with an apologetic smile. "Justin, let's not go. Let's stay home by ourselves."

His smile was amused. "Sweetheart, you're clearly in no condition for anything more taxing than sipping Bloody Marys."

She had forgotten his mocking eye; Justin never missed a flaw. He softened his words immediately by leaning over and kissing her on the forehead. "I'll go," he said. "You rest."

Leona hesitated. "I'm going crazy thinking about Faith. What happened to her money? What's the connection with her death?"

He snorted. "A disaster."

"What happened?"

"We didn't know that woman too well," Justin said. "Or at least not well enough." He shrugged. "She got herself into some scheme, I don't know what. But she never consulted me."

"Mrs. Paige is totally distraught."

"Understandable." There was that secret little smile again. "Unfortunately, the person responsible is already dead."

"Justin!"

"I'm sorry, dear." His eyes were properly contrite. "She was your friend."

It was slightly over the edge, almost lachrymose, and Leona felt a flash of anger. "You act as if you hardly knew her at all. You snapped my head off when I said I thought she was in financial trouble, and if I saw it, how come you didn't? You're the investment broker everybody consults, you were helping her with investments."

"I managed the small amount of Faith's money she chose to put in my hands," he responded tightly. "Not a cent more and not a cent less. That lady took chances and you know it, and if you're going to deny that she liked living on the edge, I don't think there's much point in going on with this conversation. Frankly, I'll be damned if I understand why Goodspeed made her his press secretary." There was a long, silent beat. "Now, can we put all that behind us? I'm working hard to position myself with Dick Sayles, damn it, and you know it. I could use some support!"

Leona was stunned by the outburst. This was so unlike Justin.

"Look"—he glanced at his watch. "You're really in no shape for any more talking tonight, I can see that. My suggestion is you go to bed and sleep it off." With that he turned on his heel and marched from the room.

Leona looked at herself in the mirror and shivered. This was the first time Justin had straight out told her she was drinking too much and she waited for her habit of angry denial to surface. It didn't happen. Instead, she stared in the mirror at the still-comely woman in her mid-forties with slightly puffy eyes and wondered just how soon it would be before everybody decided she was really a lush.

''Not long,'' she said out loud. And then wondered how she could sound so matter-of-fact.

It was half-past eleven and the crisp, white-clothed tables at Marrocco's were still mostly empty as Maggie, Leona, and Carol seated themselves around a table tucked in the corner. This wasn't their regular monthly lunch, but that didn't seem particularly important any more. They needed to gather. And they were here in these more casual, glass-surrounded environs because they couldn't face the memories of the wine room at Galileo's. Marrocco's suited them better now.

''It's been twelve days. What do we know so far?'' Maggie kept her voice low, even though there was no one near enough to hear.

Carol's response was prompt. ''Death by drowning, no proven explanation for the lacerations around her neck. And none''—she glanced at Leona—''none for the sudden disappearance of half her mother's fortune.''

''I've asked Justin.'' Leona kept her voice calm and as neutral as possible. She was not going to lose it the way she had on the phone with Sara. ''He had nothing to do with this. He counseled Faith on a few investments, but he thinks she got into some scheme he knows nothing about.''

''That's it?'' Carol was incredulous.

''Yes, that's it.'' Leona swallowed and stared hard at Carol.

Maggie hurried on. ''The Park Police are calling it suicide. The official verdict will be released tomorrow.''

''And Jack Patton wants the whole thing to go away as fast as possible.'' Carol's tone was bitter.

"Don't blame it all on him. Faith worked for Dick Sayles. He could pursue this more aggressively if he wanted to."

"He seems paralyzed—"

"On all fronts," Maggie said. "Everybody's saying he's a weak substitute for Goodspeed."

"Is Sara coming? She may know more."

Maggie picked up a piece of wheat bread and dumped a large pat of butter onto it with her knife. "She can't come today, she's working the Hill for votes." She frowned, thinking about her own agenda. She had to talk to Sara, and soon, if she was thinking of signing this book contract. The bills . . . Sara was the person to talk it out with. Sara was the person to convince.

"Sara may be in trouble," Leona said unexpectedly.

Maggie and Carol froze, menus poised in the air.

"I can't tell you anything exactly, but one of my waiters—he was doing the State Department reception yesterday—overheard one of Patton's deputies saying there's talk at the White House of dumping her for another nominee."

"Oh, no!" Maggie was aghast.

"I warned Sara. What'd he say?" Carol demanded.

"He saw my guy hovering and shut up fast. I have no idea."

"Could it have anything to do with the fact that she was a friend of Faith's?"

"Why would you think that?"

"Everything comes back to Faith."

The three friends fell silent for a long moment.

"Justin is always saying she lived on the edge," Leona ventured.

"Maybe she did."

"I'm not judging her."

"Oh, hell." Carol couldn't keep it in. "She had an awful relationship with her mother."

"How do you know that?" Maggie asked curiously.

Carol hesitated. "I guess I just sensed it."

"Are you saying that could have tipped her over the edge? Are you saying she committed suicide because she hated her mother?"

"No, no," Carol said, shaking her head. "Look, I'm just as confused as the rest of you. I mean, Faith wasn't mentally ill, or anything. We would have *known.*"

"But how does this affect Sara?"

"Well, what if they were trying to cover up a scandal? They'd dump Sara, maybe. In case she knew too much."

Again there was silence as they exchanged glances.

"Nothing can stop Sara getting this appointment. We can't let it happen." Leona's voice was tentative, but not her words. "Surely, Justin . . ." This time her voice trailed off.

Carol dug her hands through her hair. "I've thought from the beginning Patton wanted her out, and we damn well better find out why—before it happens."

Maggie felt deeply uneasy. All thoughts of doing a book had left her head for the moment. "If this gets out—"

Carol, worried too, tried bravado. "Most of the reporters in this town wouldn't see a story if it hit them in the face."

For a change, Maggie didn't bridle. Instead, it was she who pulled them back into a tight unit. "We don't want it to be a story, Carol," she whispered. "Not yet."

The late afternoon sun was dipping now below the horizon, throwing the Oval Office into a pre-dusk gloom. Dick Sayles sat behind the desk, idly strumming his fingers on the polished mahogany as he scanned a stack of papers. Jack Patton, lounging in one of the more fragile Chippendale chairs, shifted his weight. There was a loud creak.

"Jack—be careful of that chair," Sayles said, warningly.

"It's a reproduction," Patton said with a dismissive wave of his hand. He had occupied this turf longer than Sayles, and he liked underscoring the fact.

"Actually, I had them replaced with the originals."

Sayles smiled as Patton sat bolt upright. "Just kidding," he said. He turned his attention to a visitor whose place on the sofa was already in shadow. "A great British tradition, afternoon tea," he said affably. "Something very civilized about it, don't you think?"

The visitor smiled. "Always have, Mr. President," he said. He leaned toward Patton. "Jack, you want a cup?" he asked, nodding toward the silver teapot on a table a distance away from the overburdened Chippendale.

Patton rose without a word, ignoring the tea, and began to pace, brow furrowed. The bright light in the room was fading slightly to a late afternoon glow.

"You have my gratitude for checking Faith's house," Sayles said to the visitor. "She had a habit of taking things home from the office; a bad habit for anyone working here."

"Nothing showed up, as you know."

Sayles tried not to look too relieved. "Who do I thank?"

"My wife, actually," said the man on the sofa. "She was very helpful without, of course, knowing why."

Sayles turned full toward the man on the sofa, ignoring Patton for the moment. "Good job, Justin," he said.

Justin Maccoby nodded in his courtly fashion, and then poured himself a second cup of tea. His long, fastidious finger curled gracefully through the narrow curvature of the cup handle.

Patton shot a studied look and stopped pacing. "Shall we talk about Sara Marino?"

"You're still on that one?" Sayles asked, now toying with a pen on his desk. His fingers were quick and nervous.

"Perhaps this isn't the time." Patton looked meaningfully at Justin.

"Justin is a friend," Sayles said.

Patton waited for a heartbeat and then pushed forward. "I've got doubts on how good a candidate she is, Mr. President. She's got a reputation for opposing important business mergers.''

Sayles chuckled. ''Topco Entertainment? That was a hell of a lot more than an 'important business merger,' Jack. She's a trust-buster, all right. And it's won her a lot of friends.''

''A little quick off the launching pad, though.'' Patton's dissent was smooth. ''Some of the best-informed people tell me she's not up to speed on some of her biggest cases.''

''Really? I've heard the opposite.''

Patton never blinked. ''Shallow, I think that's the word.''

''I haven't heard that.''

''If there's the slightest chink in this nomination—it could happen, you know.''

''I'm sure it could,'' Justin murmured.

''A lot of people are ready to use it against you. Goodspeed was a popular president who let the bills pile up and you're still seen—I'm sorry, Mr. President, but I know you want me to talk straight. You could be held accountable for *his* mistakes as well as your own.'' Patton looked quite satisfied with himself.

Sayles sat very still. Then he turned to Justin. ''So? What do you think?''

There was the briefest of pauses as Justin gathered around him the invisible mantle of adviser. He formed a tepee with his long, slender hands. ''You do have several problems brewing,'' he said. ''The timber interests are on your neck; then there's the Arizona real estate scandal. . . .''

He was fully aware of Patton staring at him. ''Most of all, nobody's satisfied with the way health care reform got twisted out of shape. The trick now is not to scare people to death; so, in a sense, your Court nominee becomes your surrogate.''

Justin paused, studying Sayles, seeing an uncertain man still feeling his way. Not weak, necessarily, but clearly ambivalent about this Court nominee. He could hear Patton's breathing. Whatever Patton was up to, it was in his own best interest to proceed cautiously. "Rightly or wrongly, you need a team player," he said.

"There are better nominees," Patton interjected. "Sir, you have the right to choose your own nominee—and you need to consider Judge Marino's connection with recent events." He had a glint in his eye. "I assume I can say this, if Justin is a friend—our recent problem—"

Justin's voice cut in, deceptively relaxed. "Yes. Faith Paige, who certainly spent considerable time with Sara Marino. I understand it could be embarrassing."

There was a long silence.

"You know about that."

"I make it my business to know everything, Mr. President," Justin said, managing just the right tone of supportive confidentiality while ignoring Patton's glare. "That way I can serve you best."

Sayles said nothing for a long moment. "It sounds like the two of you want me to get rid of her."

Jack Patton swiftly spoke up before Justin could take the lead. "No, no," he said. "Nothing that drastic." There was silence again in the room, broken only by the distant sound of an ambulance siren on Pennsylvania Avenue.

"If I withdraw the nomination, I get a lot of people mad," Sayles said very slowly. "She's the kind of home-run nominee every President searches for. Solid small-town lawyer, prosecutor at Justice, not a problem in her writings we can find, and she's a woman. That's damn hard to match."

"Maybe she's having second thoughts herself," Patton said. "It's a lonely life."

Even Justin couldn't buy that. "Really, Jack."

Patton bristled. "What sort of life do you think a woman like that has, anyway?"

"Not so lonely she'd turn down an appointment to the

Supreme Court,'' Sayles said dryly.

''It's nothing to concern yourself about, Mr. President,'' Patton said. ''But I think I can convince her to withdraw on her own accord.''

Sayles glanced at Justin again, something Patton was getting tired of seeing. It made his own agenda even more imperative.

''What's your take?''

Justin took a long sip of tea. Too bad it was already cold, but it didn't matter. It was time to make peace with his adversary. ''I'd say, leave it in Jack's capable hands.''

Patton nodded in his direction and, in that instant, an alliance was formed.

Dick Sayles stared for a long time at the two men. He didn't trust either of them. But who did you trust in this job? He hesitated. He needed his own people, all down the line; it would take a while. And he should damn well get to choose his own Court nominee, not take somebody else's, not when it added pressure. He didn't have to walk in Goodspeed's shadow forever, for God's sake. ''Float it, first,'' he said. ''See what reaction you get, then we'll talk.'' He picked up a packet of papers on his desk and held them out to Patton. ''This Commerce reorganization. Okay, Jack? Another run-through on this?''

''Yes, sir, Mr. President. Anything you want.''

With uncharacteristic quiet, Carol Lundeen sat alone in her office in the evening's gloom. A nervous aide ventured through the door and hesitated at the sight of his boss hardly moving behind the piles of paper on her cluttered desk. He stole a glance at his watch.

''You really want us all to go home?'' he asked. ''This early?'' Congresswoman Lundeen's staff was used to grabbing sandwiches for dinner and working until at least eight in the evening, and that was in non-election years.

''Yes,'' Carol said quietly.

"What about the press package for . . . ?"

"Do it tomorrow."

"Geez. I mean"—he scrambled worriedly to cover himself—"I'm sorry, I mean—well . . ." He gulped and decided to risk it anyway. He was going back to law school in the fall so he couldn't lose too much. "Can I do something?"

She looked up, but he couldn't see her face.

"I'm fine," she said, not unkindly. "Go ahead."

Slowly the door closed and Carol barely moved a muscle as she listened for the sounds of her outer office winding down. The hum of the computers, the chatter at the Xerox machine, the frazzled voices and the urgent footsteps—all were music to her ears. Now each in turn slowed, replaced by the murmuring of astonished voices. This wasn't a sound she liked or was used to hearing, and she held still, waiting. Five minutes later the last of the murmuring ceased. She heard the outer door close, heard the turn of the key in the lock, and knew finally she was alone in the only place she truly loved. Carol tried deep breathing; maybe that would help. *Be calm*, she told herself. *You're in shock.*

"Bart," she whispered in the stillness, staring at the pictures along the wall, all those pictures of confident handshakes and smiling faces and proud achievements of the past. She found herself straining now to glimpse just one familiar face in the background, an image usually a bit fuzzy, or off to the side, or maybe just the bald spot on the top of his head, that familiar bald spot. . . .

One phone call. That's all it had taken to wipe out everything. One phone call from the guy in the background with the bald spot telling her he—how had he put it? He "needed some distance" and he was moving out, sorry, he knew she would manage just fine, she always had. He was all packed and at the airport now. He'd tell the kids himself. She'd hardly miss him.

"My God," she'd whispered in a shaky voice. "What are you talking about? Bart—this is a joke, isn't it?"

No, it isn't a joke. He was telling her this deliberately at the last moment to make it clear he was serious; there was no discussion possible. Too many words over too many years that ended up meaning nothing. He knew it was painful; he was sorry. But it was better this way.

Just before an election year. An election year! "Bart," she said, weeping finally. "You bastard. How the hell could you do this to me?"

It was a fortunate thing everyone had left the office because Congresswoman Lundeen was crying like a baby, and that would not have been good for her image, not good at all.

National Airport was a zoo, as usual. Jack Patton settled back into the soft leather upholstery of the waiting limo with the absent-minded, contented satisfaction of the fully entitled. He was on his way back from an antique show in New York that had yielded a few tidy finds for his Chevy Chase home: a Hepplewhite armchair—a beautiful piece of work, of far better lineage than those spindly Chippendales in Sayles's office—and an absolutely breathtaking cloisonné vase. He picked up the phone, his heartbeat quickening as he thought of how much more he would soon be able to afford.

"American Telecom, good morning," the operator sang.

"Si Posner, please. Jack Patton calling." Two clicks, another secretary, and then the rumbling voice of the Chairman of the board of American Telecom—the man who held the key to his future.

"Jack! So how's it going?" Very genial; they were already almost like old friends. "When are we getting you over here?"

"Soon, soon. Just a few things to take care of, first." You still had to be careful on these damn car phones.

"Got a replacement nominee yet?"

These guys didn't waste time. "Several prospects . . ." Jack started cautiously.

"But not our problem lady, right? We sure don't need an unfriendly judge." Posner chuckled.

"I think I can take care of that."

"Good! We're counting on it. This company needs you, Jack. We're waiting for you. We've got big growth plans—a helluva lot more than just movies and television this time around. We've got our eyes on a phone company. Obviously, the friendlier the legal climate for the kind of acquisitions we have in mind, the better."

A few jocular exchanges, and Jack was off the phone, his heart thumping hard. Posner's message was the bluntest yet: get rid of Marino if you want the job—and he wanted it. Sayles would never win election on his own, and he'd be damned if he'd go down with him. Nobody could take away the leverage he had at this precise moment, nobody could keep him from orchestrating his own future. Why should a trust-buster like Sara Marino stand in his way? Such a small thing. Just derail her, and he would have proved his worth to the Telecom board . . . in time to head American Telecom. With Justin's help—unwitting, to be sure—the derailment was all set.

He slammed the phone down and addressed the driver through the plastic screen. "Can we get moving? I've got an important appointment," he ordered.

So he'd be a few minutes early. That meant getting it over with sooner.

Sara gripped the arms of her chair as she stared at Jack Patton's serene, unbreachable expression. "I don't believe a word of it," she said. Her brain was spinning, her heart beating painfully fast.

"I'm sorry, Judge. This is probably nuts, but I'm sure you understand the position it puts us in."

"You'd better spell this out. Carefully."

Patton hunched forward, a frown of exaggerated proportions furrowed vertically to the bridge of his nose. "Your father is a doctor in upstate New York, right? He is also a doctor who helped sick people die."

"Doctors have patients die on them all the time."

"Not the way he handled it. He helped kill them. He did it quietly, but he did it for years."

"That's ridiculous."

"We have witnesses. I ask you to think hard how this could play politically."

"What are you saying, Jack?"

"People think they're being pushed toward accepting euthanasia, you know that. Rationed health care's a bigger flashpoint now than abortion. Hey, it's tough on politicians."

"That's your problem, not my father's. He's no killer."

Patton threw up his hands in a helpless gesture. "Look, it may appear that way to some people, you know that. I'm not condemning your father, but under the circumstances. . . ." He hesitated just the right number of seconds. "We'll do nothing. We'll let you handle it. We'll back you in whatever route you choose, I guarantee that. We could say it was your health; whatever you want. 'Judge Marino has our full respect and confidence and we wish her well in her future endeavors.' Hey, anything you *want* us to say."

Sara, outwardly composed, was frantically sifting through her options. Her own father, some kind of Dr. Death? Absurd. Totally crazy. This smug bastard facing her had something up his sleeve and she had to find out what it was, fast. "Who's making these charges?" she demanded.

"I'm sorry, I can't tell you. That would be violating a confidence. There's no fight here, Judge. Just bad history."

"You're ready to take the word of sources without the

guts to speak up publicly?" He wouldn't get away with this.

Patton hesitated, one eyebrow arching slightly. "I don't think you'd want to risk that, would you?"

"Risk *what?* My father is an honest man, a good doctor, and he would never break the law," she snapped. But Patton didn't want to be convinced, that was clear. He didn't care what the truth was.

Patton cleared his throat, enjoying his moment as judge and jury. "Your father's first name was . . ."

"George. George Marino. And don't talk about him as if he were dead."

"God, this would be terrible for him," murmured Patton, staring down at a folder of papers in his hands.

"Jack, stop this silly charade," she said flatly. "My father had nothing to do with killing anybody."

A long pause. "You're probably right," he said. "But think how difficult it would be to explain. We can't afford a press scandal, you wouldn't want that for the President, would you? This is a matter of loyalty." He stopped. "Look, no one need ever know." His voice was quite solicitous. "We've got those bases covered."

"What do you mean, you'd 'wish me well'?"

"You are a responsible, honored judge with a solid future ahead, and no one can take that away from you."

Sara's insides grew cold.

"You're withdrawing my nomination."

"I didn't say that, Sara, but in a certain sense our hands are tied. Surely you can see our position? If this gets out, your confirmation hearing could be a bloody nightmare."

This was ridiculous. Sara felt suddenly in the center of a bad movie. There was no way her father had produced this carefully orchestrated aura of crisis.

"I'm not withdrawing," she said quietly.

"Think this through, Sara. Very carefully."

Sara stood, then walked to the window of Jack's office,

staring out at the soft green lawn sloping away from the White House. "Jack, why do you want me out?"

"I don't know what you mean."

"I think you do." She chose her words carefully. "Do I in some way pose a threat to you?"

"Not at all."

"To President Sayles?"

"Anything that brings bad publicity could pose a threat to the President."

"Like a scandal?" Be careful . . .

He was silent. Then he reached into a folder of papers and pulled out an ink-smeared, tissue-thin fax. He offered it to her, his eyes veiled. "I hoped I wouldn't have to do this," he said, handing the paper to her. "But I'm afraid there's more." He cleared his throat. "You did something slightly shady yourself, Judge."

"I don't know what you're talking about."

"Your father was stripped of his medical license, I understand. And you found a way to get it back for him."

Sara gazed at him in disbelief. "He voluntarily surrendered that license."

"I believe it was the result of a settlement of a complaint against him by a colleague, am I right?"

"He was accused of nothing."

Patton studied the fax, then looked up. "Somewhat inattentive to patients, I understand. Something about substance abuse?"

Sara found herself remembering. . . . Her father, depressed in the months after her mother's death, had taken heavy doses of Valium to sleep at nights—until a nurse complained he wasn't focusing on his work sharply enough . . . a terrible time.

"No one ever said he harmed a patient."

"Some might disagree. The point is, you pulled strings to get him his license back."

"That was purely routine. When he pulled himself together, the medical society welcomed him back. They *wanted* him back."

Patton raised an eyebrow. "It isn't what it was that matters, it's how it would appear in the current political climate."

"It would be negative for me only if you allowed it to be."

"I'm not so sure we can do much for you on this one, Sara—unless you can prove you had no involvement."

This man was talking abandonment, pure and simple, and Sara was having a difficult time staying calm. "No, of course I can't prove it."

"Then you understand our dilemma."

"You *are* withdrawing my nomination, right?" She braced herself.

A long heartbeat. "We want you to make the decision," Patton said softly. "Not us."

"What's going on, Sara?" It was Amos, sounding anxious on the phone, a few hours later. "I'm getting whispers out of the White House, something's afoot."

Sara told herself to relax and accept the fact that Jack Patton intended to waste no time. The process of undermining her was under way. She shouldn't be surprised, she couldn't afford to be surprised. She must think clearly. "Amos—"

"I'm listening."

She stopped. This wasn't the right sequence. She couldn't talk about this until she talked to her father.

"I'll tell you everything—just give me a day or two."

He drew his breath in sharply, reminding her all too clearly that, as her sponsor, Amos had a lot riding on this.

"Whatever you say. But, Sara . . ."

"Yes?"

"Make it quick."

"I understand."

She replaced the phone, which almost instantly rang again.

"Hi," said Maggie with a bouncy cheerfulness that she hadn't heard in weeks. "Gotta see you."

"No, I can't. Not now, I'm sorry."

"Sara, please—I must see you."

"I'm tied in knots today with this new case."

"You can't work every minute of your life, can you?" Maggie's voice had a slightly out-of-control pitch. "Look, I'm going to be in front of the Courthouse in fifteen minutes in my car with some Fritos and a bottle of wine and two glasses, and we're heading for a shady tree at Dumbarton Oaks. Come on, Sara—it'll make you feel good to get away, just for an hour. I'll bring you back to your office after and you can work your ass off all night if you want to."

"Maggie—"

"*Please*, Sara."

So what harm would it do to relax for an hour? The idea of sharing a bottle of wine in the park with Maggie was suddenly attractive—even in the poisonously humid air of an August day in Washington. It had to be healthier than the air she was forced to breathe around Jack Patton.

"Okay," she said. "Just an hour."

"It's great wine, just not cold enough, sorry." Maggie crossed her jeans-clad legs in front of her as she poured Fiddlehead Cellars Sauvignon Blanc into a pair of plastic juice glasses picked up hastily at the Georgetown Safeway.

Sara took a sip. The air wasn't so bad on Dumbarton Oaks' soft, still-green lawns above Georgetown. "I don't care," she said. "It's good." She closed her eyes briefly in an effort to erase the pressure in her head. "You know what?" she said with mild surprise. "I'm glad you called."

"When you're reaching middle age like we are you've got to do things spontaneously," Maggie said, taking a gulp from her own glass, trying to decide what to bring up first. Sara looked tired, and she didn't want to increase the pressure on her. But she had to warn her about the rumor Leona had picked up. And if she was ever going to sign that contract, she had to bring up the book. Now. With no further delay. If she could talk this through with Sara, everything would be all right. God, it would be a relief.

"Reaching?" teased Sara.

"Sara, we'll always be reaching it; we'll never actually be there. You and me and Madonna and—"

"Princess Di and Isabelle and—"

"Carol and Leona and—"

Sara shivered, the joke dissipating. "But not Faith," she finished.

They sat in quiet companionship for a few moments, each in her own thoughts.

"I wish I could believe something—maybe a soul—survives," Maggie said.

"I'm not so sure it doesn't."

"The night we held our memorial for Faith? You said more than I've heard you say before about being Catholic," Maggie ventured.

"I don't think much about it any more. How about you?"

"Well, I guess parochial school leaves its marks."

"Indelibly," Sara said lightly. "The nuns who taught me were pretty fierce about everything, especially sex."

Maggie rolled her eyes and nodded in agreement. "A bite out of a hamburger on Friday could send you straight to Hell."

Sara was grinning now. "If you sat on a boy's lap in a crowded car, you were supposed to put a telephone book between the two of you."

"They thought of everything," Maggie said with a laugh. "But who ever went on a date with a phone book?"

"Maybe this is too personal . . ." Sara cast a quick

glance at her friend sitting cross-legged on the grass. Maggie, her hair pulled back in a knot at the nape of her neck, looked unusually casual today in a pair of jeans and a soft cotton shirt. It reminded Sara that Maggie didn't live quite the same programmed life as she did; as most people did. What, she wondered, was it like to free-lance? Did Maggie worry a lot about money? She felt bad about backing out of the *Vanity Fair* interview, but uneasy about bringing it up. Maggie didn't like excess sympathy.

"Fire away."

"Do you get lonely?" Clumsy phrasing; she could have said it better.

"I'll admit it if you don't tell anyone," Maggie said with an overly cheerful smile. Then she relented. "Sure, I do," she said. "I still miss Jim. And I miss the *Post* you know, sitting on someone's desk arguing, talking—that kind of thing." She glanced sideways at Sara. "Maybe my question is too personal, too."

"You're entitled."

"Did you ever want to get married?" she asked. "When you were living with that lawyer—"

"David."

"Right, David. Everybody thought the two of you were a done deal. If I'm prying. . . ."

Sara stretched out her legs, watching her toes wiggle. The touch of the grass was cool. "No," she said. "It's okay. I know people wonder; you probably think I'm touchy about it."

"Are you?"

Sara paused. "I don't think I am," she said "David and I were expert at juggling schedules. We'd sit at breakfast and map them out like generals planning a battle. It took two years before we realized we weren't leaving much time for each other." Said so flatly, it sounded banal.

Maggie wasn't sure if her next question was a real intrusion, but she couldn't resist. "Are you ever sorry?"

"Not about breaking up with David," Sara said, readily enough. "But I think sometimes I spent all those years working and getting ahead and never feeling I was missing anything. Then suddenly, there I was in my forties, looking up and saying, 'Well, *that* train passed me by.' " She couldn't remember talking about it quite this bluntly before. "But how can I complain about the trade-off? Look where I am. Where I go from here is another matter."

Again they lapsed into a comfortable silence, lulled by the somnolent sweetness of the afternoon.

"I don't think I've ever actually said it—but I really look forward to our lunches," Maggie said finally. "Making time for friends shouldn't be so hard, but it is."

"Maybe we don't always know when we need them."

"That's a bit unsettling."

"I suppose so," Sara said after a pause. "My father gave me a book on Clarence Darrow when I was twelve, and I knew I was going to be a lawyer before I finished it. What happens to people who don't know what they want to do or who they want to be? It's almost embarrassing to remember how young I was when I knew I loved the law. But it takes time and energy, if you're going to make it happen. So you give other things up."

Her words left Maggie feeling vaguely inadequate. "I always had my nose buried in a book," she said slowly. "But my tastes ran more to things like *Gone with the Wind*. You probably don't have much time for novels."

"No, I don't," Sara said almost wistfully. "But I wish I did."

"I guess I just like stories."

"You don't talk about it much. I think of you as the most political-minded person in our group."

"You're kidding! More than Carol or Leona?" Maggie was authentically astonished. "Leona weaves people together so well, it's almost an art form."

"But you've got the perspective of a reporter. You have

a way of standing back—of seeing us, I think. Sometimes it makes me nervous, to be honest."

"Oh, Sara, I can barely understand myself." Maggie said it with such intensity, Sara was startled. She wanted to ask what was wrong. But first she had to confide what was uppermost in her mind.

"Patton wants to dump me," she said.

"What?" Maggie's eyes widened.

"He's claiming my father was some kind of death doctor—which makes me an instant political liability. And Sayles is too conflicted to stop him."

"That's terrible! My God, Leona heard you might be in trouble, but this—" Maggie felt sick. How had Sara managed to hold this in?

"Patton says he has proof that my father helped kill dying patients. If I don't bow out, he'll leak the story. How can he do this to a decent man? Nice blackmail attempt, don't you think?"

Her tone had an edge of black humor in it, but Maggie saw the lines of exhaustion around her eyes. "It's sick, dirty politics," she burst out.

Sara stared out across the field. "I'm not the most politically minded person in the world, but I know I'm inconveniently positioned," she said. "My father's life shouldn't have anything to do with my competency for the Court, but the facts don't matter. Patton knows that. It all depends on how it plays—and he's concocted a mixture of fact and fiction that is meant to implicate me."

Maggie caught her breath.

"See? You're wary," Sara said, lifting her chin with a tightening smile. "Multiply that by every reporter in Washington, and you get an idea of what he's trying to do. The minute I leap to my father's defense, the story gets big. It's got nothing to do with the facts."

"I am *not* wary," Maggie managed, thrown off by Sara's response. "I want to help. There's got to be a way." The light was turning golden and a slight wind was rising. Maggie's head almost sank between her legs as she realized that she had a new obligation to Sara. There was no way she could bring up the book contract now; no way she could try to explain the temptation, the gravitational pull of an offer that meant financial independence for the first time in her life. How could she lay all this on Sara now?

"So why are we here?" Sara said, sensing her turning thoughts. "You've got something on your mind, some agenda, so let's hear it. Don't hold back just because I'm dumping all this stuff on you."

Maggie lifted her head. "Agenda?" she said firmly. "Sara, the only agenda is getting you on the Court."

Sara looked at Maggie's worried face and was touched. "Thanks," she said softly.

Maggie's face screwed into a tight, concentrating frown. "Sara, could this have anything to do with Faith?"

"Ah, there you go, taking the reporter's shot in the dark."

But her tone was not offputting, so Maggie pressed on. "Remember, at the funeral? You said Faith was scared, but you were vague about why. Can you tell me now?"

Sara crunched down on a Frito, not answering right away. But then she thought, maybe it was time to share this particular burden. "Remember the party?" she said abruptly.

The memories of what seemed now like a long-ago time flooded back. "Celebrating Faith's job?" Maggie said eagerly. "How could I forget it? Something happened there, didn't it? I've felt it for a long time."

Sara drained her glass and reached for the bottle. The wine was flowing now through her veins, relaxing the tension in her muscles, giving her what she knew was only temporary ease. But it felt good all the same.

"Yes," she said simply.

Maggie held her breath.

"Faith was the happiest I had ever seen her that night," Sara said. "She had the job of her dreams."

Maggie nodded, remembering. "I thought every man in the place was dazzled by her," she said. "And there she was, alone, as she always was, never needing anybody."

"That's because she had the person she needed—or thought she did."

Maggie paused, hand suspended in mid-air. "Who was it?" she asked. Slowly, she reached into the bag of Fritos and pulled out a handful, listening to the sound of them crunching between her fingers.

The sun, the wine . . . Sara felt mildly reckless. "Have you ever fallen for someone truly disastrous?"

Maggie paused a second before answering. "There was a man, a few months after my husband died. I'm still embarrassed about it."

"Well, then, maybe you'll understand. She swore me to secrecy, but it doesn't matter now. When she died, Faith was trying to break out of a relationship with a man who absolutely refused to let her go. She was growing frantic. It's the kind of thing that happens all the time, but this was different." Sara paused. "I'm telling you, it scares me. I can see why somebody could have wanted to get rid of Faith."

Maggie pulled her knees up close to her body, wondering suddenly if she really wanted Sara to go on. But the compulsion to know was too great. "Why?" she asked.

"I think she was becoming dangerous to—I don't know. But she actually did loved him."

"And you found all this out at the party?"

Sara nodded very slowly. "She told me the whole story the next day. And it's haunted me ever since."

"Maybe you'd rather—"

"No, it's time to tell you." Sara paused, staring at a softball game taking place in the valley behind them. From this distance, it looked almost like tiny stick figures in a cadenced dance. "It was quite a party, wasn't it? I had a case up the next morning so I was hunting for my coat"—she smiled faintly—"you know what it's like at Leona's, she's got more rooms than the Hilton. I wandered through half of them."

"Nobody can find a coat at Leona's."

"I couldn't find the light switch in one room—and I was pretty glad I hadn't. I saw two people standing close together in the shadows."

"What were they doing?"

"Kissing."

Maggie realized she was once again holding her breath. "Who was it?"

"Faith."

"And who?"

Sara paused, seemed to hesitate—and then said the name with great calmness.

"Dick Sayles."

CHAPTER 6

"No, Sara. I never killed anyone." The old man's voice was steady and calm. "Now you need to ask me another question, but I hope you're prepared for a different answer."

"I know it's absurd," Sara began.

"No," George Marino interrupted with the tone of quiet certitude she had known and trusted all her life. "It's not absurd, but it's going to be very hard for you to accept."

Outside his tiny one-bedroom apartment in this Buffalo suburb, Sara could hear the voices of children playing on the swings and slides of the playground next door. She remembered how he always said he liked the sound of children playing, that it was the sound of innocence too soon lost. She watched him lift his head and smile faintly.

"Hear the kids?" he said with a touch of his usual pleasure.

"Yes," she said, smiling. "The truth is, they always seem to be at recess."

His shoulders were bonier than they were on her last visit and his brown sweater—the last one her mother knitted before she died—was frayed. I must buy him a new one, Sara told herself.

"Now I've given you a moment to absorb the shock," he said gently. "So ask me the question."

"You helped people die?"

"Yes."

"You helped them commit suicide?"

"That's the word, honey."

Sara tried not to show how jolted she was. So, all right, doctors did it all the time, but she was suddenly struggling with childhood memories. She could see in her mind's eye her father's slumped shoulders when he came home after losing a patient he had struggled to save. As a child, when she saw him fail she realized the shattering power of death. How did she square that memory with the image of a man giving poison or administering a lethal needle or—or what?

"How could you? Dad—it's illegal," she managed.

"I'm not a lawyer, Sara, I'm a doctor. If a doctor can't heal, he has to help." He picked up the untouched plate of scrambled eggs and toast he had placed before his daughter, stacked the silver, and rose to take it to the kitchen. "I don't know who's claiming I was a murderer," he said with the ghost of a smile. "Maybe someone who thinks death is a problem to be solved. Want some juice?"

She couldn't quite return the smile. "Sit down, Dad, I'll take that stuff."

"My daughter, the Supreme Court Justice, clearing her own dishes? Not on your life."

"Look," she said. "Are you sure you never took it over the edge?"

"Ah, the lawyer and the doctor argue. Whose edge—yours or mine?"

"Mine." The division was drawn.

"The juice, first," he said with a heavy sigh. "Orange or apple? I think I've got both."

"Orange."

"Yeah, you and orange juice. If I'd known you were coming, I'd have bought a gallon." He gently stroked her hair and headed for the kitchen. Sara listened to the clatter of dishes in the kitchen mixed with the old man's mumbling, running monologue. He was talking to himself more, which wasn't much of a surprise. It must be lonely, living here with so many friends already dead. . . . Sara gazed around the small living room with its dining nook and noted the growing clutter. Old newspapers, stacked books, a drooping poinsettia in dusty earth. The large television set she bought him last Christmas dominated the room. Pictures were everywhere—of her mother, of the three of them, of Sara at every age. It was all normal. And yet suddenly nothing was.

"Give me the details, Dad," she said, as he walked back into the room carrying a large tumbler of orange juice. "Don't hold back."

"Remember Mr. Verzano, the man who ran the grocery store?"

"He'd give me a peach every time I picked up the groceries," she said, smiling faintly at the memory. "The pulp always caught in my braces."

"His wife got sick; maybe you remember," her father said, watching her closely. "Lung cancer, awful case. I could do nothing, no one could." A shadow flickered across his face, taking him somewhere Sara had never been. "They wanted help, the kind that counts. They knew I understood, we could talk about it. She was a brave woman. No beating around the bush."

"What did you do?"

"I gave her pills and I signed the death certificate. Heart failure."

His voice was firm and he never broke eye contact. He wanted her to agree he was right, she could see that. "So we're not talking about just withholding treatment," she said carefully. "We're talking about your active participation."

"Listen carefully, Sara. When I gave her the pills, I told

her that under no circumstances should she take an overdose because it would kill her. If you asked me, did I know what she was going to do? I'd say, yeah, I knew what she *wanted* to do."

He leaned forward in his chair and took her hand. "Sara," he said. "It was *not* a struggle for me. People understand better now, what we have to do isn't as much of a secret. If they've sat and watched people they love die slowly, they have a different idea of what's wrong and what's right. But remember this—if anybody's implying I killed someone against their will, my God—"

An instant of silence descended, freezing them both in place. The lawyer in Sara was alert: her father had just volunteered information. Or had he?

"If you think you have reason to believe someone wants to die, but they can't actually tell you"—she had to say this carefully—"is that reason to kill them?"

"I—never—killed—anybody."

The voices of the children outside had turned shrill. They filled the room and Sara's heart pounded at the sight of her father's eyes. They were dark and, yes, angry. He leaped to his feet and paced the room. "I did my best to help people and to stop their suffering, don't you understand?"

"I wish you had told me before." Sara felt her frustration rising. God, she was a judge, she had passed death sentences on people, but her father? How could he do that?

"Well, I'm telling you now." He was pacing agitatedly, wringing his hands, and Sara felt a stab of fear. His heart, she reminded herself. Don't forget his heart.

"I just don't see—"

"Pain, Sara, *pain!*" He almost roared the words. "Think! What would you do if you were faced with a desperate patient who signaled that she wanted to die? Someone with no hope, no chance of getting well?"

"I wouldn't kill her!" Sara's frustration exploded out of her. "If someone picked up a gun and said he wanted to shoot himself, would you sit there and let him do it?"

"Guns!" He snorted contemptuously. "Judges and lawyers are caught in legalisms that have nothing to do with real life."

"Legalisms? What are you *saying?*" She was angry now, angrier than she had ever been with him. "I deal with life and death in the courtroom, but, my God, when I have to, it haunts me! It isn't a power I can use as I want—it's the power of my office, and I'm sworn to respect it! How can you say these things so calmly? What the hell were you doing?"

He pounded his hand hard against a table. "Don't swear at me, young woman! You think I'm a murderer, is that it? Yes! That's what you think!"

"If you were in my courtroom, Dad, you would be! Do you understand? You *would be* a murderer! That's the law!"

George Marino whirled on his daughter, his face apoplectic. "How dare you say that to me!" he roared. She jumped to her feet. Then, so quickly it surprised them both, he raised his hand and slapped her.

The two of them stood, staring at each other, frozen in place.

"Sara, I'm sorry." He reached for her.

Crying now, she stepped back. Her fists went up to her eyes and she turned away.

George Marino sagged into a chair. "I can't believe I did that," he said brokenly.

She could not form a reply, not quite yet.

"I'm sorry, Sara."

"Dad, I'm not a kid any more," she finally managed as calmly as possible. "So don't treat me like one. You took the power of life into your hands." She took a deep breath, bent on moving away from this confrontation. It was frighteningly alien. "We're trying to talk past a gap, Dad. There's no way I could ever think of you as a murderer—

but I can't believe you broke the law so flagrantly, took it into your own hands.'' Another deep breath. ''How do you *expect* me to respond?''

Shaking, he placed his hands on her shoulders. ''Listen to me,'' he said, his eyes pleading. ''You can't put yourself in my shoes, you can't be back with me listening to sick people beg for help, I know that. Right now, this minute—stop trying to understand. Just accept. It's illogical for you not to accept, Sara, and you are a very logical person. You understand this, I know you do.''

Baffled, she stared at him. He wanted her to be logical, but he was the one arguing from emotion. The crime he committed happened, of course it happened, every day. She didn't doubt those people had suffered terribly; she could understand trying, out of compassion . . . But the law. She had to uphold the law.

''Honey, I'm asking too much of you. You're a judge. I guess I forget.'' There were tears in his eyes.

Sara swallowed hard. ''I'm a daughter, too, okay? Not just a judge.''

''How do you separate them out?''

''I don't know if I can.''

His eyes betrayed another worry. ''I don't want this to change anything for you.''

''But it already has,'' she said, struggling for the right words. ''Dad, you surrendered your medical license.''

''Because of the Valium! You know that. I was not myself after your mother died.''

''I helped you get it back. I wrote the state board, and people will think I knew you were helping people to die.''

''That's nonsense.''

''In a sane world, yes. But not in the world I'm living in.''

He sat very still. He knew what she was avoiding. ''Forget the political implications for the moment,'' he asked. ''What's changed? For us?''

"Not my love for you," she said slowly.

"Respect? How about respect?"

"I've always respected you. Do you doubt that?"

"Not until this moment," he replied.

Her gaze faltered, but then she looked him steadily in the eye. "Of course I respect you, I always have and I always will. But Dad, legally, it was wrong. I wish I had known."

"I wish I had told you," he replied.

She stood then and put her arms around her father and hugged him as tightly as she could. He was so frail. She couldn't change what had happened, but she could at least not put him at risk. And he was; she knew it in her bones. He was.

"I'll withdraw tomorrow," she said.

He pushed her to arm's length and held her shoulders with surprising firmness. "No," he said. His voice echoed definitively. "Absolutely not. I can't believe you'd even *think* of it."

"Dad!"

"Look, I'm an embarrassment now. But nobody is going to rob you of what is rightfully yours, what you are entitled to have."

"I'm not entitled to the Supreme Court, nobody is," she said. "You are not an embarrassment, for God's sake, and it's no tragedy if I don't get the job."

"That's crap." He said it so violently, she winced. "Sara, your mother was a timid woman, and I've wondered a lot, did I make her that way?" His gaze wandered to a photograph of her mother on the piano. "She was angry inside and you know it. Let's not pretend with each other."

Sara started to protest, but he gently put his finger up to her mouth. "She felt robbed, Sara, that's the word she used. And you know something? Maybe she was robbed, and maybe it was my fault. Maybe I'm the one who made her timid." He sighed, a faint sound, more like a wheeze, deep in the back of his throat. "There was no time to set things right. . . . I can't change the past, but I can make sure it doesn't happen again. Not to you. They'll go after me, right? Well, I can take anything they dish out."

"Dad, Dad." She shook her head, wishing she could make him understand. "Tell that to the *National Enquirer.*"

But he was no longer the frail man of only a few seconds ago. "If I have to," he said firmly, "I will. I'm not kidding, Sara. I want you to go for it. They won't dare dump you if you don't give up. And I assure you, there is nothing more they can do to hurt you because there is nothing more to find out."

Father and daughter stared at each other.

"It won't be a whole lot of fun," she said slowly.

"Here is what you can't do," he said with stubborn insistence. "You can't let them cheat you. You knew nothing when you wrote that letter for me—and as long as you tell the truth, they can't get you."

"Maybe," she said. "But they'll try to destroy you. I know how it works and you don't."

"Let them try."

"They will."

Father and daughter stared at each other, both uneasy. They were on a new, uncharted course.

"No, no, not the miniature Neapolitan pizzas," Leona sputtered impatiently into the phone. Sometimes it seemed the people she hired couldn't make a single sensible decision on their own; was she always going to be a one-woman show? Maccoby Caterers had a reputation in town that had to be kept up, but where were the people who could do it? Not on her payroll.

"Make the Stilton cheese and bacon gougères, Mrs. Beltson will love those—and Juan? Those great crabcakes for the main course—yes, yes, with a roasted tomato coulis;

they'll be seated by then . . . and send an extra waiter. She's cheap, she'll say she only wants two, but I know she needs three.'' She paused, listening. ''Wonderful, right—good! Talk to you later.''

Leona replaced the receiver and turned to Justin, hardly taking a breath. ''They can't do anything without me,'' she complained. ''Honestly, sometimes I—''

Justin snapped his newspaper with a touch of exasperation. ''You love it,'' he said.

''Well,'' Leona paused, disinclined to deny the obvious. ''It does take my mind off other things.''

''Speaking of other things.'' Justin patted the sofa next to him. ''Come here, dear, I have to share some news with you. Bad news, I'm afraid.''

''Oh dear, there doesn't seem to be any other kind lately.'' Leona's eyes grew rounder as she settled apprehensively onto the peach brocade and faced her husband.

''I probably shouldn't be talking at all,'' Justin began, but he was watching her closely. ''This is totally confidential and it can't go beyond us.''

She was immediately alert. ''White House?'' she said.

He nodded and sighed.

''Tell me.''

''I suppose I have to, now.'' He took her hand and squeezed. ''It's about your friend, Sara,'' he said.

''Oh, Justin.''

''She's in the process of making a very hard decision, and she's going to need your support when she does what she has to do.'' He paused. ''If you're there for her now, it may help her.'' There was just a hint of emphasis on the word ''now.''

''To do what?''

''To do the right thing—the only thing she can do, which is to withdraw her name from consideration for the Supreme Court.''

"What?" Leona sat bolt upright and began to sputter. "That's crazy!"

"I'm afraid she and her father got themselves a little beyond the law a few years back."

"I don't believe it!"

"Leona, you're a loyal friend, but sometimes even friends have to accept unpalatable facts."

Even in her shock, Leona noted how smug her husband sounded. "About Sara?" she protested. "I'm telling you, Justin—"

"Quiet now, and listen. I'll tell you the whole story."

"Carol, it's Leona. I just talked with Justin."

"Look, I'm sorry," Carol said tiredly. "Let's not go over old ground, all right? Maybe I'm wrong about Justin."

"You are."

"Okay, I'll accept that. I've got my own troubles and I don't want to argue with you."

"I overreacted too," Leona said. She paused. "I guess we're both apologizing."

"Well—"

Leona cut her off, her words tumbling out one after the other in a rush. "Listen, we have to talk. It's important. Friends have to stand together when something bad happens and we couldn't help Faith but maybe we can help Sara."

"What are you talking about?"

"Carol"—Leona's voice was scratchy with concern—"she's going to need us. This is totally confidential, we can't tell anybody except Maggie and she's at Jeff's soccer game. It isn't going to happen after all. I can hardly believe it and the reason is just heartbreaking for Sara and I don't know how to *help*."

At the other end of the line, Carol crunched her hand into a ball and shoved it against her forehead in exasperation. She had spent most of the evening ripping pictures of

Bart out of the family albums and packing up his clothes, and she was worn out from her own fury. "Leona," she said, "will you get to the point? *What's* not going to happen?"

Sara stepped off the elevator and headed for her apartment, her overnight bag hanging heavily from her right shoulder. She was exhausted. Her plane home from Buffalo had been stuck circling for an hour over National, and right now she wanted nothing more than to curl up in her living room and think about what came next.

"Sara . . ."

She looked up. Leona and Carol were standing by the door of her apartment, smiling awkwardly. Carol had the determined, take-charge look of someone about to deal with a crisis and Leona was picking at her fingernails, a sure sign she was agitated.

"Hi," she said, startled.

"The building manager let us up a few minutes ago, I hope you don't mind," Leona said. "He was afraid you'd start worrying about building security, but he recognized Carol and we—well, we wanted to be here when you came home."

Carol glanced down at the suitcase. "Quick trip somewhere?"

"To see my father," Sara replied. "Just for the day." Neither of them seemed surprised and Sara moved toward the door, key in hand. "Want to come in?" she asked uncertainly.

"Well, sure," Carol replied. "Why do you think we're here?"

"I'm sorry, I'm just tired."

"That's okay," Leona said softly. "We understand. We know about your father."

"How? This town is a sieve."

"It sure is."

Feeling somehow trapped under a spotlight, Sara unlocked the door and walked in, beckoning her two friends to follow.

Leona, always automatically the one in charge of food, slapped some cheese spread on stale crackers she had rummaged from Sara's pantry and put them in front of her friends. "I don't know how you can stay calm," she said, eyes flashing. "I've never heard of a nastier maneuver from that man. He should be shot. I simply cannot understand how he fooled Justin into believing his story."

"Considering the source? Come on, Leona, you can't be that surprised," Carol said. "Patton is very smooth when he wants to be. Why would he tell Justin, by the way?"

"Justin knows just about everything that goes on over there," Leona murmured.

Carol rolled her eyes and started to say something, but she saw Sara's expression and thought better of it. "So what happens next?" she asked instead.

"I'll figure out a way to protect myself," Sara replied. Loyalty made her choose her words with great care. "I don't think Patton can ride this very far. But I'm worried about—my father's memory."

"People aren't as shocked as they used to be over doctors' helping patients die," Leona said. "I can't see—"

"I can," Carol said. "You think there's stuff he's not telling you. Right?"

Sara hesitated. "Confidentially?" She stumbled a bit over the word. It sounded cold and unsuited to three friends who had known each other for fifteen years.

"Of course," Carol said immediately, and Leona nodded.

"I'm not sure." There, she had said it. Voiced her worst fear. "We've got a barrier between us, now," she said sadly.

"Maybe it's not as bad as you think," Leona said. "I

mean, my father and I never could understand each other. He told me cooking was a waste, that he shouldn't have bothered sending me to college.'' She paused, surprised that the memory still hurt. ''I never could get him to understand. But you've got a much closer relationship with your father.''

''Mine thought I walked on water,'' Carol volunteered, a bit abashed. ''Said he didn't want any more children, because I was perfect. It got a little lonely.'' She looked at the others with a tiny grin. ''Anybody here think I'm perfect?''

''Notice we're quiet,'' Sara teased. She felt the taut muscles in her neck easing a bit. She was almost glad Carol and Leona had shown up on her doorstep this late. ''I won't allow them to demolish my father, no matter what he did. I have to trust him, but I sure don't have to trust Jack Patton.''

''Have you called Amos?''

''Yes. From the airport.'' Thank God he had been totally in her corner, she thought. And Barney, too. ''The hearing is only a couple of weeks away.''

''We tried to get Maggie.''

''She knows.''

Carol bridled slightly. ''Before us?''

Sara shrugged, refusing the bait.

''I'll bet Patton had something to do with Faith's death,'' Leona whispered.

''That possibility hasn't left my mind in over two weeks.'' Sara's voice was almost too low to pick up.

And then Carol proceeded to shock them both. ''Hell, maybe you should pull out.''

''What?'' Sara was astonished.

''They're out to get you, and if they really want to, they will,'' Carol said. ''You know that.''

''You can't be serious,'' Leona said. ''You're talking about giving up!''

Carol stubbornly pressed her lips together and said nothing.

Sara searched her friend's face. This wasn't like Carol; she'd fight until she was the only one left standing on the battlefield. "What are you saying?" she pressed. "It doesn't sound like you at all. I can't back out. If they want me out, they'll have to dump me and do the explaining themselves. If I give up, I'd not only be giving up what I want—I'd be declaring my father a political liability and that would kill him, fast."

"Look, I'm feeling low. I can't be much of a cheerleader tonight, that's all."

In Leona's face, the light was dawning. "Something's happened with Bart."

"Lay off, Leona, please."

Sara and Leona exchanged quick glances.

"You came here to support me—what about you?" Sara persisted.

"Don't gang up, okay? It gets annoying," Carol said in her most matter-of-fact tone, stretching back in her chair to prove she was totally relaxed and in charge.

"Carol, did you and Bart finally break up?"

Carol sat quite still.

"Look, don't answer if you don't want to."

Carol's hand rose to shade her eyes. Even though they were her friends, the ones she had complained to for months about her rocky marriage, this was hard. "Yeah," she said, almost inaudibly. "News flash. He did."

"Oh, shit."

"I'm sorry."

"He said he didn't want to live in my shadow any more. He just *did* it, no arguments, nothing. Just told me it was over, packed up, and left. I can't believe it."

The three women sat silently after that for a long moment. Only when a tear trickled out past Carol's protecting hand and down her cheek did Sara move impulsively to her friend and give her a quick hug. "Can we do anything?" she said.

"What could you do? What could anyone do?" Carol replied. "It's been coming for a long time. I'll bet neither of you is surprised. Maybe nobody is, except me."

"That doesn't make it any easier." Leona said. "It's terrible to feel tricked."

"You don't have to tough it out, you know," Sara chided. "Not around us."

Then Carol startled them a second time. "Maybe especially around you," she said, a touch diffidently. "And don't ask me to explain, because I can't. It's just hard to look like a loser in front of your friends."

Sara waited for the elevator doors to close on the figures of her friends before closing her own door and latching the night bolt. Absent-mindedly, she ran her fingers over the flaking paint. She had to get this place repainted soon. She thought about Carol, remembering her stiff, desperate pride—but also remembering the years when Bart had been Carol's partner and not a problem. Did it always happen that way when people got too busy? Was that why she had dodged marriage for so long? Slowly she walked back into the living room and surveyed for a moment the one private enclave of her life. A pair of sturdy tapestry-covered sofas, at least fifteen years old, still rubbed elbow to elbow with well-scratched glass end tables that she'd bought straight out of law school. She could afford a bigger place now, but it was somehow too much trouble to pull up roots and move. She'd have to decide all over again where things should be placed; what paintings should be hung where—all the nesting decisions she never had time to make.

Back when David was around, she had thought more about that kind of thing. She picked up a badly tarnished silver frame, asking herself again why she still kept a picture of him. She had told Maggie the truth—it wasn't David she missed, not exactly. They were still friends, checking in with each other on the telephone every six months or so. No, it was just having someone around—someone reading a juicy piece of news in the morning paper out loud just when you were trying to concentrate on an important brief, or hogging the bathroom when you had to make an appointment. That's what she missed. Someone right now, this very minute, who would lie down next to her on the bed and listen to every last word she wanted to say, to pour out, about her father and about Faith and about Carol.

Sara put down the frame and walked back into the kitchen. There wasn't much she could do about the flaking paint or the tarnished frame right away (she had no idea where the silver polish was), but at least she could wash up the coffee cups and throw away those stale crackers.

The second movement of Beethoven's Fifth poured melodiously from Justin's new sound system, filling the living room with a beauty that lifted Leona's spirits. She tossed her umbrella on a chair, ignoring the fact that it was still damp, and headed for the bar. Standing in front of Justin's array of crystal glasses and decanters, she hesitated. She actually felt too excited and engaged in what was about to happen to want a drink very much.

"How is she?"

Justin was suddenly standing in back of her, his hands gently on her shoulders. Leona covered one of his hands with her own and leaned back into his arms.

"She's going to be fine," she said. "It's terribly painful, but she's strong. I'm really proud of her."

He was reaching past her for two glasses and a bottle of Cabernet Sauvignon. "Tough duty," he said kindly. "Let's have a drink."

"I think I'll wait a little."

Justin raised an eyebrow and Leona felt the urge to give a reason. "I'm just a little too keyed up," she said.

"Suit yourself," he said mildly. "but give yourself a break, you need to relax." He left her glass on the bar and moved over to the sofa, flopping down easily. "Tell me all about it."

"Justin, she's going to fight," Leona said softly. Her eyes were shining with excitement.

"What?"

"I said she's going to fight, she's not going to pull out." Leona laughed. "It's such despicable politics they're playing! Why should Sara lie down and play dead? She's going to force Jack Patton out from under his rock, isn't that wonderful?"

Justin was staring at her without expression, his glass poised in front of him like a spear ready to be lowered and thrown.

"Here I was, rushing over to administer tea and sympathy, and then I heard the whole story. I got so damn mad!" she said. "Can you get to Sayles? You have incredible access, surely you can get past Patton?"

"Are you telling me you encouraged her to challenge the White House?"

"I certainly did."

"That was not very smart." He was furious.

Beethoven filled the room as Leona stepped back from her husband's words. "Justin, how can you say that?"

He stood and strode over to her, thrusting his contorted face close to her. "Do you realize you may have just set *me* up for a disaster?" he said. "Do you have any idea how trade-offs are made? God, everything I've arranged—"

"What are you talking about?" Leona stared at him, seeing a different man. No, not different, she realized with a flash of clarity—just a man I don't want to see. "Are you telling me you were a part of this?"

"Don't try interrogating me, Leona. It isn't your style."

"Maybe it isn't my style," she retorted, stung. "But I have a right to ask. You are my husband, Justin!"

"You are a meddler, Leona!" he shot back. "A naive meddler! You have no idea what I do or how I do it, all you do is enjoy the life my work makes possible for you!"

"That's not true! My catering business—"

"Would just pay your Saks bill!"

"Why should Sara pull out?" she protested, now thoroughly rattled. "What are they trying to say she has done?"

"Don't get blinded by loyalty," he snapped. "Her father murdered people, don't you understand?"

"He's not up for the Supreme Court, even it if *is* true! Patton can't prove Sara had anything to do with it, and that's all that matters!"

"We can prove anything!" He slammed his glass back down on the bar with disgust. "You might as well start your usual guzzling, I'm going out." He stomped from the room, leaving Leona frozen in place, staring for a long moment after him.

"We?" she whispered. She turned slowly and picked up the bottle of wine. Definitely a fine vintage. Just as slowly she stood by the sink and poured it all down the drain.

The next day, Michael and Maggie moved slowly together through the crowded aisles of the Georgetown Safeway, engrossed in conversation, pausing in front of a neat display of low-fat chicken broth. It was Saturday, a busy day, and other shoppers shouldered past them as they talked.

"Jeff said to remind you to pick up fudge bars." Michael smiled slightly, nodding at the soup cans. "Not this stuff."

"I'm worried about him, he's not feeling good."

"He's probably eating too many fudge bars."

But Maggie's thoughts were back on the topic of their conversation. "What can we do, Michael?" She had told him about Sara's father, with some hesitation. But Michael's advice, his calmness, were indispensable—and she had to talk to somebody.

Michael took his time answering. "Depends on how far

Patton takes this. Sara can stonewall, but it's probably a better idea to muster sympathy for her father. Using that letter she wrote against her makes no sense. Unless they can figure out how to make it look illegal or unethical, it won't work. What works is getting Sara to crumble."

"That's what I'm afraid they'll do. She went to see her father, you know."

"What happened?"

Maggie sighed. "He told her he did what his dying patients wanted him to do and he doesn't regret anything."

"Okay, but a prosecutor still might call it murder—for which there's no statute of limitations, by the way."

Maggie caught her breath and glanced around to make sure no one was in earshot. This was a small town and they were in the most social of grocery stores. Anybody could be close by, even a Judiciary Committee aide. It wasn't impossible, given the people you routinely ran into here.

"By the way, did you know we're suing under the Freedom of Information Act to get the police report on Faith's death?" Michael said. "I'm convinced Justice is stalling. Maybe they found something in her office—what do you think? Are you hearing anything?"

Maggie turned abruptly and yanked a couple of cans of soup off the shelf and tossed them into her cart. "No," she said, too quickly.

"Maggie, your body language is not reassuring."

She started stacking the cans in the cart, at a loss for what to say.

"Okay," he said with a shrug. "We've got our pact with each other, and I won't press. But, Maggie, this book of yours—"

"What about it?"

"Aren't you in all this a bit deep?"

It opened the floodgates. "I can't write," she whispered. "I can't sign the contract." The words were tumbling out. "I wish I didn't need the money so bad."

She saw the look in his eyes but rushed on anyway. "I haven't been able to tell Sara. There's too much she's dealing with already, and how can I ask her to understand this?"

Tentatively, he reached out with his hand and touched her right temple. "You wouldn't screw them, Maggie. I know that."

"I did it to someone else."

"That's history."

"Well, there's no statute of limitations on guilt, either."

"Excuse me." A harried-looking man in white tennis shorts was pushing past her with his cart, reaching for the cans of chicken broth. "Sorry," he said, "I'm in a hurry, got a court in half an hour."

Maggie paled. "Did he hear?" she whispered.

"Let's keep moving," Michael replied. They began pushing their half-full cart down the aisle as he spoke with deliberate slowness. "For Patton to try a game like this seems out of character, unless he's got a lot more to win than he has to lose."

"I think he's using Faith as an excuse, because that's what Sayles is worried about."

"And how is he using Faith?"

Maggie flushed. "I can't—"

"Look, there are reporters swarming all over this story, and I can guarantee you nothing's going to stay secret for very long."

One thing would, she vowed. Unless it was Sayles who had wanted Faith dead.

"We're out to prove there's a mean-spirited agenda coming from the White House that's bad for the country." This time Michael broke into a full grin. "I've got an idea," he said. "You have time before the committee hearings. What about going up to Buffalo? Check things out like the reporter you are. Maybe you'll find something that helps—look at the medical records, obits, death certificates—something. You don't have to write it; just do it to help your friend.''

''If this gets out, every reporter in town will be up there.''

''You're better than they are.''

Maggie was intrigued. ''But what if he's guilty?'' she asked. ''What if he really did kill people?''

A sudden flurry of quick steps behind them.

''Well, hi, you two, what are you doing here? Looks like you're having a real serious talk, so don't let me interrupt.'' The voice was high and animated, a familiar tone pitched at a level that would always command attention.

They turned simultaneously. Right behind them—standing there for who knew how long—was Sandi Snow.

''What are you doing here?'' Maggie blurted.

''Shopping, same as you.'' Sandi pushed her cart slightly past them with a touch of self-righteous indignation. But she couldn't resist the opportunity. ''Where do I get the feeling that there's trouble brewing for Judge Marino?'' she asked brightly.

''From an overly fertile imagination,'' Michael said.

Sandi actually looked hurt. ''I've got my job and you've got yours,'' she said to Michael, brushing back a straying lock of blond hair. ''I'd think you'd understand.''

''I don't think my job—or yours—is to ruin people.''

Sandi rolled her eyes and this time sailed on by, with a parting shot over her shoulder. ''That's a bit stuffy of you, Michael,'' she said. ''Considering who you're standing in this aisle with.''

Late that afternoon, Dick Sayles paced back and forth, staring down at the gold presidential seal woven into the carpet beneath his feet, his mood so black even his secretary had retreated moments before to leave him alone. He glanced at the tape cabinet. It was locked, but the key was dangling from the keyhole. Invitingly. Tantalizingly. He turned the key in the lock, pulled open the door, and reached in. He extracted the tape he wanted and shoved it with an angry push into the VCR. He walked back to his chair and clicked it on.

It was a tape of a press briefing. A slightly fuzzy image of a laughing woman behind the shabby wood lectern in the White House press room suddenly filled the screen. Someone had said something funny; Faith Paige, a slightly wicked look in her eyes, was offering a fast rejoinder. Dark, straight hair, almost Indian black, pulled straight back into a casual ponytail . . . a face dominated by huge, brown eyes. Opened wide enough, they could feign innocence with such deft irony that even reporters who knew they were being stiffed held kind thoughts about Faith. Her suit jacket of expensive silk parted slightly; you could see a wrinkled cotton T-shirt underneath. That was Faith; always going for counterpoint. Now the smile disappeared and she was listening, every muscle still. She nodded her head a few times, then moved from the lectern, diminishing the trappings of distance between herself and the roomful of newsmen and women. She stood easy before them, both artless and artful. She was explaining something, rapidly and authoritatively.

Sayles turned up the sound.

"I can assure you," Faith's strong, familiar voice said, suddenly filling the room, "you'll all get access to the President before his press conference. Have I ever let you down?"

A chuckle from the front row. "Not yet," rumbled a male voice.

Another voice from the back seats, more fretful, where the less powerful regional reporters sat: "Faith, how come we only got a photo op this morning? Doesn't he know the voters in Louisiana want more than that when their governor—"

"There's a handout in the bins, Jerry," she said. "Anything more you need, I'll get."

"Well, okay."

"Everybody happy?" Her voice was like a bell, ringing true across meadows and fields in still air. "Now, on to the President's trip to Austin . . ."

Sayles pressed the "mute" button; he didn't want to hear the content of that press conference. He moved uncomfortably in his chair, skewered suddenly by the memory of their last conversation; the set, determined look in her eyes he could not forget.

He switched the clicker to his left hand. Slowly his right hand moved to the point below his right hip where his leg tended to ache on bad days. Usually it stiffened up only during cold weather, but other factors must be in play today. The pain was bad, vibrating from the bones where the shrapnel rested and then through his expensive summer-weight worsted suit. It wouldn't go away. . . .

He watched Faith move across the screen and back to the lectern. She picked up some papers and suddenly smiled that wicked smile again, full into the camera, before walking out of view. He pushed the clicker. One more time. Just once more, he promised himself. His leg was throbbing worse now, but he was going to sit through this, he had to see her again. "Christ, what did I do to you?" he muttered as her face came back on the screen.

He squinted. The picture was getting fuzzier, he must tell his secretary to get the heads of the damn machine cleaned. Faith was laughing . . . now she was tossing her hair. He lifted the remote control and pushed a button to freeze the picture. It was the last time he would watch, so he'd do it slowly . . . he clicked it again and Faith finished her laugh, leaned forward, her jacket parted slightly.

Suddenly the door to his office opened. Sayles jumped to his feet, dropping the remote control. Laura Sayles walked into the room, her thin wide mouth drawn tight beneath her cheekbones. She looked at him and then at the television screen. Two blotches of red began to spread across her pale skin.

"I knew you'd be watching her."

"I'm watching a press briefing, Laura."

"You don't even understand yourself, Dick." Swiftly she covered the distance from the doorway to the television set. With one finger she poked the "eject" button and ripped out the tape. The image of Faith vanished from the screen. Without a glance at her husband she took the tape and threw it. It hit one of the Chippendale chairs, leaving a sudden scratch of bare wood, before reaching the wall and falling to the floor. A thin ribbon of tape broke from the cartridge and dribbled out on the carpet. Laura Sayles stood for an uncertain moment, staring at the tape. She turned to her husband and started to say something, then thought better of it. Instead, she strode back to the door and walked out, pulling it shut behind her with enough force to shiver an eighteenth-century painting of early New York almost off the wall.

Dick Sayles stood frozen for a long moment and then slowly walked over to where the cartridge tape had landed. He stared down at it. Somewhere inside, he sensed but could not yet heed the clamoring warnings; there wasn't much time. Maybe she was right. He leaned down, picked up the cartridge, and looked at the unraveled plastic tape cradled in his hands. Then slowly, very slowly, he began winding it back in place.

Chapter 7

The door to the Beltson apartment flew open and Leona saw the huge, grateful smile on Juan's face even as she smelled the smoke coming from the kitchen. ''Juan,'' she whispered, grabbing his lapel. ''You can't fry in this apartment, don't you understand? There's no outside venting in these old buildings, I *told* you, Jenny Beltson will be furious.''

''She's not home yet,'' Juan whispered back just as urgently. ''The new cook was sautéing—''

''Did you bring a fan?''

''In the truck.''

''God, I just stopped by to make sure everything was going fine and you hand me a disaster!''

She looked up at just that moment to see Harvey Beltson roll around the corner like the tugboat he was, with—as usual—a double martini in his hand. Leona knew his habits. He was beaming, which meant he must already be on at least his third drink.

''Leona, sweetheart,'' he boomed as he spied her at the door. ''What's the chief honcho doing at Jenny's little party? I'm honored, how's Justin? Had lunch with him a few weeks ago, gotta catch up, listen, you really run a professional operation, honey, these guys are *great*."

"Thanks, Harvey," she said as lightly as possible. "I find things run best with quality checks now and then." She turned slightly to Juan, motioning him out the door. This meant, unfortunately, she was stuck talking to the oblivious Harvey until Juan got back.

"I hear your party for Governor Idelson was fabulous," she said, filling time. "Sorry I wasn't able to make it, but Justin said the Beef Wellington was wonderful."

"Not as good as yours," Beltson said loyally, his eyes definitely fogging over. Leona wondered what it was like to be Jenny Beltson, with a drunken husband and eight guests due in an hour for dinner. God, she might drink, but never before a dinner party.

Beltson's expression turned lachrymose and he put his arm around her shoulders. "Haven't had the opportunity to tell you how sorry I am about your friend. Lovely woman, tragic, really. Came from a great family; too bad, too bad. Guess she got herself a little too far out front on that oil deal of Justin's."

Shocked, Leona caught her breath.

"She was a real pal, wasn't she?"

"Yes," Leona murmured. "The oil deal, you said?"

"Yeah, Justin said she'd be a big help to us; too bad the Arabs got mad. Poor gal didn't get herself out fast enough."

"Of her investment?"

Harvey nodded. "Justin knows how to sell a deal, that's for sure. This would've been a great one. Glad we both got our money out in time. Gotta get another drink, see you, honey. Best to Justin."

The door burst open and Juan entered the apartment with a large window fan in his left hand, looking nervously in Leona's direction. She never noticed. She stood rooted to the spot, staring after the retreating figure of the amiable drunk who had just dropped a bomb into her life and her marriage.

It was late, past midnight, and Justin was supposed to be on his way to California. You never could tell, of course; Justin had a reputation for changing his plans at the last minute. Leona emerged from her husband's closet with exactly what she had been looking for: a tiny key taped to a piece of cardboard that would open the large steel filing cabinet in his office upstairs. She glanced over her shoulder. Even when he wasn't here his presence permeated the house, so she'd better get this done.

Leona climbed the stairs and tiptoed nervously into Justin's private enclave. She had chosen the curtains and bought the desk herself at a Sotheby auction, but Justin hadn't invited her in since she put it all together. The steel filing cabinet was an ungainly thing, but Justin had insisted on keeping it. Leona peeled the key from the piece of cardboard, inserted it in the lock, and twisted the cabinet drawer open. So many folders. A scrawled "White House" label was on the thickest one, and when she recognized Justin's handwriting she realized no secretary had prepared these files.

Clumsily she thumbed through them, feeling uneasy. This was flat-out snooping and she really had no right to violate Justin's privacy. He dealt in highly confidential matters and what she was poking through was absolutely none of her business . . . Then she saw a slender manila envelope tucked behind the last file. Faith's name was printed in careful letters on the upper-left edge. Leona pulled the envelope out and opened the clasp, peering in. As she expected, there were the papers Justin had asked her to find and bring from Faith's bedroom, the ones hidden in the box of notepaper; the papers he said were simply scribbles from meetings on policy issues the press had no right to see, which was why she had dutifully done her job—and not told Maggie.

But that wasn't all that was in the envelope—and Leona kept reading. Her eyes were riveted to the pages. Suddenly she cried out, put her head in her hands, and dropped the papers on the floor.

Carol squinted against the late afternoon sun as her cab drove up to the Capitol Hill townhouse she and Bart had bought for next to nothing back in an era of plummeting values. The flower boxes Bart had built were sagging and she wondered why she hadn't noticed before. Maybe because she hadn't been home in time to see the house in daylight for a long time. She glanced up and caught a glimpse through the living room of a figure with hair as red as hers and her heart leaped. Good, the kids were home.

She opened the door. "Hi, guys," she said to the two lanky teenagers sprawled in the living room. She had to repeat herself to be heard over the din of the television set, which was irritating. They knew she hated the damn thing in the living room, so why had they brought it down?

The redhead—a freckle-faced fifteen-year-old whose voice had deepened startlingly in eight weeks—glanced up and then back to the television screen. "Hi, Mom," he said. "You're home early."

"Yeah, I thought I'd bake cookies or something. Do a little bonding with my kids. You stay so busy, I never see you. Oren, get your feet off the table," she said automatically, reaching over to muss her son's hair. "Victoria, say hello to your mother."

"Hello, Mother," said Victoria in her usual bored fashion. "Oren and I have a bet. I figure it'll take you less than thirty seconds to criticize my new haircut."

Carol scrutinized the tangle of curls on her thirteen-year-old daughter's head and sighed. "It looks like you cut it with a lawn mower," she said.

Victoria snapped her fingers and glanced at her brother. "I win," she said.

"Bet's canceled," growled Oren. "You told her first."

"God, you try to wriggle out of everything!"

"Hey." Carol felt a need to pull them back to her somehow. "We've got things to talk about, don't we?"

Victoria slumped deeper into the sofa, stretching out her long tan legs. "What's there to talk about?" she said.

"Turn off the set. I want to tell you"—she paused and tried to pull back the words but it was too late—"my side."

"Oh, a battle brewing, huh? Who gets us?"

This time Carol didn't waste words. She strode over to the television set, flicked it off, and faced her children.

"Oren, get your feet off that table," she ordered. Oren obeyed, very slowly. "I know your father's been talking to you," she began. She tried unsuccessfully to be matter-of-fact. "I hope he told you that he's the one who wants the separation. I don't want a divorce, this is the biggest shock of my life. As far as I'm concerned, your father is pulling the rug out from under our lives because he's a selfish . . ."

"Asshole?" suggested Oren.

"You know I hate that word."

"It's what you're thinking. Might as well say it and get it over with."

Why were they both so surly? You'd think *she* was the one who'd disrupted their lives. "I know this is hard for you," she said more calmly. "I don't know what kind of stuff your father is feeding you, but whatever he said, it's wrong."

"You're always right, aren't you?"

Victoria's challenge took Carol's breath away, and for the first time she felt afraid. "What's going on here?" she managed.

"Ever think maybe Dad wanted to be right once in a while instead of just you?" Victoria's voice was no longer bored, it was angry, with a shading of tears.

"I don't know what you're talking about. I work hard and I've never had this kind of criticism from you before."

"Mom." Oren was unwinding himself and standing up. "You never *heard* any criticism before." And with that he turned and left the room, followed almost immediately by his sister, who stopped at the doorway and looked back at her mother. "See what happens," she said in a funny, high voice, "when you come home from the Hill too early?"

And then the doorbell rang.

Sara knew she had picked a bad time to come the minute the door swung open and she found herself staring at Victoria. "Hello, Judge Marino," the girl said, lifting her chin high. "You here to pick up the pieces?"

"You cut your hair."

"With a lawn mower, right?"

"Actually," Sara said, stepping inside, "it looks good. Kind of Shannen Dohertyish."

"Oh, God, her." But Sara had coaxed a smile.

"Where's your mother?"

Victoria nodded toward the living room. Sara walked into the darkened room, seeing the huddled figure on the sofa. "Mind if I turn on a light?"

"Do anything you want."

Sara flicked the light switch. "I just wanted to see how you were doing," she said quietly. "Sort of returning the favor."

"My kids are turning on me." Carol sounded shell-shocked.

"They're frightened, Carol."

"What's the matter with me? Go on, tell me the truth."

Sara took a deep breath and sat down next to her friend on the sofa. Carol never said what she didn't mean, that was the straightforward part about her, and Sara had to give her an honest answer. But she also had to do it gently. "You work hard and you care passionately about what you fight for,'' she said. ''But—but you can be very self-absorbed sometimes.''

''Obtuse, right?''

''A little. But very loyal and caring.''

Carol reached into a pocket of her jacket and brought forth a damp, well-used tissue. She blew her nose, hard. ''You're sugarcoating it, but I appreciate it. I haven't been paying enough attention . . .'' She couldn't go on.

''It's never too late.''

''Don't go overboard, dearie,'' Carol said with a rheumy smile. ''Bart's gone. But I don't want my kids to hate me.''

''I'm not a parent, but I think they see you as strong and powerful.''

''Oh, right.''

''And they expect you to keep their universe in shape. If you can't, it's your fault.''

''He left *me!*''

''That makes it more important,'' she said.

''It's my fault, either way.''

''In their eyes? Probably.''

''Oh, Sara,'' Carol was crying, ''I'm so *mad.*''

''I don't blame you.''

''Am I such a total shit?''

Sara moved closer, put her arm around Carol's shoulders. They felt unexpectedly fragile. ''The last thing in the world you are,'' she said, ''is a total shit. And your kids know it.''

''They'll let me know, right?'' Carol was trying to smile. ''In about fifteen years?''

Sara chuckled. ''I guess,'' she said. She looked around the room, at the newspapers scattered around the television set, at a half-eaten sandwich on the coffee table, at what looked suspiciously like a beer bottle—Carol never touched the stuff, she knew.

''The place is a mess,'' Carol said, following her eyes.

Sara couldn't deny the obvious. ''Look, go wash your

face. I'm going to collect the kids and take the three of you to dinner.'' She was probably walking into the line of fire, but somebody had to do something. Without waiting for Carol to agree, she strode from the living room, through the hall, and into the kitchen. There were Oren and Victoria, a half-smoked cigarette in Victoria's right hand. An old dog with pink skin showing through a thinning coat of hair tottered around the room, banging into the chair legs; Victoria reached out absently to scratch his neck as Sara walked in.

''Put that cigarette out,'' Sara ordered. She never stopped to think what she would do if Victoria refused. She turned to Oren. ''Go pick up the living room, Oren,'' she said, ''and get rid of the beer.''

''Who are you . . . ?''

''Hey, it's okay, Oren.'' Victoria was squishing out her cigarette in a dirty saucer. The dog disappeared under the table as the two of them eyed her carefully, waiting for her next move.

''Look, kids,'' Sara began, then stopped. She pulled up a chair and sat down. A cold muzzle grazed softly against her leg. What did she know about teenagers, for God's sake? What could she do to goose them all up a little? ''Look, I'm sorry about what's happened. I know it's changing your lives.''

''It's been coming a long time,'' Victoria said flatly.

''I know it's hard to see right now, but your mother has been hit pretty hard and she needs you both very much.''

''You're telling us we should act more mature than she does?'' Oren challenged. ''Hey, that's easy.''

These kids were tough. ''Just give her a break, that's all.'' She thought of Carol, of the long road ahead for this family. She stared at the kids, remembering how she had felt when her mother died. . . .

She folded her hands on the table and spoke with the best judicial authority she could muster. ''Okay, life goes on, and it's time to eat. If you promise to be civil, I'm treating for dinner. Now, Oren—go clean up the living room. Victoria and I are doing the dishes."

Justin was making that damn steeple with his hands again, but Jack Patton had to admit it was a good way of buying time.

"Her father? What's he got to do with this?" Dick Sayles said, staring at the two men as they faced him in his office.

"Mr. President, we don't want to burden you with details," Justin said, speaking rapidly. "But this news about Dr. Marino could be politically destabilizing. You know the uproar out there over euthanasia. The AARP's protest march here is only a couple of weeks away—just about when Judge Marino heads in for her confirmation hearing. Old people are spitting mad, Mr. President. We can't alienate them. They vote."

"I know all that, I don't need a speech," Sayles cut in irritably. "I also know I inherited a damn good nominee for the Court. Dumping her doesn't make sense."

"We're not dumping her," Patton broke in, his voice easy. "We've been handed an opportunity to make it in her best interest to withdraw, that's what we're doing. Frankly, I'm a little surprised, sir, that you don't see it our way."

"She's already turned you down, Jack."

"I think that will change. If not, it is within your rights—"

"I can't do that. She's got too strong a constituency. Dammit, she's too popular."

"With all due respect, sir—"

"You're implying that's not the real reason, aren't you?"

The tension in the room suddenly escalated. Justin and Patton exchanged a quick glance.

"Justin?" Sayles swiveled in his chair and faced his new

adviser. "What have you got to say?"

"We'll do whatever you want, Mr. President," Justin said promptly. He flashed a warning look in Patton's direction. This was his forte, playing both sides, and Patton had better keep quiet. "Let's examine the issue," he said. "There are several things at stake, not the least of which is getting you elected. We have more than this Supreme Court nomination to worry about, as I know you are aware."

"I am aware that one of those things is an indiscretion on my part," Sayles said immediately, staring back. "I'm also aware of the intermingled friendships involved."

"Sara Marino knows too much," Patton said with blunt directness.

"That's why I don't want to cross her."

There, the truth.

"Instead you want her on the Court—with information that could ruin you?"

Sayles hesitated.

Patton moved swiftly to press his advantage. "Put her front and center for these hearings and who knows what the media digs up?" he demanded. "They won't let go of the so-called mystery of Faith's death. If that money loss hadn't surfaced, we'd have the books closed by now, but we don't."

Sayles snapped back. "If she goes on the Court, I'm her benefactor. She'll be grateful. That's the way I figure it."

"You could be absolutely right," Justin said before Patton could respond. "Obviously you intend to shape a strong administration and you're committed to maintaining the integrity of an independent Court—which you would with your own nominee, too. But if you've called this one wrong . . ."

Sayles stared at him, his face completely still.

"Will you let us see how this plays out?" asked Patton.

Sayles hesitated again, clearly struggling with himself.

"I'll think about it," he said finally.

Another fast glance between Justin and Patton. Both men visibly relaxed.

"Anything else?" Sayles asked. He pushed his chair back to signal the end of the meeting.

Patton couldn't resist a parting shot. "No, sir," he said calmly. "But I would worry about something else, Mr. President."

Justin said nothing as Sayles raised his eyebrows and glanced quizzically at his chief of staff.

"What's that?"

"Mrs. Sayles," Patton said.

The room they sat in together was heavy with thick mahogany paneling, a lawyer's room; the kind of room planned originally to awe and intimidate. It was now three weeks since Faith had died. Sara sat down, nodding gently to her friends, pulling white cuffs down below the sleeves of her black linen blazer. Leona, Carol, and Maggie automatically drew their thickly padded chairs close toward her, but they, too, were almost mute. A scattering of people filed in, all silent. It was that kind of room.

A slight bustle at the door caused Maggie to turn around. A tall young lawyer in an overly cautious black suit was striding toward the front of the room, clearing his throat and shuffling papers as he moved forward.

"This isn't a complicated will," he began. "Miss Paige had a few simple bequests, with most of her estate going to her mother. Hope none of you sacrificed important appointments to come here today."

Carol shrugged slightly, conveying with body language that he was wrong on that one. She shot a glance at Sara, somewhat shamefacedly, but Sara hadn't noticed. Oh, hell, forget it. She was here because she wanted to be; there was nothing else to it.

The reading proceeded as they listened self-consciously.

Except for Sara, they were all novices to this particular ceremony. Nothing made the truth more stark: They would never see Faith again, all that was left of her were her possessions.

"I don't want to be here," Leona whispered to Maggie. "I don't want anything, I just want her back."

Maggie squeezed her hand, but said nothing. We shouldn't be here, she thought. We weren't part of the family. Why should a person's death come down to distributing things? It was like turning Faith's life into a rummage sale.

"She wanted to give us tokens to remember her, I guess," Carol said, thinking at the same time: Maybe I should update my own will. If he wasn't coming back, she didn't want Bart getting his hands on her things. She made a mental note to call her lawyer as soon as the reading was over.

". . . To my friend, Carol Lundeen, I leave my raccoon coat, with the fervent wish that hemlines stay short. If they don't, no one will know how to turn the damn thing into kitchen curtains better than Carol. . . ."

The lawyer read Faith's flip words in as flat a tone as possible, but they all still felt shaken by the irreverent tone; the normalcy. When Faith wrote this, death was not real. It was a joke.

"A little heavy, but I could line them with canvas," Carol whispered, her eyes red.

There were several more bequests read off rapidly: a set of china to a recently married cousin, a U.S. Treasury bill to her housekeeper . . . then one to Sara: the beaded, strapless gown Faith wore to Goodspeed's Inaugural Ball. "I know it'll fit, my dear Sara . . ." The lawyer was reading Faith's words in what was fast becoming an embarrassed monotone. "And you should wear it. Have some fun, kick up your heels a little more. And remember, no bra. Spoils the line."

Now it was Sara's eyes that were filling.

Maggie's turn was next.

"To my friend, Maggie Stedman, who works too hard and should look at pictures more: the album I put together of snapshots from the Ladies' Lunch vacation in Key West. I keep it in my room to remind myself of the good times. Why do you think we didn't go away together more often? It was fun, wasn't it?"

Yes, Maggie thought, squeezing her hands together. We did have fun. Oh, Faith. Why? Why?

The lawyer read on.

"And finally to my dear and stylish friend, Leona Maccoby, I leave my crystal and gold earrings, the ones I never bothered insuring. Now you can fill out those boring insurance forms, and you'll look better in them than I did."

He cleared his throat again, obviously relieved to have completed his chore. "That's all," he said unceremoniously. "This was a bit of an unusual will, as you all can see. Ah—you can go now. The bequests will be delivered within the next two weeks, just as soon as we finish the paperwork." He clutched the will close to his chest and hurried from the room. The other people straggled out after him, and in short order the room was empty, except for Faith's four friends.

Maggie and Carol looked at each other, then over at Sara, who was standing uncertainly. Suddenly Maggie remembered. She glanced down at Leona, who hadn't moved.

"The earrings—they were the ones we buried her in," Maggie said. "Right?"

Leona nodded and smiled, her face wet.

"But I hate the thought of you on that motorcycle, let alone Jeff," Maggie argued, as Michael stood patiently at the front door later that afternoon.

"Maggie, I promised him; he'll wear a helmet, don't worry."

"He's been so cranky this morning."

"Maybe a little spin will perk him up," Michael said. He gestured out to the curb. "Look—he's all excited, waiting for his ride. I'll just take him around the block, okay?"

"Why do you own that thing, anyway?" She looked past him to the curb, to the Harley-Davidson that looked to her like a bristling arsenal of danger. The city was frying, literally frying in heat, her air conditioner wasn't working well, and she felt cross. The reading of the will had brought back every moment of the awful day when Faith died, and now here she was facing a cajoling Michael, a pleading son, a decision she didn't want to make. . . .

"One turn around the block. I promise." Michael made no attempt to explain his love affair with his Harley-Davidson. He knew the difference between what Maggie could and could not understand.

Jeff, standing at the curb next to the glistening black and chrome attraction, caught his mother's worried gaze. "Mom, please?" he pleaded. "Please?"

She hesitated, looking at her son's pale face. His cold was better, but she could hear his breath, raspy in his throat. "All right," she said with resignation. "One time around the block."

She watched Michael give the go signal to Jeff; saw the two of them climb on the motorcycle, and wondered briefly if she was becoming too protective a mother. Raising a son without a father . . . Nothing seemed to make Jeff happy lately, he was grumpy and tired-looking all the time. Maybe she was too short-tempered, worrying too much about what came next. What had given her the idea she could charge up to Buffalo and hustle up some witness to clear Dr. Marino, all before the nomination hearings? The idea was nothing more than clumsy meddling; anyhow, she didn't have the money. Her route was clear: she couldn't write the book. She would tell Teleki tomorrow. But panic was seeping into her soul.

Two free-lance assignments falling through in one

week . . . what was she going to do? She was losing jobs and the whole situation was overwhelming. On top of all of the personal things, Sara was definitely in trouble. Stories were starting to buzz, no doubt helped along by Sandi Snow. She and Michael might never know how much she had overheard at the Safeway last Saturday, but Maggie felt a growing fear. She stood watching and listening from the front door, thinking about Faith's photo album . . . there couldn't be too many pictures in it. And that made her sad.

The squealing of brakes jolted her forward, moving her out the door, her slippers flapping against the cement.

"Jeff?" she hurried for the corner, trying not to run. "Jeff!"

She saw Michael. He was off the motorcycle, Jeff in his arms, walking slowly toward her.

"He fell off?" She was sobbing.

"God, no." Michael was cradling the boy close, looking worried. "He asked me to stop. Maggie, he's burning up. I think he's sick. Really sick."

Maggie punched in the numbers, her fingers trembling. Answer, answer, she pleaded. Answer . . .

"Hello?"

"Leona, it's me," she said. "Maggie."

"Maggie, hi."

"Leona, I'm at Georgetown Hospital, in the emergency room." She tried to keep her voice steady. "I need help."

"What's happened?" Leona said, instantly alarmed. "Are you hurt?"

"Jeff. Jeff's sick." She glanced back toward the admitting nurse, struggling with her fear and humiliation. The woman had been so disapproving, so witheringly shocked when Maggie hadn't been able to produce an insurance card. "We're here, okay? Please, don't ask me any questions, not yet. Let me tell you." Her voice trembled uncontrollably. "Leona, you're the richest person I know. And I need money, I need it fast."

"What?" Leona gasped.

"My insurance expired," Maggie said, her sweaty hand slipping on the receiver. "We got here and they told me my insurance expired. Jeff has a ruptured appendix."

Leona cut her off. "I'll be right there," she said. "Don't let them wait, *I'll be right there.*"

"Thank you," Maggie whispered.

Fifteen minutes later, Leona came flying through the emergency-room door, arguing at the top of her lungs with a hospital security guard running next to her. "I don't *care* if I'm parked illegally," she said, "the hell with it, take the car if you want, I'm not moving it now!" She spied Maggie and rushed over. Her hair was in chaotic wisps. "Are they operating?" she demanded.

Now it was Maggie, trying to calm Leona down. "Yes," she said, holding out shaking hands. "They said that was never an issue, but I panicked. Leona, when they ask you for an insurance card and you don't have one, it's so—"

"So frightening?"

Overwhelmed, Maggie could just nod. "I couldn't tell Michael. I would've been begging him for money he doesn't have and I was so ashamed."

Leona, calming down, reached into her purse and pulled out a checkbook. "Point me to the people I pay," she said calmly.

Hours later, Maggie and Leona stood together, staring through the window of the intensive-care unit, their breath leaving small halos of fog on the glass.

"He's going to be all right, Mrs. Stedman," said a tired-looking nurse on her way into the room. She patted Maggie's hand. "He's a lucky little boy who should speak up when he's hurting—we see a lot of young people who wait too long. Look, you can't just stand here all night, you need to get some rest yourself."

"He's going to be all right," Maggie murmured. "I've got to call Michael." And then she sagged slowly against the shoulder of her friend.

Sara dialed quickly, still stunned by Leona's quick phone call from the hospital, but Maggie's line was busy. She couldn't be home yet, her message tape must be filled. She slammed the phone down in frustration and looked at her watch, realizing she was already late for her dinner with Barney. She could call later . . . Maggie must still be at the hospital with Jeff.

She hung up and rushed for the door, thinking, as she grabbed her purse and turned the doorknob, that the good and the terrible thing was, when there was a crisis like this, life always went on. For somebody, anyhow. Somebody was lucky, somebody was unlucky, and then everybody else—herself included—ducked their heads for as long as they could. What mattered for those who ducked was simply being there, whether to comfort or to celebrate. "Returning phone messages when your friends call," she whispered out loud with a catch in her voice. "And *leaving* them when they need you."

"This place feels like a mausoleum unless it's crowded," Leona said almost apologetically as she led Maggie into the living room of her Kalorama home. It was late, past midnight. The two of them had stayed hours together at the hospital. But when Leona started to drive Maggie home, it was clear it was too soon to leave her alone. So here they were.

"I don't know why I ever let Justin talk me into this house, I never wanted it," Leona said, looking around with the eye of a detached observer. "The colors are violent, aren't they? Throw-up colors." Her eye traveled to a somber Francis Bacon over the fireplace. "Great art, I guess," she said. "Justin likes it. Me, I don't like to walk by it with the lights off."

"I can't stay long," Maggie said, moving restlessly around the room. "I've got to get some books and stuff for Jeff or he'll go nuts in that hospital."

"He won't need anything more tonight," Leona said gently. "And you're not going to find a toy store open at this hour."

"Well," Maggie was tired and flustered, "I just—I need to do something." She felt limp and drained and still not quite sure if she could stay steady on her feet for very long.

"Sit down and put your feet up," Leona said. "You deserve a rest. Hungry?"

Maggie thought about it. When had she last eaten? She couldn't remember. All she could remember was the look of recognition on Jeff's face when he came out of the anesthetic and saw her leaning over his hospital bed. Jeff was all that mattered, all there was; nothing else meant anything without him. How quickly every concern faded before this one! "I'm okay, Mom," he murmured, and then he had slipped back into sleep. "Yes," she told him, smoothing his hair. The vow she made was to herself: Her son was never going to be in this kind of jeopardy again if she could help it.

Leona guided her to the sofa. "You may not know it, but you're hungry," she said. "I'll make some sandwiches."

Maggie devoured a ham and cheese sandwich and half a bowl of potato salad with hardly a pause and found herself actually asking for more. The trembling in her hands stopped finally, and she leaned back gratefully with a second glass of wine, studying the elaborate dentil moldings that graced the huge room. "It's such a big room," she said, almost shyly. "Maybe too big for everyday living if you say so, but still a terrific room. I've always thought it must be fun to fill it with people.''

''You think so?'' Leona cast a rueful glance at her friend.

''Well, nothing's perfect, of course.''

''You can pretend it is, I've learned that.'' Her words were matter-of-fact. ''Maggie,'' she said, pouring the wine. ''Don't waste time envying me. It isn't worth it.''

''I'm not,'' Maggie said honestly. ''Not tonight. I feel like I've just won the lottery.''

Leona leaned back, slipping into a ruminating mood. ''I remember you at Vassar. You were always lucky, so lucky the rest of us could have cheerfully killed you. God, first in the class—and you still managed to attract the most interesting guys.''

''I haven't seen any of them around in a long time,'' Maggie said with a laugh.

''I used to think of you as so driven,'' Leona said. ''So *serious.* Student body president, editing the newspaper—I remember you rushing around, hair flying, in charge of everything. But always sort of—alone.''

''It wasn't that much fun,'' Maggie admitted. ''I was always worrying about what came next.''

''Maybe you should believe in your luck for a change,'' Leona said gently.

''I do. The proof is my boy in that bed at Georgetown.''

A shadow passed over Leona's face. ''I'm telling you this at exactly the wrong time, I suppose, or maybe it's exactly the right time, I'm not too good at sorting out nuances. All this''—she waved her arm, taking in everything in sight—''is just background. No more real than the scenes in a movie. Listen, nobody has it all, I promise you. Nobody.''

She stood and began walking around the room, pointing first to the sofa upholstery. ''Peach brocade, some overpriced Italian fabric, two or three hundred dollars a yard, I forget. I spent a week choosing it right after I miscarried three years ago. That relieved Justin; he didn't want a baby.

But I know I've missed something. And I regret it."

"I'm sorry," Maggie said, taken aback by the confidence. "I wish you would have told us."

"Why would I tell something that important to my friends?" Leona shrugged elaborately, but it was a weak attempt at a joke and it fell flat.

"When I had a miscarriage when Jeff was two, it took me months to get over it," Maggie said, wondering why she had never talked about this before. "It made me angry that nobody seemed to understand. They thought I was stuck on mourning."

Leona was blinking rapidly. "Yeah, well—it's a small sadness compared to a lot of others. That's what most people think."

"There's no grave, no tombstone."

"I guess we know."

They sat together silently for a moment.

"Okay, I'll admit something," Maggie said. "I *have* envied you—or been jealous, whichever it is. I'm embarrassed that you could see it." She folded her hands in front of her face and realized the words were coming more easily. "You've always seemed secure and protected. Just exactly what I don't feel, what I haven't felt in a long time. I'm nervous when I'm banging out columns or magazine pieces, and I'm nervous when the assignments aren't coming in. I always feel I'm on the edge of disaster, which isn't the best frame of mind for being a good mother or a good friend."

"And I feel like an ingenue in a bad movie."

Maggie smiled. "Now we're supposed to tell each other to stop being silly, right?"

"You don't see yourself as enviable," Leona said suddenly. It wasn't a question, it was a statement.

Maggie considered for a moment. "No, not really," she said.

"Come on, Maggie. You and I both measure ourselves

against each other and hate our trade-offs and wonder how come the other gets a free ride and we don't."

"Do we?"

"Doesn't everybody?"

Maggie shrugged. "I don't know," she said.

"I do. And you know what else? I think we've been so busy playing the game, we haven't known who we are—or who our friends are, either."

Maggie wasn't sure she was comfortable with the direction of this conversation. At the same time, it felt freeing to relax back into the sofa and say what was on her mind and not wonder how it was being perceived. It seemed a luxury, somehow. "Do you think we're really friends?" she asked.

"Maybe not as good as we thought we were."

"That scares me, Leona."

"It does?"

"It does, because I'm testing it," Maggie said slowly, rolling the words on her tongue, realizing for the first time she had finally made up her mind. "I'm going to write a book, Leona. About our lunch group. I was going to pass it up, but not now. Not after showing up at that hospital with no money and no insurance card. I never want to feel that helpless again." She thought of Jeff, lying so still and small on the narrow white bed in the intensive-care unit. He was her only loyalty now. "It's a good, fat contract. And I'm going to sign."

Leona was clearly startled. "A book? On us?"

Maggie nodded.

"Just like that, huh? Goodbye to Tom Cruise and Madonna?"

Maggie winced at the sharp overtone. Leona was angry. But when she looked into her eyes, she saw something else, something not so easily decipherable.

"Are you asking permission, Maggie?"

"No," Maggie said, a catch in her voice. "I can't afford

to, now. I tried to talk to Sara about it, but she has enough on her mind. I want to write this without violating my friendships. Do you know that?"

"Well, I hear you saying it. But how do you *do* it?"

"I don't know yet."

"God, Maggie. You take my breath away."

"Leona, I have no money. I'm hanging by my fingernails, and it makes me mad." The truth was too bare.

Leona was silent for a long moment. "We've all worried about you, actually. Ever since you left the *Post.* Don't you think you've punished yourself enough?"

"That's what Michael says."

Maggie looked so miserable, Leona reached out, patted her shoulder, and sighed. "I guess I should be horrified, but I have this problem. I think I trust you."

It was almost too much and Maggie blinked back tears.

"Now don't get drippy," Leona said gently. "Remember, you don't have to write an exposé. Anyway, better you than Sandi Snow."

"I don't want it to change things. I feel we're growing closer."

"We can work out ground rules together, maybe."

Maggie wiped at her tears. "I'll write a proposal."

"Lay out the book *you* want to write."

"I will."

They smiled at each other.

"You've got to figure out what it is you want most, you know?" Leona said. "When I think back on my brainstorm to pull everybody together, actually, I wasn't out to make friends so much. I really just wanted a good network of contacts. Tell the truth—isn't that what you wanted too?"

"Yes," Maggie said, "that's what I wanted."

"And that's what we got—you, me, Faith, Carol, and Sara. We never had to breathe each other's air up close. I don't mean we haven't come to care for each other, because we have."

"Yes, of course we have." Maggie felt obscurely ashamed that each felt it necessary to reassure the other. "I want to be a real friend, the way you were for me, today. When you walked in that door and pulled your checkbook out. . . ." Maggie couldn't go on.

This time Leona gave her a look of such sweetness, Maggie's image of her friend altered permanently. "Was I?" Leona said with a touch of wonder. "Well, so I was."

"Surprise, surprise." Maggie couldn't help smiling.

"Something's changed, I think."

"So now we don't have to debate the difference between jealousy and envy?"

Leona grimaced and shook her head. "Who cares?" she said. She stretched her arms upward, nail polish glittering in the reflected light, as if to touch the grandly scaled moldings above her head. "Isn't this wonderful? Neither of us has it all. You know what, Maggie? The edge is off. I wonder what happens next?"

The light in her eye suddenly faded. "What am I saying?" Her voice began to tremble. "I know what happens next."

Maggie looked at her swiftly, started to speak, and then waited.

"My life is falling apart," Leona said finally. "You probably aren't surprised."

"You and Justin?"

Leona nodded slowly. "I've fooled myself for a long, long time. I'm either a total idiot or a master of denial. One or the other, what does it matter?"

Impulsively, Maggie took Leona's small hand and held it cupped between her own. "In all honesty, I've been afraid of this," she said gently. She felt sudden, wondering sadness. She noticed for the first time the tiny ripple of flesh under her friend's chin; the eyeshadow that was just a little too blue. She's created herself, same as I have, she thought. We've spent all these years laughing and gossiping and giving each other parties and access to important people . . . but we're always busy. We fill our datebooks with non-stop appointments—but we pencil in our needs. Anything penciled in can always be postponed. Then we laugh and chat at the next lunch and don't worry about letting each other down, just as long as we keep our pencils sharpened. We've let ourselves create artificial selves, and now we're trying to find out who we really are.

"I've got some hard decisions ahead," Leona said quietly.

"He takes you for granted, Leona."

"No, Maggie. It's much worse than that."

"What do you mean?"

Leona was struggling, her cheeks flushing red. "Justin lives in a secret world, not a world, really—it's—it's more like a snake pit."

"Can I help?"

"Thank you. Nobody can."

"What are you going to do?"

"I don't know yet." Her eyes had a strange, lost look. "Maggie, I'm scared."

Sara hurried past the open windows of Café Atlantico on Columbia Road, and as she scanned the diners inside, she spied Barney Cassidy waving, beckoning her forward. Even in her present agitated state she felt strangely awkward approaching the table, aware she was wearing a new and reasonably stylish summer dress, all crisp white cotton with soft sheer sleeves. She had taken time with her makeup, experimenting awkwardly with a new eyeliner, and she hoped it was on straight. After weeks now of studying cases and examining issues, poring over documents with Justice Department lawyers and trudging the halls of the Capitol to build support, she wanted—she needed to think of something else.

"Did you reach your friend?" asked Barney as he rose

and pulled a chair out from the table.

"No," Sara said. "But I'll see her tonight. The hospital says Jeff will be okay—it's amazing what can happen to kids, isn't it?"

"It sure is." The feeling in his voice seemed genuine. "Poor kid. My son . . ."

"You have a son?"

"Yes. In California."

This was the most personal information Barney had offered yet, and Sara was curious. "Tell me about him," she said.

"He's six, a healthy, bratty six. Almost got killed by a car last year." Barney grimaced involuntarily. "I was holding his hand and he wriggled away. There were a couple of seconds there—hey, it's every parent's nightmare."

"Do you actually dream about it?" What a nosy question, but it was precisely the one she wanted to ask.

"Only when I'm away from him," said Barney as he signaled the waiter for menus. "I can forget it when he's here. But he lives with his mother, and I only see him on holidays and for a month during the summer. The usual divorced-father lament. But he's the center of *my* universe, such as it is. How about you?"

She felt a flash of defensiveness. "I've never been married; you know that."

"Yeah, I know." He looked uncomfortable, as if suddenly reminded that she didn't share his universe.

Sara was annoyed with her own sharpness. Slowly, she drank from the glass of wine Barney had ordered for her, and decided to be more open.

"Look, I lived with someone for seven years; the usual story," she said casually. "When he was ready for marriage, I wasn't; when I was, he wasn't." She risked a little hyperbole. "We were each clawing our way to fame and fortune and managed to hold each other at arm's length until the relationship got so thin it floated away."

But he was looking at her with such sober attention she wondered if her wrap-up had been a touch too facile.

"A lot of marriages are like that," he said.

"I've never been too curious to find out," Sara confessed. "Although I'd like having kids around."

"I miss not having my kid around."

Menus arrived and Sara chatted on, enjoying both the balmy pleasures of the evening and Barney's intelligent, quick-witted company. Their conversation roamed from her father to marriage to food, from work to the Hill, from houseplants to which was better as a pet for busy people, a dog or a cat.

Barney leaned back finally and gazed contentedly out the full-length open windows. "Great evening, isn't it?" he said. The air was surprisingly dry for the end of August, and the heat of the day had been dispelled by a soft breeze. "We've had a pretty good week," he said. "We even got Senator Perez of Florida to come out for you, which surprised me, to tell the truth. I thought he'd take some work." He laughed. "Turns out that decision you wrote in the interstate tax case really persuaded him."

It was almost too easy to talk with him. "You just never know, do you?" she said with a smile. "To tell you the truth, I'm not too comfortable with those complicated commerce clause cases. Funny, how things work."

He laughed again. "Couldn't prove it by Perez. You're an impressive woman, Sara."

There it was, the killer line, bringing her instantly back to reality. "I try to be a good judge," she said, trying for an objective tone.

If he saw her drawing back, he didn't acknowledge it. "All the good people on the Court are getting old," he said. He was toying with his glass now, turning it in his hand, looking very reflective. "We need you there, do you understand how much? Don't get put off by the politics, Sara. The battle to control the Court has gone on forever, you know that. Everybody wants an ideologue—as long as it's *their* ideologue. No others need apply."

I wish he wouldn't give me a speech, she thought—and then felt vaguely guilty. He did, after all, have a vested interest in the outcome of her nomination. "I hate to be asking this, but what happens to you and Amos if things turn ugly?"

He leaned back and gave her a long, appreciative look. "Sara, at this point, if we thought this was unwinnable, well . . ."

"You'd want me to make a graceful exit," she finished. She felt curiously relieved.

"Sure—and we'd back another good candidate one hundred percent. Unfortunately, there aren't many with your legal mind. Epstein in Philaelphia?" Barney offered a mock grimace. "He would never push for the view of search and seizure you did; you made good law in a hard area."

She decided she could offer back her real feelings. "I can tell you, when Goodspeed nominated me? I was stunned."

"Come on, Sara."

"Barney, I'm not brilliant, and I know it. I'm no wiser than a lot of people who could have been picked for this job."

"You waste time being humble, Sara."

"That's not what I am."

"Good." He grinned. "Just stay honest about that."

"I don't need reminding." She smiled, to take the edge off her words. "But sometimes I worry I remove myself too much from the fighting and the arguments."

"That's what you should do. You should be the person who can pull back and force perspective."

Same thing she had said to Maggie, Sara thought. Things were getting overly earnest, but that often happened these days. Was it she? Should she loosen up more? This time she was the one who grinned, more ruefully. "The hell of it is, I have to get down and dirty first if I want my seat on the Court."

"Down and dirty," he repeated, rolling the words across his tongue thoughtfully. "With Jack Patton, I suppose."

"Yes. But one thing I know. He's afraid of me."

Barney's eyes turned watchful. "Interesting," he said. "Why?"

"It's a matter of trust." She wasn't ready to elaborate.

Barney cocked a quizzical eyebrow, shedding one invisible hat for another. "Don't hold back, Sara. Maybe this is something we need to know."

She tried a neutral smile. "Maybe he's one of these men still afraid of women they can't control."

"Hey, haven't they died out yet?" His response was a touch too jocular.

"Come on, Barney—you know better than that."

He leaned back, studying her, as the waiter put two more glasses of chilled white wine on the table. Then he reached for one of the goblets. "Here's to you, Judge Marino," he said warmly. "These past couple of weeks have been a real treat, even if you did pull me away from making money for a while."

Sara lifted her face as if to a warming sun. Nice, she thought, with some surprise.

"All we need is to get through these hearings, and you'll be launched on a great career. Cross your fingers." He looked at her intently. "Now tell me what's going on with Jack?"

She hesitated, but only for a moment. Barney had a stake in this, too.

"There's something I need to tell you, but it's not about Jack." Safe or not, this wouldn't be easy to say. "It's about the President. I think it's at the root of what's going on."

CHAPTER 8

"A *book*?" Sara was incredulous. She stood in the foyer of Maggie's house, staring at her friend. "Maggie, are you serious? I've told you too much."

"I promise—I won't write about those things." Maggie swayed slightly, exhausted. Sara had been standing at the door when she came home, filled with concern about Jeff and holding a package of Maggie's favorite brand of doughnuts in her hands. Telling her right away had seemed best. But Sara looked so stunned, Maggie felt her resolve faltering.

A light was dawning in Sara's eyes. "You tried to tell me before, didn't you, up at Dumbarton Oaks?"

"Yes. But I couldn't, not after you told me about Faith and about Patton's charges against your father. I decided I couldn't write it, then. There's no way I'd betray you, Sara. Look, I'm broke." Maggie bit the words out as matter-of-factly as possible. Each time, something got stripped away. She hated having revealed herself first to Leona, then to Sara; hated letting it be known that she'd been dancing on a swaying wire for a long time now. Hated feeling that her friends would pity her.

Sara said nothing for a long moment. Maggie's eyes were stinging with weariness.

"You've got a son, he's sick," Sara said, half to herself. "You've been offered half a million dollars, you can't pay the mortgage . . ."

"I'm not a charity case."

"Oh, knock it off, Maggie."

The words were so quick, it was Maggie's turn to be stunned.

"You don't have to tell me that! Of course, you're not! Do you think that's what I believe?" Sara actually looked offended.

Maggie was speechless. "The rest of you don't . . ." she began.

"Don't know what it's like to stay up late at night and worry about paying the bills? Maybe not, but so what?"

Maggie bowed her head. "What are you saying?" she asked, almost plaintively, although she already knew.

"I'm saying you don't have to feel so totally isolated."

"Will you give me a chance to prove I can do this without hurting you? Or the others?"

One beat, two.

"Yes, I think I can. I'm not sure."

They stood there, silently. Then Maggie noticed drops of grease dripping from the doughnut bag. She pointed to it, and Sara looked down. With only this small provocation, they were able to look at each other and attempt uncertain smiles.

It was Thursday morning, and Carol stared at the papers on her desk. "Who did it?" she asked Molly White, the legislative aide standing uncomfortably by her desk.

"Congressman Duncan," Molly answered.

"Why?"

Molly bit her lip and glanced back at the open door leading toward the outer office where she knew several aides were listening. "He said your disclosure demands were unacceptable," she said. "So he got the votes and tabled the bill."

"Without a phone call?" Carol said, her indignation mounting. "Who the hell does he think he is? That nursing home safety bill is important, and he knows it!" She pounded her desk in frustration. "Somebody let this happen and I'm firing that person! Nobody relaxes on a bill around here, do you hear me? Nobody!"

"Nobody did," protested Molly.

Carol was on her feet now. "Call everybody in," she ordered. "Maybe this was too much for you, Molly. I put you in charge of nursemaiding Duncan and you've botched the job. I'm getting to the bottom of this."

"Okay," Molly said, dangerously near tears. "But I've been trying to tell you for days what's going on, and I haven't been able to get your attention." She gulped to steady her voice and rushed on. "You're hardly ever here, and when you are, you've got your door locked. I mean—you've hardly talked to us or anyone on the committee for over a week! I did my best, we all did our best, but you're the congresswoman!"

She paused for breath, and in that pause Carol heard the whispers behind the open door. Her wave of anger began to ebb, replaced with a sudden, overwhelming feeling of mortification. Carol Lundeen was supposed to be a master at getting bills through committee and onto the House floor. She was renowned for her tenacity and boldness, and for her absolutely top, dedicated staff. They hadn't let her down, she had let herself down. All she had been able to think about for days was Bart's betrayal and her angry kids, and now Maggie's call about writing a book—her enemies had sensed her distraction and they had taken advantage of it.

She sank back into her leather chair. The nursing home safety bill was in limbo and it was her fault. The Lundeen

Act, it could have been called, she thought wistfully. She looked up at Molly and felt ashamed of herself. Molly knew her job; she hadn't done hers.

"I'm sorry, Molly. Tell everybody skulking behind that door to get back to their desks. We've got work to do."

Molly flashed an uncertain smile and headed out the door. A moment later she poked her head back through. "Carol?" she said.

"What now?" Carol answered wearily.

"A phone call for you."

"Is it Maggie Stedman?"

"No, but she called to tell you Jeff's okay. She'll call later. Uh, this one I think you want to take."

"Who is it?"

"Mrs. Paige."

"Not again!"

Molly decided to press. "She says it's important."

Carol reached for the phone, dismissing Molly with a wave of her hand. Nothing could make this day worse, not even a call from Ruth Paige.

"Hello?"

"Congresswoman Lundeen?"

"Yes, how are you?"

"Not so good." The older woman's voice was quavering badly, as if she had aged twenty years. Carol braced herself for more questions and denunciations, and found herself wondering fleetingly how she had ever become Mrs. Paige's chosen confidante. I'm not being fair, she told herself for the fiftieth time. She's lost her daughter and her money and she has a right to feel cheated. She has been cheated. Carol's suggestion to Mrs. Paige to hire an investigative firm to track Faith's finances had yielded nothing beyond the usual bank balances, a few blue-chip investments, and a perfectly respectable real estate deal. A lot of money gone, and there was no answer why—yet.

"Nothing more from the firm you hired?" she asked as sympathetically as she could.

"No, but that's not why I'm calling. I've got something here I need to show you; it's very important."

"What is it, Mrs. Paige?" Her head was throbbing. She had to get off this phone and find an Advil somewhere in the mess of stuff in her desk. But Mrs. Paige's next words stopped her absent-minded rummaging as quickly as it began.

"I have a letter," Mrs. Paige said, as if announcing the presence of a new and deadly virus. "It's a letter from Faith. I found it in a batch of papers at her house—folded inside her Neiman Marcus bill, of all places. A very large bill, by the way."

"Is it addressed to someone?"

"Yes, it's addressed to her—her Ladies' Lunch."

Carol was too surprised to be diplomatic. "Mrs. Paige, have you read it?"

"Certainly not. But I want you to look at it. Right here. I want you to tell me if there's anything in it about my money. That's all I want to know." The older woman's voice was firm.

"I'm sorry, I didn't mean . . ."

"Please understand," Mrs. Paige finally said, slowly parsing out each word, "I do not want to read anything she might have said about me. Please come now, I need your help."

She sounded afraid, actually afraid.

"All right."

The trip was faster than Carol expected. Mrs. Paige met her at the front door of an old antebellum home that looked slightly run-down in the way that the very rich, with nothing to prove, allow to happen. She was wearing a beige knit dress finished off with a meticulous white linen collar that emphasized the tidiness of her features. Sparing few words, she ushered Carol into a living room furnished with the most weathered antiques Carol had ever seen.

Silently, Mrs. Paige picked up from a table a letter in a soft cream-colored envelope of high-quality bond; exactly the elegant kind of stationery Faith favored. The sight of it made Carol tremble.

But Mrs. Paige seemed reluctant to get on with it. "Do me this favor, please," she said. "Just sit down for a moment." She nodded toward a slightly dulled silver tea service on the coffee table. "I have some things to tell you."

"I can't stay too long, Mrs. Paige. But I'll be happy to listen."

"Oh, don't be in such a rush. You women never stop. Always rushing." Mrs. Paige's fragile, blue-veined hands fluttered aimlessly. "You have no idea how I've suffered. Faith gambled away my money."

"It's more likely she was cheated out of it." She didn't have to let Mrs. Paige oversimplify.

"Whatever. It's gone." With a sigh, Mrs. Paige collapsed into the sofa.

Carol slowly took a seat in a faded floral chair facing the sofa, studying the older woman, feeling cautious. "If I can help, I—"

"Faith and I didn't talk much, you know. She was always on and off the phone in a minute or two with her duty calls." Mrs. Paige was slowly regaining her composure. "It comes as no secret, I suppose, that we weren't particularly close." This last was said with a certain stiffness, leaving Carol to wonder if Mrs. Paige knew full well that she had been, more than once, the object of her daughter's jokes. Suddenly: "She was mixed up with some man."

It was said so bluntly, Carol wasn't sure how to respond. "I'm sorry?" she managed.

"I listen to nuances. You learn how to do that when your daughter doesn't tell the truth. I store the words so I can think later about what they mean. I memorize. But I think she was trying to tell me . . ." Mrs. Paige stopped and Carol saw a glint in her eyes. Tears? Anger?

"Tell you what?"

"That she was in trouble. She was trying to break up with somebody, but he kept calling her all the time. He was married, I'll wager. The night before she died, she called me. I thought it was the usual, but she was very upset. I think she sensed I was holding the phone and fixing my nails at the same time." Mrs. Paige stopped to dab at her eyes with a tiny linen handkerchief tucked in the waistband of her dress.

"How could you know what was going to happen?"

Mrs. Paige's short, sharp laugh was unexpected. "That's not the point. I wasn't paying attention. She was angry with me—but I learned to accept her incessant anger."

Carol wanted to get out of there. She didn't feel comfortable. "Maybe I shouldn't have come . . ." she began, starting to rise from her chair.

"Just listen!"

She sat back quickly.

"You don't know this, I doubt if anybody knows this, but I did something significant, perhaps damaging, to my daughter years ago." Mrs. Paige's hands were trembling so badly, Carol had the impulse to grab them, to hold them still.

"Faith did not feel she owed me anything." Mrs. Paige spoke more calmly now. "She was a rebellious girl and I couldn't handle her. We had terrible problems. When she was fifteen, she ran away—and when we found her, I had her committed to a psychiatric hospital. Temporarily, of course."

Carol shivered. It was too late to leave now.

Mrs. Paige shot her a sharp look before continuing. "She was only there for a month. I thought I was doing the right thing, but she never forgave me. There. Now you know."

Carol sat silent for a long moment, trying to decide what to say next.

Mrs. Paige's mouth twisted into a knot. "You have no reaction?"

"She ran away."

"Yes. She needed careful monitoring for a while. But I think the incident made her very uncertain about herself—about her emotional stability. I'm afraid there were echoes of it for the rest of her life. If I were faced with the decision again, I might make it differently. Perhaps. She may tell you that in her letter, and I wanted to tell you first."

"Mrs. Paige." Carol could hear the ticking of a clock in the next room, beating time with her own heart. "Why did she run away?"

Not a sound. Nothing except the ticking clock. The two women stared at each other, and Carol realized she had lost her chance to back off.

"You already know, don't you?"

Carol nodded slowly.

Mrs. Paige suddenly rose to her feet, and there was no mistaking the nature of the look in her eyes. "It was a lie," she declared. "A lie, from beginning to end. Her father was a wonderful man. He would never lay a hand on his own daughter! Absolutely not. Faith was hysterical; she craved attention, I'm telling you."

Carol gulped air, trying to breathe. So it was true. God, it was true. Her memory tumbled her back to a day last winter she would never forget. The day of the House child abuse hearings. . . . She and Faith were in her office watching a replay of the testimony, when Faith—without warning—burst forth with a nightmarish story. Why, Carol asked herself in anguish for the fiftieth time, why hadn't she believed Faith? Because it was too bizarre? Faith had been poised to tell more, that was easy to see. But she had responded too awkwardly, not sure what to do or how to help. Faith had drawn back and closed down; locked herself in so tight, it was never possible to bring up the subject again.

"Maybe he did. Maybe it was true."

"Nobody can convince me of that, Congresswoman Lundeen, and I warn you, don't try."

Carol tried not to show how shaken she felt. "All right, I won't," she said. "But I can't sell Faith short."

"Sell her short?" Mrs. Paige seemed genuinely shocked. "My daughter was a troubled woman. And I will not allow you to dishonor the memory of my husband. Now I think I want you to leave." She stood, stiff, straight and proud.

Carol rose, feeling more than slightly sick. "The letter—"

"I will not give you the letter, it'll just spread more scandal. I should not have asked you to come here."

Carol looked at the envelope in the older woman's hands, trying hard to think of a way to will it in her direction. But she knew it was useless. "It may tell us why she died," she said. "Anyhow, it's addressed to us!"

"It was suicide."

"What if it was murder? You said—"

"I've changed my mind. Now, go."

Carol turned, uncertain, picked up her handbag, and tried to think of what she could do to salvage something out of this disastrous encounter. "You've suffered," she said tentatively. "I know you have, and I feel sorry for you."

The skin on Mrs. Paige's face looked like powdered parchment ready to crumble into dust. "How could you dare ask me why she ran away?" she whispered. "How could you dare?"

It was still early that same evening when Carol pulled into a parking space only two doors down from her townhouse. With mechanical precision she walked up the steps, turned her key in the door, and went inside. The house was totally still and she breathed a sigh of relief. The kids were at the movies, thank goodness. Tonight she needed to be alone.

She headed for the basement stairs, descending to the cheerfully chaotic sewing room that served as her escape from work and worries. She picked up a bolt of fine navy wool and began laying it out on the cutting table. She would cut the pieces for her new jacket, maybe even get it basted together. The lining would be tricky. . . .

She sank into her chair, reached for a spool of thread, then tried to thread her Singer—tricky old thing—but she kept missing the damn needle. Her eyes were blurring. It's not really my eyes, she thought, giving up finally. I just can't focus my mind.

She heard the doorbell, a sharp, piercing sound through the quiet house. She pushed her chair back and trudged slowly up the stairs. One of the kids, home early?

"Hello, Carol."

She stared at the familiar line of Bart's angular face, at the new furrows just below his slightly receding hairline.

"Guess I hauled you up from the basement. Working on another project?"

It took her a moment to recover. Here he was, on her doorstep, just standing there, like a stranger. Maybe he tried his key and found it didn't work any more, she thought with mordant satisfaction. No one can say I don't think ahead.

"What are you doing here?" she demanded. "Where do you get the idea you can just drop in any time you feel like it?"

"Okay, so we skip the niceties," he said, his expression changing. "I'm here to pick up my drawings. They happen to be an essential part of my work life, remember? You forgot to pack them up. Does that tell you anything, Carol?"

She girded herself for verbal battle, but then she noticed Bart didn't look cheerful at all. His shirt was soiled at the collar and badly rumpled. His eyes had hollows beneath them and he needed a shave. He looked as miserable as she felt. Reluctantly, she motioned him in.

"Where are the kids?" he asked, looking around tentatively, as if he had walked into a stranger's house and needed directions to get from one room to another.

"At the movies," she said. "Look, don't think you're going to patch things up overnight. You can't walk out on me like that and figure you can just . . ."

"I'm not here to patch things up," he said, cutting her off. The very act of cutting her off came as a surprise, and Carol was momentarily speechless. "My drawings are upstairs, so if you don't mind, I'll collect them and be on my way."

She stared after him as he ascended the stairs, watching him duck his head as usual at precisely the point where his tall, skinny frame became too tall for the ceiling. It was such a familiar gesture. Carol wandered around the living room aimlessly, not sure what to do until he came down. She turned when she heard his step.

"I trust you didn't take anything you weren't entitled to."

"Oh, for crying out loud, Carol, quit being a jerk."

"How can you talk like that to me?" she said, her anger rising. "You've got a hell of a nerve, Bart Lundeen, leaving me like this, abandoning me, humiliating me, ruining my work!"

He was calmly wrapping a stack of architectural drawings with what was left of the morning newspaper next to the chair by the window. "Got a rubber band?" he said.

"Damn you!" She was close to tears.

"Look, this is no triumph for me, if that's what you're thinking."

"You're going to tell me you don't have some blonde on the side?" She instantly regretted her words. She knew it wasn't true. Had she ever really believed it was? But if it had been, how much easier to be angry—how much more explainable.

"This has nothing to do with another woman," he said. "Look at me, Carol. A real Lothario you're married to, right? This face, you think I'm screwing around?"

"It looks all right to me," she said.

He broke into a reluctant, crooked smile. "I lost the Sheridan job."

"You did?" She was startled. The Sheridans, big supporters and fundraisers, had commissioned Bart to design their new place in East Hampton. He had been poring over plans for months for the place, talking of little else. "What happened?"

"They said I'm too traditional," he said. "But the truth of it is, with you out of the picture, why should they give me the job?"

She knew she could feel righteous at the news; God, how she had been suffering! But instead she felt suddenly sick. "They wouldn't do that," she said lamely.

"Of course they would," he said. "Don't you see? It's part of why I had to leave. I'm nothing here."

There was nothing she could say. Had she done this—stripped him over the years of what made him unique and special? "You were never nothing to me," she said.

Bart sighed, twisting a rubber band around his awkwardly wrapped package. "It's late," he said. "I'm headed for Arizona tomorrow; I'll be back next week. I guess we've got to get some stuff straightened out."

"I need your advice," she blurted suddenly.

His eyes widened in surprise.

"I always could run things by you, ask your opinion."

"And dismiss it as fast as I gave it."

"No, listen. Bart, I've been down to see Mrs. Paige, Faith's mother, and she has a letter Faith wrote to us."

"Did you read it?"

"No. Mrs. Paige wouldn't give it up."

"What's the problem?"

She looked at him, this husband of many years. "I just want to talk about it."

He stared at her, troubled. "Too late, Carol."

Carol felt as if she had been caught and drawn into the center of a swirling storm. Like Dorothy, she thought a little giddily, swept out of Kansas forever. "But you're the only one I can talk to," she said with great difficulty.

"I've been talked at for years," Bart replied. He did not look happy or victorious. "Honey, you're on your own now."

She stiffened. "It's a dirty trick. I don't know how you can do this. I never will."

"Carol, you already understand."

He obviously thought he was saying something positive, which frightened her. Angry, she slammed the door on his retreating back.

It was late, far past visiting hours. Michael and Maggie had been with Jeff all evening, sharing roast chicken and Häagen-Dazs ice cream Michael had brought. Finally, reluctantly, they said goodnight and left the room.

The hospital parking garage was half empty. They stood together under the harsh illuminating light, their two dark heads bowed close.

"Thanks," she said simply.

"Maggie." He put his hands on her shoulders, lightly, making no attempt to pull her toward him.

"I don't know—"

"Do I need to make a reservation these days? Please."

What was the matter with her? She moved into his embrace. "Your place," she said. "The bed's bigger."

The first rays of morning sun crept through the blinds and touched Maggie's face. She stirred, burrowing closer to the warmth of Michael's naked body. She didn't want to get up, she thought sleepily. It was too comfortable; if her cleaning lady wasn't always so darn punctual, she could stay and not go home to let her in.

"Michael?"

He groaned, pulling the covers tighter.

"We should have gone to my house," she whispered. "I've got to leave."

"Mine was closer. And you're right, this is a great bed, when you're in it."

She stretched, realizing she was feeling some peace again. But she had to hurry. She swung both legs out of bed and onto the floor. "I'm off," she said.

"Wait." Michael turned and grabbed her, pulled her gently down and kissed her neck.

"I'll go with you," he said.

"You don't have to; it's almost fully light."

"I know I don't have to, but I want to."

The trip to Maggie's house was brief and the streets—bathed in a rosy glow—were still mostly deserted. In about half an hour the traffic would begin to pick up and Washington would lose its sleepy morning quality, but right now Maggie could see the town as she liked to think it once was—a quiet place of reasonable order. She and Michael said very little, but the silence was deeply companionable. They pulled up in front of her row house.

"See you tonight?"

She smiled and nodded, turning to put her key in the lock. Only then did she glance down at the folded copy of *The Washington Post* waiting on her doorstep. A picture of Sara stared back at her from above the fold.

"What's this?" she gasped. Quickly she picked up the paper and scanned the headline above the photograph: "FATHER OF COURT NOMINEE SAID TO HAVE AIDED DEATHS," it read. And below that: "Marino Confirmation Affected?"

"Who did this?" Maggie said. She looked up at Michael, stricken. "Who?"

Michael reached down swiftly and grabbed the paper. "Jesus Christ!" he said as he skimmed the story. "Goddamn it, we know who it is, even if her name's not on it."

"Sandi Snow." She was whispering, unable to trust her voice.

"She heard us in the Safeway, Maggie. And she put it all together." He punched the paper with his fist, his voice rising, the sound harsh against the quiet morning air.

Maggie was trembling. Why was she so surprised? It was true, the town was a sieve. Sooner or later, a leak was inevitable. "This isn't just a story, it's something that can ruin these people's lives, and I'm responsible." She was frantic now.

Michael grabbed her and held her tight, refusing to let go. "Are you kidding? Maggie, don't do this to yourself, Sara's your friend, she trusts you."

Maggie moaned. "Not any more, not after I told her I was going to write a book."

"Don't you think you underestimate her, as well as yourself? Maggie, you weren't the only one who knew. Think about it!"

"Sara wouldn't have told anybody, Michael. She only told me because her defenses were completely down."

"Patton knew, right?"

"Yes, he did, of course." But she wasn't looking at him. She wanted to, but she couldn't.

"Are you thinking it could have been me?"

"No, no!"

Michael stared at her, his eyes troubled and searching. "I can see you're determined to blame yourself," he said more calmly. "That's ego, Maggie. Not humility." Then, without another word, he wheeled and strode back down the path toward his car. Maggie took a step to follow him and then stopped. The engine roared to life and within ten seconds, Michael had sped away.

* * *

"It's me, Barney."

Sara felt a rush of relief as she quickly disconnected the chain lock on her apartment door and opened it wide. She clutched her blue jersey robe close to her body as she faced him, hair uncombed. The morning paper was spread open on the table behind her. "How did this happen?" she asked, stunned.

"It's a piece of rotten luck," he said angrily. "Let's talk about what we do now, how we start planning from here." He was staring at her. "God, you look forlorn," he said.

And then Sara's legs began shaking so badly, she all but collapsed. Barney thrust both hands out and caught her as her legs buckled. "Easy, easy," he said, awkwardly patting her shoulder. "Let's sit down, okay? I'm here to help."

Sara became suddenly very conscious of the fact that she had nothing on except a thin cotton gown under her robe. "I'll be back in a minute," she said hastily, in charge of herself again. "Please, there's coffee in the kitchen, I'll be there in a minute."

She found him rummaging for filters when she came back, fully dressed, five minutes later. "I may be out," she said.

"No problem." Barney tore off a paper towel and folded it expertly to fit the coffeepot, then began pouring in coffee. "Nice blend," he said conversationally, looking at the bag. "Glad you don't use decaf. Are you okay?"

"I am now." It took an effort to say the words, but at least now she could vent her anger. "Patton is a stupid fool if he thinks he can destroy my father or me." She reached into the cupboard for some coffee mugs and plunked them down hard on the table.

"You're sure he did it? Who else knew?"

Sara stopped suddenly, surprised by the question. She turned and moved slowly to the refrigerator and pulled out some frozen rolls, gazing at them abstractedly.

"Who else, Sara?"

"He did it." She shoved the rolls in the microwave, remembering something vague about using plastic wrap.

"What's wrong?"

"Nothing." It couldn't have been Maggie; surely.

But he was looking at her with watchful eyes. "Sara, I'm getting to know you. You may be inscrutable on the bench, but you aren't in your own kitchen."

"It was Patton," she said firmly.

"If you say so."

"If he can use the media, so can I," she said.

"Are you talking about getting down and dirty?"

The oven bell dinged. Sara pulled the rolls out, looked at them doubtfully, and put them on the table. Was she? "There's a big problem, Barney. What I know hurts Sayles, not Patton, and I've got no proof he's part of this effort to force me out."

"We can do other things."

"I called Amos," she said. "He's checking pulses on the Hill. I'll do whatever I have to do to keep my Senate support."

"What can I do?"

She smiled at him, rather liking the sight of his face at her breakfast table. "Maybe pour the coffee?" she suggested.

He scrutinized her briefly, an inquiring look in his eyes. "You're doing all right, Judge," he said, finally. "Don't know why I got a little worried."

"You've gone too far, Jack," Justin said furiously into the telephone. "I've been cooperating on your little endeavor, but you're going to get into trouble, and I don't want any part of it. What the hell are you doing?"

"I had nothing to do with that story."

"If you weren't so intent on dumping Marino to get that job from Si Posner . . ."

"All you want is to supplant *me,* right, Justin?" Jack

Patton's voice was hardly more than a throaty growl. "Well, watch your own ass. I told you—I had nothing to do with that story and I'm not telling you again."

Dick Sayles stood totally still by the breakfast table in the upstairs living quarters at the White House, staring at the morning paper. Usually he read a quick digest of all the papers, but the front page of the *Post* had been carefully folded on his breakfast plate so the picture of Sara would greet him first.

"If you're wondering who left that there, I did," Laura Sayles said as she walked into the room and settled into the chair facing her husband's. Her makeup was complete and her expression serene. She poured herself a cup of coffee from a small silver coffeepot waiting by her plate.

"If you want my opinion—"

"Spare me, Laura."

She ignored him. "If you want my opinion, that leak was pretty stupid. Unquestionably the dumbest thing Jack Patton's ever done. On the other hand"—she took a bite out of a piece of dry toast and chewed thoughtfully—"it puts you in a well-deserved corner."

Sayles stared at her suspiciously. "Did you have anything to do with this?" he demanded.

"Me?" Her eyes widened in mock innocence. "I have more sense, thank you. Jack's fighting like a bulldog, as usual, but what else do you expect when he works basically for himself? Keeping him was a big mistake; have I said that before?" She glanced at her watch. "I'm off to breakfast for the AARP parade organizers. Did you forget? Tomorrow's demonstration? Every hotel in town is filled." She laughed. "If you ever thought you could finesse thousands of angry old people, this kills that idea."

"You know what I think."

"No," she corrected. "I know where you stand. Not the same thing."

"Thanks for the vote of confidence. You seem mighty anxious to write me off as a lightweight."

Laura Sayles took a long sip of coffee. "I could use a little convincing."

"Laura, I didn't ask for this job, but I've got it and I intend to keep it," he said. His mouth was working; the veins in his forehead pronounced. "I inherited a mess. You know Goodspeed's health was on a decline for weeks before that heart attack. What could I do?"

"Right. You've got your own troubles."

"As usual, you're saying something else." His voice was sharp with frustration.

Her eyes flickered, but she finished off the toast with one quick crunch before speaking. "So what are you going to do, President Sayles?" she challenged.

"You are the angriest human being I've ever known," Sayles said very slowly, staring at his wife.

"Yes, my dear," she said quietly. "And in your busy schedule today, take a moment or two to think why."

Barney was in the car and Sara was on her way out the door to join him when the phone rang.

"Sara." It was Maggie. Her voice trembled with barely contained emotion. "Please know, it wasn't me."

"Maggie."

"I did tell Michael about your father."

Sara clenched the phone. "I wish you hadn't."

"If there's anything I'm sure of, it's this: it wasn't him. And it wasn't me."

Sara closed her eyes and leaned for an instant against the door frame. All she wanted to do right now was get off this phone and get out of the house. "Maggie," she said. "Stop, okay? I believe you."

But Maggie needed more than that. "Don't just say it," she begged frantically. "Please tell the truth. You have to do that for both of us."

Sara realized she either made a believable leap of faith right now, this instant, or a friendship was over. She took a deep, slow breath.

"All right, here's the truth," she said. "Somebody did it. You're telling me it wasn't you and it wasn't Michael, and I choose to believe you."

"That's honest. Thank you." Maggie's relief reverberated through the phone wires.

"I had a moment, I'll confess. But you wouldn't do that to me."

"Never." The word came out almost like a prayer.

"You've got your own troubles right now, Maggie. I hope your son is okay?"

"Jeff's doing fine, and for that I'm more grateful than I can tell you."

There was a moment of comfortable, shared silence that neither woman felt immediately compelled to fill.

Maggie spoke first. "I'll talk to you later."

"Take care."

Sara hung up and hurried out the door, feeling actually buoyant. A leap of faith wasn't that hard, after all.

It was a day of much political buzzing in Washington as the *Post* story went from office to office on the Hill. Cackling could be heard through the doorways of some; groans through the doorways of others. Someone was heard to remark that the least the damn paper could have done was use a flattering photograph of Judge Marino, but hey, they never were known for charity in that newsroom. The *New York Times* and *Wall Street Journal* bureau chiefs called in their White House and Supreme Court reporters and grilled them sternly. How come the *Post* got this one, you guys? they asked. Where were we? Get on it.

They got on it. By late in the day a total of twenty-six reporters had been assigned by CNN, NBC, ABC, CBS, the *Chicago Tribune*, the *Boston Globe*, the *Atlanta Con-*

stitution, the *Los Angeles Times,* and various other newspapers to get the goddamn story and give us something better than the *Post*. Even the Comedy Channel assigned a reporter. By early evening, the Associated Press had churned out several updates with fresh leads and newspapers from all over the country were clearing space in the front-page news hole for the following morning. Especially in Buffalo—which was why George Marino finally yanked his phone from the wall at around four o'clock in the afternoon, shortly after Sara's second call, no longer able to deal with another anxious reporter looking for a quote. His doorbell kept ringing. The sound by seven o'clock was like a razor blade ripping the nerves from his head and body. By eleven o'clock the media blitz was calming down (except on the West Coast, most papers already had their stories in print and the networks were finished), but it didn't matter.

It didn't matter because somewhere around eleven forty-five, probably after watching the local CBS affiliate lead its eleven o'clock news with a breathless piece that called him a "death doctor from the past," George Marino clutched his chest and moaned and collapsed onto the sofa in the living room of his small apartment. He had been through this before and he knew what was happening. He cried out. But when he reached for the alarm button that alerted the hospital he was down to one emotion, and one only.

He was mad as hell.

This time the phone rang in Maggie's house.

"Maggie."

Sara's voice was so quiet, Maggie had to strain to hear her. "What's happening?" she said, suddenly alert.

"My father had a heart attack a few hours ago. I'm leaving in a few minutes."

"Oh, God, I'm sorry." Maggie swallowed hard, forced her own voice to stay steady. "Is he . . . ?"

"The hospital says he's doing fine. It must have been the shock of seeing the coverage."

"What do you want me to do?" Maggie asked. "Sara, anything."

"Help me think this through," Sara said. Her hands were trembling, but she kept her voice calm. "I don't want Patton controlling the story. I want somebody writing who'll tell my father's side of all this—is that so crazy?"

"No," Maggie said, thinking fast. "Of course it isn't."

"You've got contacts—"

"I sure have." Maggie pulled a pencil and an old envelope from a drawer and began to scribble names.

"The *Times*, the *Post*."

"Trust me, I know the people to talk to. They'll be interested, and they'll have an entirely different take on the story."

"And Maggie."

"Yes?"

"Your book?"

Maggie caught her breath. "Yes," she began.

"Look, help me on this, and I owe you. We'll work it out."

This time it was Maggie who felt a certain lightness of spirit. "If we do, fine," she said. "But let's be clear on something, Sara. You don't owe me anything."

"There she is! Judge Marino! Hey, Judge, wait a minute!"

Sara hurried quickly through the echoing corridor of the hospital in a pair of hastily donned dark glasses—which had done nothing to hide her from the cluster of reporters encamped in the reception area near her father's room. How enterprising of them, she thought grimly as she quickened her step. They knew I would come.

The administrator of the hospital grabbed at her arm protectively, waving back the reporters and photographers. "Move back," he ordered. "Look, this is a private hospital and if you don't move back I'll have you all thrown out."

"Judge Marino, hey, Judge, will you talk to us when you come out?" yelled one.

"Later," breathed Sara, her voice close to breaking, but she knew what a hopeless declaration that was. "Sara, stay tough," Barney had advised her at the airport when he saw her off.

"You don't have to tell me," she had said, but there were tears in her eyes as she said it.

Sure, she was tough. She had to remind herself as she stared out the airplane window into the dawn light that tough was good. Repeat after me, twenty times: "Tough is good." Maybe she should just admit to herself she was scared. She pushed open the door to her father's hospital room and caught her breath.

George Marino was lying flat on his back, a weak smile on his face, as she entered the room. His face was pale as cheesecloth.

"I'm fine; go home," he said immediately in a thin, unnatural voice.

"Dad!" Swiftly she covered the distance to his bed and leaned over to kiss him. She mustn't upset him. He was doing "as well as could be expected," the doctor had said, but his tone had been guarded.

"I couldn't take one more phone call, so I faked a heart attack to get some rest," he said, patting the side of the bed. "Sit down, honey."

"I'm so sorry."

"You have nothing to be sorry about. I'm programmed for heart attacks, we both know that."

"This one was triggered by that bastard in the White House."

"It would have happened anyway, sooner or later," the old man said dismissively.

Sara looked down at her father and was saddened by how small he looked. Tired, yes. Sick, that was all right, too;

she could handle that. But small? He had never looked small. It was frightening.

"Nothing's changed, you hear me?"

"Yes, I hear you, but I'm not as sure of that as you are."

"What do you mean?" He fixed her with a pale shadow of the forbidding glare he once used on her as a child when she would not do as she was told.

"This appointment isn't worth losing you," she said, her voice cracking slightly.

"You haven't lost me."

"If that alert system hadn't worked . . ."

Marino waved his hand impatiently and Sara noted how thin and gnarled it had become. "When it's time, it's time," he said.

"I can't put either of us through this."

He raised himself in his bed, his voice indignant. "My daughter, a quitter? No!"

"Dad, calm down," she said quickly, patting his arm.

"Don't you understand? You're not just fighting for yourself, you're fighting for me, too."

"I don't give up a fight," she said. "You taught me that. But I don't want you hurt, do you understand?"

"These charges are bothering the hell out of you."

She lowered her head to hide her eyes.

He settled back against his pillow and stared at the ceiling. His face looked more drained and tired than ever, and Sara could have wept. Then she felt his hand gently close over hers.

"I love you, daughter," he said.

"And I love you," she whispered.

"Go fight for yourself, then."

"I don't want anything more to happen to you."

"Sara, Sara—maybe I've had too much influence over you, I don't know." He sighed, a heavy, sad sigh that Sara feared she would remember for a long time. She rose to go, bracing herself for the reporters and photographers jammed in the hallways outside the door.

Maggie did her job well. The AARP demonstration became a march of thousands from the Lincoln Memorial to the White House, but the papers devoted almost as much attention to human-interest stories about George Marino, the country doctor from Buffalo whose kindness his patients would never forget. "And now he lies alone in a hospital bed felled by stories branding him as nothing short of a 'death doctor,' " said the anchorman on the NBC Evening News. "It's a cruel twist to the story of a man who helped so many." The march was wrapped up mostly with video and a voice-over.

The following day, angry march organizers charged the networks with skewing their coverage to court younger viewers. "They don't give a damn about keeping anyone over sixty-five alive," declared the president of the AARP at a press conference attended by only a smattering of reporters. He also criticized the Park Police for saying only 150,000 showed up for the march when "it was obvious to anyone" that at least 300,000 people had filled the Mall. Reporters were used to hearing this complaint. It received virtually no attention.

Jack Patton sat at his desk with a cup of coffee rapidly growing cold in front of him. He had no time for it this morning, not with all the clips on the Marino nomination to plow through. The story was petering out. Unbelievable. George Marino was getting sympathetic treatment even from the *New York Post.* His heart attack had balanced out the demonstration stories and nothing, so far, was boomeranging on Sara Marino's nomination.

Patton stood and paced his office. If Justin Maccoby still believed he'd leaked the story, he was crazy. He would never have thrown it out there without careful handling and packaging. Nobody was talking at *The Washington Post,* but he'd find out who botched this if it was the last thing he did. Now what? His head began to pound and he felt the taste of panic in his mouth. He never should have promised he could pull the Marino nomination, but if he hadn't, he wouldn't be within striking range of the presidency of American Telecom. His wife, the kids—they were all sick of Washington. He'd been hinting for weeks that something good was coming, and what were they going to think if he couldn't pull it off? Sara Marino would be invulnerable heading into the confirmation hearings if something didn't break his way. What rotten luck . . .

The phone rang.

"Yeah?"

"Jack?" Tray Bingham's voice was spiraling off the charts. "What's going on over there? This is outrageous! Who's passing on stories about that doctor in Buffalo without consulting me?"

"It didn't come from here, Tray. I'm as mad as you are."

Bingham was sputtering into the phone now. "You know who I think's behind this? Sara Marino, that's who! Prissy, stubborn woman, she was out to undercut our demonstration, that's what I think. Serves her right her father had a heart attack over it!"

Patton all but froze. Of course.

"You know those damn papers did it again? We had half a million on the Mall, I tell you!"

"Yeah, Tray," Patton said quickly. He felt a certain respect for Sara. She was a formidable opponent, but there was no stopping now. "Look, I'll talk to you later. You've told me something I needed to know."

With a surge of apprehension, Leona heard Justin's key turn in the front-door lock. So he had come home after all. Two trips to California, with never a word except through his secretary . . . it was the pattern. He was avoiding her, obviously, and that bothered her even as her anger rose. What was the matter with her? Did she still care? I can't weed everything out all at once, she told herself. She heard him step through the door and walk toward the living room, and she remembered all the times she had waited eagerly as he walked toward her through that hall.

I always knew immediately by the sound of his step whether he was feeling jaunty or tired, she thought sadly, and I knew how to shape my mood as quickly as possible to complement his. I've loved him and admired him for years, and a part of me would like to believe he's the same man I thought he was—even though I know better.

Leona quickly downed a strong Scotch and water sitting next to her chair. She took a deep breath, stood, and faced the doorway. And there he was.

For a fraction of a second the two of them stared at each other like marksmen caught in each other's cross hairs. But Justin spoke first.

"Nice caftan," he said in his old, semi-teasing manner. "Have I seen it before?"

"You bought it for me," she answered. "Or at least it came from Saks with a card saying it was from you."

"So that's the tone of the evening," he said with a cold grin, tossing a brown leather hanging bag over the back of the sofa. "I'm still paying for violating your image of sisterhood, I see."

"I've come a long way from that, Justin."

There was an edge to her voice that was new, and Justin gave her a sharp glance as he headed for the bar. "So I hear," he countered, reaching for a glass. "How is Sara's father?"

"He's doing fine. She's very relieved."

"Harvey Beltson tells me you bounced into his house looking very fetching the other night, not, I hope, in the caftan."

"Harvey Beltson is a leering old fool. With a loose mouth, you might want to know."

Slowly Justin measured out his Scotch; very precise, a shot and a half. Even more slowly, he grasped a pair of antique silver ice tongs and fished two ice cubes from the ice bucket, dropping them carefully into his drink. Justin never liked to spill a drop of anything.

"And what do you mean by that?"

"He mentioned an oil deal that went bad, and said Faith was involved in it," she said, holding her chin high. "So I decided to find out the truth for myself."

"And how did you do that?"

"I went hunting, Justin, on your last trip to California," she said softly. "In your closet, first. Then in your office." This was even harder to say than she had expected. "You've been gone a lot, and I guess you could say I've been on something of a trip, too."

She really wanted another drink, but there was no way she was going to walk past Justin to the bar. Not now. "I feel like I've been—on a safari, or something. Isn't it amazing what you can find on safari?"

"You're drunk, Leona."

"No, unfortunately," she said after a moment of consideration. "I wish I were. It would be easier to be completely smashed because I don't relish facing my husband and telling him I think he is a liar and a hypocrite." There was a flash of tears in her eyes. "I'd rather be lying with a bottle outside in the gutter."

Justin's eyes looked like slits cut into a bunker, but his expression never changed. "I don't know what you're accusing me of, but your violation of my privacy is outrageous," he said. "I keep sensitive documents in that office, material no one but I should see, and you had no right—"

"No, I had no right. That's established, so don't bother getting indignant." She had to keep herself buffered from

Justin's contempt, but it was hard. "Tell me I'm wrong, Justin. We've been married a long time, and I owe you that. Just tell me I'm wrong."

"I hate to put it so gracelessly, but you're a snoop, Leona. I told you, I have sensitive . . ."

"Sensitive? Oh my, yes, very sensitive!" Her cheeks burned with sudden anger. "I found the documents, Justin. That big oil client of yours? You set up a fake company to buy land for them with Faith's money and then you gave her phony stock. But there was no oil on the land, was there, Justin? Too bad, especially after you broke every SEC rule in the book! Ah, but Justin Maccoby knew how to get out fast and leave someone else holding the bag, right? You left Faith with illegal stock in worthless land that you persuaded her to buy! God, no wonder she was depressed! Why? Why did you do it? Just to prove you could operate outside the law and get away with it?" Her voice rose in a curling wail. "Are *you* responsible for her death?"

"Leona." Justin walked over to her chair and picked up her glass.

"And what about me? You got me to bring you Faith's notes by telling me they were from an important foreign policy meeting and national security could be involved!"

Justin was filling the glass with Scotch. "Here," he said. "You obviously need this."

"Drink it yourself," she said. "You must think I'm totally stupid, Justin, you really must. I've been sitting in this house thinking of all the ways you've manipulated me and made me do the things you wanted and I'm just sick."

"Yes, and working yourself into total hysteria," he broke in. "As usual, you don't know what you're talking about. You've snooped through raw material and drawn rash conclusions that shock the hell out of me. Who do you think you're accusing, anyhow? Remember me, Leona? I'm your husband!''

''You won't give an inch, will you? I knew you wouldn't, you never do. How'd you get Faith to go along? I was such a dope, I brought you that box of notepaper and all the notes without reading them because you told me they were so important, nobody should see them. I was actually *proud* to smuggle those papers out to my very important husband—is that how you got Faith on the hook? By making her feel important while you wrung everything you wanted out of her?'' Leona tried to keep her voice hard-edged and scornful but there were tears in her eyes and she suddenly realized her words were starting to slur. No, not now, she thought anxiously. Please, not now. I need all the dignity I can muster.

''Watch those s's, my sweet,'' Justin said with a small laugh. ''If you want to pull off a good scene, you have to articulate.''

It was one of their classic moments. She stood uncertainly for an instant at the bar watching Justin pull off his jacket, loosen his tie, and rub his neck—a man at home, unconcerned, totally in charge. And at that moment she saw the minute details of the scene in a way she never had seen them before: the deliberate twist of his body away from her, the studied scorn with which he picked up the paper and began idly thumbing through it—all part of an act to show her she didn't matter; she was hardly there for him.

Such a good act, she thought sadly. It's worked so well for so many years. She was seeing new details: a slight tremor in his long, elegant hands as they flipped the pages of the paper; a tightness of his shoulders—and, with true shock, she realized something else. Justin was worried.

''I don't pretend to know everything that's going on,'' she said calmly, gathering strength from the sound of her own voice. Amazingly, her s's were under control. "But I read Faith's notes and I see what happened. She figured it out, didn't she? She knew what you had dragged her into. I saw how much money she gave you—a pretty hefty amount, Justin. And I know that oil deal was only one of the shady ventures you were involved in. I read everything."

He still had his back to her but he was no longer turning pages.

"I don't know why Faith got involved in that particular deal. She was an honest person, I'm sure of it, and I'm also sure you took advantage of that. And I think I see now why she was acting panicky those last few weeks. I saw the notice from the Internal Revenue Service, freezing her bank account. She must have been going nuts! I saw the list of friends she was hoping to borrow money from—and I see why it was in your best interest to paint her as some unstable . . ." She stopped suddenly. Oh, my God, she thought. Faith was a liability to Justin. Had he wanted her dead?

Suddenly Justin whirled and faced her. "You're talking nonsense," he said. "You've picked up a few scraps of information and built yourself a major scandal, Leona. That's fine for cocktail-party gossip, but not for real life."

"You're protesting too much, Justin."

His eyes wavered, but only for a second. "I'm tired of all this melodrama," he said. "I think it's time you took your bottle and headed for the bedroom so you can sleep it off."

She never moved. "You can't laugh me out of the room, Justin; not this time. Not ever again. You're a crook, that's what you are. And a liar."

Again they stared at each other silently. It was the longest moment of Leona's life.

"I have one question for you," Justin finally said.

"And what is that?"

"What are you going to do?"

She stared at him.

"What are you going to do," he repeated, "call the police?"

Leona blinked and froze.

"I thought so," he said. "Poor Leona. Here you are with this wonderful seamy plot and it doesn't go anywhere. What do you want to do? Destroy me? Then what happens to you? What if you're wrong?" He stepped closer, so close she took a step back. "Pull yourself together," he said. "Nobody's going to listen to this."

"Don't sneer at me," she said. "I know better."

"You know next to nothing," he shot back. "And you'll never have another chance to snoop through my papers; the locks on that room will be changed tonight." He smiled, a glimmer of the old Justin breaking through. "Why don't you treat this like a bad dream?" he suggested. "You've done some sleuthing and come up with a grab bag of facts that I have no intention of explaining to you. It's time for Leona to go to bed." He reached out to pat her shoulder but she twisted away.

"Keep your hands off me," she said. "I don't know what I can do, but I know one thing: you'll never touch me again."

"Who pays the mortgage, Leona? And who finances your little catering business?"

"God, Justin, you are terrible," she breathed. There was no sadness in her now, only cold anger. She had played the role of a slightly dippy, scatterbrained, privileged, adoring woman for a long time, and somewhere along the way she had allowed herself to believe it. *I am not a dippy fool,* she thought, *but Justin doesn't realize it yet.* At this moment, it was her one clear realization.

"What do you plan to do, Leona?"

"I don't know yet," she said.

"So have a drink."

"Give it up, Justin," she said. "That won't work any more." But her legs were shaking.

CHAPTER 9

"You surprise me, Sara."

It was Monday morning, and Jack Patton's temples were throbbing with anger, his instinct for caution thrown to the winds. His nerves were still jangled from Sayles's unexpected, furious phone call denouncing the attack on Sara's father. Worse, the American Telecom people weren't returning his phone calls. The downside of being seen as a master manipulator, he thought bitterly. They're all convinced I blew this one. She must have done it, Bingham was right.

"Sorry, Jack, you'll have to explain."

"Tipping off the media about your father? Quite a little maneuver. Was it worth risking your father's life?"

Sara heard the words, but it took her a few seconds to realize what he was saying. "You think I planted the story about my father?"

"Who else?"

There was a silence. Then she laughed, throwing him momentarily off balance. "You're so sure everybody thinks the way you do," she said. "What's your strategy when they don't?"

"Yeah, well, it sure wasn't me."

"Maybe not. It doesn't matter, he's got plenty of support now. You've read the papers?"

He tightened his grip on the receiver. "Obviously."

"Watched the networks?"

"Yep."

"*The New Yorker* is doing a profile next week, did you know that?"

"Yeah, I heard." He was sweating now. That's why he hadn't heard from Si Posner or anybody else at American Telecom. He had to be careful, don't get reckless . . . but he couldn't stop now. The hell with tiptoeing. "They're gonna need to do a fast rewrite—unfortunately for your father."

A pause. "Explain yourself."

"A relative of one of your father's patients claims he murdered her sister. Forget the fiction about helping somebody commit suicide—this is the real thing. She's ready to file a complaint."

He heard the gasp; it was worth it. He found himself savoring the chance to be morally indignant and pushed it home with relish. "This isn't some kind of ambivalent moral issue, this time. All that garbage about giving people the right to choose when they want to die? This is doing it for them."

"Spare me the moral commentary, Jack. I don't believe it."

"Maybe not, but this is potentially disastrous. You agree? If the authorities push for an indictment—and it could get to that—President Sayles might be forced to withdraw your nomination. You do understand, don't you?"

Sara didn't answer in a hurry. And when she did, it was with both guarded anger and real curiosity. "Jack, why do you want this so much?"

He stared across the spacious vista of his White House office, a few steps away from the President of the United States, thinking of the days when it had meant something—

hell, forget that, he told himself. People grow up. He focused instead on the job being dangled tantalizingly by American Telecom. If he could convince them he had the power to get rid of Sara Marino, he would be a rich man. That simple. Why did he want this? Because there was nothing else, because it was power, not noble behavior that counted, because his opportunities were slipping away. He stirred in his seat, gripped by a sudden undefinable fear.

"This may sound strange to you. But it isn't personal."

The silence on the line dragged on. He had one last card to play. "You could, of course, stop all of this from happening."

"You're a clumsy blackmailer, Jack. You've outdone yourself this time."

He couldn't read her mood. Her voice had turned cold and judicial. Patton told himself as he hung up that he had scored a big one. He told himself that over and over, but he was sweating profusely now even though the air conditioning was working fine.

Sara sat as still as possible, staring at the phone. It took a few seconds for her to realize Aaron was standing behind her, at the open door.

"Judge Marino, they're waiting for you."

She nodded, stood, and quickly donned her black robe before striding out the door and toward the courtroom.

"Last day already?" whispered Judge Lucas as she slipped into her seat. Sitting just beyond him was Judge Gonzales. He leaned forward and gave a discreet thumbs-up sign.

"How's it feel?" he whispered.

"Like I've got an appointment with the dentist," she murmured.

Gonzales chuckled. "Want to trade appointments?"

She smiled. These guys were okay; she would miss them. She picked up the gavel and looked out over the courtroom.

Several attorneys in dark suits and careful ties were shuffling papers and glancing in her direction. A certain lassitude was setting in, settling over her shoulders like a heavy shroud. There was a point, wasn't there, when the rewards were not worth the costs? Perhaps she had reached that point. She had her place in this court, and it was filled with challenges and satisfactions. She didn't have to risk everything for star status.

What did it mean, anyway, if you gave up part of what you were to get to the Supreme Court? She would call a halt to this crazy game. Her heart was pounding now. No man would go this far unless he had something very important to protect. Patton might well have had something to do with Faith's death. It was a preposterous idea, but not to be ruled out. . . . No, she couldn't give up. Somewhere inside a familiar stubbornness stirred. Not yet.

She nodded to the clerk.

His voice cut through the chamber, bringing everyone to attention. "Jones versus the Fire District of Clarendon County," he intoned. "Judge Sara Marino, presiding."

"It's just a matter of time before he self-destructs," Barney said calmly. Sara felt her tension ease as they strolled together through the lush woods of Rock Creek Park. It was late in the afternoon. The farewell party in chambers was over; the cards and jokes and gifts stacked with her books in wooden crates. The call from Barney had come at exactly the right moment. "Meet in the park?" he had suggested. "We'll walk; you'll feel better."

He was right. She did. The late afternoon sun was filtering through the trees, turning the dusty, rock-strewn path a golden hue. Sara glanced down at her new red shoes, already scuffed and covered with dust. Was there such a thing as red shoe polish? She'd probably never get around to finding out.

As they approached a tiny hollow of land within a dense

grove of trees, Barney slowed, looking around. The spot was totally deserted. With an elaborate flourish, he pulled off his suit jacket and spread it on the grass. "Rest a minute?" he suggested. "It's damn pleasant out here." His eyes swept the peaceful terrain as if it belonged to a foreign country. "No ocean, though," he said unexpectedly. "I miss the ocean. When I was a kid—"

"Sit on the jacket of your six hundred dollar suit?" she said teasingly, realizing too late she was cutting him off. "Barney, that's so reckless."

His mood turned joking. "For you," he said with an elaborate gesture of invitation, "only the best."

Sara hesitated a fraction of a second, but it was long enough. Barney, who never missed signals, reached down, picked up his jacket with a single, graceful motion, and slung it casually over his arm. "Too bad the grass is kind of damp," he said.

"I'd love to," she said lamely. "But actually, I've got a lot to do."

"No problem," he said. "It's time to head back anyway. Shall I drop you at the Courthouse?"

Sara flushed, annoyed with herself, convinced he must think now she never loosened up for long. "If you drop me at my apartment, I'll fix us a cup of tea," she said. "I'm not that busy."

"Sure, but don't think you have to," he said. His shirtsleeves were rolled up and he seemed totally relaxed, but Sara wasn't fooled. Barney knew how to look relaxed when he was thinking very hard, and he was thinking now.

The ride home was short. They knew each other well enough now to lapse more or less comfortably into silence, each in personal thoughts. But there was a strain of awkwardness, undeniable, and Sara found herself searching for a casual way of dispersing it.

Once inside her apartment, she decided to be as honest as possible. "I'm not trying to put you off, Barney, but all

I can think of is what Jack Patton is doing, and I'm frightened,'' she said quietly, sitting down next to him on the sofa. ''There, I've said it. Telling Jack off again might make me feel better, but it won't accomplish anything. He's perfectly capable of pushing this forward. If he has someone willing to make the charge and a D.A. willing to pursue it . . .''

''What does your father say?'' he asked, just as quietly.

''I haven't told him yet.''

''Do you think he's been lying to you?''

''No.'' She leaned back, avoiding his eyes. The questions she had for her father would be asked of him directly. She would not speculate; not with anybody.

''Then this will hit him pretty hard, right?''

''I can't dump it on him over the phone,'' she said. ''I'm flying up there later tonight. I really have to see his face when I talk to him and he's still in the hospital. I'm afraid.''

Barney's lean, tanned arm reached out and touched hers. ''Sure, you are,'' he said gently. ''You're afraid he'll die.''

The words were bald, too bald. ''Yes,'' she said, tensing. ''Maybe you should go now, Barney, I've got a lot to think about.'' Hearing her worst fears put into words was simply too much.

Barney gazed at her for a long moment, and then reached out, a troubled frown creasing his brow. ''Sara,'' he began. His hand was light on her shoulder; kind, caring. She made no effort to pull away. He then put both arms around her and drew her close. Still she didn't pull away.

This was crazy. What was she doing?

''I'm holding you,'' Barney said with what sounded like astonishment.

Not for long. . . . She would extract herself from this as gracefully as possible. She liked Barney; she respected him. They were rapidly becoming friends. But she was not allowing anything else to happen, she was stopping it right here. . . .

Slowly, almost awkwardly, he kissed her neck, then her face. It felt good. Something inside her was stretching, waking up. This was it; over the line. Too much. It was time to push him away and take control of the situation.

"Where did you come from?" she whispered. She opened her mouth, partly out of surprise, partly because it was exactly what she wanted to do. An image of Faith, a lonely Faith, gone finally into the water, her glittering, solitary beauty destroyed, flashed through her mind. She had been so alone. . . .

He pulled back and looked at her, eyes playful. "You're seducing me," he whispered back. "Or is it the other way around?"

He slid his hand inside her blouse, touching small breasts reaching toward his probing fingers. "Okay, so far?" he murmured unnecessarily, for Sara would no more have stopped him than she would have tried to hold back the sea. He lowered his head and kissed the hot skin. His fingers moved downward, stroking the inside of her legs.

And now she was tasting the skin of his neck with her lips, enjoying the sudden, amazing plasticity of her body. She pressed closer. . . .

Then she hesitated. Was she out of her bloody mind? This was absolutely the wrong time in her life for a relationship. If she let this man in, this particular, intriguing man . . . if she did, the entire balance was upset. What did she need him for? Her life was already complete, more or less. It was fulfilling, challenging.

He stopped, trying to read her. "This—isn't what you want?"

"I'm thinking." She kept holding herself back, running through the options, the scenarios . . . was she always going to short-change herself with her caution?

He shivered, forcing his body still. "Look," he said, his voice strained. "You want me to stop? Say so. Now, not later."

She thought about that. And then she sighed and invited him forward, and amidst the mounting warmth, it seemed absolutely the right thing to do.

Afterward, they talked. He told her about growing up in Oregon as the son of a fisherman in a struggling coastal town, about helping his father and never being able to get the smell of fish off his hands. He talked about taking a job in high school passing out campaign literature so he could get out of helping unload the day's catch. "I'm where I am today because I hated the smell of fish," he said. She smiled contentedly. He could say anything right now; so could she. He told her about his marriage, his divorce, his failed attempt to get custody of his son, and she heard the bitterness in his voice. . . .

She told him about the awkward child she had been, about trying to learn to cook when she lived with David and making a total botch of it; about her love of hiking and where was the best place to buy hiking boots, and the fervor with which her father had encouraged her to go to Yale Law School. . . .

"Sounds like you were a classic overachieving only child," he teased. "Were you the son he never had?"

Sara considered this with some gravity. "Probably, I guess. I grew up thinking more like a boy than like a girl."

"Whatever that means, any more."

She shrugged. "For me, it meant Phi Beta Kappa and no date for the Senior Prom, but that was okay. I didn't want to be trapped, like my mother."

"I wish my father had lived long enough for me to feel the same way."

She talked, finally, about her guilt about Faith, about how she hadn't paid enough attention at the right time. She told him about the crumpled, unanswered phone messages in her pocket when the news came that Faith was dead. Would returning those phone calls have changed the outcome? She didn't know, she would never know, but. . . .

"You didn't intentionally hurt her."

"But that's not the point, Barney," she said sadly. "The thing is, I didn't listen enough. Friends have to listen." She heard her own words, realized she was running the same tape through once again. "Faith was trying hard to put her life in order, the way we all do when we're in trouble, and I see her in some corner of my mind every day. The fact that I thought I was too busy to take time out for her bothers me terribly. It makes me wonder about myself—and it makes me wonder if I'll do it again, not know when someone needs me."

He sighed then. "You think you're the first person who let a friend down? Sara, Sara, you ask a lot of yourself."

He said it tenderly, and Sara felt comforted. She didn't have to prove anything to him . . . but then she saw a shadow pass over his face.

"Sometimes I wonder if I've lived in this town too long," he said, his mood turning gloomy.

"What worries you?" she asked tentatively. It felt awkward, probing a man's psyche again.

"Figuring out my life," he said, stretching back, cradling her with his arms. "To give you the most pathetic answer."

"Why pathetic?"

"How can someone in his forties still be figuring out his life? Pretty retarded, don't you think?"

He pulled her close and they talked on, building the layers of what they knew about each other. They watched the sun fade gradually from the window and the shadows deepen and still they talked. He confessed his nervousness upon first realizing his attraction: the fantasizing, the desire to touch, smell, feel.

"I couldn't believe it," he said, still sounding puzzled. "Falling for a judge—a Supreme Court nominee, for God's sake?"

Reflectively, he twirled a lock of her hair between his

fingers. "It doesn't quite fit my image, Sara. I'm known more for closing the bars on Capitol Hill than pining after proper ladies like you."

"Not so proper any more," she murmured. Curious, she asked how old he was.

"Forty-four, three years younger than you," he said teasingly. "Sorry, Sara, that's what comes from being a public figure."

"You know a lot about me, don't you?"

Once again he cradled her close, running his hands over the smooth skin of her upper arms, then down, to her waist; up, over her breast. "Pretty soon," he said, "you'll know just as much about me."

"What's Barney short for?" she asked next. He laughed. "You're probing secrets now," he chided. "Promise not to tell anyone—it's Barnshorn, after some bloody uncle with money who never came through."

"I like it," she declared solemnly. "I think I'll call you that."

"Don't you dare," he said.

She told him about her old nightmare of getting trapped in a dark room. "From the time I was ten, I've left a light on somewhere in the house, every night. Stupid, right?" But he didn't laugh, he just kissed her neck.

She felt she could tell him anything.

Finally the shadows grew too long and Sara rose and turned on the lights. But still their voices were low, their hands entwined as they stood together by the window and watched the finishing day. He would drive her to the airport. And then she would come back and they would talk again. And again and again. Of that, Sara was sure.

"Why are you here so soon? What's wrong?"

George Marino squinted as the unexpected beam of light from the hall hit his bed. Sara slipped inside, cursing the nurse who had assured her he was still awake.

"Go back to sleep," she said hastily. "I'll go to the apartment and come back in the morning. I should have waited, I'm sorry."

"You're here, aren't you?" he grumbled, tugging at the lever which raised the head of the hospital bed. "Just let me get this damn thing working, it's always sticking." The bed rose slowly and clicked into position as Marino pounded his pillows into place with sleepy satisfaction. He settled back, folded gnarled fingers over wrinkled hospital pajamas, and stared her straight in the eye.

"You've got bad news, don't you?" he said.

"It's not the best," she parried.

"You haven't pulled out?"

"No," she said. "I haven't, but something serious has happened." She paused to give him time to brace. "There's a woman claiming you killed her sister. Jack Patton says she wants to press charges."

"What's her name?" He was too calm.

"I don't know."

Marino sniffed. "I know who. Those Hegelstroms were a scrappy lot. I'm not surprised they're litigious, too."

Sara felt a tingling in her scalp. "Dad, we're talking murder charges," she said carefully.

"I know we are," he replied, still calm. "The woman's name was Sally Hegelstrom."

Sara threw her coat into a chair and paced to the window, pressing her forehead against the glass. "God," she began.

"Hear me out. She wanted help. She had no one to turn to but me; none of them did. I helped her, yes, I helped her to die when she had no other alternatives. She went peacefully, Sara. I made sure of that. I always made sure of that."

"You're saying this was a suicide?"

"Absolutely."

"Is there any way you can prove it?" she asked.

He sighed, a long, noisy sigh. "No," he said.

"Could the sister be—could she really be saying she

thinks you talked Sally into wanting to die?''

''Sara, I could sing that one round or sing it flat.''

''You're not taking this seriously enough!''

Marino threw himself back against the pillows. ''Are we starting all over again?'' he asked.

Sara took a long, slow breath and reminded herself not to lose patience. As a judge, a lawyer, or a daughter—she couldn't lose patience. ''Okay, tell me,'' she said more calmly.

''If she says I murdered her sister, she believes I murdered her sister. Her name was Ginny—Ginny something. Let's be plain about this, okay? I don't need to hide behind some sanitized construct, that's for lawyers.''

''Maybe it's a construct, as you put it, but it's still important.'' She heard the hard edge in her own voice with a twinge of discomfort. ''This woman may believe with no evidence at all that you murdered her sister—because she wants to believe it was your will, and not her sister's, that prevailed. Could that be true?''

Marino blinked in momentary surprise. Then a slow grin spread across his tired face. ''Hey, now I know why I wanted you to become a lawyer instead of a doctor,'' he said.

''Please, answer me.''

''It's a fine line, Sara.'' He closed his eyes and leaned back against the pillows. ''She can believe what she wants.''

Sara resisted an impulse to protest. He looked too tired and spent. But she needed to wring something from him for a sensible defense.

''Sara.''

''Yes?''

''None of this matters, honey, it's twenty years ago.''

''It matters,'' Sara said. ''It matters if the local district attorney decides to listen to this woman and open an investigation. Dad, please understand.''

Marino's attention was drifting. "Don't be so suspicious, it isn't worth it," he said. "I don't care about any of this any more."

If this were a cross-examination, it would be a disaster. Sara sat down in an orange molded plastic chair and stared at her father.

"Are you listening?"

"You mean, do I hear you say you don't care if you're charged with murdering a patient? Yes, I hear. And I don't believe it."

"Sara, you are just like me, do you know that?"

She stopped and looked at him, nonplussed.

"You're trying to avoid the obvious. It doesn't work for long."

"You've made it work for forty years," she retorted.

He leaned forward, his body supported on one thin arm, a very fragile arm. "I'm sick, Sara," he said with the articulation of a teacher talking to a small child. "I'm very sick, I'm stuck in this hospital that is intent on keeping me alive, but this is my second heart attack, I'm too old for all these tubes."

"So what if you're eighty-three?" she demanded. "You're getting better, don't you understand?"

"I'm patched up but it's temporary," he said. "Believe me, it's temporary. Rationing medical care, Sara? If the Court upholds the idea, I'm eminently expendable."

"Not to me, you aren't."

"Who wants to rewire an eighty-three-year-old man? Better they save a kid."

"Dad, you're tired and depressed."

"Honey, I don't want to die, don't misunderstand. I'm just stating the obvious. You've spent your life knowing how to set priorities, you know what I'm saying. I'm not at the top of anybody's list any more."

"You're at the top of mine."

"Hey, kiddo, stop personalizing this."

She smiled wanly. "Look who's talking," she said.

"Honey, I've thought a lot about Sally over the years. I did the best I could for her. She had these little kids. . . ."

His eyes were closing. She wasn't going to get any further with him, she could see that. "Maybe you should let it go for now," she said. "Get well, first."

His eyes flew open and he glared at her. "Don't tell me what to worry about," he said. "I've got my own timetable, and it's a helluva lot shorter than yours. Don't dictate."

Good, some of the fire was back. "When have I ever dictated anything to you?"

"You're trying to now."

She reached forward and smoothed a few strands of gray hair back from his forehead, swept by a deep surge of feeling.

He smiled, then closed his eyes again. Her heart twisted into a painful knot. The silence in the spare, narrow hospital room was total. Sara found herself absorbing her father's surroundings: the stale, medicinal smell, the faint odor of urine, the dreary aura of confinement. "Don't you dare check out on me," she whispered.

Without opening his eyes, he reached for her hand. "Wouldn't dream of it," he said.

"You need to sleep."

One eye flew open, fixing Sara with a baleful glare. "Don't tell me what I need," he said.

She knew what he needed. Suddenly, she knew. "You're a good man," she said simply.

"Thanks, kid," he said. He actually looked jaunty for a moment in his much-laundered hospital pajamas. "Come see me in the morning before you head back to that snake pit you live in."

"I will, Dad."

"Don't worry," he said as she stood and slowly headed for the door. "I'll be all right."

"Do you have any idea," she said, her hand on the doorknob, "how much a child needs to hear that from a parent?"

"You're the child?"

"Yes, I'm the child."

"Even if it isn't always true?"

"Even if it isn't always true."

"Then I have to send you off with one small piece of information," he said almost nonchalantly. "Nobody in Washington tipped the media. Dumb as it sounds, I did."

"*What?*" Sara froze, her feet literally unable to move.

"Crazy, huh?" He sounded amused with himself. "Don't worry, nobody knows, I was just an anonymous caller who gave them some names and told them to check it out. I had the idea I could make this guy Patton a paper tiger if I swiped his ammunition. It's like someone coming out of the closet, you know? They can't blackmail you if everybody knows you're gay." He smiled sheepishly. "I didn't figure on another heart attack."

"That's the loopiest thing I've ever heard!"

"Loopy? Hey, I like that. I don't know much about managing the news, but I did a pretty good job. Just got a little too excited about it all, I guess."

"I can't believe this." Sara wasn't sure whether she should laugh or bang her head against the wall. "What ever prompted you . . . ?"

"My dramatic streak, what else? Thought I could make people listen better."

"Dad." All she could manage was a sputter.

He turned away from her, facing the wall, and his voice was muffled. "Then again," he said, "maybe not."

Sara slapped a few pieces of bread down on the counter as Barney watched, hardly thinking about what she was doing. It was late Tuesday morning, she was just in from the airport, and bone weary. There wasn't much in the refrigerator, just some stale sesame bagels, slightly aged cream cheese, a half bottle of flat Pepsi . . . when had she last actually shopped for food? Life was moving too fast when you couldn't count on finding something in the house for a meal. But it was good to see the sun through the kitchen window, good to have Barney sitting across from her.

"Can you believe it?" she said as she piled more cream cheese than usual on a bagel. "He tipped the media himself? My own father!"

Barney laughed. "Weird," he said.

"Not weird," she corrected lightly. "Just a little crazy."

"So what now?"

"You've read the letter I wrote to get his license back?"

"Yeah, nothing damning about it. Basically a letter filled with the convoluted language of a new law school graduate, which anyone could have seen."

"So it's a non-issue."

"Yep. Patton's hanging his case against you on a pretty thin hook."

"We've known that from the start," she said, sitting down next to him at the table, staring at her bagel, realizing she was no longer hungry. "The real problem is what this woman in Buffalo decides to do. I wish my father understood better what could be unleashed. I wish he understood that I'm not the one in jeopardy, he is."

He reached for the cream cheese and spread it on with an almost languorous motion. "He seems to be the kind of guy who sees himself at the center of the universe, am I wrong?"

"Maybe all doctors do," she said. Then, after a pause, she added, "Judges, too, I guess."

"So it's his righteousness versus Patton's obsession, and you get caught in the middle."

That was too tough, she decided. "He's weary. Look what he's done to himself."

"Not to put too fine a point on it, Sara—but look what he's done to you."

She rose abruptly and began clearing the breakfast plates, replacing the lid on the orange juice with a nervous twist of her hand, tossing forks and knives with a sharp clatter onto the plates.

Barney stood too, speaking quickly. "Hey, don't take offense. I'm not condemning him, you know that, don't you? I'm saying you're caught up in his agenda at a difficult time, that's all."

Sara told herself to calm down. She needn't feel disloyal for admitting Barney was right. But this damn agenda had been forced on her father as well as on her. And what a price for him! How did it feel to lie in that hospital bed wondering when and if a third heart attack was going to hit?

"Sara?"

Sara jumped; she had actually forgotten for an instant that Barney was there. "I'm sorry, I'm just thinking about what you said."

"He's put you in a spot, Sara, and it's okay to be a little angry about that." He gave her a watchful grin. "Should I duck now or am I making any sense?"

"I'm not angry, and I don't intend to be put in a spot."

"You've got something up your sleeve."

"If this is a battle of whose character gets defamed worst, I think I can put up a fairly good fight."

His eyes grew even more watchful. "I know what you're going to do."

"I don't think you do, actually," she said.

"But—"

"I know," she said. "You think I should go directly to Sayles and tell him that I know exactly how he messed up Faith's life."

"With some finesse."

"No matter how it's done, it's straight-out blackmail. Right, Barney?"

His gaze never faltered. "Right, Sara."

"That's not the way I want to reach the Supreme Court."

"Here are your options: Pull out, and let those bastards win. Tough it out, and risk having someone testify to the Judiciary Committee that your father committed murder. If Jack wants to, he'll make it happen. Or, cut 'em off at the knees. Call it blackmail, call it anything you want. You would be laying out the truth, and you might even force Dick Sayles to act like the President he's supposed to be."

Sara said nothing, she simply picked up the dishes and silverware and walked over to the sink. She reached for a yellow scrubbing brush, turned on the water, and began methodically cleaning away the last vestiges of breakfast.

"Hey, any response?"

She dried her hands. "I've got a few ideas," she said. "But I'm not ready to talk about them."

She sensed, without looking around, that Barney was drawing back. Was she closing him out? They were partners in this, after all.

She heard the scraping of the chair behind her pushing back from the table. "I didn't really expect you to agree," he said. Was he getting up to leave? She turned around. No. Barney was stretching his legs, cradling a cup of coffee, looking thoughtful, even peaceful. He didn't want me to go to Sayles, she realized suddenly. But he had to know if I was considering it. Was it some kind of test?

"There's something else," she said, wiping her hands on a wet dish towel next to the dish rack. "And maybe what I'm going to say sounds overly dramatic, but I hope you'll listen."

"I'm listening."

"We don't know yet how Faith died. I've fantasized about confronting Dick Sayles, I can't deny it. But we can't forget that she might have been murdered. Sayles had reason to keep her quiet—"

"I don't believe it. I'm sorry, Sara, I really don't."

Sara barely heard him. "—and so did Jack Patton. And

what about the missing money? I know all the signs point to suicide, even if we can't understand why it happened. But maybe it wasn't."

Barney studied her for a second. "Something's happened, hasn't it?"

She put the towel back on the counter. "Yes," she said simply.

"Want to tell me?"

Sara paused, remembering Carol's anguished phone call telling her that there was a letter from Faith. But it was maddeningly out of reach. Carol was sure it would be in their hands now if she hadn't blundered. Maybe that was true, and maybe not, but Faith had written a letter, to them. That was a stunning piece of news. They had to get it. But how?

She told Barney; watched his eyes widen. "A letter?"

"Mrs. Paige has it."

"Well, Jesus!"

Sara raised a warning hand. "Not so fast; Mrs. Paige won't give it to us. She almost handed it over to Carol, but changed her mind at the last minute."

"*Why?* Sara, that letter is evidence."

Not before we get a look at it, Sara thought suddenly. The unbidden thought shocked her. But if Faith revealed her father's abuse in the letter, that wasn't for the police or the newspapers, was it? Unless it could somehow have been the catalyst for her death.

"Sara?"

"Sorry," she said quickly. "This has been preying on my mind."

"What's her motive? How can she keep a letter addressed to you and your friends?"

"She's doing it, that's all I can tell you," Sara said. "Probably because she's carrying around a heavy load of guilt." She sighed, "I'd rather not talk about why."

Barney pulled at his tie, loosening it, twisting the ends,

staring into the distance. When he finally spoke, his voice was soft. "There's a lot at stake here," he said.

"I know that."

"Anything that might help . . ."

"We can't arm-wrestle Mrs. Paige into giving us that letter. We have to talk her into wanting to do it."

"Yeah, okay. A lot of people are out on a limb for you, remember. I wish—" He paused and sighed deeply.

"You wish what?"

"I wish sometimes you were just a Justice Department lawyer or something—anyone but who you are."

She smiled. "Life would be simpler," she said. She turned and slowly continued loading cups and dishes and glasses into the dishwasher. But then she felt his hands on her shoulders, turning her gently around toward him.

"When this is over," he whispered.

"Don't," she murmured back, touching his lips with her finger. "Not yet."

That afternoon, Carol looked up in surprise as Sara appeared at the threshold of her office door. "Sara!" she said, rushing forward and giving her a hug. "Is he better?"

"Yes, can you believe it?" Sara said. "For a man of his age."

"It was that witch, Sandi."

"I'd be happy to blame her, but the truth will surprise you," Sara said. "I can't explain exactly why—because it doesn't make sense—but *he* broke the story."

"Your *father?*" Carol's eyes almost popped with astonishment as she sat down again.

"He's convinced he's blameless."

"Helluva time to tell the world."

Sara couldn't resist a weary laugh as she settled down in a chair next to Carol's desk. She glanced around Carol's office. "I don't get a chance to see you in your natural habitat too often." She spotted a photograph on Carol's desk almost instantly. "Why, Carol," she said, touched. "You've got the picture of the five of us on that vacation."

"I liked it a lot," Carol said, slightly abashed. "I had a copy made."

Sara frowned, thinking about Faith's mother. "What are we going to do about Mrs. Paige?"

"I don't know, she's strung very tight."

"Putting her own daughter in a mental hospital—it's hard to believe. Do you think she was trying to shut her up?"

"Maybe she thought that would convince Faith she was imagining things."

"Or let her know the penalty for accusing her father."

They stared at each other.

"Do you think we'll ever know if Faith's story was true?" Sara asked quietly.

"Maybe," Carol replied. "If we get our hands on that letter."

"Did you tell Maggie and Leona?"

"I told Maggie about the letter, not the other things. Not yet. I'll see Leona tomorrow at the Women and Justice Forum."

"So how do we get it?"

"Wait a few days, and go back to her, I guess." Carol shook her head. "Maybe we could do it together, or maybe it'd be better if the rest of you do it and leave me out. She's not happy with me, I can tell you."

"She sounds so afraid."

"How does it get that bad with your own child?" Carol's voice had a fuzzy edge to it.

"Put a lid on your imagination," Sara said quickly. "You are not some monster mother."

"Yeah, but sometimes I'm close to the edge, and that's the truth. I've got to figure out how to balance things better."

An aide's head popped through the door. "Excuse me,

but you'd better turn on C-Span,'' he said quickly. ''The right-to-work bill looks like it's coming to a vote.''

''Shit, today?'' Carol mumbled, reaching over to turn on the television set. ''Sam, see if you can stall on that Montgomery County speech tonight, I don't want to miss this one.''

Sam groaned. ''They're expecting you at eight o'clock.''

''Make it eight-thirty.''

He nodded, and vanished.

''Things don't seem important around here any more. I mean,'' Carol corrected herself hastily, ''not *as* important. Me, neither. If you understand.'' Unwillingly, her eyes strayed to the screen.

''You'll figure it out,'' Sara said with a small smile. ''We should take another vacation together. Let's really do it, it'll cheer us all up. Bring the kids.''

''Sure, why not?'' Carol straightened then, and focused finally on Sara. What had she done with her hair? It was swinging with a casual looseness as she talked, and there was a light in her eyes—leaving Carol suddenly wondering when and why these interesting changes had occurred.

''You look good, you know that?'' she said suddenly, ''Even under all this pressure.''

Sara grinned. ''Ah, so you've noticed,'' she said.

''So what's going on?'' Carol said curiously.

''Well . . .''

''Come on, you can tell *me*.''

''Well—actually, there's a man.''

Carol's eyes lit up. ''Great, you deserve it! Who is he? Can I ask?''

''Look, I know it's stupid timing.''

''Stupid? Why stupid?''

''Me? Right now? Come on, Carol, it's stupid.'' She was feeling a bit embarrassed.

''Won't you tell me who it is?''

''Who've I been spending the most time with lately?''

she said with a laugh. "It's Barney."

Carol was still smiling. "Barney?" she said. "Barney Cassidy?"

Why did she sound surprised? Or was it disappointed? Sara shifted her feet. "The very same," she said lightly.

"Wow."

The two of them stared at each other. Well, Sara told herself, no one ever said Carol held back an opinion.

"I can see you're overwhelmed with delight."

Carol was trying now for a little enthusiasm, but it clearly came hard. "I guess I never thought of the two of you as a match."

"We're not," Sara said, wishing she had never brought it up. "We just like each other."

"Hey, that's great."

"Okay, it's stupid. So what else is wrong? Why am I getting a little sweaty on the forehead?"

"Barney's a smart, interesting man, from what I hear," Carol said, still trying to sort out her feelings. "People respect him."

"Come on, Carol," Sara chided.

"Okay." Carol spread her arms, palms up. "He's had a lot of girlfriends, Sara."

"God, I thought you were going to say a lot of boyfriends."

Carol realized she was foundering, but she figured she'd better follow through now. "He has a reputation, you know—a reputation of 'love 'em and leave 'em.' "

Sara smiled faintly. "What a sweet, old-fashioned way to put it. I know all about his reputation, really."

There was a slight edge to her voice and Carol felt a bit defensive. "Hey, you asked me," she said with a shrug. "Am I the bad guy now?"

"No, no. But what kind of man do you think I should be attracted to? A monk?"

"Well"—Carol was searching—"someone with the

same stature you have, I guess.''

''What does that mean?''

''Sara, don't put me on the spot.''

''I'm not trying to. I'm just trying to ask if you're not unintentionally imposing''—Sara thought about how to phrase it—''impossible standards on me? Carol, I'm not the Virgin Mary. I'm a lawyer, a judge, and a woman.''

Carol was embarrassed. ''Oh, for God's sake, I know that.''

Sara pressed on. ''And I happen to have been positioned in such a way that I've been nominated to the Supreme Court, right? It's not exactly a crowning, Carol. Don't tell me I can only have a relationship with someone like—like the Prince of Wales.''

''Not him,'' Carol objected immediately. ''He walks like a duck.''

They looked at each other for an instant and then began laughing.

''I know what my problem is,'' Carol said, in a burst of honesty that surprised herself. ''I think I'm figuring that if I'm going to be single again, I want company.''

''Why, Carol.'' Sara was again touched. It was true, Carol had no image of herself yet without Bart in the background. He had always been there, even if he had become increasingly invisible and taken for granted. The life that seemed totally normal for Sara was alien to Carol. ''Look, you've got your kids and you've got your friends,'' she said gently. ''We're not deserting you.''

Carol suddenly got very busy straightening some papers on her desk. ''Actually, Barney's a pretty nice guy,'' she said in a slightly muffled voice.

''Thanks.''

Carol looked up and they smiled at each other.

''Can I change the subject?'' Sara asked.

Carol nodded.

''Look,'' Sara said, pulling a piece of legal-sized paper

from her briefcase. "Here's something else I know you'll be interested in." Her eyes were excited as she thrust the heavy sheet of official bond into Carol's hand.

Carol stared at the letterhead: the Senate Judiciary Committee. "Thursday," she said softly. "God, Sara—the day after tomorrow. Seeing it in black and white makes it real."

"That's right."

"Are you ready?"

"Are you with me?"

"Hell, all the way."

"Then I've got what I need," Sara said with a determined smile. "I'm ready."

Maggie sat alone in the still living room Tuesday night, listening to the ticking clock. So Faith had written them a letter . . . it made her heart beat faster to think of it. Maybe they would finally discover the real Faith Paige . . . maybe. She looked around, realizing how empty the house was without Jeff's presence. He would be home soon, and the nightmare of his being sick would fade. She couldn't wait for sticky orange juice spilled on the floor and the raucous sound of the television set. Had Mrs. Paige ever known something that good and that simple? She wanted her son home. Soon, dammit.

The phone rang, cutting sharply through her thoughts.

"Maggie, we need to talk." It was Michael. Maybe it was the calmness, the almost detached quality of his voice that gave her pause, but she felt suddenly chilled.

"I've been in Buffalo; just got back."

"Michael, you went—"

"I went because you couldn't go," he said. "And now I want to tell you what I found out."

"Can't you tell me over the phone? Is it bad?"

"I can't. Face to face. Believe me, you'll understand."

"Hurry," she said then.

* * *

Michael stepped through the front door with a friendly nod. He shrugged off his battered black leather jacket and tossed it absently over a dining-room chair as he often had before. He sat down on the sofa, clasped his hands in front of him, and quietly began to speak. "This is off the record," he said. "Totally."

"Of course, Michael. You don't have to say . . ."

"Yes, I do. What I'm saying is, I've got something to tell you—and then I'm forgetting it myself. Wiping it out of the memory bank."

Maggie felt the palms of her hands growing moist.

"You've got reason to worry about Sara, especially now. Her father, old Dr. Marino, everybody's favorite country doctor?" He smiled ruefully. "A great guy. I like him. Yeah, I spent some time with him in the hospital, not that he opened up much. But it looks like he went over the line, way over the line. At least to manslaughter."

Involuntarily, Maggie gasped. "You've found proof?"

"No, not proof. Nothing that can be laid out without question marks. I can't prove it, but I can't disprove it, either."

"Tell me, please." She said it quickly.

"This woman, Sally Hegelstrom? She's got a sister named Ginny Boseley who happens to be Patton's source. This started when she fired off a letter to the White House protesting the new euthanasia laws, mentioning—just in passing—her connection to Sara's father. She threw him in as an example of a doctor who played God with sick people's lives and said he'd never been caught. And then she said she had proof he'd killed her sister."

"And Patton jumped on it." She felt sick.

"Right. He had somebody on her doorstep a few days later."

"Go on," she urged. She needed to absorb this as quickly as possible, so she could figure out what it meant, what there was to do. But Michael would not be hurried.

"Ginny's in her sixties, worn, kind of bitter—but she remembers every minute of the last day of her sister's life. And boy, is she graphic." Michael took a deep breath. "From what she tells me, the family adored George Marino. Trusted him totally. He took care of them all, toothaches, pregnancies, whatever. Sally was bedridden with terminal cancer and just about totally helpless. Ginny took care of her, said she was ready to take care of her for life. Marino kept telling her it'd be a blessing if her sister died, but she kept insisting they could manage. She died January 14. It was her daughter Emma's tenth birthday."

Maggie put her face in her hands.

"Yeah," Michael said. "But it gets worse. The girl found the body."

"Oh, Michael. No."

"They were planning a small party that evening in Sally's sickroom. Ginny says she was in there with her sister all morning, blowing up balloons. She claims there's no way—no way in the world Sally would have chosen to die right then."

"Did Marino give her pills? What happened? Could she have accidentally overdosed on something?"

"I can tell you what they told me, that's all. Marino insisted it was accidental, but Ginny's convinced he did it. He was with Sally alone for about an hour that morning. Just the two of them—and all the balloons."

"But this doesn't prove anything, Michael. Did they do an autopsy?"

Michael shook his head. "Nobody suggested it."

Maggie found herself casting for a way out. "How could this hurt Sara?" she demanded. "No matter what her father did—"

"Simple. Patton's feeding off the anti-euthanasia fights. All he needs is a media blitz that scares Judiciary, and she's finished. Nothing complicated. Happens all the time, these days."

''No,'' Maggie said bitterly. ''Nothing complicated.''

''The Hegelstroms aren't out to ruin Sara, far as I can tell,'' he said. ''But they're mad. You can feel it and see it, even after all these years.''

''I don't know what to say.''

''Well,'' Michael rubbed the deepening lines in his forehead, ''I told you, I liked the guy—but I think he did it.''

She had to ask. ''Michael, you're not going to write anything, are you?''

Michael took a deep breath, and she could tell this had been a hard call. ''Of course not. I'm too close to you,'' he said.

''Do you feel torn?''

''A little.''

Maggie felt shaken by the loyalty she saw reflected in his eyes. She reached for his hand, squeezed it tight.

''But I've got to tell you, this stuff won't stay quiet for long.''

''What happens to Sara now?''

''Ah, the big question.'' Michael patted her hand and started to pace. He seemed on surer ground now. ''If she goes ahead, it could trigger an indictment.''

''Patton had something to do with Faith's death, I'm sure of it,'' Maggie said. ''He knows.''

''He knows what?''

Maggie stopped dead. Michael stood still and stared at her, waiting.

''Don't ask, Michael,'' she whispered. She had confided enough about what was going on; she couldn't tell him about Faith's affair, not yet. There were too many unknowns.

''Well, don't give me that kind of teaser, dammit!'' He started pacing again, this time angrily.

''I'm sorry,'' she said unhappily. ''Michael, I'm really sorry, but I just can't talk about it.'' She stood and stopped him, put both arms around him and held tight. Not telling Michael, of all people. . . . He stood there, frozen for a second. Then he put his arms around her.

"Okay, okay. But dammit, Maggie."

They stood quietly together, letting it go by.

"Michael, do you realize the hearings begin Thursday?" she finally whispered.

"Hey, am I a reporter or not?"

With some effort, he grinned at her and Maggie felt a little better. "Look," she said impulsively, "let's have a drink. Let's plan something. Let's figure out . . ."

"There's something I've never told you," he said, suddenly burying his head in her neck. "When my mother died?"

Maggie tightened her hold on him and waited for him to go on. It took a long moment.

"She wanted to die. We knew that, that's why we hid her medicines. She went down to sixty-five pounds. I remember her curled up tight, in something of a fetal crouch—it took weeks and weeks."

She simply held on to him. There was nothing else to do. "Michael."

He didn't seem to hear. "It was the worst experience I've ever been through," he said, half to himself.

"You were only a kid."

"Old enough to ask better questions. Seventeen."

"How could you know what to do?"

"Doesn't help how I feel now."

"Michael, I wish you had told me this before," she said slowly.

He faced her, looking at her as if he were seeing her for the first time. "It never came up," he said with some surprise.

She kissed him full on the lips, closing her eyes, overwhelmed. All the times he had been there for her, all the listening to her problems, all the support for her and for Jeff. . . . Her own troubles and self-pity had swallowed everything else for too long.

Somehow, it never came up.

CHAPTER 10

The grand ballroom at the Washington Hilton was buzzing Wednesday with the sound of voices and the clatter of dishes and silverware as waiters bustled about, depositing plates of broiled chicken and asparagus before hundreds of women who had turned out for the First Lady's speech at the annual Women and Justice Forum.

How strange, Sara thought, as she took her seat at the head table on the dais, two down from Laura Sayles. I am here because the Goodspeed administration wanted to showcase me as a popular choice for the Court, and now the new administration wants to force me out. I am only one day from the confirmation hearings and I still don't know what's going to happen. She smiled for the television cameras, carrying on the charade of business-as-usual, even as she watched reporters nudging each other, glancing from her to Laura Sayles. She braced herself for the questions about her father, which were bound to start coming like water through a break in a dam. Her head was still spinning from Maggie's hurried early morning call, whispering Michael's news. "Sara, be prepared." How? How did she prepare? The rumors about tomorrow were flying, and she could tell by looking at the avid, curious faces in front of her that their layer of polite containment was perilously thin. Sooner or later . . .

"Judge Marino!" called one reporter from the front row. "Where do you stand on mercy suicide?"

"Judge Marino!" clamored another, louder reporter. "Are you thinking about asking the President to withdraw your name?"

"Are you losing support in the Senate?" "Have you talked to the President about the charges against your father?" The voices were clamoring, competing. Heads were turning.

"Judge Marino."

The cluster of reporters fell silent, and Sara looked up. Laura Sayles, in a very bright blue suit, was standing next to her, smiling. Her hand was extended.

"I want to welcome you—and to congratulate you personally on your nomination."

The photographers were clicking away madly. Slowly, Sara rose and took the First Lady's hand. They smiled at each other, and Sara had the distinct impression that Laura Sayles held the handshake for several extra seconds. She's showing her support, Sara told herself, slightly shell-shocked. For whatever reason, she wants the world to know she approves my nomination.

She felt a lurch in her heart; a twinge of conscience. Surely this woman had at least some inkling of the affair her husband had carried on with Faith. Was it possible she had been kept completely in the dark? Sara stared at the very public, smiling First Lady and tried to read what was in her eyes. But all she could see was what Laura Sayles wanted the world to see. Her face was calm, her expression warm but bland; a generic expression honed through years of public life. Sara, her hand still firmly held, felt first a surge of pity, then respect. I mustn't forget, she told herself, this woman has paid a price, too.

"I have not had a chance to tell you how sorry I am

about your friend Faith's death,'' Mrs. Sayles said clearly. ''It was a tragic loss.'' She gazed gravely at the cameras and turned to take her seat. The message was sent.

Sara glanced quickly to her left, to where Carol sat at the end of this long ribbon of people behind a white tablecloth. Carol gave her the quickest of grins, over and done with in the space of a second. And the two of them sat then through the lengthy lunch, wondering what had motivated Laura Sayles to offer Sara her unequivocal support on the eve of her husband's possible betrayal.

The lunch was ending. Laura Sayles was whisked out in short order and then Sara left, encased in a tight centipede of reporters and photographers. Carol, never one to lose an opportunity, was working the floor in front of the podium.

''Carol! Carol, don't leave before we get a chance to talk!'' It was Leona, a super-vivacious Leona, bouncing across the ballroom floor toward her friend, blowing kisses and offering little flutters of her beautifully manicured hand to acquaintances along the way. The crowd parted; Carol turned and flashed a smile, ever aware of the cameras. They were both pros at this.

''Can you believe Laura Sayles?'' Carol said under her breath as they hugged lightly and exchanged feathery kisses. ''Incredible,'' Leona said, just as sotto voce. They chattered in as inane a way as possible until the TV crews got bored and drifted away.

''Meet me in the restroom, lobby level, please?'' Leona whispered. ''It really can't wait.''

Under the gaiety, Carol could see now, Leona's eyes looked desperate. She nodded quickly. ''You go first,'' she said. ''Give me a couple of minutes.'' She turned away immediately and began shaking hands with a cluster of women waiting to greet the congresswoman from Maryland, but she had a hard time concentrating on their animated questions.

As soon as possible, Carol edged out of the crowd and into the carpeted corridor, then took the escalator up to the lobby level and headed past the winding plate-glass windows to the upstairs ladies' room. When she opened the door, she saw Leona sitting alone in the deserted space. She had collapsed into a faded brocade chair and was staring solemnly at her multiple reflections in a mirror that stretched to the ceiling and wrapped around three corners.

"Anybody here?"

"No, the place is empty."

"What's the matter?"

"I can't find my lipstick." Leona fumbled with her handbag, woven of soft leather strips, finally getting it open. She pulled out a tube of pancake foundation, a mascara wand, a cake of blusher, and two small pots of dark cream. With methodical precision, she lined them up like toy soldiers on the marble makeup table. "Eyeliner," she said, holding up one of the little pots. "Eyeshadow," she said, holding up the other. "Best on the market, I get it at Bloomingdale's. Want to try it?"

Carol felt a flush of annoyance, but managed to put it aside. She leaned against the cosmetic table, her back to one of the mirrored walls, and folded her arms. "You didn't ask me in here to talk about makeup."

"I asked you in here to tell you, you were right about Justin. Carol, my husband is not a nice man."

Leona said it with a tone of desolation that made it clear the trial had been held and sentence passed. Carol could hardly believe her ears. "What are you talking about?"

"He's involved in some bad stuff. I won't be able to live with myself if I don't expose him. It's true, he was responsible for Faith losing her money."

"Are you sure?"

"Yes."

"How did you find out?" Carol felt a twinge of self-justification. Wasn't this what she had suspected from the beginning? But when she saw the tears spilling down Leona's face, she felt more shaken than justified.

"By going into his office and rifling his private papers." Leona let out a huge sniff.

Carol looked at her quizzically, raising an eyebrow. "*You* did that?"

"I had to find out what really happened."

Carol reached for a tissue on the glass-topped counter and handed it to Leona. "I'm sorry," she said with awkward sincerity. "After all, you're married to the guy."

Leona's voice echoed with melancholy. "At a certain level you must feel pretty good—to be proven right, I mean," she said.

Carol fumbled a bit before answering. "Well, if you'd asked me that a few weeks ago, I would have had to be honest and tell you, sure." Her hand reached again to the tissue box, pulling out another one which she silently handed to Leona.

"So, what's changed?"

Maybe just my perspective, Carol thought. "Well—it screws up your life, doesn't it?"

Leona mopped at her nose with the tissue. "I really loved him," she said simply.

Carol sighed. "I know you did, we all knew that."

Leona straightened her shoulders, realizing that just saying the words now would help her muster courage. "I know what I have to do," she said. "Justin set up the circumstances that caused Faith's death, I'm convinced of it. I don't know if that makes it murder or suicide, but I can't let him get away with it."

"What did he do?"

"He talked Faith into investing money in a scheme that gave her phony stock for land that was supposed to yield oil. He got out in time, but all her money was lost. Can you imagine how desperate she must have been? And mortified and ashamed and frightened?'' Leona drew a deep breath.

''Leona, she wrote a letter. To us.''

Leona gasped. ''A letter? What does she say? Oh, my God, Carol.'' Her lips began to quiver. ''Does she talk about Justin?''

Carol let herself slide into the chair next to Leona, feeling again the mixture of frustration and anger at herself for letting the letter almost literally slip from her hands. ''I wish I knew. But I don't have the letter, Mrs. Paige has it. And she won't give it to us.''

''Why not? It's ours, isn't it?''

''Sure, it's ours, but I got her angry—like an idiot, I made the mistake of telling her what I knew about her relationship with Faith.'' Carol started to say more but decided to wait. Leona didn't need another shock.

Leona's eyes turned a little wild. ''We have to get that letter,'' she said. ''Faith will tell us the truth; she always told the truth.''

''It's going to take some work changing Mrs. Paige's mind. She's fierce.''

''I can't wait. I have to expose Justin. You know what that means?'' Leona was becoming agitated. ''I have to do it, even if it wrecks his life.''

''Don't move too fast.'' Anything, for the moment, to soothe Leona. ''Maybe there's a way to set things right without . . .''

''Carol?'' Leona looked at her with surprise, but also with affection. ''You know better, and so do I. You're afraid I'm going to fall apart, but I won't, I promise you.''

Carol smiled tentatively, still watching her. ''So what do you do now?''

Leona pulled yet another tissue from the box and wiped again at her eyes. When she began to speak, Carol felt within seconds that she was braced against a bubbling split in a sea wall. Leona told what she was planning in a rushing, tumbling monotone—and for once Carol was left without a ready response.

"I'm scared to death."

"I can see why."

"My whole life with him, you know? He wasn't always like this, we used to be quite happy, actually. Justin wasn't so set on being at the center of things."

"You're probably going to tell me to keep my mouth shut for now, but I wish you'd let me help."

"You are, you are, just by listening to me."

"I've never been much of a listener, but I seem to be doing a lot more of it lately." Carol couldn't resist noting her own transformation, but Leona hardly heard her.

"Everything's happening so fast, with Sara's confirmation hearing starting tomorrow, but I've got to do something quickly. If Justin finds out what I'm planning—"

"Look, can I do something?"

"Don't do anything or say anything, not until I settle this with Justin. I mean it, Carol. Just keep listening to me."

Carol stared at Leona's pinched, determined face. She was gutsy, no question about it. I'm not sure if I were in the same position, she thought, I would be able to do the same thing.

There was a noise; the restroom door was swinging open. Carol glanced up to see Sandi Snow, eyes wide, standing at the door.

"Well, hello," she said. She wore the expression of a hawk bearing down on a field mouse. "My goodness, I certainly didn't expect to see you two friends in here. The downstairs restroom is so *crowded*—" Her eyes darted quickly from Leona's tear-stained face to Carol's unusually grim demeanor. "Looks like I stumbled onto a little problem. Is there anything I can do to help?"

"No, thank you." Leona stood with dignity, scooping

the cosmetics she'd laid out on the vanity into her purse and closing it with a vigorous snap.

"I would have thought you'd both be *ecstatic* after the little scene out there. Mrs. Sayles couldn't have been nicer to Judge Marino, wasn't that a sight to see? With all this talk." Her eyes darted again, hopefully, from one to the other. "Her father, the other things. . . . "

"What other things?" Carol bit her tongue the second the words were out.

"Well." Sandi kept herself pressed against the restroom door, holding it firmly closed against the urgent knocking of a would-be visitor. "The affair, I know it's just a rumor—"

"What affair?" It was too late to back away now.

Sandi took a deep breath and kept her voice as light as possible. "I'm referring to the rumor that Sara Marino had an affair with President Goodspeed."

Both women gasped.

"Are you kidding?" Carol managed.

"Oh, you're surprised, well, *that's* a good sign, I'm sure," Sandi said, speaking rapidly. "These rumors going around town are disgraceful, there's no other word for them, but surely you understand I have to run them by you."

"Well, that one is ridiculous." Leona's eyes were totally dry, now. Blazing.

Carol stood and moved toward Sandi with some obscure idea of pushing her out the door. Sandi was ready for her. "And Faith—poor Faith," she went on. "Have you heard about the *National Enquirer* poking around? The rumor that she was a lesbian and about to be found out? Seamy, isn't it?"

"That's just crazy."

The look on the faces of the two women was enough to make Sandi finally back off.

"Well, don't blame me," she said with aggrieved asperity. "There are all sorts of stories whirling around town, and you should be glad I ran a few by you. Now I can make sure my story has your denials *prominently* up top. 'Bye, ladies. I can see you want to be by yourselves, so I guess I'll just go get in line for the loo upstairs." And with that, she was gone.

"You know what we just did?" Carol said, stunned.

"What?"

"We just gave her an excuse to print the most outrageous rumors about Sara and Faith she can come up with."

Back at the White House, Laura Sayles stood in her bedroom and stared out the window toward Pennsylvania Avenue as she slowly unbuttoned the jacket of her blue suit. She felt a sense of satisfaction, even peace. If nothing else, she had given the media—and Jack Patton—something to ponder. And then she heard the knob of her bedroom door turning.

"Hello, Dick."

"Hello, Laura."

She turned then, and husband and wife gazed at each other like strangers.

"That was a great show of yours at the Hilton today," Dick Sayles said calmly. "Shaking hands with Sara Marino? CNN's showing the tape, over and over." There was a slight tremor under his right eye and he looked even thinner than usual.

"You find that a problem?" she answered just as calmly.

"An obvious one, Laura. I have to keep my distance politically until things play out at the hearing tomorrow. Jack is hearing rumors of real trouble."

"Jack's *making* the trouble, Dick. Don't you see that?"

He shook his head, a dismissive gesture that almost sent her over the edge. "Don't show me your presidential displeasure," she said quickly. "I'm not intimidated, because

I know how little it means. How long do you plan to stay on the fence?''

''I haven't pulled the nomination,'' he said stiffly. ''I owe her that.''

''So what? You're still hoping she'll pull out and make it easy for you. What's Patton going to hit her with tomorrow? I'm hearing all the rumors everyone else is hearing, and there are too many of them. They're being planted.''

''You know Sara Marino was a good friend of Faith's.''

''Of course I know.'' Hearing Faith's name spoken between them started her legs trembling slightly, and she chose her next words with special care. ''But that doesn't mean she isn't a good nominee. Why are you allowing Patton to chip away at her?''

It felt good, no, wonderful, to see him trying to glance away. ''Does Sara Marino know too much about your relationship with Faith, is that the reason?'' she challenged. ''Are you and Patton afraid?''

''Let it go, Laura. I want to put it behind me, but you'll never let that happen.''

''Dick, do you know what it's been like?'' she whispered.

The blood drained from Dick Sayles's face as he faced his wife. Something inside seemed to crumble. ''What do you want from me?'' he asked.

''How can you ask that? What planet do you live on?''

''All right!'' He threw up his hands. ''I'm sorry. Do you think I set out deliberately to hurt you? No, Laura.''

''That doesn't help. You never cared if I knew!''

''Why should I? She loved me, not you!''

It was all open now; raw, unleashing a blinding mix of pain and confusion. Laura stared at her husband. All the goddamn lunches and speeches and White House dinners she had smiled her way through when he was vice president, all the times she had watched him use every excuse to talk to Faith Paige, all the times she had reminded herself she had the position, she was the wife, she was the protected one! And then Faith had died, and a terrible fear had descended. . . . She took a deep, sobbing breath. If she didn't ask now, she'd never have the courage to ask again.

"Why did she die, Dick?"

Her voice sounded strained and thin, even to her. Servants might be listening outside the bedroom door, but she didn't care what happened in this damn fishbowl any more. "Or should I ask, *how?* What really happened?"

Sayles took an involuntary step back, realizing for the first time just exactly what was being asked. Here they stood, supposedly at the pinnacle of their lives, and now, finally, he had to tell her the truth. He could wipe away the fear—but at great cost.

"Are you asking me if I had her *killed?*"

"I'm asking."

"God." He stared at her for another long moment, absorbing everything about her stance—the fright in her eyes, the wary positioning of her body—before he answered.

"No, Laura, I didn't have her killed."

And then he saw something almost worse than her fear: a horrifying, naked relief. It shook him badly.

"You were trying to break the affair off, weren't you?"

"Laura—"

"When Goodspeed died, you couldn't take the chance of keeping it up, could you? She was distraught at the prospect of losing you—that's what happened, right?" But even as she spoke, Laura Sayles sensed her words rang false. Worse, he was about to set her straight; she could see that. Recoiling instinctively, she raised her hands to her ears.

Too late, too late.

His voice was flat, almost expressionless. "No, Laura. Faith wanted to dump *me.* When she told me it was over, I went nuts. I wouldn't let her go. I even threatened to take her job away. I'm sorry, Laura. That's the truth."

A single muscle in Laura Sayles's face twitched. She closed her eyes and stood very still.

"So you see, it's not the nightmare you feared, it's a different one." He couldn't erase the bitterness from his voice. "I can tell you how sorry I am that you've suffered. But I can't give you regret or penitence or whatever it is a man is supposed to offer his wife when he has to admit he's been in love with another woman, because I fought like hell to keep her. It was crazy. I never expected to be President. What do I regret? I regret making her job contingent on staying with me." He winced as he saw her face. "Yes, that's what I did. God forgive me, maybe that's what took her over the edge."

She swayed; she refused to let herself collapse. Too much yet to find out. "Did Jack know?"

"He made it his business to find out."

"So he had reason to get rid of Faith." Her fears were building again.

"Laura, she committed suicide. I trapped her, don't you see? Faith had reason to rid herself of me—and she found the one sure way of doing it."

Laura reached toward the bed and picked up her blue jacket, smoothing out the wrinkles. Carefully, methodically, she walked to the closet and removed a hanger, straightening the lapels and buttoning the jacket before hanging it up. She was actually doing something simple and prosaic for a change.

"I wish you'd just leave now," she whispered. She caught a glimpse of her husband's reflection in the mirror and thought, for one fleeting second, that his anguish might actually equal hers. But then he spoke and the moment was gone.

"Laura, we're in this together. When this is over. . . ." He stopped.

"It'll never be over." There it was again, in his eyes: an expression, just a hint of the man she once knew.

"Okay, I'll leave you alone." His voice was that of a stranger. "At least you know I didn't kill her."

She stared at him with full astonishment. "But Dick, if what you say is true—then you did."

His eyes bore through her, hardly seeing her.

"Jesus," he said softly. And he was gone.

Jack Patton drummed nervously on his desk, relieved. He hadn't realized exactly how relieved until he'd heard Si Posner's secretary pick up the phone and say, yes, Mr. Posner was there, and yes, Mr. Patton, just hold on and he'll take your call. Third try today. Just move carefully, he told himself. This was what he had built his reputation on, the ability to keep his nerve and know exactly when to act and when not to. Listening to his wife chattering this morning about looking at apartments in Manhattan hadn't helped the pressure. She was saying it too much lately; she had never liked this city. . . .

"Mr. Patton?"

"Si!" he said heartily. "How are you, Si? Haven't touched base here in—"

"Uh, Mr. Patton? I'm sorry, sir, this is Mr. Posner's assistant. He said to tell you he's tied up in a meeting, could you call him—oh, day after tomorrow? Sorry about that."

Jack's hand shook. "Yeah," he said. "Day after tomorrow, huh?"

"That's right." The assistant's voice was firm. "On Friday."

Patton slammed down the phone.

Barney's grip on Sara's shoulder was gentle as he steered her down a corridor of the Dirksen Building late Wednesday afternoon through a noisy crowd of aides and reporters to a side office with a private telephone. "Amos wants to talk to you," he whispered. "In private."

Sara tensed as she walked into a space barely larger than

two telephone booths and saw Amos whispering with an aide. He turned to Sara, his face looking old and drawn. When Barney's hand cupped protectively over her shoulder, she knew something very bad was happening.

"Bad news," Amos said.

"My father's dead." She reeled.

"No, Sara, not that."

She felt a flood of relief, then confusion. "What's happened?"

"The district attorney in Buffalo says he has a witness to the—the crime he says your father committed. The woman's sister. She claims she saw it happen. He's taking the case to a grand jury. This could mean a murder charge." He gazed at her steadily, giving her time to absorb the information.

She blinked. "This is Patton's work," she breathed.

"Yes."

"He wants revenge, he wants to kill him!"

"It's not necessarily a case, just this one sister, she's their only witness—I think." Amos cleared his throat, the way he did when he was about to say something difficult. "Sayles may use this as an excuse to yank your nomination. You realize that, don't you?"

Barney glanced at his watch. "If he does, he won't wait long. If he doesn't—"

"His hands are clean if he can get the media and public opinion to do the job for him." Sara said it herself, trying to spare them.

"The timing isn't coincidental."

"Oh, God, my poor father." Sara let out a rasping sob. "I have to warn him. I've got to go see him."

"Not now," Amos said urgently. "You have to be in the hearing room at nine in the morning. I'm sorry, Sara. Very sorry. The goddamn bastards, a sick man . . ."

Sara shook her head, stopping the sympathetic tirade. "Anything can happen now," she said. "Surely the D.A.'s not so stupid as to charge an elderly doctor with murder?''

''This one might,'' Barney cut in. ''He's ambitious as hell and probably delighted to know he'll make the top of the news tonight and headlines tomorrow morning. Our luck that he took it so far.''

''How did Patton manipulate this?''

''No fingerprints, at least not yet. This guy could easily have moved on his own.''

''I doubt it,'' Sara said quickly. ''I want someone with my father. I want him to have the best lawyer we can get. I don't want him left alone or without support for a minute until I can be there.''

''I'll take care of it, I promise.'' Barney was matching her calmness, which was steadying. She cast him a grateful look. ''We'd better get back out there,'' he said.

''I can handle it.''

His reaction was swift. ''Always, Sara? By yourself?'' Amos had opened the door and exited from the room, leaving a quick moment for him to grab her by the shoulders. With one hand, he brushed a strand of hair back from her face and gazed at her with an expression so somber, she felt her heart skip a beat.

''You don't like anybody telling you anything,'' he whispered. ''But I'm doing it, whether you like it or not. It's going to be hell out there.'' His hand was still in her hair, hesitating, hovering over her face.

She tried to smile. What else was there to do?

Then lightly, hardly grazing the skin, he kissed her on the forehead before opening the door wide.

''Did you hear the news?'' Leona had been put through to Carol instantly. ''They've got somebody accusing Sara's father of homicide! We've got to do something. What can we do?''

''I heard; it's all over town.'' Carol was thinking hard. ''I talked to Maggie, she's got ideas on how to spin the story, but this news absolutely overwhelms everything else right now. You know how it works."

"Is there any chance?"

"Leona, the committee members are running scared. They don't want the anti-euthanasia people mad at *them*."

"Which is just what Jack Patton wants them to feel."

They both fell silent, and the phone line seemed to buzz with more static than usual.

"Then you're not surprised?"

Carol sighed. "No, I'm not. But then again, I am."

"She'll need us," Leona said quietly.

"She'll need more than her friends, Leona."

Sara threw the bolt on her apartment door with relief, locking out the shouting voices, the cameras, and the chaos of the day. So this was it. The worst. Then she slowly walked into the living room and picked up the silver frame with David's picture still in it. Funny—Barney had looked at it for a long time and said nothing. Surely he knew who it was. She smiled to herself; she liked his reserve. It meant she could count on him not to push or probe without an invitation. She walked back to the kitchen, rubbing absently at the tarnished frame. Barney had been her anchor today. Never yielding, never telling her what to do or how to field the questions, just being there. She stood over the kitchen sink, opened the velvet back of the frame, and lifted out the old photograph. She stared at it thoughtfully for a second, then crumpled it slowly in her hand and dropped it into the wastebasket by the window. Then she reached into a small grocery sack on the countertop and pulled out a shiny new jar of silver polish.

She surveyed the frame. It really was beautiful. With something akin to pleasure she wet the sponge in the polish jar and began systematically to clean the silver. Time enough later to put in another picture. Time now to ride this nightmare through.

* * *

Maggie's phone call came very late, after eleven o'clock.

"Hi," she said quietly. "I want you to know there are two reporters at the *Post* and one at *Time* magazine who are very interested in the fact that a chief of staff has managed to set up a disaster scenario for tomorrow with such precision. They're absolutely fascinated by the possibility that Jack Patton may actually be out to undercut his president, and they're prepared to ask some tough questions at tomorrow's White House briefing."

Maggie had been working hard. "Thanks," Sara said gratefully. "Every little bit helps."

"What are friends for?" Maggie actually sounded cheerful.

"It's tomorrow I'm worried about right now. Nothing will step on the murder charge story for the first news cycle."

"True," Maggie said with a sigh. "You've been around me so long, you're beginning to think like a reporter."

"Or a politician."

Maggie chuckled. "Don't forget, they'll be looking for counterpoint the minute they wrap tomorrow up. Reporters get bored fast. They're looking for it now. I've got a few leads to follow up tonight."

"This late?"

"As long as it takes."

"I'm impressed, Maggie."

"Now, *that's* funny." Maggie smiled and hung up, staring at the phone with real satisfaction. Twice now, her former colleagues had listened and paid attention to her news judgment. Twice now, she had done something to help Sara. Twice was pretty good.

She glanced down at a scribbled note from Michael. Just a name and a phone number, coupled with a hunch.

"I've heard Jack Patton's angling for some big job in

cable TV,'' she had mentioned to him last night at the house.

Michael had stopped dead, the television zapper poised in his hand. ''Maybe it's more than a rumor,'' he said.

This morning, he had handed her a phone number. ''My source at the White House says Patton's been calling this number six, seven times a day. Interested?'' She took time to enjoy the twinkle in his eye. In this business, she told herself, one phone number is sometimes all it takes. If you're lucky.

She dialed quickly. The phone rang four times. Finally, a man's cross, sleepy voice answered.

''Si Posner,'' he barked.

''Mr. Posner?'' She was surprised, in spite of herself. ''Of American Telecom?''

''Yeah—wait, who's this? Jesus, do you know what time it is? Wrong number, lady.'' The phone was slammed down so hard, Maggie had to move the receiver back from her ear. But she was grinning.

Pay dirt.

Thursday morning. Sara slipped out of bed before dawn, restless, unable to sleep, as prepared as she would ever be for what lay ahead. The city slept on. She chose carefully from her closet what she would wear for her appearance at ten o'clock: a plain navy suit, simple white blouse. Her uniform, Barney called it. She thought of her father. With any luck, he was sleeping—he had sounded too calm last night, too resigned. He had already heard from the district attorney. But she couldn't have the conversation she needed to have with him, not over the phone. ''Dad, I'll be there for you,'' she had said. ''I know you will,'' he had replied. That was all they could do; the rest would have to wait. She felt fear eating at the edges of her heart. Did he really understand what it would mean to have his reputation shredded to pieces in front of the nation's television cameras? "Reputations ebb and flow," he had said brusquely. "Remember? Live long enough and everyone's a failure. Now give 'em hell tomorrow."

Give 'em hell. It would be a beautiful day, she thought, staring out the window as she sipped a cup of extra-strong coffee. It would be one of those days that no one should miss, but most everyone would, just taking time to glance out a window every now and then. . . . Were there windows in the committee hearing room?

I need to get out of here, she told herself suddenly. She finished the last sip of coffee, making a face at the bitterness of the dregs. She went back to her bedroom, slipped quickly into a pair of jeans, and laced up an old pair of walking shoes. If she planned to seize the opportunity, she'd better get moving before it got too late. She would take a walk, a long walk, instead of moping around thinking about what came next and drinking too much coffee. With some exercise, she'd be stronger and ready, she told herself, for anything Jack Patton could dish out.

The city lay still and golden under the emerging light of the day. I've lived here a long time, Sara thought as she walked up Pennsylvania Avenue, past the White House, staring up at the second-floor windows. She could hear the sound of her footsteps echoing on the pavement and she found herself searching the windows for signs of life. She wondered if Dick Sayles was awake. Or Laura Sayles. . . . Did they sleep together? What was it like to sleep in the same bed with a man when he was in love with another woman? What was it like to be trapped in a role like First Lady when the honor and the achievement and all that it could be and mean was public and public only?

Across the street, a scattering of homeless men lay curled like scrunched-up rags under jerry-rigged canvas tents in Lafayette Park. The flower beds were bright with blue violets. She remembered how awed she had been years ago, the first time she ever walked this street, staring through this iron fence at the home of the President of the United States. How strange and thrilling it had seemed to be so close to power. She had stood here on this precise spot and wondered about what was happening at precisely that moment behind the serene white facade of the White House. Maybe it was a common fantasy. I don't care much any more, she thought. It isn't the power, it's the continuity that impresses me now. Presidents come and go; some are wiser and kinder than others, but it's the system that abides.

She turned the corner at the Treasury Building, reconnecting at the park with Pennsylvania Avenue, listening to the sound of her own footsteps on the quiet streets. She had always loved the broad expanses of space in Washington, the beautifully laid-out avenues lined with trees, the accessible sky. Sara was strolling slowly, thinking, losing herself in the morning. She turned toward the Capitol, moving past the old District Building at Fourteenth and Pennsylvania, and, on impulse, mounted the slender steps of what surely was the strangest "park" in all of Washington. A flat city block of concrete, it offered tourists an architectural map of the White House etched into the concrete. No trees here, just inscriptions etched into the slabs beneath her feet. There was one, her favorite, where was it? Idly, she wandered around the park, looking. It had been a long time, but there it was, reminding her once again of the yearning for home she had felt when she first read it: "How shall you act the natural man in this invented city, neither Rome nor home?"

Sara stared at the inscription for a long moment. How indeed did one act the "natural man" in this "invented city" of noise and power? I am still searching for the answer, she thought. Maybe I always will be. Reluctantly, she glanced at her watch. Nearly seven o'clock. Slowly she turned and began strolling back to her apartment, her step quickening as her mind began reviewing what she could expect today at the hearing.

She saw a *Post* deliveryman filling the newspaper box at the corner near her apartment. She waited until he finished, jumped in his truck, and rumbled off. She approached gingerly and stared at the headline: "FATHER ACCUSED OF MURDER ON EVE OF MARINO COURT HEARING." It was what she had expected. Her eye traveled to a side story: "Friends Deny Rumors about Nominee's Sex Life." God, what was that? But what shocked her, what drove all else from her mind, was the photograph. Someone had stolen a shot of her father through the window of his hospital room, caught him with his arm raised, shielding his eyes, as if against the intruding camera.

And right at that moment, staring at that picture, she let herself finally cry.

"They aren't going to get him," she whispered to herself. "And they aren't going to get me." Then her feet moved, miraculously hurrying her home, and somehow she was not stumbling or running, just hurrying—hurrying in this town that was neither Rome nor home; hurrying back for the fight of her life. Nobody would ever be able to say she didn't go down swinging.

CHAPTER 11

Sara took her seat at the witness table, folding her hands, vaguely aware that the too-bright green felt covering the table was slightly scratchy against her skin. Facing her, past the tangled wires of microphones, were the fourteen men and one woman there to judge whether she, Sara Marino, should be the next Justice of the Supreme Court of the United States. In back of her, jammed tight into the ornate space of the Caucus Room in the Russell Senate Office Building, a buzzing crowd of spectators craned their heads, peering past the fat Corinthian columns of black marble for a better view.

Leona and Maggie—who was clutching the morning newspaper with a frowning, distracted expression on her face—took their seats along the side of the hearing room, on a curving line of chairs with a full view of the committee members and profile views of those sitting at the witness table.

"Sara's too tense," Leona whispered.

Maggie nodded. She smoothed out the newspaper in her lap and once again scanned the stories dominating the front page.

Leona glanced down with a disparaging sniff. "How

does Sandi Snow get away with such garbage? An affair with Goodspeed? If that isn't the most ridiculous rumor! I'm furious about that woman tricking us into commenting."

"Sara's too smart to go into a spin over this," Maggie said quickly. "I'll bet what really upsets her is the picture of her father."

Leona gazed at the photo, and for a second she wondered what it would feel like if that picture were of Justin. What would he do? How would he react? She drew her lips tight and started to say something, but Maggie was glancing at her watch.

"Hold my seat, okay? I've got to make a phone call," she said, her voice low.

"Now?" Leona was surprised. "They're ready to begin. Look, there's Starling."

But Maggie seemed hardly to hear her. She slipped from her seat and started working her way through the crowd to a side door where she vanished from view.

"Order, please! Order!" All eyes suddenly were riveted on the round, pink face of Arthur Starling, the Senate Judiciary Committee chairman, as he took his seat and banged his gavel once against the thick mahogany table. Obeying the signal, the buzzing hornets' nest of snapping photographers circling Sara crouched reluctantly into place.

"Showtime," whispered Amos, who was sitting on one side of Sara, with Barney on the other. He leaned close to capture her full attention. "Starling will spend ten minutes congratulating himself, so don't fall asleep." He shot a glance at her face, pale and set under the lights. "Are you ready?"

"Yes."

"You sure?" This, from Barney, his voice concerned.

"Reasonably," she said. She pressed her fingernails into the felt, leaving tiny marks of stress that no cameraman would be alert enough to catch, and forced herself into automatic. She would go through the hearing, she'd answer the committee's questions, they could do what they wanted to do; she was sufficiently detached not to take any of it personally. She had studied the cases and boned up on all the relevant issues. She would say what she had to say and be done with it. If they wanted her, fine. If they didn't, too bad; she'd survive.

"You're sounding a little flat," Amos said. "Sara, listen to me. I know we went over all this yesterday, but listen again. They'll grill you this morning, but we've got eight votes and that's all we need. If we lose any, I've got two senators from the other side ready to switch if we really need them. Cliff Borden, by the way, has a tough race next year. Without a clear thumbs-down from Sayles, he won't desert you. The important thing is"—he shifted his bulk, squinting his eyes, the liver spots on his forehead particularly prominent—"don't get forced into arguing euthanasia, any aspect of it. Nobody can get you if you don't let them. You're strong on everything else."

She began methodically arranging the papers in front of her with the same precision she used in the courtroom. It helped. But this time, she wasn't in charge. "Did you see those demonstrators outside? Waving placards denouncing me and my father?"

"Hey, he just happens to be the flavor of the day."

His jaunty tone didn't quite work. What really bothered her at the moment was an almost enervating weariness. Her appetite for a fight . . . was it dwindling?

The sound of Starling's gavel pounding again on the table in front of them cut her thoughts short.

"Ladies and gentlemen, welcome," Starling began, his voice filling the room with the grandiloquence of a high school debate finalist. "What we do here today is critical to the operation of our democracy, and I must underscore the seriousness of the proceedings. Deciding whether to send a Supreme Court nominee to the full Senate for final approval is a grave responsibility. We have before us one of the essential jobs of this Republic, the review of the President's choice of a Justice of the Supreme Court of the United States, and it is my privilege. . . ."

"Starling loves the spotlight, but he also wants everybody to love *him,*" Amos said to Sara in a low tone. "Remember that. Turn it to your advantage."

"Starling is a popinjay." Maggie had materialized again so suddenly, Leona jumped at the sound of her voice. "He's bald, did you know that? If you look close, you can see the transplant plugs."

Maggie's mood struck Leona as oddly ebullient. "Where did you go?" she whispered.

Maggie put a finger to her lips. "Later," she said.

Starling droned on, his fellow panel members doodling on invisible pads, whispering discreetly to aides, or simply staring somberly in the direction of the television cameras. John Enright, the white-haired conservative who had never quite got over his disappointment after narrowly losing the presidency to Luke Goodspeed six years ago, looked particularly dyspeptic this morning. Lips pressed tight, eyes narrowed, he projected a perpetual image of political discontent. Across from him, on the majority's side, sat Cliff Borden, his thick, restless hands moving incessantly as he waited with ill-concealed impatience for Starling to wrap it up. It was no secret that Borden, a second-term senator elected on a reform platform from New Jersey, was bored with Judiciary.

Leona and Maggie heard the sound of chair legs scraping back and suddenly there was Carol, ignoring the frowns of Senate aides miffed to see her arriving late. She edged into her seat, shooting a glance in their direction. "A lot of ghosts in this room," she said, pointing to the thirty-five-foot ceiling. "McCarthy, Vietnam, Watergate. No wonder Starling's so impressed with himself he can't shut up."

"I think he's winding down."

The three women fell silent, hands falling composedly into their laps. The networks were taping. Their friend's career was on the line, they were here to show their support and all else was on hold. Sara cleared her throat; papers rustled. She was about to make her opening statement.

"Mr. Chairman, senators, ladies and gentlemen. . . ."

It was brief; only seven minutes long. Calm, forceful, well written. Sara talked about her origins, her values, what drew her to the world of law. But her remarks were delivered in so strangely flat a monotone that Carol, Maggie, and Leona stirred uncomfortably in their seats. They glanced at each other sideways.

"She's just going through the motions," a wondering Leona whispered. "She doesn't sound like Sara."

Maggie scanned the table, focusing on Barney's presence. "Barney will tell her," she said, more positively than she felt. Her fingers worked together, separated, then knit again. "He knows she has to juice it up for the cameras."

Carol eyed Barney warily. "Yeah; I guess."

Sara finished speaking, and Starling was now smiling reassuringly. He asked Sara about a speech she had given on the role of judicial activism in the rule of law. He coaxed from her an explanation of her philosophic approach to the Constitution. She answered each question matter-of-factly, her poise unruffled. Then came questions from the other committee members, in descending order of seniority, all easy. The one woman on the panel, a newly elected Florida lawyer with a forceful voice, read from a particularly eloquent ruling on civil rights Sara had written and asked if it truly reflected Sara's beliefs. Sara said it did.

"Looking good," Carol muttered. "Boring, but good."

And then it was the other side's turn. John Enright spoke first. He glared down at Sara like an avenging angel, a pair of tiny rimless glasses slipping perilously over the bridge of his nose. "Judge Marino," he said in a rolling baritone, waking everyone up, "do you believe in this country's legal commitment to the rights of the individual—particularly the right to life and liberty?"

"Yes, I do," Sara replied.

"Well, Judge, does that commitment protect the rights of aging people to life-saving support systems? Or any of us, for that matter?"

She was prepared. "I wouldn't be able to remain impartial as a judge if I commented on a particular case."

"But there are many cases, Judge. Any one of several misbegotten state laws allow some form of euthanasia now, and you, as a member of the Supreme Court, would eventually be called on to decide whether they are legal."

" 'Misbegotten?' " Sara smiled slightly. "That's your characterization, Senator, not necessarily mine."

"But surely you have a point of view? Surely you can share with this committee your personal views on the issue?"

"No, I cannot."

Enright frowned down at the script of questions and expected answers prepared in large print for him by his staff. She had answered predictably. "Have you ever stated, to your friends or in any private gathering, whether or not you support the practice of what they're calling 'mercy suicide'?"

"No."

Carol was squirming in her chair, willing herself not to leap up and present herself as a coach. "Why doesn't she explain more?" she complained to the others. "It's not just the committee, it's the whole damn country listening."

"She's better off keeping it short," Maggie whispered.

"Are you telling us you've never talked about the issue we're dealing with here? Giving government the right to kill off old people? What do you have to say? Millions of people watching right now want to know."

Sara laced her hands tight. She sensed Amos's uneasiness and heard Barney shuffling his feet behind her. They were afraid she might trap herself, but she would ease those fears. "Like many of those people, I'm working out my views privately, Senator," she said. "I've not adjudicated any cases in this area, but I assure you, my commitment is to the Constitution and each case has to be judged on its merits."

John Enright opened his mouth to continue, but Starling had had enough. He banged his gavel, smiling broadly for the cameras, signaling the hearing would break for lunch.

People stood, stretched. The room was again a buzz of sound.

"You're doing great," Amos said encouragingly, squeezing her arm. "A few more hours this afternoon and I guarantee, Starling will wrap this up. Come on, there's lunch in the War Room, cold sandwiches, stuff like that. Barney and I will deal with the press. You eat."

Sara smiled stiffly. Why, she wondered, were men always more optimistic than women? But then she felt a hand on her shoulder, and heard Maggie's voice.

"Want company?"

Sara looked up. She was here. They all were here. Maggie looked slightly manic, Leona wan but determined, and Carol determinedly cheerful.

"Not much of a Ladies' Lunch, but better than eating alone," Leona said.

"Look at it this way." Sara focused tightly on their presence. "We've just made it a movable feast."

"Cheaper than Galileo's," Carol chimed in.

Barney took in the scene with a distracted air. He sat back in his chair, his suit uncharacteristically rumpled, watching the four women until they disappeared into the crowd.

"Barney."

"Yeah, Amos?"

"You know what's wrong?"

"Yeah, I do."

"It's going too easily."

Barney sighed. "I know."

In the afternoon, Sara answered a stream of droning questions from the other committee members before Starling got down to business and called the first witness, a former law partner of Sara's, who proceeded to field several easy questions from the panel. Finished, the lawyer stepped down, stopping to shake Sara's hand.

"I'll be back," Maggie whispered, leaving her chair.

"Again?" Leona protested.

The chair between Leona and Carol was empty, and Leona sensed Carol gazing at her. *Don't ask about Justin, please,* she prayed. *Not yet. Leave it be, for now.*

"I'm not asking, Leona." It was as if Carol had read her mind. "I just want to tell you, I think I know a little of what you're going through. I wasn't able to say it yesterday."

"Thanks," Leona said. She suddenly felt calm.

The two women leaned back then to hear a former law school classmate of Sara's answer another round of easy questions. It was four-thirty and Cliff Borden was glancing surreptitiously at his watch. Soon, it would all be over.

Maggie ignored the irritated glances of aides lining the walls near the door and squeezed past, hurrying to a small bank of aging phone booths against the wall outside the hearing room. Her fingers were trembling as she dialed. Checking Michael's computer disks had brought up all sorts of interesting information, and the pieces were beginning to fall together. Si Posner? That guy was notorious for putting together the type of shady business deals Sara opposed. If she could get him to admit to dealing with Patton. . . .

"Hello?"

Good, she had his direct line. She wouldn't have to deal with a secretary. Now, everything depended on surprise.

"Mr. Posner, I'm a reporter for the *Post* and we understand you are actively working to derail the Marino nomination," she said rapidly. "If you want a chance to talk about your role in the campaign to destroy her, sir, this is it."

"My role!" He was sputtering. "What are you talking about? I don't mess in government affairs, where did you get that?"

"Jack Patton's obviously connected to you, sir, that's no secret any more." Keep talking, she prayed. Confirm what I'm suspecting, confirm it, confirm it.

"There's no connection whatsoever! He will *not* be working here, I assure you."

"Working, you said?"

"Yeah, that's what I said. If he wants out of politics, he'll have to go somewhere else. We're talking to several people about the presidency of this company."

"Was he offered the job?"

A short silence. "Maybe he thought he was, but he was mistaken. Goodbye." The phone clicked off.

Maggie turned from the phone, her hands sweaty, absolutely elated she hadn't lost her touch—and there, through the glass door, she saw Jack Patton staring at her from across the hall. His face was pasty white. For a panicky moment she thought he had overheard her, and then she began thinking like a reporter again. "Wait!" she called, half tumbling out of the booth. "Wait, I have a question!"

He vanished through a door, but it didn't matter. He'd have to talk sooner or later. Buoyed by the almost-forgotten feeling of an adrenaline rush, Maggie edged herself back through the crowd into the hearing room—just in time to see an aide in a starched white shirt rush in and bend low over Senator Starling, whispering urgently. Starling's face fell as he stared at the slip of paper thrust into his hand. He cleared his throat and hammered with his gavel for the room's full attention.

"We have an unexpected witness," he announced, looking upset. The room became unnaturally still. Barney and Amos turned to each other, then froze. Even Borden looked up from his doodling, pencil poised in mid-air.

The cameras swung to the left. A thin woman, slightly arthritic hands fiddling with the buttons of a bright pink sweater, stepped out through a door and stood as if nailed to the floor by the shadowless TV lights.

Sara shut her eyes, waiting for the name, knowing already.

"Our next witness is Mrs. Ginny Boseley."

Sara's eyes flew open and she stared at the woman accusing her father of murder.

"Patton's lost it," Carol breathed.

"This makes the President look terrible," Leona said in shock. "Patton must be desperate."

"More than you know," Maggie said, slipping again into her seat.

Mrs. Boseley cast her eyes around the room nervously as Chairman Starling jumped up to shake her hand and thank her profusely for sharing her valuable time with the committee. Sara had the fleeting sympathy you would have for a fish arcing its way through the air toward the bottom of a rowboat. What a catch for Jack Patton. Looking slightly shell-shocked, Ginny Boseley walked toward the witness table, guided by the discreet hand of a third-tier committee aide whose name none of Sara's friends knew.

"He can't possibly pretend he's not sabotaging Sara," Carol muttered.

Haltingly, Ginny Boseley began to speak without prompting. "I'm here to tell what happened to my sister, not to say bad things about Judge Marino," she began. "I don't know her, but I sure know her father."

"And you are telling us your testimony speaks to vital character issues concerning the nominee, is that right, Mrs. Boseley?" Starling prompted. He had seen Patton through the door; the cryptic White House message in his pocket had told him what was expected of him. When in doubt, play it safe.

Mrs. Boseley drew herself up straight, exhibiting an unexpected and impressive sense of dignity. "Yes," she said slowly. "I wouldn't have known how to say it like that, but that's right. I know what he thinks and what he does, and if she helped him in any way or agreed with him, then everybody ought to know, because she's a judge and she'll make important decisions and . . ." She glanced at Starling for direction.

Barney was leaning over Sara's chair, whispering. His hand hovered over her shoulder for an instant before dropping to his side. Sara never turned.

Carol leaned forward, cupping her face with her hands. "I hope Amos is up to this," she murmured. "He can't forget the cameras for a single second. Everything shows, every fear, every worry."

"Then watch your own expression," Leona said guardedly. "There could be a camera on us."

Carol straightened instantly. Since when had Leona become so savvy?

"Mr. Chairman." It was Amos's deep, growling voice cutting through the buzz of sound that followed Mrs. Boseley's words.

Starling frowned. "Yes, Senator?"

"This witness says she doesn't know Judge Marino. She has no knowledge of her qualifications for this appointment, and therefore no light to shed on those qualifications or the lack of them. We were not advised—"

"Character, Senator! Mrs. Boseley's testimony goes to the central issue of character, which we all know is critical to any government appointment or Senate election, for that matter. Don't you agree, Senator?" Starling smiled widely, clearly assuring Amos he was still his pal, and then simultaneously launched into a heartfelt speech about the importance of the "little people of this country" coming forward to have their say.

"Wonder what Jack promised him?" Carol murmured, grinding her teeth. "That naval base they're closing in his state?"

"Look," Leona said suddenly, tugging at Carol. "It's Jack. Right here, in the hearing room."

Patton stood by the door, making no attempt to move further into the room; arms folded, expression imperturbable. Maggie's eyes traveled to Mrs. Boseley, sitting uncomfortably before an intimidating tangle of microphones and wires. Mrs. Boseley glanced toward the door, as if by prearranged signal, just as Jack Patton folded his arms and gave her a small, reassuring smile: just the slightest stretching of his upper lip. His eyes continued around the room, resting finally, with minimal expression, on Sara.

Carol looked him over with interest. "A real high-wire act." She was talking as much to herself as to the others.

"More than you know," Maggie said again, this time almost inaudibly.

Leona glanced at her curiously. But Mrs. Boseley was being sworn, her angular face frozen in stiff salute to the encroaching cameras. The three women turned their attention back to the witness table.

"Now, just begin at the beginning," Starling said. "Just tell us, in your own words, and please don't feel intimidated, we're here to help you. . . ."

"Can I start, sir?" Mrs. Boseley cut in. "I want to say my piece and be done with it."

A ripple of giggles floated across the room at the sight of the smile vanishing from Starling's pink face. "Of course," he said immediately. "Go right ahead."

The entire room was full. Ginny Boseley had been a powerful witness. There was not a soul in the room who didn't now have a vivid image of the sick young woman whose life had been snuffed out on the day of her daughter's tenth birthday party. Not a soul in the room who couldn't imagine what it must have been like for the child to find her mother dead, the sickroom filled with brightly colored balloons. Even Starling seemed momentarily at a loss for the right words to break the stillness.

"Judge Marino."

Sara lifted her face, exposing a profile that could have been cut from stone. Maggie had warned her. The cameras would reveal no private pain—she could make sure of that, if nothing else.

"Do you have anything to say?"

"I don't recognize the man Mrs. Boseley has described. My father is a healer, not a killer."

Come on, Sara, stand up for yourself. Maggie's hands were clenched so tightly the blood stopped circulating. Give them more, make them hear you; this woman's pain is real, we can all see that, but it's fed by your enemies.

"What are your views on this, Judge Marino? Is this sad tale a tale of murder?" John Enright's sonorous voice was heavy with accusation. Amos leaped up to object, but Sara spoke first.

"My views will be guided by the law," she replied. The room waited, but Sara said nothing more. She was still absorbing the image of the scene Ginny Boseley had so vividly described; thinking about a young woman's impending death; thinking about the false cheer of all those balloons. . . .

"Mr. Chairman."

This time it was Amos's voice that cut across the room. He stood, heaving himself up from his chair like a roused lion.

"Yes, Senator Berman?" Starling raised an eyebrow.

"Senator, I respectfully suggest that this hearing be recessed until tomorrow morning. Judge Marino will be prepared to answer any and all questions at that time."

"Judge?" Starling said, looking directly at Sara.

"That's fine, Mr. Chairman."

"All right. It's five o'clock anyway." Starling raised his gavel and brought it down hard on his desk. "We reconvene tomorrow at nine a.m." He stood, looking uncharacteristically relieved to get himself out of the spotlight as the room exploded in noise. Reporters pressed forward in an awkward scramble to reach Ginny Boseley, but her escort whisked her through a side door and out of sight within seconds. Flanked by Amos and Barney, Sara quickly exited through another door.

"Sara wants us over tonight," Leona said hurriedly to the others as they worked their way through the crush. Carol and Maggie nodded.

Suddenly, Carol saw an aide—Molly White—beckoning urgently from another door. "See you there," she said. With a quick wave, she broke from her friends and elbowed her way forward.

"In the next office," hissed Molly, glancing around to make sure she wasn't overheard. "Hurry, she's really upset."

"Who is? What are you talking about?"

Molly lowered her head. "Mrs. Paige," she whispered. "She's here, next door."

Carol wasn't sure she was ready for this. She squared her shoulders, reminding herself to proceed cautiously, and followed Molly. Surely—if she was very careful—she could tell Mrs. Paige that Faith had not recklessly squandered the family fortune. Maybe that would diminish the woman's fury.

She opened the door to the next room and saw Mrs. Paige's slight frame standing silhouetted by the window, staring outward. Quickly, Carol closed the door behind her.

Mrs. Paige spoke without bothering to turn around. "You wonder why I am here. I'm here because I don't sleep very well any more."

"I'm sorry," Carol managed.

"Don't be sorry. I don't want pity." The older woman turned now, her shoulders fragile, yet rigid. "This isn't the way it should have ended."

"You mean Faith's life?" Carol's head was still full of the day's events and she felt slightly muddled.

"My family. It ends with Faith. It's over. Her great-grandfather was Lawton Paige, you know. A fine, very influential man." Mrs. Paige seemed in some kind of daze.

"Your family certainly has a distinguished history." She would be agreeable, no matter what.

"More than you probably realize." Mrs. Paige seemed almost to preen. "So many accomplished men, honorable people, all of them. I cannot believe . . ." She covered her face with her hands and Carol stepped forward, wanting to do something to help.

"Faith didn't gamble your money away, Mrs. Paige. She tried to invest it wisely, but an unscrupulous . . ."

But Mrs. Paige hardly seemed to hear. "I cannot believe my own daughter brought down such shame on their memory," she broke in.

Carol froze.

"Oh, you think that's insensitive of me, don't you? You women with your careers, supporting each other, telling private things—that's not the way it was in my day. When you married, your loyalties went to your husband and family, and everything else was secondary. I've read about your separation from your husband—how can you stand it? How can you live with people knowing you failed?"

Carol was so taken aback by this outburst, she could say nothing.

But Mrs. Paige didn't notice. "I've lived my life honorably," she went on. "No one could ever accuse me of bringing dishonor to my husband." Her eyes were streaked with red.

Carol was not feeling sympathetic any more. "It wasn't

your daughter who brought shame down on your family,'' she said stubbornly. ''She—''

''And getting herself mixed up with a married man! Oh, I'm sure he was, the man I told you about. That was like Faith. Why didn't she go with someone acceptable and get married like—like a normal woman?''

''Maybe if she had had a normal father . . .'' Carol couldn't believe her own words, and a pulse began hammering in her left temple. She had blown it again, this time probably for good. Mrs. Paige was staring at her now with something akin to horror.

''I forget, you believed her. Well, I didn't.'' Mrs. Paige drew herself up to her tallest height.

''Do you now?''

The room reverberated with tension. Was she being cruel, Carol thought with fleeting confusion; was this too much to ask of any woman? Who was she to force this on Mrs. Paige when she still had her own doubts? Who had given her the right to exact revenge for Faith?

''Don't ask me unanswerable questions.'' The voice was suddenly old and soft, barely audible.

Carol drew a deep breath. ''Mrs. Paige, I owe you an apology. I'm sorry, I shouldn't have thrown that at you.''

''I throw it at myself every day. You haven't caused me additional pain, Congresswoman. Nothing can cause me additional pain.''

Carol hung her head.

''I have brought something for you.'' Mrs. Paige turned to a chair behind her, picked up her purse, and clicked open the heavy gold clasp. She withdrew the cream-colored envelope, holding it almost lovingly in her hands for a fraction of a second before turning back and handing it to Carol.

''I had no right to keep this,'' she said simply. ''No right to deny my daughter the last word. Just take it, please. I will spend the rest of my life trying to reconcile my loyalties and''—she faltered before going on—''and my feelings.''

''Thank you, Mrs. Paige.''

''Goodbye, Congresswoman Lundeen.''

''If there is . . .''

''Tell me nothing.''

The coffee table in Sara's small living room was littered with the aromatic remains of two large double cheese and pepperoni pizzas as the four friends leaned back and surveyed each other. They were groping their way through a strange, emotion-laden evening. They had begun by reviewing the events of the hearing and doing their best to bolster Sara's spirits, who was drained of fight by Ginny Boseley's haunting story. But there was much more they needed to do. Finally, they began sharing with each other all the fragments of information that, put together, might tell them what they needed to know about Faith.

Leona told them about her husband's complicity in ruining Faith's fortune. Sara took a deep breath, glanced at Maggie, and told them about Faith's affair with Dick Sayles. Then, finally, Carol brought out the cream envelope and held it in her hands, telling them haltingly about what she knew and what Mrs. Paige feared was in the letter.

They sat silently now, looking more into the past than at each other.

''We've kept a lot of secrets,'' Sara said slowly.

''We've had to.''

''Faith was trapped by her past, her heart.''

''And her lost money,'' said Leona, her voice wavering slightly. She couldn't take her eyes off the letter in Carol's hands.

''You weren't able to do anything about that,'' Sara said.

''I was blind as a stone, Sara. Don't tell me differently.''

''If you were, then I was a coward,'' Sara said, calmly starting to gather up the congealing remainders of the pizza.

She felt oddly disembodied right now.

"That's ridiculous."

"Not at all. If you should have known what Justin was doing, then I should have confronted Sayles head-on about his affair with Faith. I *knew* what he was doing. It's worse."

"Okay." Leona waved a hand with a defeated smile, and leaned over to help Sara scoop up the last crumbs from the table. She still felt angry with herself in a way Sara never could understand.

Carol hugged her knees, bending her head. "As long as we're into confessions, here's mine." She took a deep breath. "I didn't believe Faith when she told me what her father had done to her. I thought I was humoring her, actually, but Faith probably saw right through me. I couldn't believe it of her father—one of the most respected people in town? It was too incredibly strange."

"Did she guess?" They all knew the answer to that. Carol was not a woman who hid her feelings well.

"Yes, sure. I think she did. Probably why she never spoke of it again."

"Do you believe her now?" Maggie's voice was curious, unjudgmental. She was asking herself the same question.

"Yes. I mean—I think I do." Carol shook her head with a certain helplessness. "Who knows for sure? It's this retrieved memory thing: She said she had blocked it out and then it came rushing back. Maybe she believed it, but it wasn't true. Could that have pushed her over the edge? I mean—*was* she mentally ill? But I can't tolerate Mrs. Paige denying everything. She makes up her own truths."

"We have to hear Faith's side," Maggie said quietly.

It was as if everything was suspended and nothing more could happen until one of them slit that envelope open. They fell silent again.

"I'm afraid of what I'll learn about Justin," Leona said. She saw no reason to deny the truth.

Sara wiped her hands on a towel and sat down opposite her friends. "We may not find what we fear or what we expect," she said.

It was the right thing to say and it actually unfroze Carol's fingers. "Here goes," she said, ripping open the envelope. A single sheet of paper fell into her lap. Carol picked it up and hesitated. Then she handed it to Sara, as if it were the natural thing to do.

Slowly, Sara began to read.

"My dear friends," the letter began:

By the time you read this, you will probably know all my secrets. Part of me hopes you won't be too shocked, and part of me hopes you will be. Because if you are, maybe I mean something after all. How has this happened? I'm drowning in anger and fear and I see no way out. Should I clutch at all of you? To what purpose? You can't help me. Not you, Sara, or you, Carol. And the cost to Leona would be enormous.

Leona shuddered as Sara doggedly read on:

You all think of me as witty and clever, but I can't keep up the act any more. I'm trapped by someone who would rather ruin me than let me go, my mother's money is stupidly lost, and everything I value is crumbling. Sara, I wish I had your serenity. And Maggie—I wish I had your ability to step away and observe. But I don't. Pills don't help any more. I can't keep demanding attention, I can't keep leaning. If I weren't crying all the time, I would laugh: here I am, on top of the world, and it means nothing. Me, the lady who prided herself on being tough. That's the biggest joke of all. May you all never know.

Sara looked up, tears in her eyes. "She's signed it. That's all."

"That's all?" Maggie found herself swallowing a cry of protest. "Is it dated?"

"No date. She could have written it last month or the day she died."

"But—is it a suicide note? Is she telling us she's going to kill herself? What is she *saying?*"

"She's saying she's trapped."

"Depressed; she was horribly depressed."

Carol had curled herself into a tight, nearly fetal position on the couch. "No. She's saying we let her down."

The room was totally quiet, so quiet they could hear each other breathing. The paper in Sara's hand trembled as Maggie stared straight ahead and Leona raised a hand over her eyes. It was Sara who spoke finally.

"My serenity?" she whispered. "*Serenity?*"

"She felt abandoned; not tough, abandoned," offered Maggie.

"By us," Carol said, her voice faltering.

"She wanted to tell me what Justin was doing to her," Leona said, wiping a tear from her eye. "How could she hold that back? She must have thought I wouldn't believe her—but I would have helped her, I swear I would have."

Maggie's response was immediate and heartfelt. "You come through, Leona. I know."

"We should have guessed."

"She must have thought we were all shallow."

"No, she was just afraid."

"Don't you see?" said Maggie, almost frightened now. "Don't you see why she died?"

A moan broke from Leona's lips as the others stayed silent.

"She died because she thought she had no friends. That's what we've known, *that's* what we've been avoiding. We weren't friends." She was trying valiantly not to cry. What good would it do to cry? "We've only become friends after her death; we've only become real friends because she died."

"Oh, God," breathed Leona.

It was as if time and space had collapsed in on them all and for an instant they felt like trees bending before a silent wind.

Sara finally broke the silence, determined to anchor them again. "Maybe you're right, Maggie. But if she really wanted to commit suicide, we probably couldn't have stopped her. Just because we keep thinking we could have—"

"Maybe not." Carol sat up now, pulling her body forward on the sofa with heavy resignation. "But I knew more than the rest of you. I should have helped more than I did."

Sara shook her head with real vigor. "I knew about her affair, and what did I do? Not enough, I know that. But then, what could I have done? Or you, Carol? Faith chose to confide in us differently; nothing got pieced together in time."

"Well," Maggie interrupted, "I think she wanted to reach beneath the surface, she wanted to be closer to us, but everything operated against that. . . ." They considered that silently as Maggie finished her thought. "There's another possibility. Maybe I'm wrong; I hope I am. But maybe we weren't that—significant."

"How do we know?"

"If that's true, it's worse."

Again a silence, broken this time by Leona. "Maggie's talking about humility," she said. "We're not in charge of what happens. I think I understand."

"Well, the fact is, Sara's right. We'll never know." Maggie's flat reminder stopped them dead.

Never to know? When they were people committed to facts and conclusions? Faith's voice was with them, ringing in their heads, reminding them of who she had been: The perfect, beautiful creature, buoyed through life by success and luck, envied, enjoyed; the kind of friend who made one look good. The ultimate Washington friend. Their friend—an image, ultimately unknown and unknowable. Handing them finally her pain and anger, without charade. Too late. They stole quick glances at each other, thinking of other shared fragments of pride, of self-doubt.

"So maybe we never piece it all together." Carol suddenly swiveled in Maggie's direction. "Or maybe you do?"

Maggie caught her breath; this was the first reference to her book in many days. She should have talked to Carol about it more; now she had to face the edge of challenge in her friend's voice. "I have something to tell you . . ." she began.

"Let's not talk about the book," Sara said firmly. "You don't have to, Maggie. Let's take one thing at a time."

Leona glanced at the clock over the mantel. "There's nothing we can do for Faith now," she said. "It's Sara we need to worry about."

Carol nodded. "Let's turn on the news." The reminder was like a shock of cold air, bringing them back to the task at hand. Leona arose, walked over to the television set, and switched it on. All attention was diverted for the moment to reliving the excruciating reality of their long day on the Hill.

It was bad. Ginny Boseley's halting, earnest voice and the sight of her nervously clasping hands as she told her story made for powerful television. There was no way of softening the impact. Starling's stunned face ("horrified," according to Tom Brokaw's voice-over) as Mrs. Boseley came in the room filled the screen, followed by a quick cut to Sara's white, drawn face—all before the opening camera zoomed in on Brokaw at the anchor desk.

"Try CBS," Carol said sharply.

Maggie switched in time to catch Dan Rather's gloomy

summation: "Votes are being hedged tonight on Capitol Hill as Judge Sara Marino fights for her judicial life," he announced. "The nation's fear of forced euthanasia is at this point hopelessly mixed with the strange saga of her father, Dr. George Marino, who now stands accused of actually murdering a patient."

Sara cupped her chin in her hands as she listened.

"We now go live to the White House where a press conference with the President's chief of staff is about to begin."

Carol jumped, hitting her knee against the glass coffee table with a loud smack. "Moving fast, Jack," she murmured, rubbing her knee. "You're moving fast."

Jack Patton's face, somber, heavy with the burdens of his task, filled the screen. He read a short statement confirming the president's "ongoing support" for Judge Marino, concluding with the hope that the hearing tomorrow "would resolve all questions and allow this fine jurist to take her place on the Court." He paused. "Any questions?"

"Sir, would the President have pursued her nomination if he had known in advance about her father?"

"We can't answer a hypothetical question," Patton snapped.

"Are you going to dump her?" That one was from Brit Hume, blunt as usual.

"Certainly not. At this point, we're totally, one hundred percent committed to Judge Marino's appointment. She was President Goodspeed's choice and President Sayles remains behind her all the way."

"That's it," Carol said calmly. "They're telling you you're dead. My guys say calls are flooding in to the radio talk shows; they're all mad as hell."

"That guy is pond scum," Leona said, clenching her teeth.

"Oh, now, don't despair too quickly," Maggie said. If

the others hadn't been so engrossed, they would have noted she said it with inappropriate calmness.

Sara did not immediately react. "I'm thinking," she said finally. "I have a plan for tomorrow that might work. Jack can't hold this together much longer."

So do I, Maggie thought. The phone pealed sharply and she picked it up, wondering if it would be ringing the rest of the night.

"Maggie, this is Barney."

"Hi, Barney, hang on." Maggie silently handed the phone to Sara.

Sara murmured a greeting. Then, "Can I call you back later? Yes—in about an hour." She listened closely for a moment, then hung up and looked around at her friends, a quizzical look on her face.

"More secrets?" Leona asked curiously.

"Not really."

Maggie cleared her throat, ready to take the floor. "Listen," she said. "Jack Patton has a big surprise coming tomorrow morning."

They all turned to her curiously.

"I know why he wants you out, Sara," Maggie said. All heads turned in her direction. Her smile started slow, then widened. This would be almost fun. "It's all because of a man named Si Posner." She proceeded to give full details about her phone booth interview—complete with the sighting of Jack Patton—and then told them what she had discovered.

Carol let out a whoop. "He's dead, he's gone, he's buried, and he doesn't even know it yet!"

"Watch out, Carol, you're slopping the coffee all over," protested Maggie with the first lightheartedness of the night. She glanced sideways at Sara, who hadn't reacted with quite as much exuberance as Carol and Leona. "I'm going in to the paper pretty soon, it's a free-lance piece, but they want me to write it there."

The others exchanged knowing glances. "Does this mean you're going back to reporting?" Carol asked.

"Maybe. I don't know yet." Maggie looked at Sara and felt a sudden stab of worry. Why wasn't she more excited?

Sara caught her glance. Slowly, she rubbed the back of her neck with one hand, wishing she could ease the pressure in her head. "It's terrific, Maggie," she said. "But something else has happened."

"What?"

"Barney had bad news. We've lost key votes on the committee. Cliff Borden's pulling out. Patton may go down, but it looks like I will, too."

The four of them fell silent.

"No," said Maggie. She felt close to tears.

"I've got an idea," Carol said finally.

"Anything's welcome." Sara straightened up, trying to erase the slump from her posture.

"I'll make a trade-off for the votes. I can dump a bill."

"Which one?"

"Nursing homes." Carol's voice was a little too casual. "They tabled it on me, but I've almost got it pried loose. It'll cause old Enright a lot of trouble when it reaches the Senate. I could get him to vote for Elvis himself if I backed off a fight."

"Don't you dare," Sara said with unexpected firmness. "That bill is too important. We know what you've put into it."

"Nothing's sacred in this business."

"Carol, you talk so tough. And aren't you the one who told me a while back I should cut my losses and give up?"

"I was wrong."

"Carol, do you know that we see through you?"

For an instant, Carol looked a bit taken aback. But her mind was clearly on something else. "Sara, can I have the letter?" she said abruptly.

"Sure," Sara said, startled. "Why?"

"Because Faith's death doesn't have to be so damn senseless and stupid. There should be some justice, for God's sake! Dick Sayles should read this. I think he should be forced to face what he did."

"I think so, too," Maggie chimed in.

"So do I," said Leona.

"Okay, so we all want to shove Faith's letter under his nose," Maggie broke in. "But who's going to give it to him? Everybody's working for Patton, now."

"Oh, no, they aren't." They were treated to one of Carol's most triumphant winner's circle smiles. "There's one route around Patton and I know how to use it. Trust me."

They were all looking at Sara now.

"We can really give Faith the last word," Leona said softly. "Do what we wish we could have done before."

Carol was still thinking, her brow furrowed. "What's the worst that can happen? Sayles is going to let public opinion take you down unless you pull off a miracle tomorrow. This won't change that—it's out of his hands. We're not blackmailing him. There's no payoff, unfortunately, and he'll know there isn't."

"So why are we doing it?"

Briefly, Carol reflected. "To make him face up to what happens when you play around with someone's life."

"Maybe to get revenge."

This time, Leona spoke up. "What's wrong with revenge?" she said softly.

Carefully, Sara folded the note and tucked it back into its envelope. She stared at their names, printed so meticulously. Faith had wanted something to come out of writing that note. . . .

This was about survival. Not hers, but—in a sense—Faith's.

Without a word, she handed the letter to Carol, who stood and tucked it into her handbag. "I'll see you all tomorrow," Carol said, very quietly—for her.

* * *

Much later that night, Carol stood alone in one of the reception rooms of the West Wing, trying not to dwell on how many chits she had pulled to be here, at this hour, with this request. It would work or it wouldn't, and there was no use thinking at this late point about the possible downside. She had done it fast, determined not to talk herself out of it, figuring that, after all, they had served on that nursing home commission together. Still, an interior voice warned of the contradictions, the ramifications; Jesus, the political dangers, the backlash possibilities.

"Congresswoman Lundeen?"

"Yes?"

She was looking directly into the grumpy, tired face of Laura Sayles's chief aide.

"You said this was important?"

"Very."

"All right. She'll see you, but only for a few moments."

Carol followed her through a corridor, up the broad stairs to the president's living quarters, and into a small room with an overstuffed Victorian look where Laura Sayles—a plain black cardigan hanging over her thin shoulders—stood waiting for her. Carol licked her lips; she had no stomach for this. She felt herself losing her nerve.

"Hello, Mrs. Sayles."

"Hello, Congresswoman."

"I'm not sure my visit here is a good idea," she started.

"I'm quite sure it has to do with Faith Paige," Laura Sayles interrupted. Carol noticed she had her hands braced against the back of a chair, but the expression on the First Lady's face was reasonably serene. "It's okay, you know. I think I half-expected you—or one of her other friends."

"Faith wrote a letter," Carol said simply. "To us."

"So she told you about her affair with my husband?" Laura Sayles hardly blinked.

Carol couldn't help feeling a bit shocked. "Not directly," she managed.

The president's wife held out her hand. "But you want me to see it."

"We want him to see it. And you're the only person who would give it to him."

"Are you really sure about that?"

Carol respected the challenge in the other woman's eyes. "I can only ask," she said. She stepped forward and handed Mrs. Sayles the letter.

Laura Sayles slowly removed a pair of glasses from her sweater pocket. With one hand, she raised them to her face and slipped them on as she stared at the envelope for what seemed to Carol a very long time.

"I envy you and your friends, you know," she said. "You have so much freedom."

"Freedom to mess up, too."

They exchanged rather wan smiles.

"Thank you, Congresswoman."

Carol nodded and turned to leave, knowing she had been gently dismissed.

On the other side of town, at about the same time, Maggie pushed the "send" button on her borrowed terminal in *The Washington Post* newsroom. Her story on Jack Patton was complete. She leaned back in the chair, surveying the room. This familiar room. . . .

"Great story, Maggie." The reporter at the next desk grinned and extended his hand. "Nice to see you back."

"Thanks." She was slightly startled as they shook hands. She looked up. An editor was beckoning her from his glass cage. She rose and began weaving her way through the clutter of desks occupied at this late hour by only a few reporters.

"Hi, Stedman, where the hell have you been?"

"Nice to see you, kid."

Slightly dazed now, Maggie walked into the editor's office. "Good job," he said quietly. "Good reporting. You're still a natural for this business, you know."

"Thank you." She said it as casually as she could. But when she walked out, Maggie allowed herself to feel, for just this moment anyhow, very, very satisfied with herself.

The grandfather clock had just struck midnight, off by a couple of minutes. Leona checked the chimes against her watch. The clock probably needed cleaning again. Nothing in this house went for long without demanding attention. She moved about the library, finishing off a third cup of coffee, trying not to fidget as she perused the shelves and shelves of books. Some of them were old friends: dog-eared novels from college, a first edition of Edith Wharton's *House of Mirth;* others, never read: fat, daunting political biographies—I only pretended to enjoy them, she admitted to herself, because it made Justin happy. Then there were the Robert Parker mysteries, good for a quick night's read . . . she had never got around to giving them away to a school or a library. Her eyes stopped, resting on the faded white spine of a particular tall, slender volume on a bottom shelf. That old thing, still here. . . . Slowly, Leona pulled out her wedding album and opened it up.

It was as if the memories were real again, rising like pale smoke from the pages. She sank onto the sofa with the album open in her lap. There she was, in that goofy short wedding gown. Mother had been right, a long, classic style would've been better, it looked so dated now. She turned the page, gazing at a young, fresh-faced Justin, laughing, looking perfectly comfortable in black-tie—Justin was born for black-tie, she thought with a smile.

She heard a footstep behind her and looked up to see Justin in the doorway.

"What have you got there?"

"Our wedding album," she said simply. "Remember,

Justin? How it almost rained and the caterer got drunk?"

Justin's stiff demeanor loosened slightly. "You said you could do a better job than he could."

"And I did, didn't I?"

"You put him out of business pretty fast." He took a step closer, watching her with wary eyes.

"See?" She held up the book, her face bright. "Remember sweeping me up in that kiss at the altar?"

"It was the thing to do."

"Oh, come on, Justin. You wanted to."

They stared at each other awkwardly. "Have it your way, Leona," he said with a forced smile. As if to offer a touch more concession, he moved forward again, close enough this time to glance at the picture. "I had more hair, then."

"How did we get so off-course?" she asked meditatively.

"You exaggerate, as usual. Am I in for another scene?"

"Values," she said. "I'm talking about values."

"You've made the mistake of concerning yourself with things you don't understand."

"Justin, I think you really believe that." Quietly, she closed the album. "It doesn't frighten me any more. It makes me sad."

Justin was moving through the room now, straightening the magazines on the coffee table; lining them up with fastidious exactitude. He looked very busy. "You can be a charming woman when you want to be, Leona," he said. "But this talk about values is out of place. I know you. You do not have the guts to make a strong stand on anything, so why not let this one alone? Now, there's a wonderful place I've looked into, out in Iowa, where you can go for a month or two. It'll do wonders."

"To dry out? Is that it?"

"Surely you aren't about to deny you have a serious drinking problem? That would be a dreadful mistake, dear."

Ah, the tone—the authority, the tolerance of her frailties, the edge of contempt—it was all there in his voice, as it had been so many times before. And it didn't matter. "It's only fair to warn you, Justin," she said, "I've done what I had to do."

His hands froze. He said nothing, waiting.

"I told Michael about your involvement in issuing phony stock for the land you bought with Faith's money. I told him how Faith got sucked into it, and I gave him enough evidence from your files to build a pretty solid case against you. As I'm sure you're aware, he knows what to do with it."

He was staring at her, his eyes so dark with stunned malevolence she could barely see them. How they used to dance. . . . Strangely, she felt no triumph, no sense of vindication, just a deep and perhaps permanent sadness.

"You'll go down with me," he said.

"No, Justin. I'll survive." Leona rose, swiftly replacing the album in its place on the shelf, running the tip of her pale pink lacquered fingernail down its spine, tracing the lettering for one last time. "I've left my lawyer's settlement offer on your desk; you'll find it's quite modest. By the way, I don't want this house. If you sell it, you can raise considerable cash. For your lawyer's fees." She turned to face him. "You'll need it. Michael's working on a story right now."

Laura Sayles paced the length of the upstairs White House sitting room, pulling a thin robe close against the air-conditioned chill. It was already midnight, an hour now since Carol Lundeen had departed, and she had reread Faith's letter several times. A twist of pain wrenched through her stomach, but it wasn't unexpected or unfamiliar. What was done was done. There was a certain peace, actually.

Back and forth, back and forth—she stared at the paintings, the eclectic mix of functional equipment and White House antiques . . . it wasn't really her home yet. Everything here belonged to someone else's life. What would Kate Goodspeed do if she were the one pacing now? At night, sometimes, she felt the presence of the defeated and the dead in these quarters . . . too much so. But Faith was not of this historic, whispering crew. She existed now only in this letter. Laura remembered her every movement, her every gesture—all memorized almost surreptitiously over the years of Dick's secret affair. And now here was her voice once more. Pitiful, sad; but no longer hated and envied. Yes, I did hate her, Laura Sayles told herself; admit it. Who would ever believe she had hated herself too—because she could not begin to compete with the perfect Faith Paige?

She stopped pacing. Dick's right, she thought. Here is where we are, and here is where—for now—we both must stay. He should see this. Her robe whipping around her legs, Laura Sayles headed quickly for her husband's bedroom.

Dick Sayles was in bed, reading. He closed the book without a word as his wife walked into the room.

"Carol Lundeen brought me this," she said, as she stretched out her left hand with the letter.

Gingerly, he took it.

"It won't bite, Dick. But it's something you should read." She stood waiting, saying nothing, watching his face.

Sayles read. A long moment ticked by. His hand was shaking as he handed the letter back to her. There was in the gesture an element of such resignation that Laura felt a lurch of compassion.

"I shouldn't have accused you of killing her." It was very hard to say. "But you've been so detached—so remote. I've wanted to hurt you so you'd wake up."

He looked at her, an expression she couldn't identify

flickering across his eyes. He said nothing.

Laura Sayles tried again. "What this letter tells me is that Faith was depressed and maybe even mentally ill. I can see that." She tapped the letter with her finger. "She was troubled by—many things. But you, Dick, you were once a brave man. That wound in your leg didn't come from running away from trouble. If I have to put this to rest, then you do, too. If I could at least be proud of you again. . . ."

"Laura, Laura." He was shaking his head with such despondency, she became alarmed.

"What is it?"

Dick Sayles pushed back the covers and arose. He pulled on a robe lying across the back of a chair and faced his wife. She hardly recognized his face.

"There was another letter," he said finally.

"What?"

He opened the drawer of his nightstand and pulled out a second cream-colored envelope, identical to the first, which he handed to his wife. "I found it in my desk the day after she died. I've been trying to live with it."

Laura Sayles opened it and found herself staring at a piece of stationery engraved with Faith's name. Scrawled on the card were three stark words:

"You did it."

Laura looked up at him, horrified. In one searing instant, she understood what he had been living with.

"I did do it, Laura." He sat down heavily on the edge of the bed, his shoulders slumped forward. "I did it by trapping her, giving her no way out. I can't forget that."

"Dick."

"There's nothing worse."

She looked into his eyes and felt a resolve she had almost forgotten she had. "This came from a very sick woman," she said. She held his eyes with her own. "How can I help you?"

He looked stunned, at first. "You mean that?"

She nodded her head very slowly.

"Can you stand by me?"

"Yes."

"Thank you, Laura."

His voice was so low she could barely hear him. She had known in her room that this was what would be, whether there was enough heart in the decision or not. She looked down at the two notes, one in each hand, staring at them. The sadness of Faith Paige was there, yes; but the malevolence of the second note was truly breathtaking. How could anybody in their right mind be so cruel? She looked again, bringing them up close, moving to the light.

"What is it?"

"Dick—"

"What?"

"They look almost exactly alike"—she hesitated—"but they're not the same handwriting."

In Buffalo, a pallid lamp cast a faint golden glow through the window of George Marino's hospital room. The air inside was redolent with the usual mixed smells of medicine, cleaning solution, and even, on this steamy day, a faint whiff of mold. Hoisted above the bed on a spidery web of steel was the television set—blaring mindlessly as its vivid images cast harsh flashes of light across the otherwise darkening room. A photograph of Sara sat propped on the window sill. Next to his bed was an empty glass of water. The bedclothes were rumpled. Everything looked as it always did when the nurse poked her head in at seven o'clock, armed with Dr. Marino's medicine for the night.

Except for one thing: George Marino wasn't there.

CHAPTER 12

Dick Sayles strode quickly through the darkened halls of the White House, his limp hardly noticeable, nodding curtly to a few startled guards stationed along the way. He heard the muffled tones of a clock striking three as he passed from the public halls into the tightly compacted maze of offices beyond the press room. From here, he strode toward the Oval Office—stopping short at Jack Patton's door.

He turned the knob without hesitation. If the door had been locked, he would have demanded the key of a guard. But it wasn't. An oversight of Jack's.

Sayles brushed past the silk folds of an American flag and stopped for an instant at the edge of Jack's desk, realizing he hadn't been in here since Goodspeed died. Curious, how different it looked. He couldn't quite put his finger on what it was. He walked around the desk, taking in the tidy, almost sanitized surface, the lack of photographs. . . .

He opened the top drawer and shuffled quickly through its contents. Nothing. He tried the drawers on each side, checking them with efficient precision. Then he yanked at a lower filing drawer. Locked. Not surprising.

Sayles began searching for a key. When he heard

somewhere in the distance a clock strike the half-hour, he stopped and stood silently for a moment, thinking. His mouth grimly set, he took a pair of scissors, jammed them into the recess between drawer and desk, and yanked hard. It took a few minutes. But finally the lock snapped open and he pulled out the drawer. There, still in the box Leona had dutifully spirited out of Faith's bedroom weeks ago, was what he was looking for: several folded sheets of Faith's cream-colored personal stationery.

It was now six in the morning. The sun moved in stingy slices through the drawn blinds of Jack Patton's bedroom. Patton was already awake, staring at nothing, when the phone rang by the side of his bed. He reached for it as his wife groaned and rolled over, pulling a pillow over her head. He didn't bother modulating his voice.

"Yeah."

"You seen the morning papers, Jack? What sort of fix have you gotten me into?" It was a highly agitated Arthur Starling.

"I'm not up yet, Arthur," Patton said as testily as he dared. "Yeah, it looks bad for Marino and I'm as upset as you are. You hear some of those talk shows last night? It's damned ridiculous! She's a lesbian, she's dallied with some Satanic cult, she's had three abortions—people are spitting rumors all over the airwaves! Why—"

"You can stop spinning, Jack, I'm not buying it. You're out to get rid of her, aren't you? I'm looking bad, the President's looking bad, the whole goddamn thing's a mess."

Patton sat up, catching a glimpse of his face in the mirror, fractured by the slivers of light coming through the blinds. His eyes stung with fatigue and he could taste the sourness of his own nervousness. Ginny Boseley was a tricky card to play, even if her presence did set the stage for Sara Marino's defeat. What else could he have done? Using that damned letter Sara wrote to help her father had been a bust. Too obvious. Now he had to ride it out, let public opinion bring her down—and then get the hell out of this place. Fast.

"And what's this about you angling for a job with American Telecom?"

Patton's eyes flew open wide. "What?"

"*Post* story this morning, Jack. So you want out of there, huh? Don't count on Si Posner, any more. He's dumping you."

"Hell, Arthur—"

"Just get your ass out of bed and read the papers." Starling was furious. "You've unleashed one helluva firestorm, you know that? My office is swamped with calls denouncing all of us, not just Judge Marino. What do you think's gonna happen to those of us up for reelection? That's what you wanted, right? You're too goddamn smart for your own good!" The receiver slammed down in Patton's ear.

"Maggie." It was Michael, his voice hoarse. "Can you come over? I've got a surprise visitor."

"Who?"

"George Marino."

"Sara's father?" Maggie wondered for a fleeting second if Michael was joking, but he wouldn't do that. Not about this. "My God, what's he doing here?"

"He just got up and walked out of the hospital, Maggie. The guy's amazing. He's got the idea he can save Sara's nomination; don't ask me how. I don't know how he got himself out of there without being seen, but he did."

"Wasn't he under some kind of surveillance?"

"I guess they figured he was too sick to go anywhere."

"Oh, Michael, he'll just make things worse."

"I know; that's why I need you, fast. I'm trying to convince him to stay here, but so far he's not buying it. And the hearing reconvenes in two hours." Michael paused. She heard the rattling of the morning newspaper over the wire.

"I should have said it first. This is a terrific story."

"I've never had more fun writing one." She couldn't help it, she felt a quick glow. "You're the one who gave me the tip on Posner, Michael. You didn't have to do that."

"Yeah, but you're the one who followed up. Anyhow, I'll have my own front-page blockbuster in a day or two. Right?"

She chuckled. "Right."

"Remember, whatever happens today—Patton may get Sara, Maggie. But you got *him*."

Maggie walked into Michael's apartment and caught her breath at the sight of the elderly man sitting by the window, his face raised to catch the first beams of an early morning sun. He looked decidedly shrunken in a suit jacket that was almost a size too large. But the skin stretched taut across his cheekbones gave more than a hint of the strong, handsome face that had been his in youth, and Maggie could hardly believe what she saw when he turned slowly and faced the doorway where she stood.

"She looks just like you," she blurted.

"She looks a lot better than I do," George Marino said calmly. "You're Maggie, I guess."

"That's right."

Michael turned instantly and headed for the kitchen, pausing only to whisper quickly: "The hospital's notifying the authorities. They'll hold off on calling Sara for a few hours if I keep him here." He shrugged his shoulders. "What else do I do?"

She nodded and moved closer as Michael disappeared through the door.

"Why did you come?" she asked.

"After watching Ginny Boseley testify? I had to come. I want to tell those senators what really happened. And don't try to talk me out of it." His voice, which began strong, wavered at the end.

"Dr. Marino, you've been in the hospital, you've been ill," Maggie said, alarmed at his stubbornness and his fragile physical state. "You shouldn't have come. Sara—"

"Sara doesn't know I'm here." He bent his head, leaning it against the wall. "I came because your boyfriend was so good at poking around for a story, I figured he'd know how to get me into that committee room." He offered a smile. "Surprised the hell out of him when I showed up last night."

"You sure did." Maggie was trying to think what to say next when Michael came hurrying back into the room with a steaming mug of instant coffee.

Marino wrinkled his nose as Michael handed him the cup. "Don't you young people *brew* coffee any more?" he said. He took a sip. "I want to talk to Ginny," he said abruptly.

Michael and Maggie exchanged swift glances. "That's a bad idea," Maggie said in haste. "You'd look like you were trying to put pressure on her—even if they let you near her, which I doubt."

"Sara has to get out there today and try to defend me, that's what's happening," Marino said. "It's not fair. I have to help her. Ginny Boseley remembers it all wrong."

"Dr. Marino." Maggie made her voice as calm and reasoned as possible. "You'd never want to hurt Sara."

"Of course not."

"Then listen to us. If you show up in that hearing room, you will become the story, and that will hurt Sara. You'll trigger a media circus. We know."

"You're telling me the people in your line of work don't follow basic rules of decency, that's what you're saying? Great recommendation. Maybe the two of you are in the wrong business."

Michael made no attempt to argue. Instead, he too leaned forward, gazing directly into the old man's troubled face.

"So maybe they'd argue extenuating circumstances," he said. "Like you do."

"Don't talk in riddles," snapped Marino.

"I'm not talking in riddles," Michael said. "I'm talking as plain as I can. You broke the rules in your business, didn't you? In our business, there aren't that many to break. It's easier. More defensible—if it's a good story."

"Yeah, but doctors can't hide like you guys can. You kill reputations, don't you? Every day."

Michael let the challenge go. "The point is, you can't show your face in public today. You could ruin Sara's chances, do you understand? You shouldn't have come, Dr. Marino."

The room grew silent. George Marino sipped his coffee carefully, looking as if he had gulped too much air. "I shouldn't have left Sally the medicine that day," he said.

"Didn't you think twice about her kid playing outside?" Michael leaned back and Maggie could see the sweat on his forehead.

"It wasn't supposed to happen that way. I guess she couldn't wait."

"Her little girl—"

"—never forgot it. That's what keeps me awake nights. It shouldn't have happened the way it did."

Marino put the coffee cup down onto the table with a leaden motion, and Maggie had a sudden flash of how many times over the years this man must have reached for a prescription pad to order something that would help a sick patient—knowing that nothing would work.

Silence descended on the room.

The phone was ringing again for the fifteenth time in an hour. Sara dressed slowly, staring into the mirror at the oval contour of her face, the freckled skin on her delicately boned hands, the slight touch of silver hair at her temples: the image was calm and unruffled, and she had to keep it that way. Four rings and the answering machine would capture the next voice. The echo of the last ring died out; the machine clicked on. Yes, there it was, thin and pitched high: "Marino, you aren't fit to be on the bench! You're a disgrace!" The caller abruptly hung up. They were different voices each time, but all with pretty much the same message. She stopped, blouse in hand. There was an odd, bleak protection in hearing disembodied voices and not having to respond. They don't know I'm here, she thought. They can't see me standing in front of the closet in my bra, holding a blouse that I'll be buttoning up in a moment. . . . They don't know I tried to eat some toast a half hour ago and I couldn't swallow it. . . . The phone was ringing again. Sara pulled on her blouse, shoved her feet into her shoes, and left the bedroom, slamming the door behind her.

Unheard, the machine clicked on, and the sound of a worried voice filled the room: "Judge Marino, this is Holy Cross Hospital calling. We have urgent information about your father. Please call us as quickly as—" The machine suddenly cut off. The tape was full.

Leona rose from her knees after locking the last suitcase, brushing a sprinkle of fine dust from her skirt. The house was quieter than it had ever been. No humming from the radiators, no creaking of floorboards—nothing. It was as limp and exhausted as she was.

The sound of a car turning into the driveway broke the stillness, and she glanced at her watch. Seven-thirty. Good, the cab was on time. She would be able to drop her bags at the Four Seasons before the hearing began, maybe even have time to put a few things away. What would it feel like, camping out in a hotel? She looked around one last time. Strange, really, to realize she would never spend another night in this house. She had debated briefly whether that was wise, whether—as her lawyer had urged—she should stay entrenched to make sure Justin didn't spirit away some of the more valuable paintings and furnishings before a settlement was signed. But nothing here mattered any more.

It had never been a home, not the kind of home she wanted. For just a moment she allowed herself to bend under a weight of inexpressible sadness, but only for a moment. She would concentrate on the absence of agony, she told herself; remember, the agony is gone. Last night's final scene . . . would she ever forget? When Justin had finally realized she was serious, his fury had been more pathetic than fearful. For years, I've barely known him, she told herself. My marriage has been a total sham. . . .

The doorbell pealed sharply, cutting through her thoughts. Leona straightened the folds of her red silk jacket—it never had hung straight, even before it came back from that disastrous trip to the cleaners—and moved toward the door, surveying the pile of luggage in the foyer. She hadn't bothered cleaning out her closets and she was still mildly astonished at herself. Should she take the Bob Mackie gown? She opened the door for the driver, who immediately began scooping up the bags and taking them out to the cab. For one second Leona hesitated, glancing back up the stairway to the second floor. Then she smiled to herself, turned around, and reached for her purse. To hell with the Bob Mackie. Straightening, she walked briskly out of the house without a single glance back, feeling an enormous renewal of energy.

I made it, she told herself as the cab pulled away from the driveway. I made it out of there. Not only that—and here, if the cabdriver had happened to glance in his rearview mirror, he would have seen the relief on her face—she would never again have to walk around her own home with one of those bloody Francis Bacon creatures staring down her neck.

* * *

Maggie slipped into a seat next to Carol in the Senate Caucus Room, noting that her friend's eyes looked puffy from lack of sleep. The cheerful certitude of the night before was gone.

"Did the letter get to Sayles?" she asked eagerly.

"Let it play out, Maggie," Carol said with a vague wave of her hand. "You know how these things work."

"That's not very reassuring. How can I know how it works if I don't know what's playing out?"

But Carol didn't want to talk about her brief, uneasy conversation with Laura Sayles. "Your story on Patton was great," she said. "I'd rather talk about that."

"I wish I'd had it weeks ago—when it could have done Sara some good," Maggie said. She gave her friend a sharper look. "Listen, you look troubled."

Carol raised her hand slightly, warning her off. Maggie felt frustrated, but decided to leave it alone. In truth, she had to keep quiet about Sara's father, so it probably wasn't fair to push Carol. If they were lucky, George Marino would keep his promise to stay at Michael's apartment until after the hearing, but she didn't dare say a word about his presence, not yet. The possibility of this getting out made her hands clammy. Poor Michael. He didn't need the added strain, not today. He had his story to write.

"Well, look," Carol said, relenting a bit. "If you throw a wrench into somebody else's life for an absolutely good reason, you still feel like shit."

"You mean Dick Sayles?"

"No, no, not him."

Okay, Maggie thought. If there was no explanation forthcoming right now, she'd hear it soon enough.

The huge room was filling fast and the buzz seemed charged with a meaner edge. A lot of people expected blood. The sound of a gavel broke sharply through the noise as Arthur Starling—his face stitched tight, a bad sign—took his seat in the midst of his colleagues on the committee. At the table in front of him, Sara sat erect and tall, flanked by Amos and Barney. Behind her, only one row away, sat Ginny Boseley, seemingly less unnerved by the clicking cameras than she had been yesterday.

"We have serious business this morning, ladies and gentlemen," Starling announced. "In the aftermath of the events Mrs. Boseley described yesterday, I take up this gavel with a heavy heart."

Maggie tightened her lips and glanced at her friends. Starling would be quite a sight to watch as he worked his way through the minefield laid down yesterday afternoon. There were more demonstrators outside this morning, louder ones, this time with elaborate signs. Anti-euthanasia groups, whether responsible or crazy, were banding together to hold the national attention they had sought for so long.

"Did you hear the rumor about Sara slapping her law clerk?" Carol whispered.

"That's the tamest one yet."

"This hearing will not be swayed by partisan politics," Starling declared, glaring at the cameras. "But given the intensely personal story we heard yesterday about Judge Marino's father, we cannot ignore the issue that looms before us today." He cleared his throat. Then he launched into an odd hybrid of a statement: one filled with praise for Sara but laced with concern about her refusal to talk in detail about euthanasia. "On the broader issues, the issues that relate to the work you would be doing on the Court, you have not been sufficiently receptive to answering the committee's questions," he said sorrowfully, gazing at Sara. "That is, of course, your right. We cannot force you to be fully forthcoming, but it does then leave us with difficult choices. We cannot in good conscience vote for the confirmation of a nominee who appears to stonewall on issues of urgent public and political concern."

"Listen to him, he wrote this originally to support Sara,"

Carol whispered to Maggie. Her fingers worked back and forth in her lap with uncharacteristic nervousness, as if she were waiting for something to happen.

Suddenly Leona materialized and sat down in the seat next to Maggie. "Haven't missed too much, have I?" she said. Her face was pale but more peaceful than usual as she scanned the room. "Bet Michael's busy on a story," she murmured, turning directly to Maggie. There was a light in her eye.

"Yes, actually," Maggie said, waiting.

Leona reached into her purse, pulled out a small vial of perfume, and squirted it twice, once behind each ear. "I'm traveling light from now on, by the way," she said. "I just walked out on all that peach brocade."

Maggie watched Leona tuck the perfume vial back into her purse, putting it precisely back into its own little purple bag in a side pocket in her usual, somewhat precise, somewhat fussy way. Leona loved perfume. . . . Maggie looked down at her friend's nails. The skin was bitten raw.

"You left him?" Carol said quietly.

"Yes."

"Tough morning." It was said with a certain respect.

"Sssh," Leona warned, nodding toward the front of the room. Starling was saying something that was causing a stir, and the three women craned their necks to see better. Ginny Boseley was getting up, looking confused, an aide at her elbow.

"He's taking her up to the witness table so the cameras can shoot them together," Carol said disgustedly. "What cheap theatrics."

"He can't do that," protested Leona.

"He can do anything he wants," Carol replied. "He's chairman of the committee and—look, look at Cliff Borden's aide." At the committee table, with an aide whispering urgently into his ear, Cliff Borden had bolted upright out of his characteristic, bored slump and was actually straightening his tie, looking very alert. Inexplicably, Carol chortled. "You know what that kid's telling him?" she said. " 'Straighten up, your constituents are complaining.' If enough C-Span viewers complain about something, they send somebody over here fast."

Starling was pounding his gavel for order once again. "We don't want you to feel under undue pressure, Judge Marino," he said. "But Mrs. Boseley has asked to be seated closer so she can hear your answers better. Do you have any objections?"

Sara conferred briefly with Amos and Barney, but they all three knew that to raise an objection at this point would look defensive.

"No, but with this caveat, Mr. Chairman," snapped Amos. "You're dangerously close to creating a carnival atmosphere. I feel compelled to point out that this isn't a show for your constituents, it's a confirmation hearing for a serious position."

Starling flushed pinker than usual, but barely wavered. He was walking a careful line today, and if he wanted to stay in the U.S. Senate he was sticking with his gameplan. Presidents came and went; voters were forever. "I regret you are unhappy, Senator," he said icily. "But it is precisely because these proceedings are so important that we are doing this. Perhaps it isn't the traditional way of doing things, but unusual times call for strong measures. I also have an objection—I object to your calling into question the integrity of this committee."

"Hear, hear," harrumphed John Enright.

But now Amos was on his feet. "There are rules of procedure, Mr. Chairman," he said with furious calm. His shirt collar had already curled from his own sweat and the heat of the room. "You may run this committee, but you've got a lot of viewers watching you, and they'll know outrageously unfair tactics when they see them. They'll understand—"

Sara lifted her hand, cutting him off. She leaned into the microphone. "I have no objection, Mr. Chairman," she said calmly. She held up a sheaf of papers in her left hand. "I have here a statement I prepared last night in response to Mrs. Boseley's testimony, but I've decided it isn't enough. I would like to share some of my thoughts with you, the other members of the committee and"—she paused—"both Mrs. Boseley and my father, who I know is watching from his hospital bed in Buffalo."

The room grew very still. Even the photographers seemed, for a few brief moments, in suspended animation as the meaning of Sara Marino's words sank in: she was abandoning the protection of her image, her judicial restraint. She was engaging on Starling's terms.

"She doesn't have to do this," Carol whispered.

But it was Leona who hit closer to the truth. "She's got to get people to focus on her and not on the rumors; she has to take a chance."

"But she's not a gambler."

"Well, she is now," Leona replied softly. "Same as me."

Starling cleared his throat, observing Sara warily. But there couldn't be some hidden agenda, not now, it was too late. Every word she said, every expression on her face, would be under the scrutiny of millions of viewers.

"Please proceed, Judge," he said, amiably enough.

"Back off, Sara," a startled Barney said in a low, urgent voice. "This isn't a good idea, I'm telling you."

Sara briefly cupped the microphone with her hand. "I know what I'm doing," she whispered, turning her head. "Trust me."

Barney stared at her, clearly unconvinced. Then he slumped back into his seat.

"Dying isn't simple any more," she began slowly. "Many people want to choose how and when it happens. Some say, let me out of here, I want to die. And the next day they want to live. Some of us want only truth, some of us want only hope. Some of us have in our files instructions on how much care we want and some of us can't bear to think about our deaths head-on. And some of us take matters into our own hands, leaving friends and relatives to grieve and try to understand."

Maggie tightened her grip on the arms of her chair, not quite believing the direction in which Sara was going.

"I had a friend who committed suicide," Sara continued. "You all know who she was. I have finally allowed myself to believe that she did indeed kill herself: I'm convinced now there was no accident, no foul play. And now I am asking myself why she chose to die. In the end, was it a moment only—a moment that would have passed? Did she decide in a split second and would she have changed her mind one minute later? Was there a single catalyst? We'll never know." She turned slightly in her chair, addressing Ginny Boseley, who sat rigid and unmoving, hands squeezed tight on top of the bright green felt. "Could that have been true for your sister?"

Ginny Boseley clamped her lips tight together and stared straight ahead.

"It could have," Sara said gently. "We'll never know. I can only bow my head in the face of your anger and pain and tell you, there's no easy answer. My father respected life and was sworn to do no harm. You say he did do harm, but if so, it was without intent. For something else is true: there are people watching us now who would give a lot to have his name and phone number. They believe there should be limits to having one's life involuntarily prolonged. They would see him as a saviour, not as an angel of death."

"What would you do?" challenged Mrs. Boseley in a thin voice. "That's what I want to know. What would you do?"

"I wouldn't have taken on the responsibility of helping

someone die,'' Sara said. ''He broke the law because he wanted to meet a human need. He wasn't the first doctor to do this and he certainly won't be the last, but I couldn't have done it. That doesn't make me moral; in fact, it may make me a coward. I don't know the answer.''

''We don't want a lecture on moral philosophy, Judge, just an answer to the question,'' John Enright interrupted. ''This lady's sister is gone, and nothing can change that.''

''I don't deny her loss,'' Sara said, keeping her voice calm. Enright wasn't going to suck her into a fruitless exchange about Sally Hegelstrom. ''I can only pose some questions. What about doctors who increase medication when someone dying is in terrible pain? Is that wrong—if it kills them? What about doctors who don't give expensive care to someone old or poor but order up every test in the book for someone with heavy insurance? Is that wrong?''

Enright was silent. Chairman Starling glanced nervously from right to left, relieved that no committee member seemed willing to take on Sara's questions. He cleared his throat, drawing the attention of the cameras. ''What do you see as your role in this arena if you are confirmed for the Court?'' he asked a bit pompously.

''My job would be to interpret the laws, the laws that Congress enacts, not shape the moral values of a country,'' she said. ''We're all in charge of that. Nor can I tell this committee how I will vote on Congress's cutoff of emergency life-support care for the elderly. That case involves one controversial effort to deal with health costs that clash with human needs; but there will be others. The largest number of health dollars are spent during the last months, days, even hours of a person's life: so should we limit the use of costly medical technology? Eventually all of us have to make choices, and some of those choices are going to be harder than others. Which ones? When? And how? I can't answer those questions. I can only do my best to address them from the perspective of the law.''

"This isn't good enough!" The words burst from Ginny Boseley's throat in a painful wail. "I want answers, the right answers!"

Sara turned fully to her now, ignoring the microphone. "I wish I could give them to you," she said. "But I have only questions. May I ask one? If you had been in your sister's situation"—she saw in the other woman's eyes a recognition of what she was about to say—"would you have wanted to die?"

The silence that descended over the room was too profound even for Starling's gavel to violate. Ginny Boseley stared long and miserably at Sara.

"You don't have to answer that," Sara said, very gently this time. "You're not here to be judged. I am."

"I want to answer," the woman blurted unexpectedly. There was a struggle going on, only a glimpse of which came through her eyes and—oblivious to the perils of dead televised air—she gazed at Sara for a long time before she spoke again. "I don't know," she said finally. "I don't know for sure what happened. I said I saw it, but maybe I didn't. Maybe I just thought I did. I don't know what I would have done." Her head seemed to shrink down onto her shoulders with the weight of a stone. "It's true. Sally didn't want to live like that."

"Order," roared Starling unnecessarily as a ripple of applause reverberated through the room. "Order!"

Sara let out her breath, realizing only then how long she had been holding it in. She felt an almost dizzying relief. She had reached this woman, actually reached her. Ginny Boseley was not the damning witness she had seemed. She jumped slightly when she heard the sound of Barney punching his fist into the palm of his left hand and shot him a glance for confirmation: yes, she could see it in his eyes. The case against her father had just been dramatically weakened.

"She's got a chance to turn the whole thing around,"

Maggie said, astonished. She and the others craned their heads to follow the action.

"Look," said Carol, with a smile. Three aides were at the committee table whispering urgent news into the ear of Chairman Starling: the first calls were coming through. Television viewers across the nation were reacting favorably to Sara's speech. Callers were complaining that the "stupid vicious rumors" about Marino had dominated the news. Anti-Marino demonstrators outside, hearing the reports, were milling uncertainly. Things were not going quite the way Chairman Starling had expected, and his discomfiture was increased by the fact that the man who had put him in this spot was nowhere to be seen at the moment—with good reason.

He was standing in the Oval Office, facing President Sayles.

"Jack, I'm not happy with what you've been doing," Dick Sayles said, without preamble. He hardly lifted his eyes from the screen showing the televised proceedings.

"I've been simply carrying out what we've agreed—" Patton said, barely able to move his eyes from the television screen.

"Are you implying I agreed it was all right for you to destroy Judge Marino's confirmation chances?"

"Look, Dick—"

"Mr. President."

"Ah, Mr. President—"

"She's solid, don't you think?" Sayles said with imperturbable calm. "Or do you still need convincing? Maybe you've detoured a bit on this nomination, Jack."

"I do the job that needs to be done, Mr. President." Patton decided to risk more. "Like getting your love letters from Faith's office before the police searched it."

"Ah, yes. The favor for which I'm supposed to be both

eternally grateful—and guilty. Sorry, Jack, it won't work. Not this morning."

"Any job," Patton added quickly.

"Glad to hear that," Sayles said with hearty cheer. "Looks like Sara Marino will be cleared fast, all right? No big impediments still ahead, are there?"

"No, sir."

"Good." Sayles paused, then proceeded in a relaxed tone. "I've been thinking, Jack, your office is looking a little grungy lately."

"You were in there?"

"Around three this morning. Too bad your desk keys weren't handy, but I'm sure that drawer can be repaired."

Patton's face turned ashen.

"I'm not surprised that you held me in such contempt. But I am startled that you apparently held this office in contempt as well."

Patton started to speak, but Sayles raised his hand. "Spare me any explanations. Very clever, I must say. You knew Faith hated to write out anything by hand, so duplicating her handwriting wasn't that great a risk. Unfortunately for you, I had the chance to compare your note with a letter Faith wrote to Sara Marino and her friends. My wife helped me on that one, actually."

"Your wife?"

"Yes, my wife."

The room fell silent, but Sayles never took his eyes off Jack Patton's face. "Amazing, isn't it?" he said softly. "People don't always react the way you expect them to. I must admit, I'm a little curious as to whether that note in my desk was planned in advance or whether you just stumbled on the stationery in the packet of stuff Justin's wife brought out of Faith's house. But it doesn't matter—your contempt comes across the same. Why'd you do it, Jack?"

Patton stared at the cold, questioning eyes of the president and felt as if the room were tipping first one way, then another, and he was sliding, helpless, with it. It was the question that would haunt him, he knew it already. What *had* prompted him to think writing that note was a brilliant way to keep this greenhorn president in line a little longer? The sweat was collecting in his shirt collar; in the palms of his hands.

"It was a terrible mistake," he said.

"You bet it was. By the way, I found Maggie Stedman's story this morning mighty interesting. You and Si Posner, huh? You were in one helluva hurry to jump ship, Jack. Rats do that, I understand. But this ship isn't sinking, not if I can help it."

There was nothing to say. Patton stood facing the president, wondering now only how long it would be before he could leave the room. He had to figure out a plan.

"We need a few changes around here, I've decided. Every new administration has to shake itself up after a while. And this one is just getting started."

Jack Patton stared stonily straight ahead. "Yes, sir," he said.

"You're fired, Jack. I want your desk cleaned out within the hour."

"I'd appreciate a little time to get my affairs in order, sir."

"You're not getting it. The air around here stinks." Sayles stood abruptly. "Don't figure on enlisting Justin Maccoby, Jack. He's never seeing the inside of this office again, either. Goodbye."

Patton turned and left the room, wanting now only to reach the protection of his own office. But his secretary—the expression on her face showing how quickly she had sensed trouble—was standing by the door. Silently, she handed him a phone message: Michael Bitterwood, *Post* reporter, wants info on Maccoby oil deal. Call, please. Urgent.

Jack Patton's hand trembled as he took the message and

went to his office, slamming the door behind him. He'd better talk to Justin before Bitterwood called again. Quickly, he dialed. Five minutes later, he stared at the wall opposite his desk, realizing how completely his carefully constructed world was crumbling around him. He stood and walked around his office, the office he knew so well. He gazed at the two quite wonderful Cézannes, placed precisely to catch the entering morning sun. Morning visitors to this office—totally unaware their appointments were scheduled to coincide with the illumination of the paintings—were always impressed. It was quite a nice bit of theater, really.

He pressed the intercom button on his phone.

"Miss Goodwin, I need the number for a local attorney—Edward MacDonald."

He heard her inhale sharply. "The criminal lawyer?"

"Yes. Hurry up."

He dialed another number. Slowly.

"John!" he said heartily when the phone at the other end was picked up. "How's that talk show of yours going? Remember our chat about life after the White House?"

"Terrific job, Sara."

Amos was clapping her on the back and Barney had grabbed her hand. Sara stared at them, one after the other, slightly stunned.

"Sara," Barney said quietly. "It's over."

She heard them, but she couldn't move. She turned her gaze to the senators in front of her as they pushed their chairs back from the long table, whispered, conferred with staff aides and—amazingly—smiled and nodded in her direction. She could hear behind her the buzzing excitement from the crowd. How strange. She had been so deep in her own thoughts, she hadn't even heard the bang of the chairman's gavel. Was it really over?

"You were great, Sara. We'll get a read from the committee in a few hours—after they've checked the political winds, naturally. But I'm telling you, I think you've pulled it out."

She turned slowly toward Barney, noticing immediately a deep, vertical furrow in the middle of his forehead. Had that appeared only in the last couple of weeks? There was an instant of awkwardness; each saw it in the other's eyes.

"With your help," she said.

Barney shook his head decisively. "No, I gave bad advice. You did it on your own. Hey, one of these days, you'll be Chief Justice." He smiled again, with a little more reserve than she realized suddenly she wanted to see.

"Oh, sure, maybe in a hundred years," she said, adding quickly: "I'm still the same person I've always been." Who was she reassuring, she wondered: herself or Barney?

"Yeah, me, too."

"That doesn't have to be a problem, does it?"

"Guess we'll find out."

Sara hesitated. She felt a certain reserve herself, after all. This wasn't the place or the time. They stared at each other for just an instant. The crowd was pressing close, she could hear the laughter, the applause. Think about it later, she told herself. . . .

The hell with that.

Impulsively, she held her arms out wide and Barney grabbed her in a tight embrace, holding her tighter than she had ever been held before.

"I'm so proud of you," he whispered into her ear, "so proud."

The crowd descended, enveloping suddenly; a cheery, happy crowd filled with praise for the excellent performance of the woman surely now about to receive the blessing of the Judiciary Committee followed by the almost certain confirmation of her appointment by the entire U.S. Senate. Sara smiled up into their faces, acknowledging their compliments, laughing when her friend Maggie rushed up and gave her a hug, and then quickly, so quickly, she was pulled up and absorbed into the crowd of people and cameras that saw her as the next page of Supreme Court history. And Barney still sat there at the witness table, watching her as she was swept up and then disappeared from view. His expression was hard to read.

"Cassidy? Barney Cassidy?"

A man with the stubble of an overnight beard was leaning close, almost whispering into his ear.

"Yeah." Barney braced, pulled himself back from the inevitable interview.

"Look, I'm Maggie's friend at the *Post,*" said Michael Bitterwood. "I think you know who I am." His lanky body was taut, like stretched wire. "Something's happened."

"If you want to talk to Sara . . ." Barney began.

"Forget that; I need your help. Fast. Sara's father."

"What about him?"

"He was here—and now he's disappeared."

There wasn't much time. Hurriedly briefed by Michael, Barney dashed from the committee room as Michael managed for a brief instant to pull Maggie out of the crowd. He whispered the news and she turned white.

"How?" she managed.

"I was faxing copy," Michael said rapidly. "It took forever. When I checked on him, he was gone."

"Gone! How? When?"

"He was talking to himself when Starling moved Ginny Boseley up to the witness stand," Michael said. "Goddamn it, I should've known that would upset him. I ran in there when Sara started testifying, but he was already gone."

Maggie's heart was pounding hard, but she had to respond to the distraught expression on Michael's face. "You couldn't exactly lock him in," she said haltingly.

"Doesn't work, Maggie. I still feel like shit."

"What do we do?"

"Try to find him. Barney's out looking. Any ideas?"

"I think he'd try to come here, wouldn't he?"

"Unless he couldn't make it."

Maggie shivered. "Let's call the police."

"I have."

Maggie shot an agonized glance in Sara's direction. "I don't want to ruin this for her. If we can find him—"

"My thinking exactly. But if we don't find him. . . ." Michael glanced at his watch, trying to balance the perils involved. "Maybe half an hour? Can you make an excuse to keep her from calling him?"

"I'll try." This was one assignment Maggie would happily have passed.

The overcast sky above the deserted Supreme Court Building began spilling out rain. It came first as heavy, fat drops plopping onto the parched lawns and dry pavement east of the Capitol, but motorists—wise to the ways of a Washington summer storm—switched on their lights as the sky grew darker. Government workers clutched briefcases and purses and hurried quickly for shelter as they listened to the deep rumblings of approaching thunder. Then suddenly the rain came in furious cascading sheets, hitting the pavement like buckshot. Barney cursed his faltering windshield wipers as he drove slowly up Constitution Avenue. When he reached the top of the hill, he turned onto First Street and pulled over to the side of the road. It was as if someone had thrown a bucket of water in his face. So it was not surprising that he didn't quite believe his eyes when he saw an elderly man dressed in a suit and tie sitting in a crouched position on the steps of the Court, approximately halfway to the top.

"Jesus," he muttered. He yanked at the handbrake and jumped out of the car. By the time he had covered the distance between the car and the steps, the rain was slowing. The skies were already lightening.

"Dr. Marino?" he said, out of breath as he reached the man on the steps.

"You folks get rainstorms that don't even take the heat out of the pavement," said the old man, frowning up at him. "Touch these steps, by God, they're all wet but they're still hot."

"Are you—"

"Yes, I am. And who are you?"

"I'm Barney Cassidy. A friend of your daughter's."

"Yeah, I've heard of you."

"What are you doing here, Dr. Marino?"

Marino glanced up the steps behind him almost wistfully. "Got too tired. Couldn't reach the top."

Barney hesitated, glancing at the wet, steaming steps. Then he yanked up the trouser cuffs of his pants and sat down. "Why were you going up there?"

"To find Sara. Hell, I thought the hearing was being held here. I got lost, young man. I'm just an old coot from Buffalo who's managed to destroy his daughter's career." Marino's voice faltered. He stopped, cradling his head in his hands.

"You didn't do anything of the sort. She turned it around today."

Marino lifted his head and stared at the younger man with the weariest eyes Barney had ever seen. "Say that again."

"She's okay, that's what I'm saying. People were calling in from all over the country praising her, even before she stopped speaking. All those heroes on Judiciary are back in her corner. She's a shoo-in for confirmation."

"Ginny Boseley?"

"Backed off her charges." Barney couldn't resist a grin. "You're not a fugitive from justice, after all."

Marino let out an explosive sigh of relief. "She's won, you're telling me. I walked away too fast."

They sat quietly, each in his own thoughts.

"I guess this puts Sara on another plane from the rest of us. My own daughter. Seems strange," Marino said finally.

"Yeah, I know what you mean." Barney hardly attempted to disguise his glumness.

Dr. Marino shot him a glance. "Don't let yourself get overly impressed."

Barney considered that without comment. "Shall we get out of here?" he suggested. He had to move this guy along fast; he didn't want Sara panicking.

There was a brief silence. "Give me a couple of minutes," Marino finally said.

Barney peered closely into his face, realizing for the first time that the older man was clearly exhausted. He felt like an idiot. Why hadn't he focused on the fact that Sara's father shouldn't even be out of his hospital bed, much less sitting on the steps of the Supreme Court in a rainstorm?

"I'll help."

"No. I'm okay. Two minutes. Does Sara know I'm here?"

"We haven't told her yet."

"You'll take me to her?"

"Of course."

He seemed satisfied. He sat back and closed his eyes. "Okay, Barney, now tell me why you're feeling a little down."

"I am?"

"A little."

Barney shrugged. "Things don't always work out the way you think they will, that's all."

"Yeah? Tell me about it. What's this got to do with Sara?"

"Well—" Barney suddenly longed for a cigarette. He hadn't smoked in fifteen years but felt at this precise moment an almost overwhelming desire for an unfiltered Camel, even a soggy, broken butt from off the street. Anything. "I probably won't see that much of her from here on," he said, elaborately casual. "You know how it is. Lining up the votes and fielding all the crap has been kind of fun. Now I've got to go back to my own life—making money. I'm just another lobbyist."

George Marino considered that in silence, kneading his gnarled, heavily veined hands thoughtfully. "Well, maybe you're right," he said. "You've got to be pretty special to keep Sara's attention."

"I never was in her league, she just thought I was." Was he really saying these things? Barney found himself fidgeting, pulling at his shirtcuffs with nervous fingers.

"Yeah? You seem smart," Marino said affably. "But then what do I know?"

Barney smiled at him. "No reassurances?"

"No, sir. I made my mistakes and you'll make yours, but she won't be so busy she can't spare a few minutes every now and then for a cup of coffee."

"Thanks, that's reassuring." He kind of liked this guy.

"Just stick to your guns, is all I'm saying."

"I intend to." Barney realized he felt better.

"I've been thinking about Ginny Boseley," Dr. Marino said, changing the subject. "I've got this idea that it would be good for her and me to have a talk. What do you think?"

"What would you say to her?"

"I'd tell her how sorry I am," Marino said simply. "Sounds dumb, I suppose. But I want to tell her the things her sister told me before she died."

"She might spare you a few minutes over a cup of coffee. I heard on the radio the Buffalo district attorney's dropping the murder charge, by the way."

They smiled at each other.

"Let's go," Marino said, standing abruptly, stretching his legs.

Slowly they walked down the still-glistening steps, the older man leaning noticeably against the younger one. At the bottom, Marino stopped and looked back, staring up at the imposing facade of the Court.

"I'm glad I came," he said, half to himself. "At least I've seen the place from the outside."

"It's even more imposing inside, but you'll be here for the swearing in. You'll get a full tour of the place then."

George Marino frowned slightly as he turned away. "Maybe," he said.

"Come on, the car's right there across the street." Barney couldn't think of anything else to say.

"Illegally parked, I see."

"Hell, meeting you was worth a fifty-dollar ticket."

Marino looked up at Barney, this time with considerably more than a flash of interest. "You're okay, young man," he said. "Now take me to my daughter."

It was nine o'clock and the uproar was over. Barney had left quickly after delivering a very tired George Marino to his daughter's doorstep. Exhausted, Sara tiptoed past the door to the extra bedroom, listening. He was sleeping peacefully. Tomorrow would be soon enough to decide whether he stayed here or went back to Buffalo; right now it was simply an enormous relief to have him safe. God, how loyal he was: to make that trip. . . . She closed the hall door and stood for a moment in the living room, still absorbing the impact of today's incredible events. The news reports had been positive and the first tapping of public opinion had indeed shown a shift in her favor. Judiciary aides were giving the clearest signal: it was thumbs up for her nomination.

Slowly, Sara let out her breath. By God, she was going to be a Supreme Court Justice. She laughed out loud and began to whirl around the room with the exuberance, if not the skill, of a ballet dancer, stopping only when she heard the sharp peal of the doorbell.

Still flushed, Sara opened the door. There were Maggie, Carol, and Leona, hoisting a magnum of champagne.

"Ladies' Lunch," Leona announced, eyes dancing. "Wrong time of day, and we're going to drink it, but it's going to be the best one we've ever had."

All laughing now, they crowded into the narrow kitchen of the apartment. Sara began hunting for wine glasses, which she eventually found in the dishwasher.

"Sara, you were wonderful!"

"God, what a day!"

"Here, I brought some crackers, yours are always stale."

The glasses were out, and Sara was pouring as everybody talked at once.

"Look out, you're slopping it, that stuff's precious!"

"Did you hear Carol's news?"

Sara stopped pouring, glancing up. "No, what?"

"Laura Sayles was the messenger who took Faith's letter to the President—she called tonight and thanked our old friend Carol, here, for recruiting her." Maggie said with a grin. "She said it was exactly the jolt her husband needed. He got rid of Jack Patton today—just booted him out the door. *Something* worked."

Carol tried to look appropriately modest as she reached for a glass. "That is one strange marriage," she said casually. "Interesting woman, lots of steel, but we'll probably never know the whole story, although my contacts. . . ."

Carol launched with her usual enthusiasm into the kind of inside-the-Beltway detail they all knew so well, and for a few minutes they listened. But then Sara's attention turned to Maggie.

"Something's happening with you," she said quietly, observing her friend with interest. At some point they had to talk about the book, she told herself. Soon. Not yet.

It was Maggie's turn to try and appear modest. "Michael and I are getting married," she said in as offhand a way as possible.

"That's wonderful!" Sara and the others, their glasses all filled, lifted them in Maggie's direction.

"Here's to you both."

"God, it took you long enough to figure it out."

Maggie grinned happily. "That's what Jeff said, can you imagine? My kid, knowing more than I did. He's coming home tomorrow."

"I'm taking my kids on a trip," Carol offered unexpectedly. "Nobody has to tell me it's high time I paid attention, I know it." She glanced at Sara with a wry smile. "Ever been to Yosemite? The kids want to go. You know, they've got that geyser. 'Old Glory.' "

Leona giggled. "Carol—you mean 'Old Faithful.' "

Sara laughed. "Carol, it's not even Yosemite. It's Yellowstone."

Carol was undeterred. "Whichever. A geyser's a geyser." For just an instant, she showed a spark of her old, slightly wicked, humor. "Unless it's in my district, and then I have to know."

"Heard from Bart?"

"He called the kids," said Carol, a little wistfully. "He's designing some kind of new city which sounds great. They said he's really excited about it. But they didn't give many details, naturally. Not to me."

The others glanced at each other, but said nothing.

"Are you going back to the *Post*?" Leona's question to Maggie was a bit abrupt, but in the midst of this wonderful, noisy moment, anything was appropriate. They all paused, curious to hear the answer.

Maggie took a deep breath. "They want me back. I think I want them back, too."

"Which means?" Sara was trying to be careful.

"Which means, I'm not writing the book." Maggie's voice wavered slightly. "I'm not selling out my friends. Not that I won't try to salvage that lucrative contract, you understand. I'll suggest a new twist, 'The Women of Washington,' or something like that. What it's like to succeed, the pressures."

"If the editor doesn't like it?"

Maggie shrugged, a little too elaborately. But her heart was in her words. "I'm a reporter again. I'll find something else."

Another toast ensued, and by now, still crowded together in the small kitchen, Leona sitting on the counter, they were into their second glass of champagne.

"Was it hard today?" Sara asked Leona in a lowered voice. Again there was a small silence. The fragile one of the group had probably gone through more change today than any of them. And it involved a lot more than just walking out on a marriage.

Leona's head felt as bubbly and light as the liquid in her goblet, but her voice was quite steady. "Sure, it was." She paused for a second. "And then again, it wasn't, because Justin isn't the person I used to know, and I've finally stopped pretending. And if Michael's story puts him in jail, so be it. I feel free, you know—more independent than I ever have." She stretched out her arms and flexed her muscles, laughing, just to show them she meant it.

"We'll drink to that." Carol's voice was quiet as she raised her glass, followed immediately by the others.

"Sara."

They all turned in Sara's direction at the sound of Maggie's voice. "We're very, very proud, you know that. Incredibly happy and proud at what you've accomplished. Here's to you."

"I couldn't have done it without the three of you." Sara's voice was tremulous. "Do you all know that? Every step of the way, you've been with me. My toast is to the four of us—the Ladies."

"Well," Leona cut in. "For that, we'll have to drink another round."

They laughed, Sara poured, and their glasses were filled again. By now, Sara had joined Leona on the counter, swinging her legs over the side. Carol was leaning against the broom closet, while Maggie was sitting cross-legged in front of the refrigerator. They dissected the day's events, talked about Ginny Boseley, Sara's father, Barney (Sara had a particular light in her eyes when she talked about him, but Carol refrained from saying anything embarrassing), and what came next. Finally, Sara raised her hand.

"Okay, last toast," she said. She looked at their faces, thinking of all the years. "We've shared a lunch date every month for longer than I can remember," she said slowly. "We began as a group of five—and I think we always will be."

The tiny kitchen grew very quiet, and although no one moved, they felt a sense of drawing even closer together. The flat, shadowless fluorescent light from above lit their glasses as they held them high.

"To Faith." The name came from Carol like a sob.

"She should have had this."

"She should be here."

"She deserved better."

"Let's try and say it exactly as we mean it," Maggie said. "This—right here in this kitchen—is a true party of friends."

"This is the party Faith should have had."

Sara's voice was quiet, definitive. "Yes," she said, raising her glass one last time. "To friendship. And to justice—and not just the kind you find in a courtroom."